GRACE
IS
GONE

ALSO BY EMILY ELGAR

If You Knew Her

GRACE
IS
GONE

a novel

EMILY ELGAR

HARPER

NEW YORK . LONDON . TORONTO . SYDNEY

HARPER

Originally published as *Grace is Gone* in Great Britain in 2020 by Little, Brown UK.

GRACE IS GONE. Copyright © 2020 by Emily Elgar. All rights reserved. Printed in the United States of America. No part of this book may be used or reproduced in any manner whatsoever without written permission except in the case of brief quotations embodied in critical articles and reviews. For information, address HarperCollins Publishers, 195 Broadway, New York, NY 10007.

HarperCollins books may be purchased for educational, business, or sales promotional use. For information, please email the Special Markets Department at SPsales@harpercollins.com.

FIRST U.S. EDITION

Library of Congress Cataloging-in-Publication Data has been applied for.

ISBN 978-0-06-294563-1 (pbk.)
ISBN 978-0-06-297210-1 (library edition)

20 21 22 23 24 LSC 10 9 8 7 6 5 4 3 2 1

This book is dedicated to my wonderful parents,
Edward and Sandy Elgar.

Thank you feels so inadequate for all the love you share—
but it's all I have—so thank you.

GRACE
IS
GONE

Prologue

Megan

Grace doesn't know, but every night around 2 a.m. I go to her. It started when she was just a toddler, but still, so many years later, I creep into her room and roll back her duvet to check that her bony chest is still fluttering, her weak heart still doing its best. Tonight is one of those nights I try to be brave, stop myself. I stare at the ceiling, make my legs heavy.

Stay put, I tell them.

I try to think about something else. I plan what Grace should wear when we visit the new pediatric unit in Taunton in a couple of weeks; we might be photographed. But even that won't stick. I don't see Grace smiling for the camera, a pretty clip in her short, spiky hair. I see her in bed, across the hall, her rosebud mouth gasping for air, her lips turning gray, then blue. I see her green eyes, naked without their glasses, fearful, desperate, searching for me in the dusky light of her room, and then before I know it I'm out of bed, across the hall and by her side. My hand goes straight to her warm chest. It rises and falls, slow and dreamy, just like it should. But that's not enough. I lean over her, my cheek an inch from her mouth. I feel the breeze of her, her little life puff warm and rhythmic against my skin. She's OK. Only then does my own breath catch up with me.

I rearrange her hands under her favorite daisy-printed sheets and stroke my palm lightly over her body, the sweetest little mound. She's out deep tonight. Dr. Parker said the antibiotics he prescribed after her operation will make her sleep heavier than normal. It's nothing to worry about.

I pick Flopsy up from where she's fallen on the floor, gray ears sticking out at angles, and sit her at the top of Grace's pillow. It's a habit, that's all, this checking on her. Her windows are definitely locked. The nurses say it's normal, totally natural. They touch my arm and say they'd be the same after everything we've been through. I plump the heart-shaped cushion in her wheelchair. They're not only talking about Danny; they're talking about the time Grace was rushed to hospital foaming at the mouth, the time we finally decided the only way to get nutrients into her body was through a tube in her stomach, the time *he* tried to take her like he took my Danny. I pause in the doorway, watch my little mouse sleep for a moment. I always leave her door open so I can hear her call for me if she wakes, or is woken.

My bed sighs under my weight, and as I turn off my bedside lamp I think how the nurses have no idea what they're talking about. It's not what's already happened that keeps me rushing, terrified, into her room at night. It's the invisible bomb I hear ticking over our heads, the precious seconds we have left together that are starting to run out, like water through cupped hands. It's the horrific promise of what I know will come. That one day the locks will slide back, the handle will slowly start to turn, and then there will follow those practiced, determined footsteps and no matter how fast I run to her, how much I plead, there is nothing I can do to save us both.

1

Cara

I hold my finger on the bell for number 52 Woodgreen Avenue for longer than is probably polite. The ringing is urgent, but that's good, I want them to know I'm in a rush. My Monday lunchtime shift at the Ship starts in half an hour.

I imagine Grace inside, her little owl face swiveling towards the noise in a way that makes her seem so much younger than most seventeen-year-olds, her thin arms somehow maneuvering her chair down the wide corridor towards me, Meg in her uniform of slippers, leggings, and oversized T-shirt padding behind her, a kindly, dependable guard dog. "Just coming!"

I nudge my leg against the tote bag full of summer clothes—washed, ironed, and folded—ready for Meg and Grace. Mum and her friends have been collecting them for weeks.

Come on.

I take my phone out of the pocket of my ripped jeans, look

at the blank screen, and put it back again. The paint on Meg and Grace Nichols's house is fresh and gives off a chemical tang in the early June sun. Naturally, they went for pink. Mum said the Wishmakers, the charity who adapted the house for Grace's wheelchair, repainted last month. Next door, the red paint on Mum's woodwork is peeling away like burnt skin.

Where are they?

I press the doorbell again. They're always in. Maybe Meg is helping Grace in the bathroom? Or perhaps they're in Grace's bedroom, Meg changing Grace's feeding tube—I think she has to change it every week. Last Christmas, Grace lifted her Santa Claus sweater to show me the new hole in her stomach. It looked like a tiny eye socket with the eyeball plucked out. It seemed bottomless, Grace a doll with all her stuffing pulled out.

"Weird, isn't it?" she said, looking straight at me. I shrugged and turned away so she couldn't see how queasy I felt.

I glance at my phone again. Maybe I should just leave the bag here on the doorstep? I could write a note? But I know Mum will be pissed off if I don't give them the clothes in person. She's been saving them for me to bring over, like it's a special treat. Mum visits Meg and Grace a couple of times a week, sometimes coming home dewy-eyed. It's as if, for her, spending half an hour with Meg and Grace is some kind of religious experience. She says Grace always asks her what I've been up to, if I've been dating, that kind of thing. Mum is always trying to get me to visit them. I tell her I've been too busy this year, retaking my A-levels, working at the pub, and dealing with the breakup from Chris. I finished my exams two days ago and I've run out of excuses, so here I am. The truth is, I never know what to say to Grace these days. It feels mean to tell her about my life—my plans for university, how I'm going to get out of Cornwall as soon as I can, that I'm saving for a big trip to India next year—when her big weekly event is a trip down the beach with her mum.

I press my face to the mottled glass door. Although adapted for Grace's wheelchair, the layout of their bungalow is exactly the same as Mum's and probably very similar to the other one hundred and something houses and bungalows on the Summervale Estate. I can't see much; the glass makes everything look like it's underwater. My hand finds the door handle, squeezes. The inside air greets me first. It's warm, fuggy with Meg's air fresheners with names like Summer Daze that make my nose itch. I know because my mum buys the same ones.

"Hello?" I call into the thick silence of their house.

"Meg? Grace? It's Cara. I've got those clothes . . ." I stop as I turn into the sitting room. Everything is pristine as always. The beige three-piece suite is plump, the armchairs facing the sofa as though holding their own tea party. Polished photos of Meg and Grace, framed in hearts and stars, shine from the mantelpiece. But behind the sofa, my eye catches. Something is out of place, something is there that shouldn't be.

"Grace?" I move slowly, but fear comes quickly. Grace's wheelchair has fallen on its side. Her little toy rabbit and the heart-shaped cushion she sits on have skidded across the linoleum, towards the kitchen. The sight jolts me into action, and I rush around the sofa, imagining Grace's tiny body bruised and broken, her glasses smashed. But there's nothing, or almost nothing. On the floor lies Grace's diary, the same one I noticed wedged between her hip and her chair the last time I saw her, just a month ago.

Unless she's in bed, I've never seen Grace out of her chair. She's been in a wheelchair for as long as I've known her, over half her life. I pick up the diary. Down the hall, behind Meg's bedroom door, a clock chimes the half hour. A tap drip-drips. The noise shifts the air, helps me find my voice, and I call out again.

"Guys? Meg?"

I safely stow the diary in the bag of clothes and leave it in the hall. I'll give the diary back to Grace when I see her.

I make my way slowly down the corridor. With each step I take, fear tugs at my stomach, makes me alert. Somewhere a fly whines, blood rushes in my ears, the tap drip-drips. The door to the toilet opens suddenly and I cry out, my body jolting with shock, but it's just Cookie, Grace's ginger cat. Cookie ignores me and pads across the corridor, mewing as she slips gracefully into Meg's room. I follow. Now there's a new noise, a hum, like static. I tell myself, desperately, that it might be the radio. Maybe that's why Meg and Grace can't hear me?

But as I get closer, I know the humming sound isn't mechanical. It's deeper, weirder . . . organic. The back of my hand strokes the smooth, cool wall. The smell of cheap vanilla, so sweet it's almost putrid, blooms inside me like mold.

"Hello?" I don't recognize my voice, cracked and small. Fear grips like a hand squeezing my throat. I'm about to push Meg's door but it opens wide at the slightest touch, as if eager to give its secrets away.

I see the bluebottle flies first. They circle above her like tiny vultures. Meg is twisted around the bedsheets, her body brittle and too still to be resting. Her face is gray, her gaze clouded, but fixed on something living eyes can never see. Her mouth is a rictus of fear. Her forehead has collapsed in on itself, no longer a shape, just a dark mass of sticky pulp. Blood stains the sheets, halo-like behind her. Her bruised leg and arm hang over the edge of the bed and from her pink-painted fingertips her blood drip-drips.

2

Jon

As I stand in the middle of a field, looking down at a dead sheep and wondering for the fifty-third time that day what the hell has happened to my life, my phone buzzes with a text. As the farmer, Mr. Leeson, nudges the bloodied sheep with his foot, as though prompting the poor dead animal to confirm that it was definitely "those bloody travellers and their bloody dogs" that ripped her esophagus from her throat, I remind myself this is my second chance. That I'm lucky to have this job, and a way to keep my son Jacob in my life. Not everyone gets a second chance. Mr. Leeson bends low into the mud towards the dead sheep, allowing me to surreptitiously check my phone. I hope it's a text from Jacob—Jakey—but the screen says *Ben*.

Six months ago, a text from Ben wouldn't have been anything remarkable. But then I wouldn't have been standing in a boggy field looking at a dead sheep because just six months ago I was busy doing real investigative journalism. The last time I saw Ben was the last time I wrote anything of my choosing. A personable freelance photographer, Ben took the photos that accompanied the article which, in a roundabout way, led me here, to this field, on this dank early June day with Mr. Leeson and his dead sheep.

"So, are yer going to talk to them then?" the farmer asks, showing me blackened gums that look like their own crime scene.

I shove the phone back down into my pocket. "Sorry, Mr. Leeson. Who is it you want me to talk to?"

"Them gypsies . . . them travellers, what yer call them. Are you going ter talk ter them or is it up ter me and my shotgun?" Mr. Leeson lifts his flat cap off his head and wipes his greasy hair with a mucky hand. I have the impression he's hoping I'll choose the latter option.

"How about I go and talk to my editor about a story and we'll—"

"All the story you bloody need is right 'ere." His heavy boot is back on the sheep's head. I wish he'd stop. I know she's dead but her eyes are still open, and it's muddy. It starts to rain again.

"I heard you're from London," Mr. Leeson says with a familiar mixture of disdain and pity. The "poor sod" following the statement is always silent. I don't want to get into this now. Telling people how I moved here to Cornwall for my wife, my son, for a better life is like being forced to repeat a joke you know isn't funny again and again. I snap the rubber band against my wrist. The rubber band was suggested by Dr. Bunce, the relationship therapist I'm seeing twice a week with—and at the behest of—my wife, Ruth. The little shocks of the rubber against my skin are supposed to stop negative thoughts. It doesn't work, of course—instead I have a new tic to accompany all the shit going on in my head.

"I'd better be getting on," I say, declining to respond to Mr. Leeson's statement. The Cornish rain is already soaking through my thin London-bought anorak and my glasses have started to steam up. I'm only standing in this God-forsaken field because I didn't know how to tell Mr. Leeson that I didn't want to see the mutilated sheep he found this morning—the third already this summer.

I'm here reporting for *The Rambler*, a magazine dedicated to all things Cornish and outdoors, and we're supposed to be talking about the farmer's preparations for the Ashford Agricultural Show next month. I'm here to talk winning sheep, not dead ones with jellied eyes.

Mud sucks around my Converse as we walk across the flat, boggy field towards the farmyard. I shake Mr. Leeson's hard hand, say sorry again about the sheep, promise to be in touch about the story. As soon as I sit behind the wheel I wipe my glasses with my sleeve and reach for my phone to read Ben's text.

Jon mate, long time no see. Thought you'd want to know. Police just removed a body from the Nichols place on Woodgreen Ave. Break-in gone wrong? Fucking nuts. The body looked too big to be the girl. Ben.

A robbery in the small town of Ashford is headline news, but a possible murder is beyond comprehension. I read the text again.

From anyone else the "too big to be the girl" bit would sound monstrous but I know Ben just wants to reassure me it's not Grace in the body bag and I'm grateful for that. But still, *shit*, does that mean it's Meg? Ashford's darling, the perfect mum, dead? Murdered in her own home?

I wonder where they've taken Grace. To a neighbor's? The

police station? I imagine her mute with shock, trembling in her wheelchair, clutching that stuffed rabbit like a much younger girl. I hope someone will know how to comfort her, that they'll call the doctor, help calm her down. I can't imagine the trauma will do her already-weak heart any good.

Out of the grubby farmhouse window Mr. Leeson is staring down at me and frowning. His lips move, presumably saying something to Mrs. Leeson—perhaps he's finally noticed, is telling her he remembers my face on the front of the *Ashford Echo*—before he walks away from the window.

I tap out a response to Ben's text: Thanks for letting me know.

My car skids in the mud as I pull out of the farmyard. Hands firm against the wheel, I remind myself why I mustn't go to Woodgreen Avenue. The police, the restraining order, the custody agreement. I snap the rubber band.

I glance at my watch. Ruth and I have a session with Dr. Bunce in forty minutes. Ruth sent a text to remind me this morning. As I drive down the bumpy farm lane, I reason that the ten miles to Dr. Bunce's incense-scented treatment room on the other side of town should only take twenty-five minutes tops at this time of day. I snap harder. The skin on my wrist turns pink.

All I can think about is Ben's text, about Meg and Grace. Could it have been a break-in gone wrong? Somehow I don't think so. Human decency aside, what idiot would target the most beloved family in Ashford? But the idea that it was a personal attack is hardly easier to fathom. My thoughts drift to Simon, Grace's dad. Mentally unstable and deemed a danger to others, Meg had kept him away from Grace for most of her life. I'll bet all fingers are already pointed at him.

I remember the one and only time I spoke to Meg about Simon.

I was interviewing her and Grace for the article that was about to ruin my life, though I didn't know it then. They'd welcomed me warmly into their home, though underneath there was a disappointed, restless feel, like the aftermath of an argument. I had an unusual feeling of wanting to leave as soon as I arrived, but Meg and Grace smiled at me, told me they'd made cake, and looked at each other like teenagers about to burst into giggles, then apologized, said they were nervous, excited. They sat next to each other, Grace's small hand always reaching to hold her mum's. They finished each other's sentences. Grace spoke in a little girl's voice despite being a teenager and Meg's accent had the full, rolling vowels of someone who'd spent her life in the South-West. Meg showed me albums full of photos of Grace in different hospital beds, doctors and nurses posing at her side like playground buddies. It didn't take long for me to realize that Meg didn't understand why the Wishmakers had put us in touch—perhaps the Wishmakers didn't understand the purpose of the article either—so it was up to me to explain.

"What, out of interest, were you told the article was about?"

I directed the question at Meg. She had short, loosely curled brown hair and a full face, unremarkable looking until she smiled. Then, it was like being given a bowl of something warm and delicious. Her brow creased as she tried to remember what she'd been told.

"Maggie said you were writing about how families cope in times of difficulty. That you'd want to know about our challenges with Grace's health." In a quieter voice she added, "Maybe a bit about Danny too."

I shifted in my seat, uncomfortable under their expectant gaze. I chose my words carefully, suddenly aware of how fragile they both were.

"In part, yes. I want to hear, if I may, about both those things. But the article is also about the new branch of Dads Without Borders in Plymouth. So, I do have some questions about Grace's dad and what happened in your relationship with him."

A frost seemed to pass across Meg's face and her eyes became hard, unseeing. Grace turned anxiously from her mum to me, then back again.

"What do you want to know about Simon?" Meg's mouth pinched with the question.

"Do the two of you ever speak?" I knew from having interviewed Simon that they didn't, but I wanted to hear her side of the story.

"To the man who is responsible for my son's death? To the man who used to be physically violent, who tried to kidnap my daughter? No. I don't speak to him." There was a sob in her throat and her face reddened, while the color seemed to drain from Grace's already pale skin. Meg's words built an invisible wall between us. Simon was clearly not a topic for discussion. Grace stared at me, and behind her glasses I saw her eyes had blurred with tears. Her hand searched across the table; she needed to be held by her mum. They found each other like magnets. I apologized, asked to see the photos of Grace in hospital again to calm Meg, to lighten the mood. Later, when Meg stood up to go to the toilet, she winced, rubbed her lower back. When she saw me looking she shook her head like it was nothing. "Old back injury," she said, "from a long time ago. He pushed me down the stairs." She put a hand on Grace's shoulder in a way that meant she didn't want to say anything more about it.

As soon as Meg was out of the door, Grace leaned forward in her chair and asked in a whisper, "Have you seen him? Have you seen my dad?"

14

The memory comes back to me, clear as a day, and as I pull onto the main road a sign reminds me how close to Woodgreen Avenue I am right now—just five minutes away. I could drive by the house, see what's going on. I won't even get out of my car. No one will notice I'm there and no one need ever know I went. And I'd still be at Dr. Bunce's in plenty of time. So why not? Once I've been, my curiosity will be sated and I won't need to go again.

Fuck it.

I turn off the main road.

The Summervale Estate is a maze of identical Spam-colored houses built in the nineties, an uninspiring lump a couple of miles outside Ashford. Only a handful of locals actually live in the town now, most of them having sold up to rich families looking for a holiday home with sea views years ago. I don't blame them. Many of the people here found themselves newly poor and unskilled after the collapse of the tin-mining industry in the nineties, so when the estate agents told them what their tiny fishing cottages were worth they were already packed and ready to move to new-build suburbia.

I creep slowly on the approach to the Nichols's bungalow and set myself some rules. I won't get out of the car. I won't talk to anyone. I'm here only as a concerned Ashfordian, not as a reporter. I don't know if restraining orders still apply if the protected person is dead, but I can't afford any trouble.

I don't remember the last time I was here, six months ago. I don't remember because I'd drunk the best part of a bottle of Jack Daniel's—and I'm not a drinker. I don't remember banging on the door, screaming at Meg and ripping up the front garden that volunteers from the Wishmakers had planted. I don't remember breaking their sitting-room windows with one of my dad's old golf clubs and I don't remember the police tackling me to the ground.

It's stopped raining by the time I park outside number 50, close enough to see what's happening but far enough away to hopefully avoid being recognized. The police have cordoned off the area outside Meg and Grace's house. Two uniformed police officers stand stock-still, hands clasped, outside the front door. The curtains are drawn in the big front window but the lights are on. One of the police officers is smiling slightly, delighted perhaps that something big, a drama like on telly, is at last happening here in Ashford. The pink bungalow looks just the same, though freshly painted, and I notice guiltily that they've replanted the garden. There's a new-looking VW Caddy in the driveway, a Wishmakers sticker in the window; it looks specially adapted for Grace's wheelchair.

There's a loud smack at the window and a damp-looking palm lands flat against the glass. It's Ben, cradling his camera like a baby. He bends down to look through the passenger-side window, his Italian features folding into a wide, easy smile, before he opens the door.

"All right, mate!" We shake hands before he steps into my car, kicking away the empty cans and crisp packets that litter the floor. "Thought you'd come down. I was having bets with myself, wondering whether you'd stay away—"

"Good to see you, Ben." The only way to get Ben to stop talking is to regularly interrupt him. "I'm just here out of concern, as a neighbor, not for work. Is it . . . is it Meg?"

Ben nods his head slowly, sorrowful for a moment. "It's a fucking tragedy, mate. Something bad, and I mean *bad*, happened here. Remember my wife's mate Remi, goes out with Sam over there?" Ben nods his head towards the smiling police officer and keeps talking.

"Sam told me that Meg's skull was smashed in using an iron bedside lamp, *in her own bed*. Sounds totally fucking brutal. 'Frenzied' is the word everyone's using. Anyway, the neighbor found the body, and on top of that no one knows what's happened to Grace. Mate, I know it sounds mad, but it's looking like some-one's taken her."

No, no, that can't be right. Ben sees my frown, the confusion.

"I know what you're thinking. Of course, it was the dad—who the fuck else would kidnap a disabled seventeen-year-old kid, right? Sam said they're already trying to track him down—last seen in Plymouth—but no luck yet—"

We both turn towards a movement in front of the house. A dark-haired young woman I recognize, wrapped in a gray blanket, is being ushered slowly out of number 52 by two female police officers. One of the officers is carrying a tote bag over her shoul-der. The young woman is Cara Dorman from number 53, Meg and Grace's next-door neighbor. Cara's mum, Susan, clad in bright red chinos and clutching Grace's ginger cat, walks shakily behind them. They keep their heads down, respectful; stare at their feet. Ben clutches his camera—"Gotta go, mate"—before scrambling out of the car and lifting his camera to his shoulder like a hunter with a rifle.

Everyone on the street turns to watch the somber procession as they shuffle slowly past the Nichols's car and onto the pave-ment. Ben's camera pops. They're walking right towards me and for a mad moment I think they've come to arrest me for breaking the restraining order, but the police officers and Susan keep their heads low, like sad, wilting flowers. Only Cara lifts her gaze. She glances at me where I'm parked across the road, her brown eyes wide, wild like they'd scream if they could, but she doesn't recognize me, and then she looks away again as she is gently ushered up the brick path and through the door to number 53.

Once the door is shut behind them a tension settles coldly in my chest; it pulls and tugs, makes my hands grip the steering wheel. The pain's familiar. It's the same pain I felt when my son was diagnosed with leukemia, that sat in my chest the whole time he was in hospital. Two years on and he's in remission now, thank God. His hair has grown back blonder and he plays football four times a week. It's Ruth and I who didn't recover. Jakey's illness put a strain on our relationship, but it was my badly judged article about Meg and Grace that marked the beginning of the end. A court case, a restraining order, and a difficult separation later, here I am. Back again.

I close my eyes, rub them under my glasses to try to stop an image of Jakey, sick and in hospital, from coming into my mind. Instead I see Grace, remember her showing me the assortment of pills she had to take every day. Blue for her muscles, white for her stomach; she held out a pink pill for me to see.

"This one, this is the most important, this keeps me alive. I have this one twice a day," she said in her singsong voice. "It keeps my heart from stopping."

I watched as she swallowed the pill as easily as a drunk with vodka. God, where are those pink pills now? How long will it be before she starts to weaken without them? I imagine her heartbeats becoming soft, irregular, like a wind-up toy running out of energy. I rub my hand over my face because my eyes have filled and all I can see is the photo of Grace we used in the article. She had a new beanie hat covering her bald head, her smile so wide her eyes disappeared behind her huge glasses. And as I try to rub her image and the tears from my eyes, I hear her again—*It keeps my heart from stopping*—and I know that Grace must be found quickly before she fades and fades and there is nothing left.

The sound of my phone ringing pulls me back from losing it completely. Ruth's name flashes on the screen. I turn the keys in the ignition and as I pull away my tires squeal, which makes a couple of police officers look up. I glance at my watch. *Fuck, fuck, fuck.* It's 2:52 p.m. I have eight minutes to get to Dr. Bunce's before Ruth loses her shit. I answer, and press the speaker button on my phone.

"Jon?" Ruth's beautiful, husky voice fills the car.

"Oh hi, love," I say, not looking properly as I pull out of the estate, wiping my eyes.

"You sound stressed. Why are you stressed?"

There's never any lying to Ruth.

"No, no, I'm just, um, the traffic's just a bit tight."

"Well, where are you?" I imagine her outside Dr. Bunce's in her own car, peering down the road perhaps, hopeful that I'm about to appear. She thinks the sessions will help us figure out how we co-parent Jakey, but I'm hopeful they'll make her realize how good we are together and bring her back to me.

"Just coming from an interview, sweetheart. I'll be there in about fifteen minutes." The GPS says twenty-eight minutes.

"So you're going to be late," she sighs, as though me letting her down is inevitable, like I am the cross she has to bear. My stomach tightens.

"A few minutes late, and I'm sorry, but I am on my way. Why don't you get started? I'll be there before you know it."

"Because this is supposed to be *couples* counseling, Jon, and when one half of a couple can't be bothered to turn up . . ."

"I can be bothered, Ruth. I'm clearly bothered. I'm just a few minutes late because of work and I'm sorry. Look, the longer you talk to me the less time you have to tell Dr. Bunce what a massive pain in the arse—" but I know Ruth's stopped listening because in the background she turns up the news on the radio. I catch a few words clearly: "body," "Megan Nichols," and "missing."

"Ruth? Ruth?" I ask, but she's not listening to me anymore.

"OK, see you soon, Jon," she says, distracted by the news story. She hangs up as I move into the fast lane.

I'm twenty minutes late by the time I pull up outside Dr. Bunce's Victorian terrace. My wrist smarts; I've been flicking the elastic band nonstop. I ring the doorbell and hear the shock of it reverberate throughout the house. Dr. Bunce likes to move slowly, not because she's old—she's only in her mid-fifties—but as if she wants to convey that life is something to savor, a fine wine. *Hurry the fuck up.* By the time she's opened the door and I've kicked off my shoes on her cool mosaic floor I'm at least three minutes later. I apologize, which she accepts with a gentle nod of her fine, gray-haired head. The therapy room is sparsely furnished and always smells freshly vacuumed. Ruth is sitting in one of two armchairs opposite Dr. Bunce's larger chair, a box of tissues in front of her. Her wavy blond bob curls behind her ears; the dimple in her chin is visible, which means she's trying hard to stop her chin from wobbling. She pulls the sleeves of her red sweater over her hands as I bend to kiss her cheek, as I say, "Sorry, sorry I'm late."

I sit in the chair next to Ruth, my heart still in fluttery panic in my chest, not yet tuned in to the stillness of the room after the speeding and swearing of the last twenty-eight minutes. Ruth glances at me, her eyelashes dewy, before she turns back to Dr. Bunce, who sits opposite us, her fingers raised in a steeple, her head angled slightly to the side like a thoughtful hen.

"Ruth, are you happy for me to share what we were talking about before Jon arrived?"

Ruth nods. There's a tissue scrunched into a ball in her hand. Dr. Bunce turns to me.

"Jon, Ruth was explaining how she feels you're not committed to these meetings and, by extension, no longer committed to making your marriage work." Dr. Bunce speaks like she moves, slowly and clearly. My words sound loud and boisterous in comparison as I twist in my chair towards Ruth.

"No, come on, please. This is the first time I've been—"

Ruth's forehead knots and her green eyes darken as she interrupts. "It's the second time you've been late, and I know you lied about where you were earlier."

"I didn't lie."

"You said you were working, at an interview."

"I was . . . I . . ." I feel heat flush my cheeks.

"I heard about what happened to poor Megan Nichols on the radio. You went to their house, didn't you?"

"Ruth . . ." I glance at Dr. Bunce but she's no help. She's looking at me, after the truth as well.

"I knew, I just *knew* you wouldn't be able to stay away."

I snap the band on my wrist. Dr. Bunce sees, arches an eyebrow. Out of the corner of my eye I see Ruth glance at Dr. Bunce for support before turning back to me. I don't look at Ruth as I try to explain to her as calmly as I can: "Megan Nichols has been murdered, her disabled daughter kidnapped."

"Exactly. That's why you of all people should show some humility, some decency. And if that's too much like empathy, then at least show some respect for the restraining order. What if the police had seen you?"

"I only went out of concern, Ruth, nothing more. I won't

21

go again." I'm surprised to hear that my voice has grown into a shout. Ruth's eyes widen. I've overreacted. I force a calm I don't feel into my tone. "Look, maybe I shouldn't have gone, but I knew them both a little and I interviewed Simon. You know I always thought he was treated unfairly. I can see the same thing is going to happen—"

"Jon, listen to yourself!" The tendons in Ruth's throat swell as she shouts. Jakey once told me "that means Mummy's really cross." "The woman's son drowned when he was four, her daughter's severely disabled, and the father of her kids pushed her down a flight of stairs when she was pregnant and then tried to kidnap their daughter, and you're protecting *him*? Jesus!" Ruth sits back in her chair as though exhausted by my stupidity, looking at Dr. Bunce like they're a team. The therapist strokes the air with her hands, as though it's the air and not us that needs calming. But I don't see her, not really. Instead I see Grace again, smiling, holding out that pink pill. Dr. Bunce asks something about what me visiting Woodgreen Avenue means in terms of our relationship.

"It means Jon cares more about trying to save his professional reputation than saving his family," Ruth says, matter-of-fact and keeping her eyes on Dr. Bunce, a child telling a teacher about another's naughty behavior. I'm shaking my head before she's even stopped talking.

"That's bullshit, complete bullshit."

"OK, can you tell us what it means for you, Jon?" Dr. Bunce's steady gaze settles on me like a blanket.

"It means I've got shit time-keeping skills."

After the last couple of sessions, Ruth invited me back to New Barn Cottage, the home we converted just outside Ashford. We picked Jakey up, had a family meal together, then, after I put Jakey to bed, Ruth and I stayed up, drinking wine. Last week we kissed and it felt like the first time, only better; the love came back in a flood. But today the tendons in Ruth's throat are still twitching as we leave Dr. Bunce's in silence. Once in her car, she snaps her seat belt around her and I have to tap on her window before she winds it down, and it's only then I see she's crying again.

"Oh God, Ruth, look, I'm sorry. It was a stupid thing to do. I should have come here straightaway, but don't make it into something bigger than it is. We were doing so well."

Her eyes dim as the tears pool, and she says, "I was starting to think these sessions were about more than just Jakey. I was starting to think they could help save our marriage. But if you're late and don't take them seriously then I don't think we've got anything left to talk about."

I watch as Ruth drives away. She's right, of course, she usually is. I need to stay away from Summervale and the whole case. Now is a time to focus on rebuilding my family and my career. It's not a time to be digging around for an angle about a murder and kidnapping; there'll be plenty of reporters doing that already. Though those other reporters won't have met all three of the people involved . . .

All three of them.

Did I just think that? Assumptions are so contagious and so slippery. It's so easy to assume Simon is involved in all this. I sit in my car and snap the band on my wrist to try to stop thinking about Meg, Grace, and Simon when I should be thinking about Ruth and Jakey. My bones feel heavy as I turn the key in the ignition, but I don't start to drive, not yet. I don't want to go back to the flat I refuse to think of as home, but I have nowhere else to go. I still need to write the article about the summer fair; it's due tomorrow. If I focus, I'll get it done in a couple of hours. Then what?

I wish I had a friend, someone I could meet for a pint and a chat, but I left all my real friends behind in London. I scroll through my phone, try to find a name, someone I can call who lives near Ashford who isn't better friends with Ruth than me. Becks and Clare went to school with her, so they're both a no, and Laurence, who lives round the corner from my flat, was her first boyfriend, so he's a definite no. Besides, since the article and the tsunami of vitriol against me, I know none of them would relish being seen with me in public. Which just leaves Dave.

I feel a new kind of loneliness, staring at Dave's number and realizing it's come to this: Dave is my only chance of seeing a friendly face tonight. Dave is a middle-aged policeman I met by chance after a row with Ruth and an angry stomp to the pub. I've only ever contacted him when I wanted the inside story on something for an article, but I'm desperate, and Dave's been through an acrimonious separation so he might understand. Before I can change my mind, I text him: "Pints tonight, mate?" And as I drive slowly away I feel worse than I have in weeks, lonely and very much on my own. Ruth said the meetings with Dr. Bunce would help, but she was wrong this time. Therapy really is complete bollocks.

3

Cara

"You know you can cry if you want to," Jane, the family liaison officer, tells me as she places a third cup of tea in front of me, the other two poured stone cold and untouched down the sink. She scoops away the ragged tissues Mum's left littered on the coffee table. I get the impression Jane likes to be in perpetual motion, like she doesn't want her thoughts to settle. On the sofa next to me, Mum squeezes my hand. Our skin feels damp where we touch. She's been gripping on to me for over an hour now.

"Car's not much of a crier, are you, love?" Mum wipes my fringe out of my eyes with her fingertips. Mum's face is blotched, swollen, her eyes even bluer than normal with all the crying, mascara streaming down her face in dirty rivers.

"She's like her dad. He never cried. Doesn't matter though. I cry enough for the both of us, don't I, love?" She kisses my forehead and I let her hold me; I know she needs to feel me close. She becomes still, stares into space as though she could stare herself out of the room, back to yesterday when her friend was still alive. Her lungs heave a couple of times and I know she's about to start again.

"Who . . . who could do such a horrible thing to such a good person?" she asks no one in particular. "I can't, I can't . . ." but her voice turns to a wail, her tears crash, wash away whatever it was she was about to say. I press my ear against her chest and listen to her heart, imagine little pieces of it breaking away with each racking sob. Jane stands, watches us for a second before her radio crackles and she hurries to answer it in the kitchen. As soon as we got home from my recorded interview at the police station Jane drew the sitting-room curtains so we couldn't see the journalists and the photographers outside, but we can hear them. Tense voices, the odd cough, and every now and then a laugh, a reminder that this is just another Monday for them.

In the kitchen, Jane speaks into her radio. "OK, I'll let them know. Over." My neck feels stiff. Mum's arms relax around me, so I take my chance and sit up.

"DCI Upton and DC Brown are just finishing up next door. They'll then come over here to ask a few more questions, if that's OK?" Jane looks at us.

Mum squeezes my hand one last time before letting it go.

"Cara told them everything already at the station . . ."

"It shouldn't take long. They want to speak to both of you this time, more general questions about Megan and Grace."

Jane and Mum keep their eyes fixed on me. They've been like that for hours, like they expect me to do something at any moment and don't want to miss it. I nod, unsure whether I'll be able to find my voice.

"If it gets too much at any point or you need to take a break, you just let us know, OK, Cara?" There's a thin line of coral lipstick around the outside of Mum's lips. I nod at her, but I know she wants to hear me say it.

"OK, yeah." The words are sore in my throat and I stand, unsteadily, as Jane and Mum stare, wide-eyed.

"Toilet," I tell them. There's one just off the kitchen, but I decide to walk to the bathroom at the end of the hall instead. It'll give me a bit more time alone, free from their staring eyes that make my skin prickle. Our bungalow has the same layout as number 52. Before I can stop myself, I glance at Mum's bedroom door, the twin of Meg's. Drip, drip. My mouth tastes like rust, like blood. I see Meg's dead eyes, open but unseeing. I lean against the cool corridor wall to steady myself, turn away from Mum's door. I breathe deep and slow, wait for my heart to settle, and let my eyes slide across the walls. They're bursting with life and memories— Mum's a sentimental hoarder. I spot an excruciating poem I wrote about autumn when I was ten.

> Red leaves dance to the ground,
> Soft and without a sound . . .

It's framed next to a photo of Granny and Granddad grinning in deckchairs on Ashford Beach. There are countless photos of me, all the way from blubbery baby to unsmiling teen. A couple of cheap watercolors Mum's had forever and a few framed posters. I've never understood why Mum bothers putting stuff up. No one ever sees it apart from her, which kind of defeats the point. But now I take comfort in these simple things. They're like a stitch holding together the world before I found Meg's body with the world now, just a few hours later—the safe "before" and the terrifying "after."

My eyes stop suddenly. Next to an embarrassing KEEP CALM AND CARRY ON poster is a framed photo of me and Grace. I haven't looked at it, really looked at the photo in months, maybe years. The photo was taken at Grace's thirteenth birthday party. The huge helium "13" I gave her is attached to the back of her chair, next to me, where I'm leaning low so our heads are level for the camera. Grace is wearing a bright blue wig; a birthday badge on her chest says TEENAGER! We're both grinning, but behind her glasses Grace's eyes are fixed towards the camera while mine are cast sideways, towards Grace, like I'm checking she's having a good time. Those were still the days when Meg would let me take Grace to the beach. We'd come home with red, windburned cheeks, sticky from ice cream, big smiles on our faces, and a feeling that everything was OK because we had each other. Grace loved the beach but she hated the water, never wanted to go near it. I asked her once why she was so frightened and she whispered "Danny" and I knew not to ask anymore. It can't have been soon after that photo was taken that I met Chris and let my whole world shrink to fit him. Chris teased me for being friends with a disabled kid five years younger than me. At the same time, Grace's fits got worse, and then it was too dangerous for me to take her out on my own. I started to see less of Grace, and when I did see her, often during one of her frequent hospital stays, she'd be hooked up to cruel-looking machines and an unspoken question in her eyes—*Where have you been?*—made me feel hollow with guilt, which only made me turn away from her more.

The doorbell rings and I hear Jane call "I'll get it!" like we're at her house. I quietly lock myself into the bathroom before she steps into the hallway and sees me.

I've already met the two police officers. They took my statement and DNA swabs a couple of hours ago at Ashford police station, while I left Mum wailing into Jane's arms. DCI Upton has a strong face; she looks like the type who runs marathons for fun. DC Brown looks almost withered next to her. A skinny man so covered in freckles they've even reached his lips and the insides of his ears, he follows Brown like an apologetic shadow.

I know I'll need to face Upton sooner or later, so I head to the kitchen. Jane swiftly clears Mum's magazines and unopened mail from the table and the four of us sit.

"Thanks for seeing us again, both of you. I'm sure you're exhausted so hopefully this won't take too long." Upton keeps her eyes on me as she talks.

Next to me, Mum runs her long nails through her rust-colored hair and rests her elbows on the table, leaning in towards Upton and Brown, not crying anymore. She's reapplied her mascara and coral lipstick.

"Oh anything, anything we can do to help. Isn't that right, Car? Have you got search parties out yet?"

Upton nods. "We're doing everything we possibly can to find her but the next few hours, as I'm sure you're aware, are critical. The more information we have, the better our chances of finding her. Can you think of anyone who would want to hurt the Nicholses?"

Mum's eyes start welling up again and she chokes out a name in a strangled sob.

"Simon. It has to be him. He's crazy, unhinged, he . . ." she sniffs and shakes her head violently, steeling herself. "He's done it before, hasn't he? Kidnapped Grace? And he was violent before that too. Pushed Meg down the stairs when she was eight months pregnant. That's why she went into labor early. Meg told me once that the doctors think that's why Grace had so many troubles." She whispers "troubles" like it's a dirty word.

Brown scribbles in a skinny pad. Upton keeps her eyes fixed on Mum and nods.

"Yes, we've got a record. Ms. Nichols called the police on a number of occasions reporting threatening behavior from her ex-husband. We've been told Simon had been calling the house, apparently trying to contact Grace."

Mum nods, looking from Upton's eyes to Brown's notepad. "Honestly, she changed her number so many times but somehow he always managed to track it down."

"Was she scared of him, do you think?"

Mum nods so hard I think she's about to come off her chair. "Of course she was. Mostly scared for Grace, of course. Stress really isn't good for her heart or her epilepsy. I'll never forget, soon after they came down from Plymouth and moved in next door, the girls were playing in Cara's room and Meg sat right where you are now and told me about Simon. It was the first time I'd heard about Danny, her little boy, how Simon was supposed to be looking after him but he was pissed, didn't keep a close enough eye on him as he played in the sea, a couple of hours north of here, over at Port Raynor Beach. His tiny body washed up two days later." Mum starts crying again. I stroke her shoulder; Jane offers another tissue. Upton shifts in her seat like she doesn't have time for tears as she asks, "And their relationship came to an end soon after their son's death?"

"I told you at the station already," Mum says, dabbing the tissue under her eyes, checking for mascara. "I wouldn't call it a relationship. Simon was the abuser and Meg was the victim." Mum squeezes the tissue in her hand before adding, "Look, shouldn't you lot be out there trying to find Grace instead of asking us the same questions again and again?"

Upton holds up her hand in apology and says, "I know this is distressing, Susan, but I'm just trying to get the facts straight. I can assure you there are already highly trained search teams working around the clock to find Grace. Now, can you tell me a bit more about what happened after Danny's death?"

Mum sniffs, dabs her nose with the tissue before she starts talking again.

"Simon started drinking more after Danny died and Meg kept on trying to leave him but he begged her to take him back, wouldn't leave her alone. It took some time, but Meg finally found the courage to leave him once and for all, for Grace's sake more than anything, and the two of them came here for a fresh start when Grace was seven. Honestly, I remember thinking it was the saddest story I'd ever heard. I couldn't believe one woman could go through so much and now . . . and now this has happened I . . ." Mum covers her eyes with a tissue, forgetting about her makeup. Her shoulders shake. Jane puts a glass of water in front of her.

"Please take your time, Susan," Upton says. "I know how hard this must be." She turns to me.

"You were close to Grace, is that right?"

"Oh, the two of them were like sisters," Mum says wetly, fanning her hand in front of her eyes to try to stop more tears. Upton looks at me but Mum keeps talking. "It was so sweet: when Grace was about nine and Cara fourteen, they'd play dress up and Cara would push Grace all the way to the beach. They tied balloons to Grace's chair. Remember, Car? How you used to tie balloons to her chair?"

I nod, feeling all the eyes in the room on me. Grace had just seen the Pixar film *Up* and thought if she got enough balloons she'd sail away. She saved up her pocket money for months. I didn't have the heart to tell her it would never work. Besides, it was adorable how much she believed in magic.

"But you saw less of her in more recent years, is that right? When you were living in Plymouth?"

I nod. I'd moved to Plymouth to live with Chris after I dropped out of school at seventeen, cocky and sure I could handle life. I worked in a pub and then got a job as a receptionist in a small local estate agency. I pretended I was happy wishing away the weeks, drinking away the weekends with Chris and his mates. It was when Chris started talking about babies that the panic set in. I felt trapped, knew I had to get out. I had to at least try to do something with my life. So just over a year ago I moved back in with Mum, signed up at college to take my A-levels, and got a job at the Ship.

"I didn't see Grace so much when I was living in Plymouth. I was there for a few years." My voice is small and I feel Mum swell with words next to me.

"Well, yes, partly because Car was in the city, but also they started doing all those tests on Grace's heart because of the arrhythmia, and then of course her seizures became more severe and she couldn't swallow so she became very weak. With all of that, Cara couldn't take her out anymore in case something happened. It wouldn't have been fair on Cara to be put in that position."

It was just a month ago, a sunny day in May, the last time I went over to see Grace. I was busy studying for my exams and she begged me to take her to the beach. She wanted to go, just the two of us, but I'd heard how bad her seizures were now, how her eyes rolled and her lungs refused to behave like lungs, how she'd spasm so hard she once fell out of her chair, smashing her front tooth on the pavement. Her epilepsy was harder to manage because of her muscular dystrophy. The seizures would strike without warning, at any time. Meg said she'd come to the beach with us, but Grace wheeled herself back to her room, mumbling "Don't bother" over her shoulder. When I told Mum later, she reminded me Grace was still a teenager, prone to testiness like anyone else, despite being sick.

"So you grew up seeing Grace's health struggles?" Upton is looking at me, but Mum answers yet again.

"Oh, Cara was brilliant with Grace when she was little, she'd even help Meg with her medication, remember, Car? That was when you said you were going to be a doctor."

I don't remember that, but I do remember a few years ago, the summer before Grace's thirteenth birthday, waiting, nervous, in the hall while Meg went into Grace's room to see if she was awake. Grace had just had a huge seizure and Meg said she was still groggy. It was August, the sun blistered, I was in flip-flops and had my swimming costume on under my shorts, ready to rejoin Chris and his mates for flirting and cheap booze on the beach. The coconut oil I'd slathered all over my skin curdled in the humid air of number 52; I wanted to get out of there, but then I heard Grace crying so I pushed the door open a couple of inches. Meg was sitting on Grace's bed, her back to the door. The curtains were drawn, summer and all its energy pulsed just behind the thin orange fabric like a heart. An ice-cream van chimed outside, jarring with Grace's warm room, tangy with sweat and vomit. Meg turned briefly, a small, sad smile on her lips as she tilted her arms so Grace and I could see each other. Grace's eyes were open, they flicked towards me briefly, but her body looked floppy in Meg's arms, wasted and strangely without form, like all her bones had withered away. I realized she wasn't crying, her face was dry, but she let out a whimper, raw and desperate. I felt embarrassed, she sounded so animal. It felt impossible she could be wasting away in this stifling room when half an hour earlier my legs had been wrapped around Chris's waist in the sea, his stubble grazing my face. Grace's pain felt so abstract, I couldn't comprehend it and, being there in her room, I realized my life would be easier if I didn't try. Meg, sensing my alarm, stroked Grace's damp hair off her forehead, rocked her broken daughter gently in her arms, and spoke softly.

"I'm not sure today's the day for visitors, Cara. I'm sorry."

I was already backing away, relief rising in a wave. I ran away from them, back towards summer, towards stolen cider on the beach and more salty kisses with Chris. I wish I could go back to that moment, shake myself for being so selfish, so shortsighted. My friend was suffering and I should have done something, anything, to make things better for her.

Across the table, Upton is still staring at me, quizzical, her eyebrows slightly raised.

"I wanted to ask you both about the journalist, Jon Katrin. He interviewed you, didn't he, for an article in the *Cornish Chronicle*?"

Next to me, Mum snorts with disdain.

"He came over here for ten minutes, I'd hardly call it a proper interview, but that's his style of shitty journalism, excuse my French. He asked me what Meg and Grace were like, what I thought of Simon, and that was it. What do you want to know about him for? It's Simon you need to focus on."

"We're keeping all lines of inquiry open at this stage. What did you think of Jon Katrin, Cara?"

Upton keeps her eyes on me as Mum says, "Cara only met him after the interview, on his way out. Isn't that right, Car?"

Upton's still looking at me, waiting for a response, so I shrug and mumble, "Didn't think much of him."

I'd been at college all day and had come back half an hour early to meet the journalist Mum and Meg were so excited about, but he already had his coat and Converse on, ready to go, by the time I arrived, Mum visibly wilting with disappointment behind him. He shook my hand and grimaced when he saw the thick book in my hand, and said, "God, I remember studying *Middlemarch* at uni, almost drove me mad." Then, with a wave to us both, he was gone.

"His article was a disgrace. Meg said when she read it she felt like she'd just been chucked down the stairs again."

Upton listens quietly, lets Mum vent.

"She was devastated. I mean, imagine, she lost her little boy and then dedicated her life to caring for Grace only for some bloody reporter—that Jon whatshisname—some *man* to tell the world he thinks she wasn't doing well enough because she wouldn't let the violent bastard near Grace. Honestly, I was seething for her, for them both. Seething."

Mum pauses for a moment, sniffs. Usually when she's wrong, I have no problem letting her know, but suddenly I realize I don't know what's right anymore. Everything feels out of focus, blurred. I used to think the reporter, Jon, was suggesting that Danny's death was an accident and that it was unfair for Simon's life, and his relationship with his daughter, to be completely destroyed because of an accident. I remember at the time I kind of agreed with him, but then Jon got pissed and tore up Meg's garden just before Christmas, smashed a couple of windows, and Mum acted like she'd been proven right: men like Jon and Simon were selfish, dangerous bastards. End of story.

Mum keeps talking. "You should talk to Martin from number thirty-seven, he leads all the community watch stuff round here. It was Martin who called the police when Jon went mental, smashing Meg's windows. I was out at work, in the salon. Thank God Grace was in the hospital at the time, so neither of them were home, but it shook us all up, didn't it, love?" Mum nods at me.

I know she wants me to agree with her, to show Upton and Brown what a terrible man Jon is, but I don't know him so I just say, "Someone posted a photo of his little boy online when he had cancer. Apparently that's what tipped him over the edge." Mum stops nodding and just stares at me, so I add, "Obviously, though, he was stupid. Doing what he did next door, I mean."

Upton nods. "So you felt a bit sorry for him?"

I feel Mum bristle next to me. "Of course not!" Upton narrows her eyes at Mum, before Mum adds, "Why are you asking about him when we all know who did this?"

Upton keeps her face impassive. "Susan, we are focused on finding Simon, like I said. But I'm asking about Jon Katrin because he'd been aggressive towards Megan and Grace in the recent past. Was there anyone else Megan or Grace ever mentioned: boyfriends, other family?"

"No, no one."

"How about Grace—any relationships? Friends?" Upton perseveres. Mum curls a strand of hair around her index finger.

"Grace was always too sick to go to school, of course, so she was homeschooled when she was well enough. She made some friends online, though. She was always talking to other disabled kids, giving them advice, making them feel better." Mum pauses, squeezes her eyes shut, thoughtful for a moment. "But Meg never really talked about her family. Her dad's still alive but he's got

Alzheimer's, lives in that big home just outside Plymouth, Resthaven I think it's called. Meg didn't get to visit as much as she wanted; it was hard being a full-time carer. Her mum died from breast cancer when Meg was really young, twenty-one I think, and then her brother moved to Australia a few months later. Meg always said her friends were her family."

With a loud mewl, Cookie leaps up onto the table. Brown leans back in his chair, cups a hand over his mouth, and mumbles "Allergic" as he stands up from the table. I raise my hand towards Cookie, let her rub her cheek against my knuckles, and Mum coos in a baby voice, "Of course we hadn't forgotten you, Cookie, you're family too," before she starts crying again and the meeting is over.

I let Mum tuck me into my single bed. She's smiling faintly for the first time all day. I know she likes it when I feel like her little girl again. She places a sleeping pill next to a mug of warm milk. "Just so you know it's there," she says. She took her pill twenty minutes ago; her words are already slurring. She kisses me, reminds me I can come into her bed if I need to, before I am, at last, alone.

I make my body go completely floppy to try to help my mind relax, but it doesn't. Everything seems to be marching through me at once. I don't know how I feel because I'm feeling everything, no single emotion rests for long. As soon as I feel thick with sadness, a blaze of white anger passes through me, and then the anger is immediately replaced with a deep, queasy guilt. I'm a hostage. I see Meg's dead, bulging eyes again, I hear the drip, drip. In death she was staring so hard, like she was trying to get one last message to the living world. I know what she wanted—the only thing she's ever wanted: for Grace to be safe. My eyes start to blur and I feel tears rise up in me in a sickening wave. I try to focus on my breathing but my head is too full of noise. My eyes dart around my small childhood room, searching for something to calm me, but there's no respite to be found in the bowing bookcase of A-level textbooks, the chest of drawers laden with dusty, cheap jewelry and half-empty body sprays. The floor is littered with clothes from the last few days and one wall is lined with boxes, stuff I still haven't unpacked since I left Chris's. I feel entombed by it all, by all this stuff. Sweat clings to me in a fine, cold film. Desperate to get out, I decide I'll run the half mile down to Angel's Bay—let my confusion toss about with the waves. I'm sure Mum won't hear me: she'll be asleep by now.

My feet drop, leaden, out of bed, and as I bend for the jeans I left crumpled on the floor I kick something soft. The bag of carefully laundered clothes meant for Grace tilts and then collapses to the floor. As it does, something thuds. I stare unblinking at the thing on the floor: Grace's diary. My memory comes back to me in slow, persistent pulses. I picked up the diary, splayed right in front of me. I picked up the diary and, with my hands full and nowhere safe to put it, I dropped it into the bag. I forgot about it, didn't tell the police. Will I get into trouble? My eyes are fixed on the diary, right there on the floor in front of me, and then I pick it up for the second time today. It shakes in my hand. On the pink cover, Grace has written her name and address. Underneath she's put PRIVATE in capitals. I go to open it then pause, uneasy, like I'm snooping. But I remember Meg's eyes again, unseeing but desperate. I picture Grace lying cold and terrified in a disused mine somewhere. *No.* I run my fingertips over the cover. Grace would understand me reading her diary, she'd know I was trying to help. It's what Meg would have wanted.

I stumble back to sit on the edge of the bed. I slowly open the cover and it's like opening a music box, Grace's childlike voice taking over in my head, telling me about her small life.

10 November 2018

Mum keeps asking when I'm going to start writing in this diary. She says Lola—one of her favorite nurses—asks her about it every time they speak. That's because Lola gave me the diary. She gave it to me when we were in the hospital two weeks ago to see another consultant about my heart. Lola has this theory that it'll be good for me to write about how I'm feeling "physically and emotionally." She's a counselor as well as a nurse and is always talking about something she calls "mind-body connection." She knows other sick kids who kept a diary and said it really helped them. I asked her who they were, but she just smiled and touched my cheek and said she couldn't tell me. I was only asking because there was this boy who was on the ward with me a few months ago, he had cerebral palsy and he was always writing stuff down with his one good hand. Mum doesn't seem convinced that it will work for me either, but anything Lola recommends Mum reckons is worth a shot, so I'll do it for her.

I asked Zara about diaries yesterday when we were in the salon. Susie was painting Mum's nails a bright purple color I picked out, the two of them chatting as usual. I was in the hairdressing part of the salon, watching Zara sweep the hair off the floor. Some of it was brown, some gray, and some blond. It was all swirled together like melting ice-cream flavors mixing in a bowl. It doesn't seem right that some people have so much hair they leave great big clumps of it cut and abandoned on the floor like that. Looking at it made me touch my bald head through my beanie and try to remember what it was like to have hair, proper hair, not just fuzz.

It's just hair, Grace. You're just as beautiful without it.

That's what Mum says. Sometimes Mum takes me to try on wigs and we make faces and take selfies with bright pink hair. We put the photos on Facebook and get hundreds of likes. She always knows how to cheer me up.

"What do you think people write in diaries, Zara?" I asked in the salon.

Zara stopped brushing for a moment and smiled at me like I'd just said the most adorable thing ever and said, "I don't know, Gracey, what do you think people write in their diaries?"

I knew I should have asked Sylvia instead. Sylvia volunteers at the library and she's like a book herself, full of useful words and experiences.

"Don't know," I said. "Secrets, I suppose?"

"Well, there you go."

"But what if someone doesn't have secrets?" I asked.

"Oh, everyone has secrets," Zara said with a wink. *She always winks at me. I don't know why. It's not like we share any secrets and I've never seen her wink at anyone else.*

And then Zara had to go and answer the salon phone and I was left sitting there, surrounded by dead hair, wondering if she's right, does everyone have secrets? I looked at Mum and Susie, who were still talking about Cara breaking up with that boy Chris, even though she dumped him months ago. The two of them are like radio presenters when they're together, always, always talking even if no one is listening. It must be hard having secrets and talking so much, one of them could pop out so easily.

I feel a bit jealous, I suppose, of all those people with secrets, things they hold close, just for themselves. I don't have secrets, not really. But I'm going to work on getting some. Not just things that we aren't supposed to talk about, like farting or Dennis the butcher's bad breath or Dad. Or things like Danny and what Mum was like before I was born because other people know those things so they're not really secrets, they're just sad memories, and no one likes to talk about sad memories. I mean proper cross-your-heart secrets. Now it makes sense. Lola gave me this diary so I have somewhere to keep my secrets, something to confide in. It'll be like having a new friend, one who's always happy to let me whisper in their ear. I'd like that, especially now Cara isn't around so much. And the next time someone says "Everyone has secrets," I'll be able to nod in a knowing way because I'll have this diary and it will be full of them.

We left as soon as Mum's polish has dried, and no one noticed when I picked up a curl of golden hair on the ledge below a mirror. Zara missed it when she was cleaning up. I rubbed it between my finger and thumb and put it in my pocket. No one else knows I have it but me. Secret number one.

Love, Grace xxx

41

4

Jon

The Best Year Yet: Plans for Ashford's Award-Winning Summer Fair Gathering Pace.

The cursor blinks at me on the empty screen, the computer equivalent of tapping a watch, as if impatient for the first word of the article. My hands hover over the keyboard. I always work in the kitchen with the radio on, but today the words "kidnap" and "Grace Nichols" carry through the flat, so I kick my chair back to turn it off before I sit back down at my desk. The bloke reading the news won't have met Grace, of course, won't know how tiny she sat in her chair but how huge her smile was. I pull my glasses off to rub my eyes before I position my hands back over the keyboard, try to recall what it was the mayor said about the fair. My fingers start to type but I can't focus. My thoughts keep drifting to Meg and Grace and Simon, their faces filling my mind.

Grace and Meg were very similar, but there were a few things about Grace that reminded me of Simon. Did they both have blue eyes? Or was it the way Grace spoke, the soft inflection of her voice that made me think of her dad? Now I come to think of it, I can't remember what Simon's voice was like. I stop typing. I *could* listen to the tape from my interview with him. No. Come on. I force my eyes back to the screen to read, with dismay, the words I just typed. All I've done is write out the headline for the article again. Bloody idiot. I drop my head to my desk with a groan. This is so fucking painful. Why do I have no energy for what I should be doing but boundless energy for exactly what I shouldn't?

Ten minutes later the article is abandoned and I'm rifling through the box under my bed, already feeling less tense. Ruth used to joke, though now I think she means it seriously, that the only thing I'm fastidious about are my work tapes. Every important interview I've done is recorded on tape and stored in a carefully sealed plastic box, labeled in black felt-tip, and ordered alphabetically. Most reporters don't use tapes now, everything is digitized, but I straddle both generations and can't resist the security of hard copy. I trace past interviews with boxers, ex-politicians, disgraced bankers, and musicians until I get to the "stories in progress" section. *Davis: Simon Nov. 2018.*

I had wanted to write about the effect of tragedy on families. How some manage to drag themselves up from grief together, and others buckle and fold. Jakey was in the middle of another grueling round of chemo, our family was suffering. I couldn't write about illness, there was enough of that at home, so I decided to write about "act of God" tragedies, car crashes and freak accidents. Right from the moment I had the idea, I saw the article take shape in my mind. I wanted to talk about how most adults know the cold horror of near misses—that moment you don't see the cyclist in your rearview mirror, the second you take your eyes off your toddler to inspect the price of bananas in the supermarket. Most of us have felt how terror turns blood to cement in your veins, the shriek that rises in the throat like bile, but then the cyclist skids to a stop or you see your toddler hiding behind a shopping cart and relief, like bleach, strips you clean. Never again, you tell yourself, never again will I forget to check the mirror, or let her out of my sight. But some parents, like Simon Davis, don't get a second chance.

I was introduced to Simon through a contact at Dads Without Borders, a national charity that supports fathers' rights. Seeing as he was just over an hour away in Plymouth, they suggested an interview. The charity warned me Simon had "episodes" of poor mental health and that he'd struggled with depression since his son's death, but he was, at the time, quite balanced and agreed to the interview. Sitting on my bed, I slide the tape into the Dictaphone and press PLAY.

The noises from the steamy café where I interviewed Simon puff and clatter from the small speaker, pulling me back to the day we met. I remember his watery eyes scanning the café before he saw me waving at him from my small round table. He walked as though some unknown force was pushing him down from above, shoulders hunched, eyes fixed to the ground, as if in constant apology. He had prematurely gray hair and his clothes bunched around his frame, like he used to be bigger. He was an ordinary man who wore an extraordinary sadness.

"So, just for the record, can you please confirm you're Simon Davis and you're happy for me to record this interview." My voice is clear, confident. I remember the relief I felt when I was at work during that time, the professionalism a protection against the other me, the me I tried to hide, the vulnerable father of a sick son.

"Yes." Simon's voice was just a whisper. He clears his throat, makes an effort to speak up. "Yes."

"Can you tell me, please, in your own words, what happened on June the sixth ninety-eight, the day your son died."

Simon's voice is plain, almost matter-of-fact, as he talks, but I remember how his eyes darted around the café.

"It was Meg's birthday, so I'd taken the Friday off work. I was an accountant back then. I know, hard to believe really, but I was. I'd booked us a weekend away at Port Raynor Beach. We were staying in the static caravan site there, I don't know if it's still going. You know it?"

I probably shrugged, less interested in this setting-the-scene stuff than what came after. Simon keeps talking.

"I'd heard about the beaches down there, how they'd be deserted even on a hot weekend in June. Meg used to tease me about being a boring accountant, so it was a good surprise. As soon as we got there, Danny wanted to go down to the beach, it was all he could talk about. He kept saying he was going to catch a whale in his little net." Simon stops, clears his throat. "He loved whales, I don't know why."

"So you went to the beach?"

I wish I could smack myself for sounding impatient.

"We had a picnic on the beach." Simon either doesn't hear my irritation or it doesn't bother him. "I'd bought a bottle of wine."

Later, Meg claimed he'd been drunk.

"While I cleared away the picnic things, Meg went back up to the caravan to get Danny's armbands. He was so excited."

"Where was Danny at this point?"

"Splashing in the shallows. He kept shouting he'd seen a whale in the distance, on the horizon. I promised him we'd go out together, once his mum was back. He was a good boy, he didn't mind waiting, just kept chattering away to himself and digging with his spade in the wet sand."

"And then?" I ask. Simon clears his throat; a waitress calls out an order. "Then I saw those boys. They were only about eight, identical. I thought it was a bit odd they were on their own, running like hares down the path to the cove. Danny stopped digging. He loved older boys. I remember he stared at them, the sun shining behind him. I called the boys over, I wanted to make sure they were OK, they were shy, you know, didn't want to talk to a stranger. They went crashing into the sea with Danny instead. They were all splashing about, having fun. Danny was laughing. I kept sorting out our stuff. It makes me sick now, knowing that was the last time I'd hear him laugh, that I was busy packing away our picnic rubbish at the moment he needed me the most." Simon clears his throat again. "It was only a couple of minutes. I thought it was good for him to be playing with older boys, but when I looked up the brothers were splashing each other and I couldn't see Danny—"

I turn the tape off. That's when Simon started sobbing and I knew it wouldn't be right to press him for details. Besides, my mind's always been limber for disaster; it colors in most of it. I picture how Simon would have scrambled to his feet and run to the water, his eyes desperately searching for a flash of Danny's hair, his swimming trunks, anything. I can see him pulling his T-shirt off as he splashes into the surf, all the while screaming Danny's name. But no matter how much he screams, the sea gives him no clue, the waves roll black and uncaring around him, carrying Danny's limp body further and further away. I imagine how small Simon must have felt in the face of such great terror; it's how I felt when I thought we might lose Jakey. But whereas Jakey was spared—thank God—Simon wasn't so lucky. Perhaps I was wrong to empathize with Simon, maybe I had let my fear of losing Jakey color my judgment and took his side too quickly.

I take a deep breath and, as I exhale, I pick up a notebook from the box. It's the notebook I used while researching the article. One page has the corner turned down, a reminder to myself to go back to it. It's an interview with a Dr. Nina Rossi from Plymouth. I remember she was one of the senior doctors at the practice where Grace was registered. At the bottom of the page I've scrawled a note in pen:

> *Uncomfortable answering questions about Meg and Grace—why?*

I cast my mind back to the interview. I knew Grace's old GP had moved on to a new post but thought it'd be helpful to meet Dr. Rossi anyway, to get the medical perspective on Grace's limitations. As one of the senior doctors at the practice, she dealt with all media inquiries. Nina Rossi was an upright, tense woman who clearly had little interest in talking to me beyond parroting facts. Her answers are straightforward but I remember feeling she was holding something back. I let myself imagine for a moment that I'm writing an article on Meg's murder and Grace's disappearance. I'd go back to Plymouth, interview Dr. Rossi again, sniff out any other old contacts. No one would ever talk to me in Ashford now, but maybe I'd have more luck further afield. It's not going to happen, though, I tell myself. A fantasy, nothing more. My phone starts to ring, shrilly interrupting my thoughts. It's Jakey—I feel my whole world brighten.

"Dad!" He sounds out of breath, excited, and before I can

say anything he says, "I made the team, Dad! I'm on the football team!" Tears prick behind my eyes, tears of gratitude, relief. He is safe, better than safe: he's healthy and happy.

"Mate! That's amazing news! God, I'm so proud of you! Are you striker?"

But on the other end of the line Ruth is calling his name.

"Coming, Mum!" he calls back.

I picture him hurrying towards her, his too-big backpack banging against his back, his school blazer falling off his shoulders, the gappy-toothed grin he'll greet her with.

"Sorry, Dad, gotta go. Mum's taking me out for pizza to celebrate."

I clear my throat before I say, "OK. Have a good time, mate. Love you, Jakey."

"You too, Dad," he says before the line goes dead and I'm left with a hollow ache: grief for the family we once were. Two years ago Ruth and I were told to think about how to say goodbye to our son and today he's playing football for his school team. We're proof that sometimes people do get second chances. Is it possible Ruth and I could have a second chance too?

I look at my watch, realizing the ten minutes I promised myself has somehow melted into half an hour. I shove the box under my bed and force myself back to my computer. An hour later I've written six hundred words about sheepdog trials and giant vegetable competitions, and with a quick glance at my watch I rush out to meet Dave.

Dave is already sitting at a corner table. The Red Dragon, his favorite, is an old-fashioned pub and I have to duck to avoid destroying a bunch of dried hops hanging from the ceiling. Dave has a wide, jowly face and strangely delicate features, a button nose and rosebud mouth that would be sweet on a young girl but don't work so well on a balding forty-something man. To be honest, if Dave wasn't a policeman we wouldn't have seen each other again after that first night. But most good reporters know how important it is to have an ear in the police station, so I made sure we kept in touch. But tonight, I remind myself, I'm meeting him as a friend. Dave's facing the door, absentmindedly tearing up a cardboard beer coaster. He hasn't got himself a drink because the unspoken deal is that I buy the drinks and he talks about local police stuff once his tongue is loosened. Tonight, I don't care. I just want a drink. I wave at him and his brow relaxes as I head to the bar, ordering two pints. Dave keeps his eyes fixed on the beers as I carry them over to him.

"Ah, cheers, mate," he says, lifting his pint as soon as I've put it on the table in front of him.

"How's it going, Dave?" I ask, sitting on a small stool opposite him. Dave shrugs as he drinks.

"Karen's going for the jugular again," he says.

This is why I texted him. Dave's as soft as a marshmallow and loves to talk about his ex-wife, whom he still clearly loves. I nod and murmur agreement at the right moments. Karen's started dating and Dave is understandably cut up about it. I wonder whether his sensitivity is why Dave's never been promoted, why after fifteen years he's still only a constable in the macho Ashford police force. As Dave finishes his pint I'm about to take the opportunity to start talking about Ruth when the barmaid changes the channel on the television to—in what must be a first in the history of the Dragon—the news. Dave and I swivel on our stools towards the screen as the reporter addresses the camera outside number 52 Woodgreen Avenue.

"The police are appealing to anyone who knows or has seen

Simon Davis, a forty-five-year-old Caucasian man, to contact the police on the number below. If you see Mr. Davis you are advised not to approach him, but to contact the police immediately."

A grainy photo fills the screen, not a great shot. People can't have been in the habit of taking photos of Simon if this is the best they have. He's smiling, head tilted at the camera, his eyes half-shut. He's standing as though he has his arm around someone's shoulders but they've been cut out, giving the sinister impression Simon might be holding on to them. His hair is longer, messier than I remember, his features smaller in a fuller face. The reporter keeps talking.

"Search-and-rescue groups are preparing to work through the night in their effort to find Grace Nichols. Concerns are growing for the seventeen-year-old, who has a complex history of health conditions, including an extremely rare type of muscular dystrophy. South West News has been informed that Grace also had problems with her heart, and epilepsy, for which she needs daily medication. Stress and anxiety are known to worsen both conditions, so it is of upmost importance that Grace is found as quickly as possible. Her neighbors and friends are understandably very concerned for Grace and are making an urgent appeal to anyone who might provide information on her whereabouts." The image snaps to an interview prerecorded earlier today. The woman is middle-aged, with unnaturally bright red hair that falls in waves below her shoulders. Her face is puffy, her blue eyes flick from the camera to the reporter, and as she talks a dimple winks in her cheek. Susan Dorman, Meg's next-door neighbor and a regular on local forums. She was one of the ringleaders in the hate campaign against me after the article went live—CornishSuse. I look away from her face on the screen, my fingers gripping my pint glass. CornishSuse was there days after the article was printed, watching from across the street when some yob spat on me and told me to fuck off back to London. I was still more confused than angry then. In my mind, all I'd said in the article was that Grace might benefit from having her dad in her life, that their estrangement was a decision I felt had been made for her rather than by her. Although I could never say it out loud, especially now, I still stand by the article. It was meant in good faith. It was what I did after that photo of Jakey was posted—getting drunk and angry—that I regret. It never crossed my mind that the article would upset people the way it did—it was like I'd attacked every Ashford mum individually. I had to hide out in Ruth's parents' house for two days after that. Now it seems they were right and I was wrong after all; Simon is dangerous, a sick man capable of terrible violence. I begged Ruth to move back to London but she wouldn't budge. I had no choice. I had to stay in Ashford. Thinking about Ruth reminds me why I called Dave in the first place.

"I was going to say, actually, mate, Ruth's making me go to therapy . . ."

But Dave isn't listening. Without taking his eyes off the screen, he shakes his head and shushes me. He wants to listen to what CornishSuse has to say.

"I live next door to Meg and Grace. They were more than just neighbors, they were our friends, our best friends, and they never did anything to hurt anyone. Everyone loved them."

"Can you tell us a bit about the reaction from neighbors and friends about what's happened here?"

"Oh God, everyone is crushed. Absolutely crushed. We know we just have to focus on finding Grace, which is what Meg would want us to do. Until we find her, until we find her safe, we won't be able to mourn our friend properly. Which is why we're organizing our own community search teams. If anyone would like to come and help us, we're running a twenty-four-hour Find Grace headquarters from the Style Rooms Hair and Beauty Salon on Pembroke Road on the Summervale Estate. There'll be community searches going on round the clock, so please come by if you'd like to help."

"Ha! That'll piss Upton right off. She's not one for police and community cohesion, says amateurs only bugger things up, make it harder for the professionals." Dave is talking again, but I don't turn to look at him because at the bottom of the screen a line of red ticker tape starts to roll: BREAKING NEWS: POLICE HAVE REVEALED IT IS ESTIMATED THAT OVER £3000 IN CASH WAS TAKEN FROM THE MURDER AND KIDNAP SCENE AT 52 WOODGREEN AVENUE.

Dave reads, nods, and smiles in a smug way to show he already knew about the cash, before he wiggles his empty pint glass in the air and says, "I'm still thirsty, mate."

I walk dutifully back to our table clutching pints for us both, while trying to think of a way to move the subject back to safer ground. But Dave is fixated on the Nichols case, staring up at the TV, nodding his head. To be fair to him, police business is the reason I usually get in touch and he's clearly primed to tell me what he knows. I don't want to be rude and, besides, I can't deny I'm not interested in getting some insider knowledge, even if it turns out to be nothing. I follow his stare to the TV. The picture has changed to the press interview with DCI Upton and I know he's waiting for me to ask.

"You knew about the cash?" I say, gesturing at the screen.

Dave shrugs, his mouth turning down like a sad cod, his head wobbling back and forth like he's trying to make up his mind whether to talk. It's a pantomime. He's desperate to talk.

"You knew," I say. Dave breaks into a grin and leans towards me, hunching over his pint.

"Upton reckons Simon Davis tried to make it look like a burglary gone wrong, what with the cash and their laptop being taken. Apparently it was well known Megan didn't trust banks." I've tried to resist, but it's like a switch has been turned on and I've come alive again. Suddenly, I'm me again, the old me, a journalist on the scent of a huge story and I need to get Dave to tell me everything he knows.

"And there are no other suspects?" Dave, I know, likes it when I make it sound like he is the whole force.

"Not at the moment, mate—Simon's a violent man, he'd even tried to kidnap Grace when she was small and we know he was having money troubles, been on the dole for years, can't hold down a job. Claimed it was because of mental health problems. There's no doubt this was him."

"What about forensics?" I can see the moisture from Dave's pint on his bottom lip.

"Nothing's come up yet. It was all planned. He wiped the lamp or was using gloves, and they're saying he probably wasn't wearing shoes—took them off so he didn't make any noise. He knew what he was doing, that's clear enough. The rest of the house is full of the girl's and the victim's DNA, plus quite a few other sources. We're checking all their friends and neighbors when we speak to them."

I nod.

"The phrase I like to use is 'every contact leaves a trace.'" Dave pauses, to let the well-known police wisdom he's claiming as his own sink in. I've heard it before, but I don't tell him that. Dave raises a finger. "But the key thing to remember, Jon, is that the evidence might not be left at the scene. I call this 'reverse contact.' So the perp could have taken evidence of contact away with him. He might have traces of the victim's DNA on the clothes he was wearing, for example." Dave nods his head as he waits for me to take it on board. He should have been a teacher instead of a policeman.

"Sounds like Simon thought it all through carefully, especially for someone so mentally unstable." I've always railed against assumptions of criminality, but Dave has confirmed what I already knew: there is no other possible suspect. Meg's and Grace's lives were so closeted—they weren't involved in any shady dealings that might implicate them. Besides, I don't want to make it sound like I'm defending Simon and risk making myself even more of a social pariah.

Dave shrugs. His eyes flicker towards the sports news that's now on the TV as he says, "Apparently he'd go up and down. Must have planned all this on an up. If I'm honest with you, mate, he'd been suicidal before. I reckon he decided to take his daughter with him. It's like what you said in the article—he didn't think it was fair that Megan kept him from Grace. I think he wanted to punish Megan in the cruelest way he could think of for keeping him away."

I hate that he's saying the worst possibility out loud, as though the saying of it makes it more likely to be fact. Even worse, I hate my work being involved, albeit indirectly. I know the story already but I don't want to lose Dave to the football so I say, "Remind me about the first time he tried to take Grace." Dave fixes his eyes on me as he takes two big gulps of his pint, stifling a burp before replying.

"The girl, Grace, was small, only six, she'd just been discharged from the hospital. It was the first time she'd been in— meningitis. Simon and Megan had at last gone their separate ways by this point. He was pissed off Megan hadn't let him see Grace in the hospital. He still had a key to the back door and when Megan went in to check on Grace one night just days after she was discharged her bed was empty. Blues and twos tracked him down, driving south just a few miles out of Plymouth. Must have scared the poor little thing shitless."

"She was six?"

"Yeah, so?"

"Just a couple of years older than Danny when he drowned."

Dave makes the cod face again, before he lifts his glass, shrugs, so? Although officially cleared of any wrongdoing or neglect, so many years after the tragedy Simon is still widely held responsible for his son's death. Dave's eyes glide back towards the football scores.

"So, you have any idea where Simon is now?" I ask, wanting to keep Dave talking.

He snorts. "As if I'd tell you, mate. More than my life's worth. But the truth is, they could be anywhere. If they're still alive, and if he's got any brain cells, he'll have left the country already."

"With Grace?"

Dave shrugs again, smiles from the corner of his mouth, but he's trying too hard, I can tell he doesn't have a clue. Anything he does know is locker-room gossip from the station, based on conjecture, nothing more. Upton has enough sense to keep lowly constables safely away from anything important. Dave burps softly into his hand, his forehead creases, and he looks up at me.

"What's your theory, then?"

I keep my face open. "What do you mean?"

"You must have a theory, asking me here, getting involved when you of all people should be staying well clear."

"Not really, mate, no theory. Honestly, I got in touch because

I wanted to tell you about these bloody therapy sessions Ruth's insisting on, but then the news came on and, well, it's difficult to think about anything else, isn't it?"

Dave laughs, guttural, into his beer. Clearly he doesn't believe a word. He probably thinks, like everyone else, I'm here to defend Simon. But it's different now. Before recent events, I felt sorry for Simon. I could tell he loved his family, but since that sunny June day over twenty years ago he'd been in perpetual freefall, trapped in his own scream. He'd been punished again and again for a moment's distraction. The man lost everything he loved in a single moment. His life was my worst nightmare. I felt sorry for him. But a violent man with nothing to lose is dangerous, and now I know he was the only person who would have a motive to murder Meg and kidnap Grace.

I feel Dave still looking at me, but he's not smiling anymore and his glass is on the table, a sign he's about to get serious again. He burps quietly under his breath this time before speaking.

"Look, we both know from personal experience how shit it is not to be allowed to see your kids every day, and I know, in a way, you feel a bit sorry for the bloke, and I don't blame you, mate, but if he really did that to someone, to the mother of his child—"

I hold up my hands, shake my head at Dave. "Dave, I know, I know Simon probably did it. I didn't say anything about him, did I?"

Dave narrows his eyes and gestures at his face to show he's mimicking me as he says, "Yeah, but you were getting that look."

"What look?"

"The sort of constipated look that means you're thinking something nuts."

"Look, Dave, most likely Simon is guilty. It's terrible to think, but he probably killed Megan and took Grace. What I want to know is why, and why now? Grace, if she's still alive, is going to be eighteen in a few months. If she wanted to see him, like he claimed, why didn't he just wait a bit longer until she could decide herself?" As I talk, I feel another, bigger reason tugging at the corner of my mind, but as soon as I try to focus on it, it slips away again.

Dave glances over my shoulder at the screen again. I turn; they're showing a repeat of the clip of Cara, covered in a gray blanket and being led away from number 52 by two police officers. Cara's mum walks behind, clutching Grace's cat. A police support officer drapes an arm around Susan's heaving shoulders.

"That's it!" Dave says out of the blue, snapping his chubby fingers. "She works in the Ship"—he nods towards the screen— "or at least she did last summer. I knew I recognized her from somewhere."

The Ship is a big pub on the harbor. Like most places in Cornwall, it's quiet in the winter and bloated with tourists in the summer. The kind of place that sells fluorescent shots for a quid on the weekends, it's generally ignored by locals but not, it would seem, by Dave.

"Who? The mum?" I ask.

"Nah, the mum's got that salon, hasn't she? I mean her daughter, Cara, the one who found the body," Dave says, keeping his eyes on the screen.

"Is she working there again this summer?"

Dave shrugs. How should he know? He takes a big pull on his pint before turning away from the screen and forcing his eyes back to me.

"So, go on then, mate, what was it you wanted to tell me about Ruth?"

But now I'm thinking about Meg and Grace I can't even remember why I needed to talk about Ruth. It's like my head is full of tiny doors concealing different aspects of who I am and only one can be open at a time. Now the door to Meg and Grace is wide open, swinging on its hinges, and the Ruth door is firmly locked and bolted. So I just shake my head and say, "It's not important anymore, mate. Look, it's been good to catch up, let's go for a drink again soon, yeah?"

I leave Dave before he's finished his pint but he doesn't seem to care. It's a relief to be outside, walking home in the cool, dark night. I snap the band round my wrist so hard it breaks. "Fuck," I say out loud as the limp rubber falls to the asphalt. And because it feels good I say it again: "Fuck, fuck, fuck." Ashford's deserted, as though it's 4 a.m. on a Sunday night, but for once I don't miss the bustle of London, the wired feeling of being constantly in a race with nine million other people. Tonight, the stillness helps me think. While I was talking to Dave about Meg and Grace, all the unfathomable shit with Ruth and the future of our marriage melted away. For a while I understood who I was, and I didn't ache anymore because my brain was busy, active with other people's lives, other people's pain. If Meg and Grace give me a purpose beyond myself, is that really such a bad thing?

I've tried to ignore it, but I can't anymore. Meg might be beyond help but, despite what Dave thinks, Grace could still be alive. I don't have much faith in the local force, not if Dave's anything to go by. I was good at my job—great, in fact. I always found the leads that others couldn't. What if I could find Grace?

I think fleetingly of Ruth, imagine her scornful expression as she tells me I just want to salvage my career. But this is about more than that. Grace is a very sick, very vulnerable child. Like my child once was. What if it was Jakey who'd been taken? We'd do anything we could to get him back. I'm one of the few people who have met Meg, Grace, and Simon, who have met people from their past. I'm in a unique position.

The restraining order flashes into my mind. I'm probably Ashford's public enemy number two, after Simon. The police haven't been in touch yet but I'm sure they will be—it's lucky that I met with the organizers of the summer fair the night Meg was murdered. But I'll still need to be careful, not do anything too public. For once, I can't wait to be back at the flat. I want to have another look at my notebook, see if I turned down any other pages apart from the one about meeting Dr. Rossi.

I quicken my pace. I'm certain Simon was involved in Meg's death and Grace's kidnapping, which makes the article I wrote quietly supporting him even harder to bear. For the first time I question my judgment. I looked into Simon's eyes and saw a troubled but innocent man. Am I the only one who didn't see him for what he was? How could I have got it so wrong? I resolve, here and now, to use my experience and what I know to help Grace. I'll use all my resources to find her, and then, when she's safe, I'll write an article, the best article I've ever written. I'll apologize for what I wrote before and tell Grace's story, all of it. It will be a tribute not only to her safe return but also to Meg's memory. I feel twitchy for a pen and paper as the words take shape within me. The shamed reporter who helps find Britain's most vulnerable victim, not only saving her but also saving himself in the process. Bloody hell, my road to redemption could be brilliant. I quicken my pace as the betting shop below my flat comes into view. I wish I could call Ruth, talk through the idea like we used to. But of course that's the last thing I'm going to do. First, I need to find Grace, and then I need to write the article, and then maybe, just maybe, my family will come back to me.

5

Cara

DCI Upton and DI Brown came over this morning as soon as Mum called in about the diary.

"Did you read it?" Upton asked, expertly raising an eyebrow. I met her eyes, managed not to blink.

"No, of course not. It's private."

Next to me, Mum's bangles chimed as she shuffled in her seat. She knows me better, of course, knows I'm lying. It seems to me that anyone who says they didn't read the diary of a kidnapped person is untrustworthy or stupid, or most likely both. Incredibly, Upton seemed to swallow my lie. I tried not to think about the carefully photocopied diary under my bed in case she could read the truth in my face as she told me again how much I'm helping Grace by helping the police. I'd been too upset to read it properly and what if Grace had left a hint or a clue that the police, not knowing her, would miss? I wanted to go back when my head was clearer.

I'd cried quietly in my room for hours after I read the diary. There were seventy-three entries in total, each one full of Grace's sweetness. Taking a lock of hair from the salon was the naughtiest thing she'd done, for God's sake. She had more to be miserable about than anyone I've ever known—stuck in her chair at home most of the time, a dead brother, and an actually crazy dad. God, it used to make me depressed just thinking about her life—which is why I avoided it as much as possible. But in the diary Grace focused on the good: the support they received, the fun she and Meg had, the love between them. I feel tears start to burn behind my eyes and I don't want Upton to see so I blink them away.

The police officer on duty at our front door tips his hat at Upton and Brown as they leave. There are only a handful of news vans left now outside number 52; it looks strangely sparse.

Mum closes the door quietly behind them and slowly turns towards me.

"You know Jane gave me a number for a counselor, a woman who's specially trained in working with victims of trauma."

Is that what she thinks I am now? A victim?

"I know, Mum, you said, I just don't want to right now, OK?"

Mum looks at me like I'm something she just can't understand.

"It's free, Car, for as long as you need."

"Yeah, you said that as well."

Mum's brow crumples, so I move in for a hug. Her hair is crisp with chemicals against my face, her body taut as a wire, and I know mine must feel the same. I wonder which one of us will snap first. When we pull away, she wipes the tip of her finger under her eyes, frowns at the smudge her tears have left.

"Oh for God's sake, I must remember to bring that waterproof mascara back from the salon today."

She squeezes my arm and walks towards her bedroom, still

dabbing at her eyes. I don't follow her in case Meg's in there waiting for me. Drip, drip. So I wait in the hall next to my baby pictures while Mum changes.

"You're opening the salon today?" I'm surprised—she didn't say anything about work. Mum set up the salon after Granddad died ten years ago. Like most of our neighbors, she sold the three-bed Victorian cottage right on the harbor, the house where she grew up, when a couple from London looking for a holiday home offered over three hundred grand. She bought our bungalow and had enough left over to set up her hair and beauty business. She called it the Style Rooms and I've always hated it, not only because it caused me no end of grief at school as I romped around in skinny jeans and Dr. Martens, but because Mum loved something I never understood. She loved turning perfectly normal women into frozen mannequins of themselves. They'd come out with PVC-shiny lips, dangerously flammable hair, and a petrified look. I've grown up a bit, though. At least I can bear to say the word "salon" now instead of just mumbling "Mum's work."

"Obviously not for clients, love. I told you already, it's going to be the HQ for the Find Grace campaign. We're going to get search parties together—we can't rely on the police to do everything. It's time for us to pull together, to help, and there's the vigil to organize. It's what Meg would've wanted." For the first time since I found Meg, Mum seems more like her old self; she seems better now she has a plan. Ever since Dad left to start a new hippie life living off grid with his girlfriend in Scotland fifteen years ago, Mum's always needed to keep moving, to keep busy, as though she's constantly trying to outpace any feelings she doesn't want to settle for too long. I don't say what I'm thinking, that Simon—if he has Grace—could have her locked up hundreds of miles away from here. But I know if there's a chance, no matter how minuscule, that Grace is just down the road, Mum won't rest until the whole area is searched. It's the doing something that's important for her—and for the community—now.

"Sounds like Martin and Sylvia's idea," I say instead. Martin and his wife, Sylvia, live opposite us. Martin heads up the local community watch group. Most weekends they can be found in their fold-up chairs by the side of the road, trying to catch speeding drivers.

"Actually, it was my idea," Mum calls from her room, "and Zara was the first to agree with me." Mum employed Zara, a hairdresser, five years ago and the two of them had been firm friends ever since. Zara has a penchant for huge earrings and, like Mum, bad men. Things haven't been easy between them recently. I'd come home one night in March and found Mum crying and halfway through a bottle of white. A customer claimed Zara had stolen her diamond engagement ring she'd had in her handbag during a haircut. She'd shown it to Zara to get her advice on how to have the stones reset, but when she got to the jeweler's the ring wasn't in her bag. Mum threatened to fire Zara, but then realized the salon would sink without her. A thin truce was declared and when I asked Mum if the ring was ever found she turned away from me, muttering something about water under the bridge. Mum comes out of her bedroom wearing jeans and a white T-shirt with Grace's smiling face on the front. She hands me a folded, identical T-shirt.

"Mum! You've never worn a T-shirt in your life!"

Mum shakes her hair back. "Well, I've never run a missing-person campaign either, have I?" she says, defensive, wobbling as she bends to slip on her heels. "A printer in town heard what happened, he knew Meg and worked through the night putting them together, bless him. Martin dropped these ones over first thing. Quickly, Car, put it on and then we can get going."

I don't need to say anything. Mum looks up at me.

"Oh, Car! You're not coming, are you?"

"I thought I'd go back to the pub today, just for a few hours."

Her jewelry jangles as she stands and looks at me, disappointed I'm not joining her.

"Really?" she says. "Is it a good idea to go back so soon? What about tonight?"

"I'm only doing a half shift, I'll be back way before the vigil starts."

"But I thought you could help me with my speech, Car . . . I . . ."

"Come on, Mum, you know I need the money and—"

The doorbell rings so I don't have to say how, more than money, I need time away from concerned glances, endless mugs of tea, and whispers about the effects of trauma. I need to think about something other than the horrible things that could be happening to Grace right now. I need to see if I can feel normal again, even if it's just for an hour or so.

Mum walks with fast, small steps like a seabird running from the surf and opens the door to Martin and Sylvia, who are also wearing campaign T-shirts, with reflective vests over the top. In their late sixties now, they're like the parents of the whole estate, keeping an increasingly disapproving eye on everything that happens to anyone who sets foot on Summervale. They've been here since the estate was first built and love to talk about how much better it was, how much better people were back then.

"Morning, Susan! Ahh, Cara, good to see you," Martin says, tilting his head to look at me. Sylvia, by his side, smiles at me and pulls me in for a short, tense hug. "You're joining us today, are you?" Martin asks.

I explain that I can't and Martin lifts his eyebrows in a way that suggests he should have expected as much from someone of my generation. Mum gives me her car keys so I don't have to deal with the bus today. On the road outside, a delivery van pulls up and, staring at the reporters next door, a man hauls a box up the path towards us.

"Oh, this'll be the T-shirts" Mum says, casting a quick smile at the deliveryman and scribbling her name on his electronic pad. "Let's get them straight into your car, Martin."

"No room, with all the vests and maps. We'll have to leave them here for now and I'll pick them up tomorrow. We've got plenty for today," Martin says, pulling on brown faux leather driving gloves before turning towards his car, ready to leave.

Mum steps over the box and says to me, "Love, would you mind?" But I'm already bending down to pick it up.

"I'll put it in the storage room, Mum."

"Thank you, love," she says and kisses me hard, so I feel the stamp of her trademark coral lipstick sticky against my cheek before the three of them fold themselves into Martin's small car.

The peace of the house is a relief. I carry the box into the tiny room where Mum keeps all the stuff she can't bear to look at every day, but also can't bear to throw away. There are a few suitcases and a wardrobe, but mainly it's full of Granddad's things. His old suit jackets and coats are piled over his favorite easy chair as if he'll pop back any moment to grab one—"Silly me, going out without a coat." I wish he would. It's been ten years since he died and I miss him more than I've ever missed Dad.

I put the box down on the floor next to a larger box that has Meg's writing in black Sharpie on it: *M & G—stuff for tip. Thank you! xxx.* Typical Meg, to leave kisses even on a cardboard box. I don't know why it's here. Mum probably offered to get rid of it for her and forgot about it. It's also typical of Meg to tape up a box that was destined for the dump, but then, she was fastidious about everything. Mum said carers had to be—if Grace missed a pill or an appointment it could be life-threatening. There was never any room for mistakes or forgetfulness; her life was about care and precision. I run my finger over the three kisses and remember how much I loved Meg's hugs. Her hugs were strong and warm, they were gifts—I always felt surer of myself after one.

I slide my finger along the box until I get to a loose bit and, without thinking, start to pull the tape away. I don't know what I'm expecting to find. Some little fragment of Meg, perhaps, something that will make her feel more alive than dead. But inside there's just the usual household detritus—an old kettle, some rusty tools, a moth-eaten blanket, two pairs of shoes with holes in the soles, a broken plastic plant pot, all jumbled together. Now I've cleared some space, I see that everything was resting on a sketchpad. I pull it out to have a look. Grace used to love drawing. Shamefully, I realize I don't even know if she still does. The sketchpad is skinny; most of its pages have been torn out. There's just one of Grace's drawings inside. My breath catches as I realize it's one of her special thank-yous. Grace went through a stage where she'd obsess over making thank-you cards for anyone who helped her and her mum. She'd labor over each card for days, carefully thinking through what she should draw, practicing what to write in the note again and again. They all followed a theme: a colorful scene on the front, with the name of the person Grace was thanking concealed somewhere within the picture. This one is a bunch of balloons. I imagine Grace drew it when she was much younger. In each colorful balloon she'd drawn a letter, spelling out the name "Dr. Rossi." I run my fingertips over the drawing, imagine Grace humming, head cocked to one side and bent close to the pad as she colored in each balloon. My throat feels tight suddenly. I open the card, inside is a note with carefully joined-up writing:

> *Dear Dr. Rossi,*
>   *Thank you for giving my mum a job. She's so happy! Thank you for always making sure me and Mum have everything we need. We are lucky to have friends like you!*
>
>   *Big Kiss,*
>   *Grace xxx*

I read the note again and again until my voice becomes Grace's voice and she feels a bit closer, a little safer. I put the card carefully to one side and, as I drop the now-empty sketchpad back in the box, a small envelope I hadn't seen before slithers out of the pad. On the front, Grace has written:

> *Granddad*
> *Resthaven Nursing Home*
> *Plymouth*

I turn the card over. It looks as though Grace had sealed the envelope and then opened it again. I slide my finger inside the ragged edge of the opening and pull out a small photo. The tightness returns to my throat, gripping harder now. The photo is of a man, old and crumpled in his chair, but his rheumy eyes sparkle as he looks at the little girl sitting on his lap. Grace looks about three in the photo; she's turning her small face back towards the old man. Behind them both, with one hand on the old man's shoulder and the other on Grace's knee, is the youngest, slimmest Meg I've ever seen. There's nothing written on the back of the photo and, uncharacteristically, Grace didn't write a note, or it's been lost. This photo—this memory—was something Grace clearly wanted to share with her granddad, so why did the photo end up here, waiting to be taken to the dump? Sitting here, surrounded by his scuffed shoes and his dusty books, I think how I'd love to get a message to my granddad if I could. Clearly Grace, at one time, wanted the same. The burn in my throat has at last given away to tears. I sit on the floor and cry as I stare at the picture of Grace as a toddler. I could have been so much better, I should have been kinder, more patient, more like the big sister she always wished I'd be, the big sister she so badly needed. I let myself cry. But I know it's pointless, there's too much, I'll never be able to cry my guilt away. When I can't cry anymore, I wipe my eyes and decide to look up the full address of the care home and the doctor's office. I'll post these remembrances from Grace to Dr. Rossi and to Grace's granddad. There may not be much I can do anymore, but I can do this small thing. Glancing at my watch, I realize it's 10:45 a.m. already. *Shit.* I grab a couple of envelopes from the kitchen and shove them in my backpack. I'm going to be late.

I drive through the estate, past the squat row of red-brick shops— the newsagent's and the post office, the Star Inn with its blacked-out windows, the butcher's, and finally the Style Rooms. There's a short queue of people standing on the pavement outside the salon and Sylvia, clutching a clipboard, is talking to them. Inside, Mum's leaping around like a cricket, talking quickly on her mobile, and Martin is bending over a map alongside volunteers in his reflective vests. In the window there are three huge posters of Meg and Grace holding hands, with a number to call underneath their smiling faces. I only recognize some of the volunteers, neighbors mainly, standing on the pavement waiting to be told what to do.

A balding bloke perhaps in his late thirties stares at me with cold eyes as I pass, and I realize, if Simon doesn't have her, the person who took her could be anyone, someone we know, or someone we've never met. They could even be one of the volunteers outside the salon now, pretending they don't already know where she is.

I drive on into town. There's not a lot in Ashford now, away from the harbor. I get why the tourists don't bother coming here anymore. What few independent shops there were when I was growing up have been replaced by chains and brands. The hippie shop where I got my nose pierced when I was fifteen is now a mobile phone shop; the Corner Café where I once took Grace for hot chocolate while Meg did some quick shopping is a Starbucks. Even the sea around Ashford feels industrial, as flat and gray as a parking lot. I park behind the pub. The Ship is blessedly anonymous, one of those pubs people generally only come to once. It's still before opening time and Brian, the owner, who looks like a potato with his round cheeks and prematurely hairless head, opens his arms to me as soon as I walk through the door. He wipes his doughy hands on the cloth over his shoulder, tilts his head, and hugs me. It seems like people are always tilting and hugging when they see me now.

"Don't forget what I said on the phone: you just leave any time you need to, OK, Car?" he makes a point of saying before going back to polishing the beer taps.

The decor in here hasn't changed in decades, the fake fishing nets hang from the ceiling like great spider webs and the floor is tacky under my sneakers, but it's a relief to be somewhere without any memories of Grace—Meg would never let her go anywhere so mucky. I fill a bucket with soapy water and carry it out to the front, the harbor side of the pub. The first job, as always on an early shift, is to scrub off the white bombs of seagull shit that have exploded on the outside tables. Far above, the gulls glide smugly. I remember Grace pointing out how their scratchy cawing sounded like they were screaming my name: "Car, Car!" I dunk a brush into the warm water and, with my head down, start scrubbing the wooden tabletop.

"You've got an audience." I look up and see a man in his mid-forties opposite me, with a brown beard, glasses, and a geeky-looking anorak. It takes me a moment to place him as the journalist the police brought up yesterday, Jon Katrin. He nods to a spot just a couple of feet away, where a huge seagull flaps from the pavement onto the table and, standing on its drinking-straw legs, fixes a blank, disapproving eye on me. I clap my hands at it, try to shoo it away, but it only flaps its wings a couple of times. Clearly I'm not nearly scary enough to make it budge.

"Stubborn bugger," Jon says, before lifting his arms like he's about to take off himself and shouting *Coooorrr* at the bird. The bird cocks its head and looks mildly amused before flapping its wings and hopping lazily down from the table.

"Thanks," I say, even though he didn't really do much to help, then I go back to my scrubbing. Why is he here? He's caught me off guard. The police told me not to talk to the press, but it's Mum who'd hate it most.

Before I can figure out how to tell him to get lost he says, "One of them dive-bombed and took my son's ice cream clean out of his hand a few days ago. Scared us both stupid."

"It happens," I say, shrugging and not looking up as I keep scrubbing, hoping he'll hear the lack of interest in my voice. Even though the first table is white with chalky shit I move on to another table just so I can turn my back to him. But he's like a seagull himself, unafraid to stick around even when it's obvious he's not wanted.

I remember the photo of him posted and shared on Twitter and Facebook six months ago, being led away from number 52 by the police after he smashed Meg's windows. His glasses were almost knocked off his nose, his mouth frozen around an ugly "F" at the camera, his hair wild. After his article about Meg and Grace was published, everyone was so angry. Mum, Zara, even Sylvia took to the internet to write all sorts of nasty stuff about him. They said they had to speak out and defend their friend. Jon didn't reply to any of the online comments, but then someone tipped him over the edge by anonymously posting a photo of his sick kid in the Summervale News Facebook group. Whoever it was had left a comment but hadn't had the balls to post from their real account: Perhaps Jon Katrin should spend more time looking after his poor son than poking his nose into other people's lives.

The image got thousands of likes and hundreds more comments, things like I don't know what must be worse for the poor kid, having Jon Katrin as a dad or having cancer.

I was busy at college and working at the pub while all of this was going on, too consumed by my own life to get involved in any of it beyond listening to a couple of Mum's rants. I didn't say anything, but I thought they were going too far. I remember how Mum's hatred of Jon lit her up, how there was talk of little else in the salon, how sometimes it seemed like she was enjoying it. I remember reading about Jon's arrest in the *Echo*—it was framed as "Drunk local journalist in twisted 'revenge' plot against Ashford's best mum." The article mentioned that when he was arrested Jon had been shouting about something to do with his son—that stuck with me—but I don't remember anything else. In the end, the fact it was his first offense meant he got away with a fine, community service, and a restraining order, which made Mum pull at her hair and mumble something about the world going to shit.

He looks a bit more together now than he did in that photo. Neither of us has said anything for a while when he moves to the front of the table.

I stop scrubbing and frown up at him as he says, "Look, I didn't plan on turning up like this, I live just up the high street, above the Ladbrokes. I'm trying to finish an article about the summer fair, but I can't concentrate, I keep thinking about Megan and Grace. So I decided to go for a walk to clear my head, then I bumped into you."

I stand up straight, to look directly at him. "Yeah, but you didn't exactly bump into me though, did you? You must have seen me and decided to come over."

He raises his hands and says, "No, you're right, sorry. Wrong choice of words." He drops his hands, shrugs. "It just felt serendipitous, is all."

I shake my head. "I'm not talking to journalists."

"How about ex-journalists?"

I roll my eyes at him, drop the brush into the soapy bucket, planning to go inside and tell Brian not to let Jon into the pub, when he says, "Look, I just want to try to help. I know my article . . . well, I know I made some mistakes and I want to try to make up for them."

I stop walking because I hear the guilt in his tone; I recognize it from my own voice. I wasn't a good enough friend to Grace, I know how regret can beat away like a drum. In the past few years I've not been there for Grace, and now she's gone. I turn around to face Jon as he keeps talking.

"Look, I only want to try to help find Grace. I am, or was, a good journalist. I'm also the only investigative journalist who met them all, even Simon. If there's a chance I can help Grace, I have to do everything I can. I've tried, but I just can't sit on my arse while a sick child is missing. I keep thinking if it was my son that had been taken—" He stops suddenly, looks up to the sky, and works his jaw. "God, sorry, I don't know why I'm telling you all this. I'm meeting a doctor in Plymouth tomorrow, someone who used to know them, but apart from that I'm around. I'm just going to leave my card on the table—"

"What's the doctor called?"

He's quicker at clocking my interest than I am at concealing it. "Dr. Nina Rossi, I met her before . . ."

But he doesn't finish his sentence because he's seen the recognition spread across my face, the surprise. As he says the name I see each letter carefully written in colorful balloons in Grace's childish handwriting, the same at seven as it was at seventeen. I push my fringe off my forehead with the back of my hand, leaving a wet smear of soap bubbles across my skin, but I don't care.

I try to keep my voice light as I ask, "Why are you seeing her?"

"I met her last year, when I was researching the article. She didn't tell me much, but I had a hunch then that she knew more about Grace than she was letting on." He shrugs again. "I thought it worth talking to her just in case I was right. Do you know her?"

I think about the message inside Grace's card, thanking Dr. Rossi for getting Meg a job. I never knew Meg worked back then, but then Meg never liked to talk about their lives in Plymouth. Mum said it was too painful for her, that it only reminded Meg of Danny's death and Simon's cruelty. I turn to face Jon. Behind his glasses his eyes are wide, fixed like he's studying me, waiting patiently for me to tell him whatever it is I need to say.

I shake my head. "No, I don't know her, I . . ." I stop myself from telling him about the thank-you card, remind myself I don't owe him anything—that I shouldn't even be talking to him.

"Good luck with whatever it is you're trying to do, but don't talk to me again," I say, turning to leave. He doesn't try to stop me and the water from my bucket sloshes, wetting my jeans as I walk quickly back into the dark safety of the pub.

As I walk through the pub towards the kitchen, I realize the chefs, the kitchen porter, and two of the other waitresses are sitting at a table with Brian. They stop talking and all of them turn to stare at me, their eyes full of fascination and horror. It's obvious they've been talking about me.

"Here she is!" Brian says like he's greeting a puppy, and suddenly I feel as if I've just been pushed onto a stage, the spotlight on me, everyone staring, expecting, *waiting* for me to perform when all I want to do is hide. I drop my bucket to the floor, not caring about the carpet, and run to the toilet.

It's a relief to lock myself away in the tiny cubicle, even if the smell of partially digested cheap alcohol and bleach makes me gag. I slide my back against the door and cover my face with my hands. My cheeks are wet with tears I hadn't realized I'd been crying.

Shit, shit, shit.

Why have I lost it again? It's Jon Katrin's fault. Talking about his guilt, how he's decided to do something, anything, to help Grace even if it gets him into more trouble. I was Grace's friend, I *am* her friend, and what am I doing to help? Nothing. All I'm doing is scrubbing bird crap off tables.

There's a gentle knock on the door, followed by Brian's voice raised in a way he must think sounds concerned.

"Cara, sweetheart? You OK in there?"

I wipe my hand across my hot eyes and make my voice steady as I say, "I'm not feeling well, Brian. I think I'll just go home if that's all right?"

"Of course, Cara, you just take all the time you need."

I open the door and Brian's face is all worry as he puts a sweaty palm on my arm, his eyebrows knitted together, and he tilts his head as he says, "Cara, have you heard of post-traumatic stress disorder?"

I have a disorder now?

I shake my head as I push past Brian and say, "I'll call when I'm ready to come back." Ignoring all the curious eyes that blink out at me from the darkness of the pub, I grab my bag and coat from behind the bar and let the door bang behind me.

The seagull is still back standing on the table I'd been scrubbing just minutes before, and there's a white rectangle under the salt shaker. I pick up the business card and read Jon's name, his contact details. Not wanting Brian and the others to know I was talking to a reporter, especially not Jon Katrin, I shove his card into my pocket and fall, with relief, behind the wheel of Mum's car.

I don't feel ready to go home yet, so I drive on past Mum's towards Angel's Bay and pull over when I see a postbox. I take the two envelopes out of my bag. One is addressed to Dr. Rossi at her Plymouth office and contains the thank-you card from Grace, and the other, with the photo, to Mr. Charlie Nichols at Resthaven Nursing Home. I wrote a brief note to send with each of them, explaining that I'd found the card and the photo and that it felt right to pass them on. I'd signed off "Kind regards" followed with my best signature. It all felt quite formal. My hand pauses in the mouth of the postbox. Suddenly I don't want to let them go, as though by dropping the envelopes I'd be letting another part of Grace disappear. I pull my hand back and stare at the addresses. What if I didn't post them but gave them to Dr. Rossi and Charlie in person instead? They're both in Plymouth, after all, and I don't have anything else to do now I don't need to go back to the pub any time soon. Maybe Dr. Rossi would tell me more about the Grace and Meg she knew over coffee. I could curl up in an armchair opposite Charlie, like I used to with my granddad, and listen to his stories about what Grace was like as a baby. It would be a small, good thing I can do. I feel a bit better, lighter. I picture Grace smiling, glad that I'm going to meet these people who, at one time at least, were important to her.

Full of memories of me and Grace, I walk along the beach to while away a couple of hours, and by the time I get home Mum is sitting at the kitchen table chewing the end of a pen and staring fixedly at an unmarked piece of paper in front of her. She gets up, relieved to have a distraction, kisses me, tilts her head to look at me, hugs me, and kisses me again.

"How was the pub?" she asks.

"Fine. Just normal," I lie.

"Brian looked after you, did he?"

I shrug, pour myself a glass of water. "How's it going with the volunteers?" I ask before drinking the water in one go.

"Amazing. People are really coming out of the woodwork to help, but of course I'm not surprised: everyone loves them. There's been a good turnout from the Wishmakers too. If only I could say the same for the police. Upton called me today and basically asked me to call the whole community search off. I almost told her that if they were doing their job properly they would have Grace safely home already. Simon's dangerous, but from what Meg told me about him, he's too stupid to be some kind of criminal master-mind," Mum says, sitting back at the table and sighing as she looks at the blank page in front of her before turning again to face me.

"I spoke to Jane today as well, Car, she was talking about that counseling again, she was saying how—"

"Mum," I cut in, "did Meg ever have a job?"

Mum's eyes dart to the far corner of the ceiling, as though something's caught her attention up there or as though she doesn't want to look at me. She frowns. "What's brought this on?"

"I'm just curious. I know she never worked when they moved here, but before, I mean, when they were in Plymouth, was she ever able to work then?"

Mum leans back in her chair and sighs again, but this time at me. "Cara, being a single mum is the toughest job you can imagine, let alone when you're a single mum to a very sick child . . ." Her voice has a frayed, defensive quality.

"Mum, I didn't mean it like that. I'm asking because I found a—"

"And I'm trying to answer, but you're not listening to me." She smacks her hand down on the kitchen table. We both stare at it, surprised by her overreaction. She closes her eyes briefly and comes to stand opposite me.

"Look, Car, I'm sorry, I didn't mean to shout. I'm just worried about how you're reacting to all this. Like I tried to say earlier, Jane and I were talking today and she said that counseling—"

"I don't want to see a counselor, Mum, I want to find Grace." I sound angrier than I mean to.

"I know you do, love, we all do, but you've been through a huge trauma. I know you're trying to battle on, pretend like it never happened, but that can't go on forever, Car, you'll make yourself ill." Mum pushes some hair back behind my ear. Her long nail against my skin makes me shiver. I pull my head away and she looks newly hurt. Her hand drops to my shoulder.

"That's exactly what you do, though, isn't it? Battle on. Why aren't I allowed to do the same?" I ask, my voice calmer.

"But I didn't find her, did I? The police haven't been calling you to tell you to keep an eye on me, have they?"

"They've been calling you about me? Why?"

"That's what I've been trying to tell you. They're *worried*, Cara, like everyone else is worried about you."

"I'm all right, Mum, I don't know what else to say." I know now is probably not the best time to ask a favor, but I have to try. "Can I borrow the car for a few days? I can't face the bus, there are still reporters around."

Mum's hand drops from my shoulder to hold her waist, her eyes narrow. She shakes her head and splutters a small, exasperated laugh. "Have you even listened to a word I've said?"

"What if I agree to call this counselor woman? Then can I have the car?"

But Mum's shaking her head.

"I'm not giving in to emotional blackmail. You can't be that worried about reporters, otherwise you wouldn't be going to work, and besides, I need the car to ferry search volunteers. You know I don't think you should be back at the pub so soon, but if you must go to work I'll drop you off and pick you up after your shift." Mum slumps back down at the kitchen table and, cupping her hand around her forehead, mutters, "I still haven't written anything for the vigil tonight."

Part of me wants to sit down and help her, but a bigger, noisier part is too angry with her for standing in the way of my plan. I can't afford a taxi all the way to Plymouth and the bus route is terrible. I'll have to change buses twice, it'll take hours and means I probably won't be able to see Dr. Rossi and Charlie in the same day. Mum's treating me like a kid, just like everyone else, telling me I have a disorder, that I'm traumatized. It's like they want me to collapse, like they'd be happy to see me fall apart—*just like they knew I would*. If Mum had given me the chance, I'd have told her about the card and the photo. I was even going to suggest we go to Plymouth to meet Dr. Rossi and Charlie together. But not now. I shove my hands in my pockets as I walk out of the kitchen and brush my thumb against the smooth surface of Jon Katrin's card. He's going to Plymouth tomorrow . . .

I squash the thought before it's even taken shape. I can't ask him for a lift. I sit on my bed, back against the headboard, and remember how he looked at me today. It was almost as though he recognized something in me. It was the first time in two days that I didn't feel like I was playing the lead part in a tragedy written by everyone else except me. He didn't patronize and he didn't treat me like I was sick. He just wants to find out the truth. I pull my laptop onto my knees and type "Jon Katrin journalist" into the search bar. There are hundreds of references from Facebook and local forums about the Meg and Grace article, but I decide not to read them now. I want to know who he was before he came to Ashford, before that article. I read a piece he wrote about the MPs' expenses scandal and another about Islamophobia. I'm impressed; his writing is left-wing, feels thoroughly researched and considered. He won a litany of awards and was well regarded before he left London and his career nosedived. I'm about to start a third article, about a Christian cult, when there's a gentle knock and my door starts to open. Mum's perfume arrives before her, the smell of chemically reproduced flowers. She's fully made up, ready for the vigil and the cameras.

She hands me an identical T-shirt and says, "Here, I thought you might want to wear this."

I take it from her. "Thanks, Mum," I say, letting her stroke my hair a couple of times. It's our code, our way of letting each other know we're not angry anymore.

I hold Mum's hand as we walk out into the dusky pink early-evening light. They would have liked that, Meg and Grace, the pink light. The atmosphere is hushed, a little nervous. No one has done this before, gathered together to mourn but also to hope. People hold candles in jars, passing a flame to each other with sad, mild smiles—what else can they do? The candles dance, trapped and beautiful. Grace's face is everywhere I look. She's staring up, chin thrust forward, grinning into the camera. That's how I remember her. Grace spent her life looking up. Unlike most girls her age, she never learnt how to pout. She always smiled with the abandonment of a toddler—chin raised high, cheeks puffed out like dough balls.

I squeeze Mum's hand and we walk towards the crowd.

"Oh, I almost forgot." Mum stops and takes a badge out of her pocket, the same photo of Grace printed on the front.

"Maggie from the Wishmakers had them made up," Mum says before pinning it with shaky hands just above my heart. I kiss Mum's cheek, a camera flashes.

There are more people here than I anticipated. They stand in small huddles, like sheep in a field when it rains. I spot Martin and Sylvia, of course, and Zara, who waves at me but is then nudged by the guy next to her to stop. A nurse, Lola, who used to visit Grace at home is standing next to an elderly gray-haired man I think might be Dr. Parker, Grace's GP. Barry, who is as yellow and wrinkled as the roll-up cigarettes he likes to smoke, is standing with his wife, Marie, who smiles a small, wobbly smile at me. Barry and Marie lived next door to Granddad before he died. From a long line of tin miners, Barry was forced into early retirement when all the mines closed in the early nineties. There are many more faces I don't recognize, some moved by tragedy, and others—I imagine—who are drawn to it. Could one of them know where Grace is? I don't see Jon. The crowd opens, like a slow wave, parting to allow Mum to walk to the front.

There is something a bit sacred about Mum tonight, like she rules in this weird new hierarchy. A few cameras click and, like fingers on piano keys, they seem to set the mood: tense, like we're all holding our breath. A couple of photos of Grace and Meg are on easels at the front of the crowd, just where number 52's lawn begins. The one of Meg is the photo all the news channels have been using. She's younger than she was when she died, slimmer. It's close up, but still a flattering photo. Her face is at an angle to the camera, smiling like she's mid-laugh, her brown hair just brushing her shoulders, the freckle below her right eye visible. It was the one Mum gave them to use: she knew Meg liked it. But when I look at it now, Meg's forehead starts to crack in on itself like a dropped egg, her eyes staring but empty. A camera flashes and I quickly look away.

Mum and I make it to the front of the crowd. Standing next to the easels is an older, thin-faced man in a black fleece and black flat cap who moves towards us and kisses Mum on the cheek. He's wearing a Find Grace badge. Someone puts an arm around me. I turn and see Molly, my old friend from school. She's got her baby, Zack, in a stroller and is moving it gently back and forward. She's heavily made up as always, false eyelashes, foundation, the works. Sometimes I think Mum wishes I was more like Molly.

"Car, it's so good to see you." I feel her acrylic nails dig into me as she squeezes my shoulder. "How are you, after everything?"

"Ummm." I don't know what to say. More cameras flash. Just

in time, Molly tenses with a pose, sucks her tummy in, before she turns back to me.

"Stupid question. You must feel completely fucking nuts. Look, can we go for a drink next week? You know, talk about it? I just want to make sure you're OK."

That's bollocks, of course, she doesn't want to make sure I'm OK, she wants the gory details. She wants to hear how Meg's blood was so dark it was almost black. But I can't blame her, I'd have been the same, wouldn't I? Molly's boyfriend, Paul, is one of Chris's oldest mates, it was how Chris and I met. But Molly hasn't returned my calls since Chris and I broke up, since I said I didn't want to live in Cornwall for the rest of my life, have three kids by the time I was twenty-five, and stay in a job I hated. Since I said that basically I didn't want Molly's life.

Another camera flashes. Molly looks around to see where the photographer is, but then an older woman behind me hands me a jar with a candle lit inside and she nods towards the front lawn, where the man in the fleece is standing on a platform I didn't notice before. He raises his hands towards the crowd, but he doesn't need to wait for us to stop talking. We are already silent. Molly's arm falls from my shoulder.

"Thank you all for being here. For those of you who don't know me, I'm David Raffin, CEO of the Wishmakers. It has been decided that a funeral will not be held for Megan until Grace has been found, so myself and Susan Dorman, along with other friends and community members, decided to organize this remembrance event this evening, for a period of loving reflection on the life of Megan Nichols. We are also here to ask you—whether you have a religious faith or not—to hold both Megan and her daughter, Grace, in the light, to send them your love and strength at this most difficult of times, and to pray that Grace will be found, safe and well, very soon." There are a few shy claps of support from the crowd before David says, "Now I'm going to hand over to Susan Dorman, Megan's neighbor and closest friend."

Mum steps forward. David gives her a hand up to the platform. She unfolds a crumpled piece of paper, it flutters in her hand like a wing. She looks up at the crowd in front of her. We stand, candles raised, like devotees, and I see a flash of fear in her eyes. She looks quickly down at her notes again.

She stammers on the first two words and, unlike David, keeps her head lowered, eyes fixed on the page in front of her as she speaks.

"I met my . . . I met my friend Meg when we were both young single mums to gorgeous little girls. Neither of us thought we'd be on our own with small daughters, struggling to pay the bills. Meg moved next door with her daughter, Grace, to escape a violent and dangerous man. We became close immediately. Our girls loved playing together, they used to pretend they were sisters."

Mum pauses. Her eyes trace the crowd; I think she might be looking for me. I stand on tiptoes, will her to see me but she doesn't, so she looks down at her notes again.

"I remember the first time I saw Grace have a seizure, years ago. It was shocking and I felt completely useless. But Meg knew exactly what to do. She calmly held Grace's arms by her side so she wouldn't hurt herself. She soothed Grace until the spasms ended. Afterwards, when Grace was in bed, I got upset. I'd never experienced anything like it, never seen firsthand what it means to care for a sick child twenty-four hours a day, seven days a week. And when I asked her how she coped on her own, she said simply, 'To me, Grace is perfect just as she is. I will love her and care for her come what may.'"

Mum pauses, closes her eyes to swallow. As she says the last few sentences, a dramatic crack runs through her voice; it sounds as if it's running through her whole body: "That was Meg in a nutshell—she was all love and care for others. I have no doubt Meg protected Grace with her own life when she was brutally attacked two nights ago, and now we owe it to Meg to do the same. I promise my best friend, Meg, I will not rest until we find Grace. Come what may."

There are a few slow, self-conscious claps; people look around, unsure whether to join in or not. Mum's crying again. David pats her shoulder and then hugs her. The cameras pop. David helps Mum off the makeshift stage. I move forward and take her hand, squeeze it because I can't hug her now I'm holding a candle.

"Was that OK?" Mum asks.

"They would have loved it," I say, meaning it, and Mum smiles. We both bow our heads as the local vicar moves to stand where Mum just stood. "Let us pray," he says. And as I listen to his words about love and faith I close my eyes and see Grace laughing beneath a beanie hat, her cheeks pink with joy, and then the pink becomes blue from the lights of the ambulance that so often came to take her away, as though even the smallest sip of happiness would make Grace sick.

After the vigil a few neighbors and friends came back to Mum's for tea and cake. Zara suggested everyone chip in for wine, but Martin felt that was too celebratory. People needed to be somber tonight.

When most people have left, I sit at the kitchen table, sipping tea with Sylvia and Zara. Sylvia tells us in a low voice, so Martin can't hear, how she'd dreamt about Grace, saw her walking out of the sea. Zara, fondling her fake gold dangly earrings, nods along with Sylvia and says she felt Meg's spirit the night before, heard her begging her to find Simon. I keep quiet as I get up to see if we have any biscuits. I think about what I'm going to do tomorrow, whether to text Jon and ask for a lift, or whether that'd make me as mad as everyone thinks I am. Once everyone's left, I'm going to read his article about Meg and Grace and then I'll read some of Grace's diary again before I make up my mind whether to get in touch or not. It's good to have a plan. Even such a short-term one distracts me temporarily from a recurring image of Grace on the floor of a dark basement, a blindfold over her eyes, her hands bound, alone but still crying for help.

16th November 2018

Something amazing happened today. Something so amazing I can hardly believe it.

Mum was just about to give me my drugs through Peggy (that's the PEG tube that runs into my stomach for food and drugs—Mum gave it a name to make me feel better, she always knows how to make me laugh)—when the phone rang. It was Maggie from the Wishmakers. Mum told me to ignore it, but I'd been waiting for this phone call for two weeks. I couldn't let it ring out, lifesaving drugs or not. Sorry, Mum!

"Hello, Maggie?"

"Grace? Is that you?"

"Have you decided, do you know who's going?" My heart was thumping so hard I thought it might actually burst out of my chest, but then Cookie leapt up onto the bed, mewing for attention, and I twisted around too hard, trying to shoo her away, pulling the pink skin around the

opening in my stomach. The shock of the pain made me shout and Mum took the phone from me.

"Maggie, sorry, this isn't really the best time."

"No, Mum, Mum, please just ask her about the Big Trip, please!" I gasped, pulling my pajama top down in case Peggy had started bleeding. I didn't want Mum to see. I knew she'd hang up on Maggie immediately if she did.

Mum looked back at me, nodded, and smiled. She put the plastic syringe full of mushed-up pills back into its sterile plastic container.

"Actually, Maggie, Grace is driving me crazy. You'd better just tell me now whether she's been accepted or not."

The words seemed to hang around me, suspended in the atmosphere.

"Uh huh. OK. Okaaaay. Hawaii?"

And that's when I knew. I've thought about the Big Trip hundreds of times a day for two weeks since Maggie and I filled out the application and sent it to the Wishmakers head office in London. This was the last year I had a chance of being chosen, my last chance at going away to another country.

My back groaned as I pulled myself to sit up in bed but I hardly noticed. I'd convinced myself it wasn't going to happen because I wanted it too much. If I want something too much, I always jinx it.

Mum was still talking into the phone.

"OK, thank you, Maggie. Yes, yes, she's delighted, we both are. Yes, I'll chat with Grace and then, if she's feeling up to it, we'll come in on Tuesday as you suggest to talk through all the details. Thank you, Maggie." She looked as startled as I felt when she hung up the phone. She stared

at the receiver, blinking at it like she'd never seen one before.

"Mum?" I said, banging the side of my bed to snap her
out of it because she was just standing there in the middle of
my room, blinking at the phone, and then she was shaking
her head and smiling at the same time.

"They've got a place for you, Gracie!" she said, and she
came over to me in a rush and bent down towards me so
her eyes could tell my eyes that this was real, this was really
happening.

"Oh, my darling, finally!" she said, her smile almost
too big to let the words out. She kissed me all over my face
then, making me laugh so much my glasses went wonky
and then they fell off my face, which made us both laugh
harder. But then Mum said this: "Oh, Mouse, what will I
do without you for ten whole days! I'm going to miss you
while you're off swimming with dolphins and working on
your tan."

She winked at me and I knew she was joking, but I
felt myself go rigid. Who will make sure I've got the right
meds? Who will check on me in the middle of the night? I
think Mum saw that I was scared because she took my hand
and squeezed it. I squeezed back twice, which means "I'm
OK," because there's no code for "I wish you were coming
to Hawaii with me." I don't want her to worry, she's always
worrying about me—it's all she does. So I put on a big
smile and pretended that I wasn't scared to go without her.
Another little secret.

Lots of love, Grace xxx

6

Jon

"Mind if I put the radio on?" Cara asks from the passenger seat as I turn onto the main road towards Plymouth.

"Sure," I say, and switch it on for her.

I had doubted whether Cara would pick up the business card I left on the table outside the pub, let alone use it, so her text had come as a surprise. Apparently, she had something she wanted to give Dr. Rossi and she needed a lift. I had left it until this morning to answer, unsure about the wisdom of driving around with a young woman I barely knew. What if someone saw us in the car together, recognized us and posted something, a photo of the two of us, online? That would have Ruth running to the solicitors to file for divorce in no time. Not to mention that I hadn't actually arranged a meeting with Dr. Rossi, strictly speaking. Still, the professional part of me was thrilled at this chance to get to know Cara, maybe find out a bit more about Grace and Meg.

When I rung Dr. Rossi this morning I'd fully expected her to ignore the call—I don't think either of us enjoyed our last meeting much. She'd ended the interview after five minutes, saying she couldn't help me any further and that I was not, under any circumstances, to use her name or quote her in the article. My plan was to tell Cara that Dr. Rossi had canceled our meeting at the last minute, but that if she wanted to tell me anything about Grace and Meg I'd be happy to meet.

But Dr. Rossi had answered the phone.

"I have back-to-back patients for the next two weeks, Mr. Katrin, and frankly I don't understand why you want to meet. I told you last time, Megan and I haven't spoken in years." Her voice was clipped, like she was in a hurry to get rid of me so she could begin her busy day.

"It was actually Cara Dorman, Megan's next-door neighbor, who wants to meet. She has something from Megan and Grace she wants to give you."

There was a pause at the end of the line, a breath held, and I knew that I had Dr. Rossi's full attention.

"What is it?"

"Honestly, I don't know. But it must be something specific to you. She thought you'd be interested in whatever it is." She was quiet for a moment, a busy kind of quiet, like she was trying to figure out what to do.

"Fine. I can meet you in my lunch break, for ten minutes. I'll be in the playground behind the office."

I was stunned. Clearly Dr. Rossi was interested in whatever Cara had to give her. I still had no clue what it was, but—decision made. I was driving Cara to Plymouth whether I liked it or not.

Now, a few hours later, with Cara in the passenger seat next to me, I feel less wary about giving her a lift. With my beard and scruffy hair I look different from how I looked six months ago and the chances of us being recognized, especially miles away from Ashford, must be tiny. I'm here to help Grace, but I still feel the reporter in me sit up, pen poised, ready to take notes for any clues. We haven't spoken much yet, which is fine, I don't want to push her. She keeps flicking through the radio stations until she stops on a report about Grace's disappearance. Sitting low in her seat, Cara keeps her eyes fixed straight ahead as she listens to information she's probably heard hundreds of times already. She listens intently, as if there might be a secret, some code hidden in the reports.

The car fills with the voice of Simon's neighbor. I've heard it a few times already: "Simon's always been a quiet bloke, keeps himself to himself sort of thing. Looks like he wouldn't hurt a fly, but mind, it's those ones that you . . ."

I feel uncomfortable listening to this stuff about Simon with Cara next to me. I don't want her to associate me too closely with him, like everyone else does. I lean forward, changing the channel to a love song, before flicking to the local radio station, and a news bulletin.

. . . *The police are still focusing their efforts on finding Simon Davis, father of the missing Grace Nichols. CCTV footage shows Davis boarding a train to London the morning after the murder, but they haven't as yet released any further details on his whereabouts. The public is reminded not to approach him but to call the police immediately if they see him. Police and community groups are continuing to search the local area for any sign of Megan's daughter, Grace Nichols. Now over to Sabrina for the weather. Sabrina . . .*

Cara doesn't stir; we've both heard the updates before. I flick again, on to a program about a group of parents who are teaching their kids how to speak Cornish, before changing back to the love song.

"So, mind if I ask what it is you want to give Dr. Rossi?" Cara glances down towards the crumpled backpack in the foot-well next to her scuffed Dr. Martens boots. With a blunt nail she picks the skin around the nails on her other hand, glancing at me quickly before replying.

"Grace used to make these personalized thank-you cards for people who helped her and Meg somehow. Mum got one for do-ing a half marathon to raise money for her wheelchair a couple of years ago. Anyway, I found one for Dr. Rossi that she never sent. She'd written a note in it and everything, so I thought she should have it."

That's it? A thank-you card? I don't know what I was expect-ing, but certainly something more significant, more substantial than something she could easily have posted. Cara seems to pick up on what I'm thinking.

"I was going to send it, but, like you said, I couldn't just sit around and keep pretending Grace hasn't been taken. It might not actually help find her, but at least I can do something I know would make her smile." Cara looks fierce for a moment, defensive.

I clear my throat, tell myself it doesn't matter how insignificant it is. Dr. Rossi was still intrigued enough to agree to a meeting.

Suddenly Cara turns to me and says, "So what was Simon like when you met him?"

The abruptness of her question takes me by surprise. I decide it's best to keep things vague.

"Depressed, lonely, misunderstood, or so I thought at the time."

"And now? What do you think of him now?"

"Well, if he is behind all of this, then I think he's a brilliant manipulator and I'm even more of an idiot for supporting him in that article."

"And if he's not?"

I feel my forehead fold into a frown. "I think it's unlikely he's not, to be honest. There are no other suspects, no one they knew had any kind of motive, and the chances of this being a random attack and kidnapping are so remote that—"

"So you think Simon killed Meg? That he has Grace now?"

She knows I'm stalling, that I'm skirting round the question. Suddenly it's like I'm the one being interviewed. I fumble for the elastic band on my wrist, forgetting it has snapped.

"That seems to be the most plausible explanation, yes. Don't forget his mental health has been deteriorating since Danny died, and he'd been violent in the past. Also I think the fact that he's not come forward to clear his name is pretty damning."

Cara nods, turns her dark head to stare out of the window, the countryside a blur.

"So, did you tell your mum I was giving you a lift today?"

Cara snorts. "No! She thinks I'm working at the pub. But she's so wired with everything, she won't know I didn't go in."

Great. Cara lying to her mum will give Susan and her mates another reason to hate me. But I remind myself that Cara's an adult, she can make her own decisions and, besides, Cara instigated all of this. I haven't done anything wrong.

"And you? How are you doing 'with everything,' I mean? Walking into a murder scene is pretty rough, especially when you know the person." I glance over at Cara. Her eyes widen, her pale skin blushes, she looks like she's about to be sick, but she just shrugs.

"I feel better when I'm busy," she says.

"So, what does your dad reckon about all of this?" There's

been plenty about Susan in the news reports, but nothing about Cara's dad. Cara glances quickly out of her window before looking straight ahead. She keeps picking the skin around her fingernails.

"I have no idea, he hasn't been in touch. He lives in Scotland with his new family, they're kind of hippies—don't have a telly, that kind of thing—so he probably doesn't even know what happened." Cara pauses, before she adds, "He's nothing like the dads in your article, if that's what you're getting at. I don't have a restraining order against him or anything. He just kind of opted out of being my dad a long time ago."

Before I can say anything she turns to face me and asks, "What about you? How's your son?"

I feel her eyes move. I know she notices my jaw tighten. I force a lightness I don't feel into my voice.

"He's good, just made the school football team actually, he's playing—"

"So he doesn't have cancer anymore?" Cara interrupts. She's not interested in hearing about Jakey's football. I let her question hang for a moment. She's skilled, I'll give her that: deflecting my questions, turning me into the subject, but nevertheless I don't like it. She's looking at me like I owe her something. Perhaps she's right. What was it Dr. Bunce said that made Ruth snort with laughter? "Honesty demands reciprocity" or something like that. If I want Cara to be honest with me, I need to choose what to give her in return. I want her to trust me. I shift in my seat.

"So you read my article about Grace and Megan?" I say, and out of the corner of my eye I see her watching me.

"Of course: everyone in Cornwall's read it. I looked it up again last night."

I nod and try to swallow the thick, familiar lump of anguish that lifts to my throat whenever anyone mentions that article.

"I'd forgotten the bit about 'A parent's job is to lay the foundations for their child to flourish as much as possible—and sometimes this means making hard decisions, ones we would rather not make, for the child's happiness.'"

"You memorized it?"

"It almost read like you resented Meg, when all she was doing was her best in really shitty circumstances."

I nod. I know. I know all of this. I'm glad I'm driving, that I have an excuse to avoid eye contact. My hands have become moist where they grip the steering wheel.

"You're right. I was angry. I'm not trying to justify anything, but the doctors said Jakey only had a fifty-fifty chance of surviving and my marriage was falling apart. I think I was going through some sort of delayed shock. Ruth and I were barely talking, it was all so painful. I felt like I was losing them both: Ruth and Jakey. So I suppose in some crazy way when I met Simon I felt sorry for him and pissed off that Meg was able to keep Grace so close and Simon so far away." As I say the words I feel the thudding truth of them. I'd never told anyone that, never even been able to admit it to myself. The ball in my throat softens.

Cara doesn't say anything for a moment and I panic that I've said more than I should. I try to think of a way of making it all sound better, making me sound better.

"I'd always worked for big national papers. If I'd known that article would affect the community in the way it did I would never have sent it to the editor."

"Well, I suppose the editor shouldn't have published it, should they?"

I swerve into the slow lane, too close to the front of a truck. The driver beeps but we both ignore him. I glance over at Cara. She's still looking at me.

"I've been looking into being a journalist," she says, shy suddenly. "I read that the editor is ultimately responsible for what they publish, not the writer."

Cara's just said what I've never dared say aloud in case it sounded like I was trying to pass the blame on to the young, inexperienced editor of the *Cornish Chronicle*. But she's right. Cara turns back to face the road and we're both silent for a moment before she asks, "Did you ever find out who posted the photo of your son on Facebook?"

My neck prickles as I picture Jakey as he was then; skin translucent, his head hairless, his body so thin he looked like he would break at the slightest touch. He's smiling in the photo, giving a brave thumbs-up, but he was in Ruth's arms in tears again straight after it was taken. The image still haunts me. I press my window down and breathe in the highway air. It is acrid and chemical, like sickness, but I breathe it in anyway. I need it to shift the memory of Jakey in his hospital bed. I close my window, clear my throat.

"A copy of the photo was found on a computer at the hospital where Jakey was being treated. It could have been one of the nurses who set up the account and posted the photo, or someone else working there. Someone Megan and Grace knew who took offense on their behalf, probably."

"You don't like talking about it, do you." It's a statement, not a question, and I know it's her way of telling me to stop trying to get her to talk about finding Megan's body. She knows I don't want to talk about Jakey; she's just trying to make a point. I lean forward and turn the radio up.

The children's play area, just behind the office where Nina Rossi suggested we meet, turns out to be a broken seesaw, a slide covered in graffiti, and a couple of chain swings that look like they could easily split a child in two. Unsurprisingly, it's empty. Cara kicks away a couple of cider cans and we sit on a damp bench facing the back of the office. Cara carefully takes an A5 envelope out of her backpack and says quickly, "Look, don't take this the wrong way, but maybe you should wait in the car?"

"What?"

But she knows I heard what she said, so she keeps talking. "It's just I think maybe on my own it'll seem less kind of . . . confrontational, I suppose." She looks at me, can tell I don't know what to say, and shrugs. "This is all just quite private, you know, it might be emotional for her. I don't mind if you want to talk to her on your own after, I just don't want her to think you're writing an article, that's all."

Suddenly, I realize Cara is worried about being associated with me as much as I am about helping her. But still, there's no way I'm waiting in the car.

"Cara, I organized this, and besides I didn't drive all this way to . . ." but I stop talking because Cara isn't listening, she's watching a woman walking towards us at an efficient clip. Dr. Nina Rossi has the upright, steady walk of someone who knows exactly where they're going. She's wearing a two-piece suit, the type favored by civil servants and politicians, and has short, neat, gray hair. As she approaches I see there's a dullness in her eyes, her mouth leaden and unsmiling like it's been that way for so long you'd need a chisel to change it.

We both stand and she nods at us, putting her hand out to Cara first.

"You must be Cara," she says, and Cara, rather sweetly, does a tiny deferential bow of her head as she shakes Dr. Rossi's hand.

"Yes, hi."

"I'm sorry you've been caught up in such an awful tragedy," she says, before turning to me.

"Hello, Jon." Her eyes narrow, like my name is an aggravation. Her skin is smoother than most women's her age, perhaps from care, but more likely from lack of any real sadness or joy. She looks like she plateaued long ago, her feelings a hand of cards she holds carefully away from other players' prying eyes.

"So, you said Grace had something for me?" She looks directly at the envelope Cara's clutching in front of her. "Is that it?" she asks, looking from Cara to me like a hassled teacher needing a quick answer.

"It's from Grace," Cara says, trying to smile at Dr. Rossi, who looks blankly back at her. "A thank-you card she made for you, for helping her and Meg."

Dr. Rossi turns to me, her tone skeptical as she asks, "You drove all this way to give me a thank-you card?" I lift my shoulders, shrug, and Dr. Rossi's eyes become small, glinting from me to Cara and back again as she says, "What do you know?"

Before I can think of the right way to respond, something that will make Dr. Rossi reveal why she's so on edge, Cara jumps in.

"Nothing! I just thought you should have it, since Grace made it for you. She must have been grateful to you."

"Well, I can't think why. I was never Grace's or Megan's doctor; they saw a colleague of mine." There's something rehearsed about the doctor's tone, as though she's been practicing, reciting the sentence over and over.

Dr. Rossi holds out her hand towards Cara, waiting for the envelope, but Cara doesn't move. Instead she says, "Grace wrote a note—she wanted to thank you for getting Meg a job."

Dr. Rossi drops her outstretched hand.

"Ah, I interviewed her for a part-time admin role here. It must have been that."

Why does she sound so relieved?

"We didn't know Meg worked here," Cara says.

"Only for a few months. It wasn't worth my time training her up, to be honest." Dr. Rossi glances at her watch. "Look, I said I only had a few minutes. I'm very sorry about what's happened to your friends but I need to be getting back to my patients."

Cara looks downhearted. This wasn't the meeting she'd hoped for. "So why didn't they send it to you years ago?" she asks, confused.

Dr. Rossi looks briefly up towards the heavy sky, exasperated, as though it's Cara's fault the clouds have gathered.

"I honestly have no idea, now please . . ." Dr. Rossi reaches for the envelope again and Cara slowly places it in her hand.

"Right," Dr. Rossi says, like she's rounding off an appointment with a patient. "Thank you." She speaks curtly, glancing at me one last time. We watch as she walks quickly away, pausing only to open and read the card before she scrunches it into a ball and drops it into a trashcan.

"What a bitch," Cara says, stalking after Dr. Rossi. I'm worried she's going to charge into the office after her but instead Cara stops at the trashcan, takes out the card, and is straightening it out in her hands by the time I catch up.

"She's a strange woman, Cara."

"She's a cow."

Cara sounds more angry than hurt.

"I thought she'd be happy to have the card, that we'd chat a bit about Grace maybe. I never thought she wouldn't give a shit, chuck it away. God, I feel like an idiot."

"Hey, you're not the idiot, she is," I say. My hand is suddenly on her shoulder; it feels important she believes me. She glances at it before I pull it awkwardly away. "But I think you're wrong about one thing—she clearly did give a shit."

"You think so?"

"Yeah, you heard how defensive she was, asking us what we know." It's like hearing the old me talking when I'd just had a breakthrough on a story. A familiar feeling, like bubbles bursting, lifts into my stomach.

Next to me, Cara's biting her lip, and frowns towards the office as she says, "She was a bit weird, wasn't she? It was like she was hiding something and was worried we'd find out about it."

"I think you might be right. You've got good instincts."

She tries to smother the smile that flickers across her face but she's not quick enough. "You think so?"

I nod. "You need sharp instincts to be a decent journalist, and instinct is something that can't be taught."

Cara glows a little and I feel the first drops of rain on my cheek.

"Shall we get going?" I say.

Cara nods and we start walking in silence, but before we get to the car she stops by another bench and asks, apropos of nothing, "Why are you doing this?"

"I told you already: I want to find Grace, or at least help if I can."

"Because you messed up before?"

"Partly, yeah. But mostly because I just want to help."

"And you're not helping because you want to write an article?"

I lift my gaze to the sky so I don't have to look her in the eye. "I want to find Grace. I want to find Grace soon, while she's still alive."

Cara looks directly at me as she says, "Will you let me help?"

"Cara, I'm not sure that's such a good—"

"You said yourself just now I've got good instincts."

"Cara, I don't want to get you involved in all of this . . ."

She looks crestfallen, thin, and dejected standing in the rain.

"It's really going to bucket down. We should get back to the car."

Cara blinks a few times, as though trying to chase a thought away, before she shrugs and starts walking towards the car.

The traffic looks heavy all the way to Resthaven Nursing Home, the roads like blocked arteries. We join the queue as raindrops hammer the windshield. Cara turns the radio on again and is staring out of the window when my phone starts vibrating. I shuffle it awkwardly out of my pocket, balancing it on my thigh as I hit the speaker icon.

"Dad? Dad? You there?"

"Hi, mate! I'm here, how you doing?"

"Dad, Mum says I'm not allowed to play *World of Warcraft* anymore, which is really unfair because everyone, *everyone* at school is on it and I'd just started chatting to this kid who lives in Hong Kong and he's going to tell me this secret about how to get past—"

"Woah woah woah, hold on, Jakey."

Whatever had Cara's attention outside has lost it now. She's turned back, her head pressed against the headrest, staring straight ahead, the faintest smile on her lips. I turn to her, mouth "Sorry." She shakes her head to show she doesn't mind. She's listening, how could she not? I've already had a £250 fine and three points for talking to Jakey on the phone while driving but there's no way I'm hanging up on him. It's the best part of my day.

"Jakey, mate, if your mum doesn't like you playing the game she must have her reasons. How was school today?"

But Jakey ignores my question. "No, Dad, she doesn't know what she's talking about, she just got ragey and changed the Wi-Fi so I can't log on to it anymore without her putting in a password."

I could listen to him all day, even when he's moaning.

"Your mum has a point, Jakey. I mean, you know that you have to be careful of strangers on the internet, we've talked about that before. She's just looking out for you."

"Yeah, but he's twelve and he lives in Hong Kong!" He punctuates the words like I'm still learning what they mean.

"You don't know that for sure. Besides, your mum will be more nervous than usual. You heard what happened?"

"Yeah." His tone drops, his voice softens. "You mean that girl. She's sick, right?"

"Yes, Jakey, yes she is." Although now in remission, Jakey hates hearing about other sick children. He knows better than anyone how sickness, real sickness, strikes at random.

"You knew her, the missing girl, didn't you, Dad? Are you helping the police find her?" I feel Cara shift beside me but don't look at her.

"Something like that, yeah."

In the background Ruth calls my son's name. I picture her at the bottom of the stairs, one foot resting on the penultimate step, her short, wavy hair pinned behind her ears. I dress her in jeans and a simple white T-shirt, always my favorite outfit on Ruth. She calls again.

"Well, she's lucky she's got you helping her, Dad. Gotta go, speak tomorrow, yeah?"

"OK, Jakey." Ruth doesn't know he calls me every day. "I love you," I add, but he's already hung up. My phone clatters as I drop it into the pocket in my car door.

In the passenger seat, Cara's turned fully towards me. She's staring at me, studying me as though I've suddenly grown a snout or wings out of my ears.

"What?" I ask, darting my gaze from her to the road and back again. She doesn't flinch. Have I got a sandwich crumb on my face or something? I strain to look in the rearview mirror but it's hard to see with my beard and I don't want to creep into the car in front.

"What?" I ask again.

But she just shakes her head and stares out of the windshield. I recognize this silence, how she shifts around in her seat. It's like she's had an idea. Ruth always told me I go quiet and stare when I have a realization that I'm not ready to share. It's odd, but I see parts of myself in Cara. She has a determination for the truth, and a willingness to take risks, both of which I've always had in spades. As we drive to see Grace's granddad I realize I'm glad Cara's next to me and for the first time in a long while I feel a little less alone.

7

Cara

It was Jakey, talking about his computer game and the creep in Hong Kong that made my memory crack, slotting together again like a jigsaw. I stare at the rain streaking against the window and remember Mum's last birthday. It was February and the plan was to have cake and tea at Mum's but Meg said Grace was having a bad day. She'd started on some new medication and had been up with diarrhea and vomiting all night. I always found it strange how Grace's body had its own set of rules, like the sensitivity used for others didn't apply—it was always "diarrhea" for Grace, never "upset stomach" like it is for the rest of us.

"Well, if you two can't come to the cake, then we'll bring the cake to you," Mum told Meg in a sparkly voice. So over we went, Mum carrying the elaborately iced cake Zara had made with the same reverence as a sculpture on a plinth, Zara and

Sylvia chatting behind her. Number 52 smelled ripe, the air stale and queasy, but none of us said anything. Meg hugged us all in turn.

"Am I glad to see this one!" she said, pulling me towards her. *I've got you*, her strong muscles seemed to tell my weaker ones. *No matter what, I've got you.*

"Hi, Meg," I said over her shoulder, but I don't think she heard.

"Mouse was saying just earlier how much she hoped you'd be coming." Meg grinned at me, her pretty round face soft and sweet as cake mix. She cupped my cheeks briefly between her warm palms, still smiling. I could never help but smile back at her.

"I've just got Mouse out of bed. Will you go and find where she's hiding, Car?" I nodded, before Meg added, "And tell her off if her nose is back in that computer, will you?"

Grace's bedroom was like a kid's room—Harry Potter posters, an army of stuffed toys on the duvet—and simultaneously like how I remember my granddad's: the oxygen canister, the pills by the bed, the fixed-arm supports, the commode tucked discreetly beside a bookcase. I felt nervous suddenly. I always felt nervous seeing her those days. I felt like a bad person around her. Grace was in her chair, wearing a blue knitted bobble hat, her back towards me, absorbed in her computer which sat on a little desk against the wall. She didn't turn straightaway, but I saw her back flex and knew she'd sensed me standing in the doorway. Her computer screen flashed as she closed the page she was looking at, but she wasn't quick enough for me. I saw a message board and a cartoon avatar, a lanky, long-limbed, shaggy-haired kid called *GoodSam*. Whatever they were saying to each other, Grace didn't want anyone else to see.

"Mum, OK, OK, I know, I'm turning it off," she said before she spun her chair around to the left, to face me.

"Cara!" she said, her eyes light, surprised behind her round glasses.

She was wearing a pair of my old pajamas I hadn't seen in years, a snowman stitched to the front. At seventeen, she still didn't have any boobs, her body strangely ageless, suspended in sickness. She reminded me of a school trip my class went on years ago to a medical museum, where our biology teacher showed us a baby preserved by a Victorian surgeon in a jar. Like that baby, Grace always seemed to me both ancient and impossibly young.

"I thought you were Mum!" she said, spinning her chair to the right and then to the left, her version of moving nervously from one foot to the other. I walked towards her. Since we stopped seeing each other much, I didn't know how to greet her anymore. If I bent down to kiss her I felt like I was kissing a granny. Hugging her was just way too awkward, but touching her shoulder felt too formal, weird in a different way. So I did what I always did: I left it up to Grace. My old pajamas sagged around her thin arms, usually covered in tiny bruises from all the injections. She lifted her hand up to find mine, light and delicate as an eggshell. I let her hold my hand for a moment and, through her touch, I felt the whole world between us.

"Your mum said I had to tell you off if you had your nose in the computer."

Behind her glasses, Grace's eyes rolled like marbles.

"She's got this theory that it's bad for my headaches to look at a screen, so she only lets me go on the Wishmakers forum, says I should support other sick kids. She says it's a way we can give back to the charity for helping us so much." Grace shrugged as she spoke, resigned to the fact that screens were just another thing she had to avoid, which was basically everything from horse hair to the internet.

"Oh," I said, because I didn't know what else to say and I couldn't imagine Grace's life. I decided to change the subject.

"Sooo . . . who is *GoodSam*?" I said in the same tone I used when I was younger, talking with my mates about boys we liked. I knew the longer I stayed in Grace's room, the longer I could avoid the questions about boyfriends and university applications that were sure to be waiting for me in the sitting room. Grace colored and looked away. I knew that feeling, knew how it was to panic that secrets you didn't want to share were about to be exposed. Grace was embarrassed.

"Cara, please don't say anything, he's just a boy is all, a boy I've been talking to on the forum."

"You fancy him, don't you, Grace?"

Her cheeks went red and I realized, appalled, that her eyes had become watery with tears.

"Please, Cara, please don't say anything. It's nothing. He's sick like me. I'm just trying to help him."

I put my hand on her shoulder, felt her bones and thin muscles jump away from my touch.

"Grace, I fancied loads of boys when I was seventeen. It's OK, I won't tell anyone."

Her eyes widened with relief. "You won't say anything?"

"Promise," I said, perching on the edge of her bed. "But you're sure he's not some internet freak?"

"No! He's lovely, he wants to meet up, but . . ."

"But what?"

"Look at me, Cara." Grace lifted her skinny arms to show

me her deadened legs in the chair, as though I'd never seen them. "He'd never fancy me."

I tried, I tried desperately to think of the right thing to say, to tell Grace that was superficial bullshit, that she was the kindest, sweetest person I knew, but I wasn't quick enough and Meg's voice traveled down the hall. "Grace, Cara!"

And Grace pushed herself past me, towards the door, to call back to her: "Coming, Mum!"

In the sitting room, Grace sang "Happy Birthday" louder than any of us and then sat silent as we ate Mum's cake, heavy with chocolate icing. She kept looking at the cake, following it as fat slices were raised to open mouths. Meg kept a slice back in case Grace's diarrhea was better later and she could swallow a few bites. I wanted to talk to her about *GoodSam*, tell her that if he was a decent guy he wouldn't care about her chair, about her epilepsy, about any of it. But even if I had found the right words, we were never alone together again, so she never knew.

Jon's quiet next to me. I'm glad he doesn't try to chat. It gives me the chance to take my phone out, go on the Wishmakers website. The same photo of Meg and Grace that Mum's got up in the salon window fills the screen. I click on the button for the forum, but the car slows and next to me Jon says, "Here we are," and a large sign by the side of the road tells me we're pulling into Resthaven Nursing Home. It is a low, squat building covered in stucco. The parking lot is practically empty; not many visitors, then. Jon stops the car but doesn't move to open his door. Instead, turning to me, he says, "You know what, Cara, if it's all the same to you I think I'll sit this one out. My dad was in one of these places for a while. I'm not a huge fan of them I'm afraid."

I shrug, I don't mind. Besides, now all I can think about is getting home to my laptop and trying to find *GoodSam*. Suddenly I feel as though I don't have time for the long, cozy chat I had pictured having with Grace's granddad.

The door buzzes to let me in before I've even pressed the bell and a thin nurse in her sixties says, "Hello, can I help you?"

"I'm here to see Mr. Nichols, please."

"Do you mean Charlie?"

"Yes, Charlie Nichols. I am, or was, a friend of his daughter, and his granddaughter. I was passing and wanted to say hello."

The nurse lifts a hand to her mouth.

"You knew that poor woman? We've all been watching it on the news, it's a horrible, horrible . . ." She stops, looks at me, tilts her head, a wrinkle forming in the middle of her brow. "You're not the next-door neighbor, the girl who found her, are you?"

I look away, nod, and before I know it she's patting my back as I sign my name in the visitors' book, then walking me down the long corridor.

"Charlie doesn't know what happened, of course. He doesn't come out of his room much now to be honest—he's not one to socialize. Yes, hello, Cynthia," she says to an old woman with no teeth. The old people we pass gawk at me like kids who have forgotten it's rude to stare.

"He's harmless enough, but he does get very confused with his illness. If he starts getting rowdy you just pull his alarm bell and leave the room, OK?" The nurse stops outside a beige door, identical to all the other doors we've passed. "I'll come and check on you in a couple of minutes anyway, OK?" She knocks once, but doesn't wait before slowly opening the door.

"Charlie, you've got a visitor!" she calls in a loud voice.

His room is small, boxlike—it looks like a hospital room,

not a bedroom. It's like he's just moved in; the walls are blank. Everything—from the sheets on the bed to the chair he's sitting in—looks standard NHS.

He's facing the window but his chin is slumped to his chest so he can't be looking out. His hair is a white cloud above his head and his skin has a silvery quality, like wood left outside too long. He opens his eyes a crack, chews on his mouth, like he's waking it up to say something after a long time. His brow is fixed in a scowl. Suddenly I have no idea why I'm here.

"Well? Who is it?" His voice sounds corroded from lack of use. "Come here so I can see you if you won't bloody talk."

I feel like I'm walking towards an old dog, one who could nip me without warning. I try to smile as his watery eyes slip over me.

"I'm Cara." I make my voice warm.

"Are we related?" More scowling.

"No, no we're not. I'm here because I know . . . because I lived next door to your daughter, to Megan and Grace."

A corner of his mouth turns up involuntarily, he chews it again.

"I don't have a daughter." His words are clearer now. I don't want to challenge him, I'm afraid of upsetting him. Maybe the nurse showed me to the wrong room? But this man is the man from the photo, so he must be Charlie.

"Y'hear me? I said I don't have a daughter and I don't know any 'Grace.'"

I find the second envelope I put in my bag this morning and take out the photo of Charlie, Meg, and Grace as a toddler.

"Look, this is her, Megan, your daughter." I step closer to him. His old flesh shakes, the corner of the photo curls as he stares at his younger self. His scowl deepens, but he doesn't say anything, so I point to the image and say again, "This is Megan and this is Grace, Meg's daughter, your granddaughter."

Both Meg and Grace are beaming at the camera like their lives depend on it. It seems impossible those two smiling faces could be related to this man who, though small and shaking, is hard as a knot. His rheumy eyes wince down at the photo and he raises one shaky finger, twisted and gnarled as ancient oak, and holds it over the photo; it shakes like he's casting a spell.

"That's not Grace." He hisses something then; it sounds like a name but I can't make it out, and before I can say "Pardon?" he lurches forward in his chair. Spit gathers at the corner of his mouth and he lifts his clouded eyes to me.

"She's sick!" he shouts. "Don't you people understand? She should never have been born! She's sick!" His mouth curls and quivers around his ugly words.

I pull the photo away. I don't want him to see them anymore. I want to shake him, kick him for saying this shit about Grace, but his whole body is already rattling as he keeps shouting, spitting and hateful. I can't be near him, this hard ball of bitterness, so I turn and run out of his room, past a nurse who's walking fast towards us, her mouth a grim, resigned line.

"What happened?" she asks but I don't stop, I can't because he's still shouting, his words chasing me down the corridor. "She's sick! She should never have been born!"

Jon's staring out of the windshield into space when I run back to the car. I'm too upset to be embarrassed about crying in front of him. He hands me tissues and tells me his dad had dementia, that towards the end Jon tried to stop his mum from visiting him because she'd always leave in tears after he'd called her by the wrong name or said something hurtful. He says it's the cruelty of the disease, not Charlie himself, that I shouldn't take anything he said seriously.

He's right. I raise a small smile and a damp "Thanks," and I'm relieved Charlie and his rattling words don't follow us as we drive back to Ashford in silence.

Mum must still be at the salon because the house is empty when I get home. I go into my room and try to smooth out the photo and the thank-you card as best I can, prop them up against the water glass on my bedside table. I was stupid to think Dr. Rossi and Charlie would be glad to have them. Jon must think I'm a child, crying when my naive plan didn't work out. I'm surprised he didn't laugh in my face.

I sit on my bed and balance my laptop on my knees to log on to the Wishmakers forum again. I'm curious to know more about *GoodSam*. Was he just a kid Grace helped, or was there something more going on between them?

I make a profile to access the forum. I choose the name *StillSearching* because it's exactly the sort of name my tortured seventeen-year-old self would have been pleased with. In order to find *GoodSam* I need to behave as much like Grace as possible and hope the website treats me like it treated her, with the same pop-ups, the same suggestions for other users to connect with. *StillSearching* is a seventeen-year-old disabled girl from Cornwall whose interests include painting, the beach, and movies. She's on the forum to make new friends and talk about life as a teen living with disabilities. I find a picture of a pretty but not too memorable teenage girl from the internet.

Welcome, *StillSearching* to the Wishmakers
forum for teens!

CONNECT, CREATE, SHARE

I click on the CONNECT tab and type "*GoodSam*" into the search bar. It comes back with one result. *GoodSam* is still registered; I recognize his avatar immediately. The cartoon boy with floppy hair grins out from the screen in primary colors. His profile is hidden; he has to approve me before I can see anything more about him. All I can see is the date he was last active on the site. My mouth dries, my heart fizzes. The last day *GoodSam* was on the website was the third of June, the day Meg was murdered, the day Grace was stolen. It could be a coincidence of course, or perhaps he's too upset to go back on the forum, knowing that Grace is missing. But what if it's not? Grace never had a boyfriend, never really had any male role models in her life—what if this *Good-Sam* knew how to manipulate that? What if he has her now? The thought makes me grab my phone, scroll through my contacts until I get to Upton's number. But it doesn't ring, immediately clicking through to her voicemail instead.

"DCI Upton, it's Cara Dorman. Can you call me back when you get this? Thanks."

I slip my phone into my pocket as I hear Mum's key in the door and then her call: "Car?"

I come out to the hall to meet her. Her hair, although thick with spray, hangs defeated and limp around her face, wet from the rain. She hates it when her hair isn't right, but she won't care once I tell her about *GoodSam*. I rush towards her.

"Mum, you remember Grace used to chat with other kids on the Wishmakers forum?"

She looks up at me slowly. I can tell from the dark circles under her eyes and the lack of makeup that she's been crying again.

"Just let me take my shoes off, Car." Her voice is whispery, all the energy drained out of it. She uses my hand to balance as she slips her heels off her feet. I follow her as she pads into the sitting room and flicks on the TV; the news is always playing somewhere in our house now. "As well as intensifying the searches, the police are scouring hundreds of hours of CCTV footage in the hope it will help them find Grace Nichols. The public are reminded that if anyone has any information on the whereabouts of Simon Davis to please—" Mum mutes the news anchor.

"Did you get my message about picking us up something to eat?"

I remember now: she texted in the car but I was too busy at the time trying to remember anything else Grace might have said about *GoodSam* to register.

"You forgot, didn't you?" She rolls her eyes at me as her shoulders drop even further towards the ground and her hand lifts to squeeze her temples. "I haven't had anything since breakfast. I can't think straight I'm so starving." She walks past me as she pulls her phone out of her pocket and lifts it to her ear.

"Hello. Yes, can I get a large ham and mushroom please." She looks round at me to see if I want a pizza too but I shake my head. I can't think about food until I've talked to someone about what I've found. Now Mum's here, the urge to tell her fades, it doesn't feel right somehow. We've never been close in the way she wishes we were—best friends sharing secrets and confiding in each other. We're no Meg and Grace. I know she thinks it's because I'm too like my dad, independent, a lone-wolf type. Besides, this thing with *GoodSam* could be nothing and I can see Mum's exhausted, she's got enough on her plate. I realize with a flash of guilt that I'd rather talk it through with Jon. After all, he's a journalist, he'd be able to think about it rationally rather than emotionally, know whether it's something worth pursuing or not. I go back to my room, take the photocopied diary out from under my bed, and slide it into a large brown envelope. Putting it in my backpack, I walk quickly down the corridor and say, "Just popping out, Mum, won't be long."

I quickly pull the door shut behind me and pretend I don't hear her calling back, "Where are you going, Car?"

The shingle grinds together like broken teeth as Jon walks up to where I'm sitting on the beach at Angel's Bay, just below the spot where Grace and I used to fly our kites. It's stopped raining but the downpour has softened the vivid summer colors, the early-evening sky like a vast watercolor above us.

Jon didn't sound particularly surprised when I called him. I told him I had to tell him something. He didn't ask what it was over the phone, he just said, "Where shall I meet you?"

It was a relief to know he was coming. *GoodSam* might be nothing, but if it wasn't? I needed Jon's years of experience to help me figure out what to do next.

"You OK, Cara?" he asks, looking at me carefully before sitting tentatively on the still-damp shingle next to me.

I can't wait anymore. I breathe out and tell him about seeing *GoodSam* on Grace's computer, that I think she liked him. I tell him about the last time he'd logged on to the forum. Could *Good-Sam* have helped Simon find Grace? Or, even worse, could *GoodSam* be Simon himself? He listens to it all without interrupting, just raising a single eyebrow. It feels good to be listened to, really listened to, and now I've started talking I find I don't want to stop.

"There's something else as well."

I reach for my backpack and Jon shifts uncomfortably next to me against the cold, sharp shingle, but he doesn't complain, he just waits as I pull out the brown envelope and pass it to him. Slowly he slips the carefully photocopied pages out of their envelope. He inhales sharply, his gaze leaps as he sees the word *Private* followed by Grace's name on the front. He runs a hand across the cover and doesn't take his eyes off it, as though worried it'll disappear if he stops staring at it.

"Where did you . . . ?"

"It was at their place. It had fallen by her chair that day I found Meg. I made a photocopy before I handed the original over to Upton."

Jon is slowly shaking his head, his whole face breaking into a wide smile. "You're a bloody genius, Cara." His voice is raised in excitement. I let out a little laugh. I don't think anyone's called me clever, let alone a genius, before.

"Seriously, picking up the diary and making a copy is—" but he stops talking because my phone is ringing. The screen says it's Upton. I show Jon, he frowns, and asks, "You know why she's calling?"

"I left her a message. I was going to tell her about *GoodSam*, just before I called you."

For a second Jon's face darkens, before he says, "Don't answer, not yet. We need to think this through before we speak to her." I like the sound of the "we" more than I like the idea of speaking to Upton, so I nod and mute my phone before dropping it back into my pocket. I can call her later. Jon looks back at the diary in his hands; the pages quiver with his excitement. He opens the first page, his big hand strange next to the love hearts Grace doodled in the margin. He allows himself to read the first couple of lines before forcing himself to stop. The shingle crunches underneath him as he stands, being careful not to bend the photocopied pages he's holding.

"OK, I think we need to think carefully about what's best for Grace here. What's most likely to help her. For all we know, Upton might already know about *GoodSam*, we don't know, but what we do know is that *GoodSam* has no idea who you are, who *StillSearching* is. That's a huge advantage and one that might help us find Grace. You've handled this well, Cara. You really have."

He smiles down at me, and I look at my lap so he can't see how I want to cry and laugh at the same time. I know he's being a bit patronizing, but I don't care. I'm helping, that's important. Jon keeps talking, and I don't stop him, I want to hear more good things. I want to believe everything he says about me, want to believe I'm the clever, shrewd person he sees, not destined to live the same life as Molly and Mum and everyone else in Summervale.

"Setting up that profile was a smart move, really smart. If we tell the police about this they'll get straight on the forum to find *GoodSam*, and you know what'll happen? First they'll shut down *StillSearching* and won't let you anywhere near it, then there'll be ten middle-aged policemen all suddenly trying to chat with *Good-Sam*. He'll spook immediately and I guarantee, I *guarantee*"—he repeats for emphasis, holding my gaze—"he'll disappear."

"But what about—"

"Cara, I've seen it before, trust me. Remember that boy, Adam Rufton, who went missing from Southampton? The family is suing the police for negligence and I hate to say it, but they have a point. Adam might still be alive if they hadn't been so heavy-handed. They knew Todd Mather, the bloke who took him, was unwell. All Todd's doctors, everyone who knew Todd, all the mental-health experts, told the police the way to deal with him was to be gentle, to talk to him, reassure him. They told the police that it was when Todd felt threatened, vulnerable, that he was likely to lash out and become violent. But what did the police do when they found that old farm where Todd was holding Adam? They organized a raid, went in with their battering rams and guns. They scared Todd shitless. That's why he killed Adam and then himself, and that's exactly why I think we should be the ones to contact *GoodSam*, find out who he is and what, if anything, was going on between him and Grace before we tell the police."

He doesn't take his eyes off me but starts nodding his head slowly, and even though I've never had any reason to doubt the police I find myself nodding along with him.

"What should I say to Upton?"

Jon looks back out to sea, as though the water might have an answer.

"Why don't you just say you were calling for an update, that you wanted to know if they had any new information, that's all." Jon must see the uncertainty I feel flicker across my face.

"Remember, Cara, we don't know who *GoodSam* is. He might not have anything to do with Grace's kidnapping. We shouldn't waste Upton's time until we know more about him. What does Grace say about him in the diary?"

He carefully flicks through a few of the pages before he looks at me. I'm embarrassed. I've read the diary so many times now but I hadn't noticed—Grace doesn't mention *GoodSam* anywhere.

Jon only needs to glance at me before he says, "What, she didn't say anything about him at all?" He fans the diary in front of him, making Grace's small secrets wink out at me from the pages. I nod and he looks straight ahead towards the horizon for a moment. He scratches his beard before turning back to me. "That's strange. Did the two of you talk about boys much?"

I shake my head. Meg talked more about boys than Grace. It never really occurred to me to talk about that stuff with Grace. After all, she'd never even been kissed. Or so I had always thought. But I want to give him something else. I want, I realize, to impress him again.

"She does talk about someone calling the house phone, though.

117

Look." I reach up and take the photocopied diary from Jon, leaf through the pages until I find the entry, point to it. "Here. She says Meg got really pissed off with whoever it was who kept ringing. There was one time when we were at Meg's house, having cake for my mum's birthday, when the landline started ringing. I remember thinking it was weird that Meg went into the kitchen to answer. Everyone was chatting, so I didn't hear what it was about, but Meg hung up quickly. When she came back, her cheeks had gone red, like she was embarrassed or pissed off. I remember Grace smiling up at Meg from her chair. Meg saw, but she didn't smile back, which was odd because everyone was always smiling at Grace. Maybe it was *GoodSam* trying to reach Grace and she knew it was him? That's why Meg looked weird but Grace was pleased—he'd been trying to get in touch with her?"

Jon raises his eyebrows, nods, and sort of shakes his head at the same time.

"Could have been him, or it could have been her dad of course. Can't imagine Megan would have been happy about Simon calling."

Jon sits back down next to me. We sit in silence for a few minutes before I ask, "So what now?"

"Well, I'd like to take the diary away with me, just for a little while, so I can read it carefully—if that's OK with you?"

I don't like the thought of being separated from it, from this last piece of Grace, and I hate the thought of someone else reading her secrets, but I remind myself Jon might see something that I missed. Finding Grace is more important than her privacy.

"OK. What about *GoodSam*?"

"Keep checking the forum, see if he comes online, and, if he does, call me before you do anything, OK?"

I nod agreement and I can see he's twitching to leave, desperate to read her diary. I can't blame him. I was the same.

"I'll give you a call, yeah?" he says as he stands, causing a small avalanche of pebbles to fall into each other. I nod again and he tucks Grace's diary under his arm, lifting his hand in a small wave before turning and walking quickly away. I keep my eye on the pages under his arm until both disappear from view.

30th November 2018

Today it all went wrong again. I could hear Mum coming into my room to get me an hour after my first syringe of food and drugs. I could hear her but I couldn't see her because my eyes wouldn't open.

"Come on, sleepyhead," she said and pulled the covers back. Behind my eyelids everything became a bit brighter. I heard her suck in her breath. "OK, Gracie darling, you're OK," she said, and then I heard her pressing keys on her phone to call an ambulance. I felt the foam around my mouth, felt my mind unclip itself from my body. I seemed to float up to the ceiling like a balloon.

"Not now! Not this today!" I wanted to scream but I couldn't because my tongue was dead in my mouth.

Today was meant to be a big day. I was going to meet the other kids going to Hawaii. I was going to have a whole day with them, maybe make friends. Mum and I had planned it all. I was going to wear my new jeans and a sweater that used to be Cara's, with the stars and stripes flag embroidered on the front. Today I was going to be funny and friendly and kind, like a normal teenager. But instead I'm on another hospital ward with two old women who frown and chew their mouths when they see me, because there's no space for me on the kids' ward. Today all my muscles ache from the seizure and a tooth in the back of my mouth has crumbled because I was grinding my teeth so hard. Today another doctor is scratching her head and saying "More tests?" like I'm a crossword she can't figure out.

They thought the epilepsy was a hangover from the bacterial meningitis I had when I was little but now they reckon, with my arrhythmia, it could mean something else is going on with my heart. I didn't recognize the doctor but Mum did. She's good like that, she says it helps to make a connection with the doctors and nurses. I pretended to be asleep, worried that if I tried to talk I'd only cry and that would make Mum cry, which is worse than anything. She's better at talking about what's going on anyway.

"Are you OK, Megan?" The doctor had a quiet, posh voice.

"Oh, don't worry about me, Sarah, I'm just devastated for Gracie. She was supposed to go to Hawaii in a week's time with the Wishmakers. She's never been abroad, never been anywhere. It's all she's talked about. I'm sad for her, that's all."

"I'm so sorry, Meg, really I am. You know it could be her heart causing these new seizures, but until we know for sure we just can't risk her traveling. It must be a long flight to Hawaii."

"I was worried you were going to say that." Mum sniffed. She tries hard not to cry in front of doctors but sometimes she can't help it.

120

"She'll be devastated, but you're right. It's not worth the risk. I'll call the charity now to get it over with."

"Perhaps they could put her on the list for the trip next year?"

Behind my eyelids I could see Mum shaking her head. My stomach felt like a ball of stale chewing gum. Of course they won't change the rules just for me. I'll be eighteen next year, this year was my last chance and my stupid, broken body has messed it up for me again. When I was on my own for a moment I made my hand into a fist under the covers and thumped my chest to show my idiot heart how it should beat, slow and regular like everyone else's. The movement pulled the cannula in my hand and made me out of breath. I let myself imagine the dolphins, picture how it would feel to be with new friends in the sunshine just one more time before I closed the door on them for good. I won't let them back. Like Mum always says, we're not hippos, we don't wallow. Besides, there are so many other people worse off than me. I might not be able to move my legs and the seizures are painful and my heart hurts but I have more love in my life than most people. I have Mum.

"They'll be along with something to help you sleep in a moment, love." Mum shuffled the visitor chair close to my bed, careful to avoid the tubes that ran in and out of me. She had been picking at her nail varnish, which always means she's been worrying.

"Mouse, listen to me, I just spoke to Maggie." But I kept my head turned away from her. Squeezed my jaw to make it sing with pain so I couldn't hear properly. But Mum saw what I was doing. She squeezed my hand, to tell me to listen.

"Maggie spoke to David, who runs the charity. They had an idea. There's a reporter, a really well-known one, Jon something, who wants to write an article, I don't know what it is exactly but if it's through the Wishmakers it'll be something about brave kids like you living good lives even when really tough things happen to them. David reckons this Jon would love to interview you. Isn't that great, darling? There'll be a photographer and everything apparently."

I didn't move and I didn't say anything. So Mum kept talking, her face hopeful as she tried to make me feel better, just like she always does.

"Just think of all the people you could help, Mouse, so many more than any trip abroad. You'll be an inspiration to hundreds, maybe thousands, of kids and their parents. Imagine, a kid who's just been diagnosed with MD or epilepsy might read it and feel a bit better—wouldn't that be great?"

I should try to be more like Mum, try to think about others before myself. But I still wish I was going to Hawaii instead of having an article written about us. That's another secret: I'm not as selfless or as good as Mum.

A nurse appeared. Neither of us have met her before, but everyone knows about us.

"Hello, Grace," she said, her head cocked at an uncomfortable-looking angle. "I'm Faye. I'll be keeping an eye on you tonight." She smiled at Mum. "Good to meet you, Ms. Nichols."

Mum smiled back and told the nurse to call her Meg, like she always does.

I couldn't roll over on my own, so I just smiled and

waited while Mum and Faye talked about what I would need during the night, when the doctor would be back in the morning, where Mum would sleep. She's spent so many nights at the hospital she sometimes jokes the visitor's chair is her second home. Poor Mum.

Love, Grace xxx

8

Jon

I kick the sheets off my bed and roll to my left in the hope that a new position might bring some rest, some sleep, but my mind chatters away like a chimp. Reading Grace's diary was harder than I imagined. She was so good, and the bond between her and Meg was extraordinary. Why didn't I write an article celebrating their relationship instead of questioning the way Simon had been treated? For the first time, I understand why the community was so angry with me.

It's been three days since Grace went missing, three full days without any medication. Whenever I close my eyes I see a tiny mound in bed under white hospital sheets, the face changing from Grace to Jakey and back again. I sit up. Drink a pint of water. I need air, that's what I need. I need something to remind me life exists outside my tiny one-bed flat, outside my own head. The bedroom window opens on to the lower high street but the sitting-room window is bigger, and opens to a series of wheat fields that eventually lead to the sea. There's no breeze coming in from the street, so I pad across the sitting room, open the window wide, and feel my lungs expand like balloons as they fill.

Get a grip, Jon, get a fucking grip.

I take another lungful of air as a ghostly cry is carried along on the warm night. The cry comes again and again, like someone calling, pleading. I think of Meg. I think of Grace.

The shout comes again, clearer now, and I realize it's her name: "Grace!" It's like the night itself is calling for her to come home.

Am I actually going fucking nuts?

The shouts get louder and then I see glinting lights, like fireflies in the distance, and I realize it's not Meg's ghost and it's not the night calling her name, it's a search party. A very human search party with flashlights, loud voices, and reflective vests. They must be doing a sweep of all the fields that run down from the town to the beach.

"Grace! Grace!" they call. Before I can talk myself out of it, I grab my jeans from the bedroom floor and pull on a T-shirt. As I worm my feet into my Converse, I look at myself in the hall mirror to reassure myself that I look different from how I looked just before Christmas. I have a beard now, thick-rimmed glasses, and I've put on a few pounds since Jakey went back to school. Even if Susan and her mates are out there searching, especially in the dark, they're unlikely to recognize me from the photos online. But I shove on a navy baseball cap just in case before I head out into the warm, salted air.

The bright moon hangs above us, lighting the way for the searchers as though it too wants to help find Grace. I read a couple of articles from the national papers claiming volunteer searches can hinder rather than help investigations. They said the searches around Ashford are well intentioned but unprofessional, random sweeps across the countryside into old abandoned mines and farmhouses, and that untrained eyes can miss key pieces of evidence. But neither the volunteers nor the police have found anything yet, so the jury's still out as far as I'm concerned. And instead of a disorganized rabble, the search seems well organized. Most people have flashlights and the lines look ordered, the volunteers walking perfectly in time and only a few tasked with calling her name. They all keep their eyes fixed on the ground as they brush through the golden wheat fields. It seems unlikely she would have been taken across this field—it's well used by dog walkers in the day and is too close to the high street to be private—but perhaps they're searching the more public areas at night. Statistically, time is running out for Grace and there must be hundreds of square miles to search. I fall in step next to a woman at the end of the line. She's around my mum's age and wears a Barbour jacket under her reflective vest.

"You look like you're thinking about joining us," she says when she sees me.

I nod. "Would that be all right?"

She throws me a reflective vest from her pocket.

"Course! Grace needs all our help. Come next to me, I'll get Martin to budge up a bit." She calls to the man next to her: "We've got another joiner, move up the line!" The words echo along the volunteers and a space is made for me, and suddenly we're together, the wheat scratching at my legs, and I feel calmer as I search in gentle time with these good people doing what they can to help.

Once we reach the end of the field the lady in the Barbour sighs and, unzipping her jacket, sits on a log. She pats the space next to her and smiles at me, like she's expecting a little lap dog to leap up next to her. She pulls a thermos out of her huge pockets.

"A break at last!" she says with a chuckle as I come to sit next to her. She offers me a plastic mug.

"Oh no"—I wave my hand—"you've been out here much longer than I have—"

"Oh away with you. There's plenty for us both."

I take the cup and have a sip of tea. The tea is good—sugary and flavorful. I feel the woman looking at me.

"So, if you don't mind me saying, you looked a bit dazed when you joined us earlier. Wake you up, did we?" she asks in her warm Cornish accent.

"Oh no, I always look like that," I say with a smile, which she returns. "No, no, you didn't wake me. I have trouble sleeping sometimes so thought I'd make myself useful."

"Good for you!" she says, taking my empty mug. "We need all the help we can get, what with the police being so bloody useless—they don't seem to understand how much Grace will be suffering after three days without her meds." She shakes her head. "Sorry, but I just get so upset with it all. I'm Maggie, by the way," she says, raising the cup in a silent toast before taking a sip. Maggie. A small bell in the back of my mind chimes but I'm too tired to figure out why.

"I'm Jon. So did you know Grace?"

Maggie looks suddenly stern.

"Oh no, love," she says, "we'll have no past tenses, thank you very much. But yes, to answer your question. I do know Grace, knew them both, Grace and her mum." As she says it she leans forward and I see her T-shirt has the Wishmakers logo on the front. I remember Grace talked about a Maggie in her diary and my mind snaps like a twig: she's Maggie from the Wishmakers.

I spoke to Maggie when I first called the charity to ask if they had any families I could interview for my article. Although I told Maggie I was working with Dads Without Borders, I suspected she didn't understand the real intention of the article, that I was on the side of the dads kept from their kids rather than the mums doing the keeping. Maggie immediately started telling me about Grace and Meg. She told me earnestly how Meg had called her just a few hours earlier, how devastated Meg was that Grace could no longer go to Hawaii. Maggie said an article about them could be the boost they both needed. I should have said something, explained the article in more detail, but even I'd heard about Meg, Grace, and Simon on the Ashford grapevine. I wanted to interview them as much as they wanted to be interviewed. I needed them for the article. I found it easy to shush my conscience and ask Maggie to give them a call.

I have to go carefully now. Although we never met in person, I can't risk Maggie recognizing me. I want to keep talking to her—she was close to Meg, she might know something.

"You're Maggie who works for the Wishmakers, aren't you?"

She looks puzzled, then nods.

"That's me." She looks at me more closely. "Don't I recognize you from somewhere? I can't for the life of me figure out from where."

I try not to panic.

"Oh, I have one of those faces. My wife, Ruth, was friends with Meg—that's how we got to know them." Maggie sips her tea as she listens.

"I remember Ruth saying how disappointed both Meg and Grace were when she couldn't go on the Hawaii trip," I say, keeping my tone light.

"Oh I know, poor mite. She would have loved it—all that sunshine, the lovely hotel. But it wasn't meant to be. First all the trouble with the passport, then she was admitted to hospital again. That was it, I'm afraid, there was no way she could go."

Maggie passes the cup back to me.

"Her passport?"

"Oh, it was a silly thing really." Maggie looks around her at the other volunteers, who are standing in small groups talking quietly, eating chocolate bars and smoking.

"I'm ashamed to say I got a bit frustrated with Meg at the time. Not her fault, she had more than enough on her plate. But she was usually so good with paperwork, so organized. Anyway, we've got more important things to worry about now, haven't we?" Maggie looks over again as a low ripple of outrage runs through the group of volunteers. I only catch the odd word, but it's clear they're talking about the police, frustrated they don't seem to have a clue where Simon has taken Grace. I need to keep her attention— I have the feeling Maggie is someone who'll keep talking if I ask the right questions.

"Ruth and I are about to apply for a passport for our son, actually. Is it as painful as everyone says? I'm rubbish at admin stuff."

"Oh, it's not that bad. You just have to get everything together and make sure you've dotted all the i's and crossed all the t's. Megan's problem was that she never got hold of a copy of Grace's birth certificate. That was all. I had all the other forms, all the signatures, the money ready to go. I asked again and again, even gave her the number to call to get a duplicate. She would have got round to it eventually, I'm sure, but then, like I said, Grace went into hospital so . . ."

A man with a laminated map around his neck and reflective trousers and vest blows a whistle for us to regroup. Maggie pours away the rest of her tea on the stubby ground and nudges me.

"That's Martin, one of the organizers. Ignore him at your peril," she says with a wink.

I stand and give Maggie a hand up. Next to Martin I'm surprised to see the farmer, Mr. Leeson, and shivering next to him the woman who works with Susan—Zara—in huge hoop earrings. All the news reports keep saying how loved Meg and Grace were, and here's the proof.

"Actually, I'm going to head home, try to get a couple of hours' kip before the alarm goes off. But good to meet you, Maggie," I say, not wanting to risk being recognized by one of the others.

"Good on you, Jon." Maggie pats me on the back before rejoining the huddle of volunteers.

As I walk back across the field I think about what Maggie said. I understand how any parent, but especially the parent of a disabled child, would be nervous about them going away for the first time. From what I've heard, Meg always put Grace first, no matter what. What stopped her this time? Could Simon have had something to do with it? Was Meg worried about Grace going abroad, or was she frightened that a passport would make it easier for someone to take Grace far away, against her will? I remember what Maggie said about Grace's birth certificate and an idea starts to form. As Ashford comes into view ahead of me the first rays start to lighten the sky and I quicken my step.

As soon as I'm back in the flat I make a big pot of coffee and open up my computer. The supposedly free genealogy sites won't give me the detailed information I need without my credit card details. I know I still haven't paid the minimum payment and I'm almost at my overdraft limit, so I dial the only number I know by heart. I let the phone ring and ring until she finally picks up.

"Mum?"

"What is it, Jon? Is it Jakey?" Her fear crackles down the phone line.

"No, Mum, no—he's fine." Idiot. I forgot. The last time I woke her so early was when Jakey was readmitted with an infection and I just needed to hear her voice. "Sorry for calling so early. I have to ask you something."

"Jon, it's half past five in the morning!"

I picture her in her tiled Victorian hallway in Islington. She'll be wearing her burgundy bathrobe, Agnes her rescue Scottie dog at her slippered feet. I love how Mum's world remains the same while the rest of London changes around her, as quick as the weather.

"Sorry, Mum, I sort of forgot what time it was . . ."

"Rubbish," she scoffs down the phone. "You just had an idea you thought couldn't possibly wait until a decent time. So come on then. I'm awake now, you'd better tell me."

Suddenly I wish I was there with her, in my warm childhood home.

"I wanted to ask about that family tree stuff you got into a while ago."

"It's called *genealogy*, darling."

"Right, well, how did you do it? Do you have an account to look up birth certificates and stuff?"

In spite of the time, I hear Mum smiling down the phone. It's rare anyone asks her how something works now—she still uses a pocket diary and would never trust GPS. Like her home, Mum stopped changing somewhere in the mid-eighties.

"So how's Ruth?" Mum asks before we hang up.

"She's good, sends her love."

131

"Things getting better between you two?" she asks hopefully, and for once I want to bring her good news.

"I think we're getting there, Mum. I think we're going to be OK."

"I can't tell you how glad I am to hear that, darling," Mum says with a sigh before she yawns and I tell her to go back to bed and that I love her, and I hang up the phone.

Outside, the gulls are already circling in the pink sky. I can't hear Maggie and the other volunteers anymore. Perhaps they've finally called it a night. I pour myself more coffee and type Mum's username and password into the genealogy website. I don't know exactly what I expect to find, but this missing birth certificate is all I have to go on. I type in Grace's full name and her place of birth: Plymouth. But the search comes back with no results. I try just "Nichols" and "Plymouth" and now there are a couple of hundred results. I scroll down the first page—most of them are male—and am about to try a third and final search when the last entry catches my eye.

Name: Nichols, Zoe Grace Megan
Place of Birth: Derriford NHS Trust, Plymouth
Date of Birth: 10/09/1998

The first name and the year of birth are wrong—I've never known Grace to be called Zoe, and Grace is seventeen, born 10 September 2001, not 1998. But it's too much of a coincidence to ignore. I lean in so close I can see each individual pixel. Under my glasses, I press my thumb and forefinger onto my eyelids and rub. I repeat my search—looking first for Grace Megan Nichols born in 2001. Again there are no results. Instead I search for Zoe Grace Megan Nichols born in 1998. One result.

It doesn't make sense. Did Grace change her name? But why would she change her birthdate? If I'm right about this—and I think I am—then we were wrong. We were all wrong. We'll never find seventeen-year-old Grace Megan Nichols because she doesn't exist. But, according to these records, twenty-year-old Zoe Grace Megan Nichols does.

I sit, numb and mute, for an hour on the sofa, a film forming over my untouched coffee. I keep hearing Grace's high-pitched, girlish voice in my head. She had always seemed young for her age, but that she's an adult, not much younger than Cara, seems inconceivable. Why did Meg lie? And Simon—surely he'd know his daughter's real name and age, why didn't he raise the alarm? Perhaps they were both protecting Grace, keeping her in the pediatric system for as long as they could. Perhaps someone in the NHS made an administrative error and Meg and Simon realized that if they didn't correct it Grace would get better care for longer? That makes sense, that I can understand. But what about Grace? Was she complicit, or did she never know her real name? Her real *age*? The questions are thick, heavy in my head, and when I try to pull them apart they seem to stretch and expand like toffee, making even less sense than they did before.

The sun has risen fully when my phone starts ringing on the coffee table, shocking the silence.

"Jon? Mate, you there?" Ben sounds slightly out of breath, like he's rushing somewhere.

"I'm, I'm here," I say, my own voice a surprise.

"Look, mate, sorry to wake you but I thought you'd want to know. I'm headed to the Point. Apparently the police search team found some clothes, a dress looks like, washed up on the rocks. Word is it matches what Grace was wearing the last time anyone saw her."

The line starts to crackle, losing reception. Ben keeps talking, but then the line breaks. It doesn't matter, though. I know everything I need to know. I grab my house keys, wallet, and the blue cap and, forgetting the time and the fact that I have neighbors, I let the front door slam loudly behind me.

9

Cara

I forgot to close my curtains before I went to sleep, so the sun wakes me. My eyes haven't fully opened but I reach for my phone and open the forum. *GoodSam* still hasn't replied to the message I sent as *StillSearching* last night on a whim: Hi GoodSam, I'm new to the forum. Your avatar is cool—sometimes I wish I could be a cartoon version of myself. Where did you find it?

I feel like a geeky adult trying to be a teenager, but I think the tone is about right. I know Jon said we should wait to see if *GoodSam* comes online, but he also didn't say anything about sending him a message. I close my curtains before getting back into bed. I need to try to get more sleep, but just as I close my eyes the door creaks.

"Mum?" I call out to her, lifting my head from the pillow.

She opens the door slowly. She looks hollow, her face sharper without all her makeup.

"What's happened, Mum? What is it?"

She sits gently on the edge of my bed, runs her bottom lip through her teeth, before she tells me that a navy dress has been found by the police, washed up on the rocks at the Point. I used to have a navy dress with little silver stars on it when I was a teenager. I hadn't known Mum had kept it and given it to Grace until I saw her wearing it one day. It had become Grace's favorite. Could she have been wearing it when she was taken?

Grace was terrified of the sea. Her whole body would shake if we got too close to the water. She didn't need to say it, but I know she was terrified of the water closing in on her, filling her lungs with salt, terrified of what happened to Danny.

Mum's too upset to drive, so she lets me take her car. She won't go to the Point, says she couldn't bear it. She's going to the salon to be with Zara.

"Don't go there, Car, why don't you come with me instead?" she pleads. But I'm already out of bed, pulling on my clothes. She knows I won't go with her, so she just goes back to running her lip through her teeth and she doesn't say anything when I grab her car keys.

Before I leave, I kiss her and promise to come and see her in the salon later.

On the drive to the Point, Upton calls my cell phone. I answer this time. She'll only call Mum if I don't pick up.

"I'm sorry we didn't speak yesterday, Cara. What was it you wanted to say to me?" she asks. Wind echoes down the phone; it sounds like she's already at the Point.

"Is it Grace's dress they've found? Does it have stars on it?"

"I can't talk about that, Cara. I'm sorry. What did you want to tell me yesterday?"

She won't tell me whether they've found Grace's dress or not, but she wants me to share everything I know with her? I remember what Jon said about that poor Adam kid, how he was murdered because the police screwed up the investigation. I won't let the same thing happen to Grace.

"I was calling for an update, that was all."

"You're sure? Because remember, any detail, no matter how small, could be really helpful."

"I'm sure."

She exhales like she's already having a bad day and I've just made it a bit worse. But I don't care. I've had enough of everyone, apart from Jon, treating me like a traumatized child. I hang up, and as I turn onto the road to the Point, I realize I don't care about anything anymore, my exam results, getting into uni, being single—none of that troubles me. Now I only care about Grace.

The waves beat against the rock at Grey's Point like the sea is angry with the land, trying to teach it a lesson. Granddad told me once that people have been jumping from here since the Middle Ages; still today there are at least a handful of deaths reported every year. I can see why they choose this spot. The Point looks sure to do the job. It must be two hundred feet high. Pointed rocks jut into the foamy water like angry fists, but the soft colors where the horizon meets the sea makes it feel like heaven is just one step away. There's a Samaritans advertisement in the parking lot, which is already busy, even at eight in the morning. I notice an ambulance and two police cars amongst the family SUVs. I try not to look at them. I've seen Grace wheeled into an ambulance too many times. I don't want to see it again, one last time. Just before I get out of the car, my phone makes a sound I haven't heard before. I glance at it. I downloaded the Wishmakers app last night and *GoodSam* has come on to the forum. There's a tick next to the message I sent, telling me he's read it, but he hasn't replied yet. Just an hour ago he seemed so important. Now I can't think about him.

There's a clutch of dogs walkers, talking quietly to one another, and a few photographers are here already too. A single policeman in fluorescent yellow is stopping them from walking out onto the Point. Jon texted me on the drive so I know he's already here, and I spot him standing a few feet away from the others on a patch of grass covered in daisies. A man with dark hair, holding a camera with a huge lens, is talking animatedly to him, but Jon isn't listening, I can tell: he's too still. Underneath his cap his eyes are fixed on the sea. The man with the camera has to nudge him before he sees me. Jon nods, but doesn't smile as he starts walking towards me. The man tries to walk with him but Jon shakes his head, nods towards the police officer at the Point, and he dutifully turns around, walks back in the direction Jon suggested. Jon gestures for me to keep walking further up the path, away from the Point. He's right—it would complicate things if anyone saw us together. I wrap my cardigan around me and pull the hood over my head. We're the only people walking away from the Point. As I walk, I realize I'm heading towards another moment where everything will change, and I'll think back to now, to this moment, when the world was still whole, and wish I could go back. It's strange to feel sorry for my future self, to mourn what has not yet happened but what I'm sure is inevitable.

The path narrows into a one-person track. Pretty yellow gorse flowers hide the spikes that seem to strain towards us on either side. Jon holds the kissing gate open for me.

"You OK?" he asks as I walk through. His eyes are bloodshot. Has he been crying? And suddenly I know I'm not OK, nothing's OK. I want him to see I'm falling apart without having to say anything. I don't want to know a world without Grace in it. I want a second chance, a chance to be her friend again, for things to be like they used to. He puts his hand on my shoulder, pats a couple of times. I widen my eyes to try to stop myself from crying.

"She's dead, isn't she?" My voice is a whisper. Jon gently moves me off the path, walks me behind a gorse bush. He puts his arm around my shoulders, bends his head so he's close, facing me. I wonder if this is how he comforts Jakey.

"I'm not going to lie to you, Cara. I was just talking to Ben, a photographer friend of mine, and he told me the police believe the navy dress Grace was last seen wearing has washed up. It's ripped, but they don't know whether it was ripped by someone or whether it was ripped by the rocks. I'm so sorry."

"Did it have little stars on it?" Tears are rolling freely down my cheeks now.

"Stars? I don't know, he didn't say."

This gives me a tiny sliver of hope. If it didn't have stars on it, if it's not the same dress, there's still a chance, isn't there?

Jon's arm drops from around my shoulders. He glances out to sea before he says, "Ben has a contact in the police, they said there's no DNA evidence connecting Simon or anyone else on record to the murder scene. Simon must have been lucid enough to do his homework, to keep himself well covered. They also said the post-mortem tests on Megan's body came back negative—apart from signs of struggle there were no drugs in her system, no signs of sexual assault . . ." Jon trails off. I'm glad, I don't want to hear any more about forensics and autopsies, not now, not here. But I notice how restless he is, how his eyes dart about, and I know there's more he needs to say.

139

"What is it? You're not telling me everything. Have they found something else?"

"No, no, nothing like that."

"Simon, then?"

"No sign of him either."

"Then what is it?"

I wipe my eyes with my sleeve. "Jon! Tell me!" I almost shout.

"OK. But first I need to know if Grace was ever known by any other name."

"Meg called her 'Mouse' but she was always Grace to everyone else. Why?" He tells me about Meg, about how she didn't complete Grace's passport application, about an issue she had with Grace's birth certificate. I'm confused, starting to lose patience when he asks, "Do you know Grace's birthday?"

"Tenth of September, I think."

Every birthday Meg made her a pink cake she couldn't eat. Grace liked to blow out the candles.

"What year?"

I think about it—I know I missed Grace's last few birthdays. "Two thousand one, I guess?"

Jon shakes his head, shows me the screenshot. It takes me a moment to process. It's the birthdate for someone called Zoe Grace Megan Nichols. Zoe? I've heard that name recently. It takes me a moment, but then I remember the thick air of the nursing home, how Charlie's wrinkled mouth whistled around a word when I showed him the photo of Meg and Grace—he could have been saying "Zoe."

But it's not Grace, it can't be, the year is wrong.

"It must be someone else with a similar name. That's all."

Jon shakes his head. "With exactly the same middle names? Born on the same day, in the same city? I've searched the records—

there was no Grace Megan Nichols born in Plymouth on the tenth of September 2001. This is too big a coincidence to ignore."

My mouth feels ashy. I swallow and tell Jon about Charlie, what I think I might have heard. He's right, it's too big a coincidence. Jon doesn't blink as I talk, just stares at me and says, a crackle of excitement in his voice, "This must be her, then. Grace isn't Grace, she's Zoe. She's twenty and she's called Zoe."

My legs feel watery suddenly, like I can't trust them to hold my weight. I hear Jon saying my name, but he sounds far away. I slump to the ground. I want to lie facedown on the grass, to touch something real, to feel the earth's solidity beneath me. I wish I could burrow into it, hide at least for a while until things make sense again. But I can't because Jon's sitting next to me and he's passing me a bottle of water, telling me to drink. I drink. It helps a bit.

"Grace is twenty?" I ask. I used to call her my little sister. She was so small. Jon nods.

"She's almost my age." I try to picture Grace older, as a woman smiling in her wheelchair, not a girl, but I can't focus on the image. I realize I never imagined her growing up, becoming an adult. My voice is small as I ask, "Why? Why would she want to be younger?"

"I've thought about it and the only answer that makes sense is that pediatric care tends to be much better than what's on offer to adults, especially in Plymouth. Maybe it was something that started out as a white lie—a fib on a form—and then Meg found she had to maintain it. Maybe admitting to the lie felt worse than just going along with it. And the name, well, maybe they both just preferred Grace? Maybe she just felt like Zoe never suited her and it didn't seem relevant to tell anyone? People change their names sometimes, don't they?"

Yes, yes. This is good. This makes some sense.

"Meg did anything she could to get the best care for Grace," I say. Mum always said Meg knew more about Grace's conditions than the experts themselves. She had been known to drive up to London and back in a day just for Grace to have a single test. Grace's health was the most important thing in both their lives and I have no doubt that Meg would stop at nothing to get Grace the care she needed, even if it meant lying for years about her daughter's age. I don't judge her for it.

"I thought maybe Dr. Rossi knew she'd been lying and that's why she was so defensive yesterday—she didn't want to be involved," Jon says. He's right. She must have thought we had proof that she knew Grace—I can't imagine ever calling her Zoe—was older, there could be professional implications for her. She must have been relieved when she found out it was just a thank-you card.

"What should we do?" I ask.

But Jon doesn't answer because he's staring at his phone, which is vibrating in his hand, his thumb hovering over the answer button like he doesn't know what to do. He answers. I can just make out a woman's voice. She sounds stressed, her voice taut, like she's about to snap.

"Of course I haven't forgotten we moved the time, Ruth. I'm on my way right now." He looks at his watch, springs to his feet, and rubs his eyes under his glasses.

"I'm fifteen, maybe twenty minutes away." Jon grimaces, looks at his watch again.

There's an angry shout from Jon's phone and then nothing as the woman hangs up. Jon shouts "Fuck!" into the wind before he bends down towards me.

"Look, Cara, I'm so sorry but I've got to run. I'm really late for an appointment with my wife." He grips my upper arm, too hard for it to be reassuring. It's almost like he's the one who needs to hold on to something stable now.

I twist slightly under his grasp. His grip loosens.

"Sorry. Just promise me you won't do anything, like go to the police, without talking to me first." His eyes bulge, his mouth looks ugly behind his beard.

"I won't, I promise," I say.

"Good. That's good. We'll speak later," he says before standing up and jogging away down the path.

I lift my hand to my face; my cheeks are wet. I lie back. It feels so easy to let myself dissolve. I shake with soundless sobs, Grace's smiling face so clear in my mind I feel like I could touch her. I cry. I cry because I never knew her, not really. I cry until my throat is sore and my face swells. I cry until I feel completely empty. When I finally stand, I walk away from the path, towards the cliff edge. My body is so heavy it feels like the earth is pulling me, dragging me down. I hear the seagulls circling overhead, hear Grace giggling when she said it sounded like they were screaming my name. I look down at the white sea below and think how easy it would be, how easy just to let myself go. I stand at the edge, close my eyes, and see Grace in front of me again, laughing, holding her arms out to me.

"Woah, you're making me nervous. Maybe step back a bit?"

I open my eyes. The photographer Jon was talking to earlier is just behind me, beckoning me to come back. I'm aware suddenly how I must look, standing at the edge of the cliff, my face swollen, eyes red and raw with sorrow. I wipe my face and step back, next to him.

"That's better," he says, smiling at me. He offers me his hand—it's warm. "I'm Ben."

"Cara."

He nods like he knew my name already.

"Do you think Grace is dead?" I ask.

He looks down at his sneakers, gray with age, kicks one foot against the other and says, "Shit, I don't know. Probably. That's what the police are saying. They've got boats and a dive team out now, apparently. I don't know why they're bothering really, the bodies will come in on the tide most likely."

"Bodies?"

He looks away from me, as though he's said something he shouldn't.

"Yeah. The police reckon Simon probably jumped with her. He had a history of mental illness, apparently he always got worse over the summer, around the anniversary of his son's death so . . ." Ben keeps talking, but I've stopped listening. Simon's mental health deteriorated over the summer because that's when his life started to fall apart.

"What's the date today?" I ask, interrupting Ben.

"Sorry?"

"The date, what is it?"

"The seventh, I think."

"The same day." I say it out loud, forgetting Ben is standing next to me.

"What was that?" he asks, cupping his ear towards me, away from the wind.

I don't want to tell him what I think I'm starting to understand. Simon timed it. He leapt off the Point with Grace the same day Danny died.

"Nothing," I say, turning away from him. "Nice to meet you, Ben."

I'm about to walk back to the car—I want to be on my own to

think—when I hear the distant whine of a speedboat engine. Ben hears it too and we both turn back towards the sea, Ben gripping his camera. The seagulls swarm and scream above as if in warning, as if they already know what's happened. The noise is coming from a bright orange police motorboat traveling at full speed, its hull rearing up against the waves. A shout comes up as paramedics clutching medical cases run through the crowd towards the path that leads to the beach far below, a team of police following them. The police immediately start trying to draw the crowd and the press away from the path, pulling the overly curious back from the edge, shouting, "Get back! Keep away!" They link arms to create a barrier between the crowd and the path. Ben runs towards the action, to jostle for a space at the front, but my feet have suddenly become rooted in the earth. The boat has almost reached the beach and I watch as two people in black wetsuits jump into the shallow surf and heave it up onto the sand. There's another person in the back of the boat; they're bending over something, or someone. The first paramedic arrives on the beach just as the boat is pulled up onto the sand and the third person carefully stands, keeping their head bowed over the white body in their arms. Even from here I recognize the limpness of her arm as it dangles in the air and it's clear that, where there should be movement, a pulse beating through her small body, there's nothing. Where there should be life, there's only death.

12th December 2018

Jon Katrin came last week, with this photographer, Ben. I was wearing my new gray beanie but I didn't feel much like having my picture taken. I used to have thick, blond hair before I got meningitis. Now when it grows it's like the downy feathers on the baby birds Mum likes to watch on nature programs, scrawny and thin. But at least it's something. My hair started falling out again last month, I don't know why. I tried to hide it from Mum but she came in while I was in the bath the other night with the razor and her face all creased with worry.

"I'm so sorry this is happening again, Mouse."

"It's not that bad, Mum, it still covers my head."

"Please don't make this harder, love. Please don't make me go and get the photos."

I tried not to let her see my tears when the blade touched my scalp. I know it's for the best. I don't like to look in mirrors but Mum took photos of me once when my hair was falling out so I could see how bad it had got and I understood then why she needs to shave my head. What little hair I had left hung scraggy and limp against my flaky scalp. I didn't look like a girl—I didn't even look human. I looked like something that had been buried and dug up again. Mum's right. Even being bald is better than that.

Mum bought me the hat afterwards, as a present for being brave. I hope she didn't see how sad I was. She'd been fussing over the interview all week, buying flowers and hoovering all the furniture. Cookie and I just stayed in my room, out of her way. I chatted on the Wishmakers forum to a younger kid who has muscular dystrophy. Most of the people on the MD forums are boys. Zara teases me that they're all my boyfriends, but they're not. They're just glad someone else knows what it's like to be left in a chair at the bottom of the stairs in public. Like Mum says, it's good to feel like I'm helping others.

"You look pretty, Gracie," Mum said on the morning of the interview, kissing my nose like she always does when she's excited. "Hat looks fab."

I wheeled after her as she went through the house straightening straight pictures and plumping already plump cushions.

"Did Maggie say what questions he's going to ask?"

"Not really, just that it's about single-parent families and living with disabilities. He'll probably want to know about your meds, daily life, the usual sort of—"

She didn't get a chance to finish because the doorbell rang. Mum jumped upright like she was on a spring.

"Oh God, Mouse. He's here!"

Jon Katrin is tall with curlyish brown hair and some stubble with bits of gray in it. He was dressed a bit like a teenager—jeans and a raincoat. He pulled off his Converse sneakers at the door and I felt Mum raise an eyebrow behind me. She doesn't really like it when men wear sneakers.

"Cool hat," he said to me.

I don't get to meet new people much, especially not dad-aged men, so I asked loads of questions. He told us his wife grew up just outside Ashford, that they moved down from London for a better quality of life, amongst other reasons. I didn't believe him when he said he loved it. He teased me, said he thought he was supposed to be the interviewer. Mum laughed and squeezed my hand once so I knew it was OK, he was only joking.

It was all going fine until Jon asked about Dad. He's off-limits, him and Danny. We don't use their names—it upsets Mum too much. And me. We never talk about Dad but I know Mum worries about him. Especially since he

147

started calling. Last week I even unplugged the phone. I wanted Mum to have some peace.

I tried to distract Jon, showing him the photos from hospital again, talking him through my meds and my feeding tube. He said it was amazing I could remember them all. I felt a glow of pride at that, but later Mum said he shouldn't have been so flippant.

"Only someone who doesn't understand how one pill can mean the difference between life and death would say something so silly."

Mum liked Ben better than Jon but secretly Jon was my favorite because he liked my hat.

But that was then. We hate him now, since he wrote that stupid article. It was in the newspaper today—Mum went out specially to buy it and has been crying for hours. She keeps asking me if she's a good mum. I hate it when she asks me that because no matter how much I tell her she's the best mum in the world I know it's not enough. I hate Jon Katrin for making her feel like that. He says in the article Dad should be allowed to see me but he doesn't know anything about us. I don't need Dad, I just need Mum.

I read the article quickly when Susie came over to comfort Mum. I was so pink in the photo I looked like a strawberry and the hat didn't look cool, it looked stupid. There were just little slits where my eyes should be, I couldn't see any bones in my face at all. This is why I don't look in mirrors. I threw the newspaper across the room when I saw it.

Susie's been over a lot, she swears she's going to put things right, says her and Zara and Sylvia have already got a plan. Mum kept crying and crying. I just sat by her side and held her hand. It was horrible. Then Cara came round and smiled at me carefully, like her smile could hurt me. This is how she is with me now. Her hair's growing, it's really dark and thick and shiny. I tried to picture how it would feel, soft like melting chocolate around her shoulders.

"All right, Grace?"

I nodded and shrugged.

"What about that article, eh? My mum's fuming."

"I shouldn't have worn that stupid hat," I said, and she grinned at me, like she was relieved I said what she'd been thinking. We don't see each other as much as we used to, but when she comes over I try to talk about normal stuff like TV and shopping. I wish I could ask her more about Chris, about boys in general. But I don't because I think it'll only make me seem weird.

"Fancy getting some chips?" Cara asked. I tried not to look too excited as I nodded.

"Better just go check with your mum," Cara said, and I sank a little in my chair as I followed her into the kitchen. I know Mum needs me close when she's sad.

Mum wiped her eyes and stood to give Cara a hug.

"You get more and more gorgeous, Cara." Cara smiled in thanks, as though it was nothing.

"Grace and I are just going to go and get us all some chips." I saw the worry move across Mum's face like a shadow. Susie put an arm around her.

"I'm not sure that's the best plan just now, girls. How about Cara runs out and brings us four portions back? What do you think, Cara?"

Cara looked at me. I shrugged and she said, "Fine by me."

Susie gave her money to get the chips, and Cara headed out the door. And now I'm back in my room, alone, trying to block out the sound of Mum crying.

Lots of love, Grace xxx

10

Jon

I'm sweating and over forty minutes late for our session. Dr. Bunce opens the door agonizingly slowly.

"Thank you," I say, pushing past her, coughing on the incense smoke in the hall.

"Shoes," she says.

I go back and kick my Converse off next to Ruth's sandals. Ruth is sitting quietly in the therapy room. She doesn't shout at me when she sees me—not a good sign. She shakes her head, and turns away when I try to kiss her cheek.

"Ruth, don't be like that. I was working. I'm sorry, I really am, you know how important you are to me."

But Ruth waits for Dr. Bunce to sit in her chair before she says in a calm, well-trained voice, "Jon, I've decided I want us to formally separate."

I look from Dr. Bunce to Ruth and back again.

"Ruth, don't be like that. I'm late, that's all!"

But she shakes her head slowly, as though what is going on inside is physically weighing her down.

"No. I told you how important these sessions are to me, and therefore to our marriage. You chose to completely ignore me, which is symptomatic of our entire relationship. You've placed me in a horrible position. I have a choice: either I stay with someone I don't trust, or I hope I'll find something better. I've chosen the latter."

"No, no, I think you're the most important—"

Dr. Bunce's alarm rings and she says, "That's time."

"Oh come on!" I appeal to Dr. Bunce, but she just raises a sharp eyebrow at me, playing the headmistress.

Ruth stands. "Thank you for helping," she says to Dr. Bunce.

They smile at each other, like the two of them share an understanding. Her composure is aggravating. This whole fucking thing—the incense, the lotus poster in a frame—it's all so fucking aggravating.

"This is absolute bullshit," I say, in the wild hope that one of them might come to their senses and agree. But they both carefully ignore me and Ruth follows Dr. Bunce in her slippered feet out of the therapy room. My shoes are still warm as I try to squirm my feet inside, not pausing to put them on properly. I'll talk to Ruth once we're outside, on our own, but Ruth's out of the door too quickly. I kick my sneakers off again so they don't slow me down and, holding them, ignoring Dr. Bunce's requests to let Ruth leave, I go after her.

"Ruth! Ruth, wait!" I shout.

She's not quite running. Instead she's walking at a frantically fast pace that is somehow more dramatic than running. I'm a good few feet behind her. Tiny pebbles on the pavement sting and nip at my feet, making me tiptoe. I gain on her as she searches for her keys and, finding them, clicks her car unlocked. I fall on the passenger seat door and then throw myself in, next to her. She doesn't look at me. She's one of those people who sometimes finds drama funny, Jakey can always make her laugh when she's trying to tell him off, but this gravity is new. She seems too weary, too worn out to laugh. The muscle in her neck pulses.

"Ruth, look, I'm so sorry. I was held up at work—"

"I listened to the news on the way here, Jon. I know that poor girl's clothes were found. I know you've been to the Point. I know that's why you were late. You're choosing them, even though they're probably both dead now. You're still choosing them over us."

"I'm not choosing them, I'm just finding out some stuff that suggests things weren't quite as they made out . . . They'd been lying, Ruth, they'd all been lying and I need to find out why. Today is the fourth day Grace will go without her medication—"

"She's probably dead, Jon! They're probably all dead, they don't have to worry about their problems anymore, they don't exist! But your son and I do, our problems are real, very real, but you still, you *still* choose them."

It's almost a relief to hear her shout at me. She'll start crying in a moment.

"Ruth, look, I think I might be able to find out what happened to Meg and Grace that night—"

"You're calling her Meg now? Like she was your *friend*? Get out," Ruth says, still pointedly not looking at me. "Get out now or I'll call the police."

"Ruth, don't be nuts . . ."

She rummages in her bag, pulls out her phone, makes me watch as she dials the police.

"Shit, OK. I'll go." I open the passenger door a couple of inches and Ruth turns the key in the ignition. She always leaves the radio on when she drives, and a news reporter is reading the headlines: *Breaking news this afternoon: South West Police have confirmed that after an extensive manhunt, Simon Davis has been taken in for questioning in connection with the murder of Megan Nichols and the disappearance of their daughter, Grace Nichols . . .*

Ruth clicks the radio off and, turning to me with a sad smile, says, "Look at you. You can't wait to get out of here now, can you? To find out what happened from your buddies in the police. What is it that makes you so obsessed with them, Jon? They're a family, that's all. A family who couldn't survive the terrible tragedy of their son's death and it fucked them all up. It happens every day—families falling apart. Strange how clear it is when it happens to someone else's family and how hard it is to see when it happens to your own."

"What are you saying? Ruth, we're nothing like them."

"Just go, Jon. Please. Just go."

I'm too tired to fight anymore. I get out of the car and stand in the middle of the quiet cul-de-sac, staring as Ruth drives away. Simon's been found at last, which means Grace—or Zoe—is closer to being rescued and Ruth wants to leave me for good: seismic change squeezed into a few short moments. I'm aware Dr. Bunce will be watching, but I don't care. I hate to think how she's probably been leading Ruth, encouraging her to leave me when she doesn't even fucking know me, doesn't know us, not really. Suddenly I remember the satisfying weight of my dad's old golf club in my hands as I swung at Meg's windows, how the sound of breaking glass was the sweetest thing I'd ever heard. It was a stupid thing to do but, Jesus, it felt good.

I glance back at Dr. Bunce's front room before I make myself breathe out, sit on the curb to put my sneakers on, and calm the fuck down. I don't want to go to my car, not yet. I want to stay here for a little while longer, as though by being here what happened will start to make some sense. Above me, a group of screaming swifts duck and dive for invisible insects. I see Ruth's point more than I let on. I think she knows I get it, that's what drives her so insane. Our marriage is hanging by a thread and the one thing she asks of me to help save it, I fuck up. But when I think about stopping, like Ruth wants me to, I realize my reasons for wanting to help run too deep. At first, I only wanted Grace's safe return and, if I'm totally honest with myself, my redemption. But now I'm starting to understand the power Meg and Grace have over the whole town. I think about Mr. Leeson, Zara, and Maggie at the night search. These people, brought together by Meg and Grace. Meg and Grace were protected and cared for like broken children by the whole community. They were a common cause, a tiny family everyone could fight for, everyone could love. I didn't know it at the time, but I understand more now. My article did more than bruise Meg and Grace, it insulted everyone in Summervale, and they retaliated with a smear campaign, baiting me with the one thing they knew I couldn't ignore: my son. I don't think their response was justified, but perhaps my article wasn't either. This isn't about Simon, Meg, and Grace, it's about the bigger family, it's about people fighting for their lost community, for their lost identity. That's why all this is so important. That's what I can't explain to Ruth, because she wouldn't understand. She was raised just outside Summervale, she's one of them. When I defended Simon, I was attacking her hometown for supporting Meg and Grace, and deep down I don't think she's ever forgiven me.

I'm shaken from my thoughts by my phone buzzing in my pocket. I've missed three calls and have a text message, all from Cara.

Call me.

She'll want to talk about Simon's arrest, maybe seek reassurance that his arrest means we're about to find Grace, or Zoe. But I can't offer her any until I speak to Dave and find out more. Why is Cara different from everyone else in Summervale? I can see her vulnerability, the way she looks at me like I'm a baffling but longed-for rescuer. She's smart, and her instincts are sharp. I wasn't lying when I said she'd make a good journalist. She grew up next to Grace, she saw more than anyone. I think we both know that Grace is Zoe, and that this is the first of many secrets. I think she wants to find out the others as much as I do.

I stand up from the curb, slow and weary. My joints creak like they need a good oiling; the last few days feel like a decade in my bones. Not knowing where to go, I walk slowly back to my car. I'll go home, that's what I'll do, I'll go home and see if Dave wants a pint this evening. I glance at Dr. Bunce's house, resist the urge to wave as her curtains twitch. The sun is high now, but on the horizon there are dark, angry clouds gathering in the west, towards the Point.

On the drive, my head is thick with exhaustion. I need some rest before I can think clearly about Ruth, about Grace, Zoe, about any of it. I'll read the diary again once I've had some sleep.

I'm waiting at a red light, straining to not let my eyes close, when my phone starts ringing. I glance at it, expecting to see Cara's name on the screen. But it's not Cara. It's a withheld number, which always means one of two things: it's either a trash call or it's important.

"Hello?"

"Mr. Katrin?" The woman's voice is clear, the voice of someone who has been expertly trained.

"Speaking," I say, trying to match her professionalism.

"Mr. Katrin, my name is DCI Upton, I'm calling from Ashford police station."

"OK. Can you hold the line for a moment please?" The lights have turned green. I need to get off the road to concentrate. The car behind beeps as I pull up at the side of the road, forgetting to signal. I turn the engine off and say, "Thank you for waiting."

But Upton doesn't respond, she's not calling to be thanked.

"Mr. Katrin, you might be aware that I'm leading the investigation into the murder of Megan Nichols and also into the disappearance of her daughter, Grace." She pauses.

"Yes, I've seen you on television." I cringe as soon as the words are out of my mouth.

"Right. Well, you might have seen we arrested Simon Davis today."

"I just heard on the radio. Where was—"

But she answers before I can ask my question.

"As you probably know, he got a train to London the day after the murder. We've been working with the Met, trying to locate him, when today a member of the public identified him on a train to Plymouth, where he was detained. Two of my officers are currently questioning Mr. Davis but I'm afraid he isn't being cooperative. He's made an . . . unusual request."

"Right."

"He says he wants to talk with you."

I bang my head back against the headrest. Is this a joke? "With me?"

"In any other circumstances, I'd dismiss his demands. But,

you see, it's rather delicate. I can explain everything when you get here."

I remember meeting Simon in that café, how he moved slowly, like it pained him to be alive at all. Talking to him, I felt the full horror of the fragility of life, how it could have been me sitting where he sat, how close my own son was to death, how my own neck had been in the noose. It was like meeting a nightmare version of myself. I felt a sort of tragic kinship with him then. How would I feel about him now, knowing what he might have done to Meg, to his own daughter?

"When do you want me to come in?" I ask.

"Immediately, if possible. I can send a car if you want."

"No need. I'll be there in twenty minutes."

I put my foot down hard on the accelerator, all the exhaustion I felt just moments ago replaced by adrenaline. What if the dress wasn't Grace's, what if she is still alive? If I don't fuck up, I could help save her. And, in the back of my mind, I think how this could be the interview of my career, a story that could be reprinted for years to come, translated into many languages.

Simon wants to see me, will only talk to me. He must think I have some kind of authority. Perhaps he wants me to tell the world what he's done. Perhaps I'm the only journalist he knows. Or perhaps he wants to talk to me because I'm the only person who's ever listened to him. I don't know, but it feels like my chance, possibly my only real chance, to help Grace, and there's no way I'm going to let her down.

I swerve into the fast lane, feeling the world open up before me because Grace might still be alive and I feel like I'm driving away from the wreckage of my old life and towards a brighter, better future.

11

Cara

Down on the beach the police put a tent over her. They won't tell us anything. The crowd jostles around me. Whispers of "What's happened?" or "Is it the disabled girl?" make me want to hide. I need to leave, I need to be with Mum. My body moves robotically, getting me first to the car and then driving me to the salon, to Mum.

The salon is only slightly less busy than it's been all week. There's a small group of people outside on the pavement in front of the photos of Grace and Meg on display in the window. I don't know most of them but I spot Brian from the pub; I know he sees me, but I don't acknowledge him. I just need Mum. It's busy inside but the atmosphere is heavy, it's like walking in to the end of a disappointing party. There are balloons around the corners of the room, tied to the dryers and stuck onto the mirrors. People I know and some I don't stare and nudge each other when they see me.

Dennis the butcher is standing by the door, with Barry and Marie. Dennis puts a heavy arm around me and says, "Martin called us from the Point. We're so sorry, love," into my ear. I picture him in his white apron, hands inside a pig's ribcage, smell the iron tang of blood and instinctively pull away.

Either Zara or Mum have stuck search maps of the local area on all the walls, but no one is looking at them anymore. What's the point? Everyone's exhausted, their Find Grace T-shirts are crumpled now—some of them have been up for the last three nights looking for Grace. Some of them, like old Dr. Parker, are so shattered they look numb, and are perhaps secretly relieved that their searching might be over. Others, like Zara, are wet-faced and angry. She calls "Cara!" when she sees me and pulls me towards her thin but strong body.

"Your Mum'll be so pleased you're here, babe."

She holds my hand firmly, the way Meg used to, as she leads me past Molly, who smiles at me as she rocks Zack in his pram, past the farmer Mr. Leeson, past Sylvia, who squeezes my arm, past the vicar who prayed at the vigil, and past others I don't know until we get to Mum, who sits at the head of a trestle table. Mum sits still and upright in her chair; her makeup's been wiped or cried away. She looks more herself than usual, more beautiful despite her tear-stained face. I want to fall on her, drop my head into her lap, but something stops me. Mum is trying to hold herself together; she knows that if she gives in to sorrow everyone else will too. There's a pink cake in front of her; only a few slices have been taken. David from the Wishmakers sits next to her, his head in his hands.

Mum's hand trembles as she reaches for me.

"Cara, love, I'm so glad you're here." She sees me looking at the cake.

"Zara made it for Meg's birthday today. Meg never celebrated when she was alive, it was always overshadowed by the anniversary of Danny's death. We thought . . . oh, I don't know . . . we thought it would be a nice surprise for everyone. We thought it'd be something positive we could do, you know, keep people's spirits up. Silly really." As well as the cake there are sandwiches, and crisps laid out in bowls, untouched on the table. I think of Danny, of Grace, and standing there, holding Mum's hand and staring at Meg's birthday tea, I realize this is it: we've almost run out of hope.

"Mum, I've just come from the Point." Mum closes her eyes, she doesn't want to hear it.

"We know, love. Zara's cousin Remi is dating a police officer. He told Remi that they found a body, that they're trying to identify who it is. He said they're moving quickly, there were crowds there, he said, they don't want it getting out on social media before they've released a statement."

An older woman in a Barbour jacket starts gently crying in the corner and David stands to comfort her. Mum looks at her and says to no one in particular, "Poor Maggie's been up all night searching."

Mum rolls her bottom lip between her teeth. We both watch as David whispers something in Maggie's ear, and Zara inspects Molly's cuticles while Dennis takes a huge bite of cake.

I realize none of these people knew Grace, who she really was. We all act like we did, of course, but did any of us really know her or did we just like to think we knew the sweet girl in the wheelchair? We didn't want to think her life could be complicated—not simple, smiley Grace. Grace who made all of us feel better about our own lot.

"I know it's an awful thing to say"—Mum talks in a whisper,

more to herself than to me—"but a part of me is glad Meg isn't here, that she can't go to Grace's funeral, that she doesn't have to go through the agony of losing another child." My stomach plunges. Has she already given up on Grace? If she gives up, then so will everyone in this room, so will I. But then Mum squeezes my hand harder, shakes her head again, and at last looks at me.

"Your hands are freezing, love!" Mum gestures to David's empty chair. "Come on, sit down with me so I can warm you up."

I pull the chair closer to Mum, who uncrosses her legs and starts rubbing both of my hands between her own. Neither of us says anything. We look each other in the eye and I feel like I see her clearly now, know her better somehow than before. I'm devastated for her, but I'm also prouder of her than I've ever been. My mum, who is so much more than what most people see. She keeps her voice small, her words just for me as she says, "You know, Car, whenever you and I had one of our bust-ups I'd always go to Meg for advice, she'd always know what to do. Even though Grace was younger than you, it was like she knew how to raise a teenager. She was always so wise, so calm when it came to Grace."

We both stare at our hands as she rubs warmth, life, back into me. If I don't take my eyes away it's almost like we're alone.

"Did you and Meg always tell each other everything, Mum?"

"She was my best friend, love. I never kept anything from her."

"But did you ever get the feeling that there was stuff going on with Meg, stuff from her past that she didn't tell you?"

The words are out of my mouth before I even knew I was thinking them. Mum stops rubbing, pulls her hands away. I look up at her, her lip reddening as she starts to bite it again.

"What are you talking about, Cara?"

"It's just, you were saying that Meg knew about teenagers. I was wondering if Grace ever seemed older to you?"

Mum is looking at me like she doesn't recognize me, like I'm a stranger to her.

"What do you know that you're not telling me?" she asks, her voice shrill, her numb state giving way to panic. "Cara, I don't know what you're trying to get at, but I'm only just holding it together so please don't—"

Mum stands so suddenly her chair falls with a clatter behind her. The noise shocks us both. People turn to stare. She says "Sorry, sorry" but her words are muffled because she's covering her face with her hand. Martin moves forward to pick up her chair and Mum says, "No, it's all right," more to herself than to Martin, "I'm all right," before she breaks and starts crying into her hands, really crying, the deep, guttural kind that's rarely public. She makes noises like I've never heard before: raw, animal.

Zara drops Molly's hand and moves towards us. The whole room seems to hold its breath, everyone waiting for what will happen next. I've never seen her like this, so stripped back, so exposed. I want to go to her, hold her, but I don't because this is my fault. I've upset her, I've made things worse, by being here I've made things worse. I shouldn't have come, I have to get out of here. As I turn to leave, someone moves forward and tries to take my arm to stop me but I shrug the hand away. I don't want to be touched, they don't feel like the hands of a friend. People stand back from me as I stumble, blinded by my own tears, towards the door. Outside, the air feels thick with rain. I scramble in my bag for Mum's car keys and run without looking across the road. A car screeches to a halt just a few feet away from me. The driver beeps his horn and a man calls out of the car window, "You bloody idiot!" but I hardly hear him. I feel as though the whole world is staring at me as I drive away.

Not knowing where else to go, I start driving back to the Point. I want to feel the same wind Grace felt, hear the same waves hitting sharp rocks. I want to know that real, solid world—to get away from the horrifying freefall of Mum's agony.

But when I stop at a crossroads, about to turn right, a road sign pointing left catches my eye: PEACEWAYS CREMATORIUM AND CEMETERY. I must have driven past it hundreds of times but I've never turned left here. Danny's buried there, I'm sure of it. No one's mentioned Danny all day. It's as though he's quietly died a second death through his mum and sister. Grace told me once about visiting his grave, how Meg had bought the plots surrounding it. Grace said it was weird to think that one day she'd be buried there, next to her brother. She showed me a photo on Meg's phone. I only glanced at it for a moment; the stuffed toys they'd left propped up next to the headstone sent a cold shiver straight through me. I try hard to remember anything else from the photo but all I can see is a weeping willow tree in the far corner.

I turn left and drive down a long, well-kept road, and park next to an empty hearse. I don't take my phone with me, I need some peace. Clouds have gathered again, like an avalanche in the sky. They look swollen with rain so I grab Mum's red raincoat from the passenger seat as I step out into the chilly air. I shiver: even June feels like winter here. The graveyard is made up of a series of different areas that seem to go on forever, a maze of death and decay. Some of the older graves, green with moss, have collapsed on one side over the years. The newer ones stand proud and sturdy, like whoever lies below is still trying to fight off death.

The red-brick paths are slippery and so are the steps that join up the different levels. Everywhere I look there are routes leading to more graves. I feel like the only living person for miles. I walk randomly, stopping to read any headstones that catch my eye.

I put the hood up on Mum's raincoat, but the patter of raindrops on it is too loud. Drip, drip. I pull the hood down again, let my hair get wet. The air is thick, it smells of freshly cut grass and fungus; a few seagulls scream in circles above. The rain clouds have darkened the sky so much the day seems forced into early twilight and I'm suddenly aware that I'm in a graveyard, on my own. Usually I'd be spooked, but I feel oddly calm here amongst the graves and I realize how exhausted I am, how much I'd love to lie down on the soft, damp grass and join the endless sleep for a little while.

It's starting to rain harder now so I head for the edge of the graveyard, to shelter in the line of trees there. A raindrop runs, like a finger, in a cold stream down my back. I shiver and pull the hood up again. The light is a sickly yellow now, the day slowly being smothered by the gray clouds. I look back at the crematorium for reassurance. The building looks like a tiny model from here; another car is in the parking lot, the headlights on already in the murky light. I decide to turn around, but as I turn back towards the parking lot something familiar hooks my eye. I recognize the gentle shape, the drooping branches in the strange light. There could be a hundred willows in this graveyard, but this one's not much further down the path—it marks the beginning of a small wood on the edge of the graveyard. Now I'm here, I want to find Danny's grave. I need to see the place where Grace might soon be buried too. I bite my bottom lip as I feel the tears build, but I don't want to cry now.

As I walk closer, I know it's his grave. It's on its own, adrift from the others, looking strangely lonely, cast out. As I walk towards it, I feel an uncomfortable pressure in my back, a prickle like I'm being watched by hundreds of silent eyes. The rain falls harder now but I don't stop. My feet slip about in my flip-flops, mud bubbles between my toes. The rain sounds like thunder in my ears, hits my eyes like tiny wet darts, and the gulls scream. I keep my head down as I walk. It's only when I'm close that I look up, and that's when I see them. A person is kneeling just to the side of Danny's stone. They're being careful not to put any weight on his tiny grave, as though worried they might hurt him. A small hand, mucky with earth, strokes the curve of the headstone. They're wearing a too-big man's raincoat. I stop still, but my mind cartwheels. They're distracted, running their hands back through the earth and whispering to Danny, so they don't see me for a few seconds, until they feel me staring and their eyes snap up to mine. In the second our eyes lock the world I thought I knew disappears forever because I know those eyes. I've seen them laugh and I've seen them raw with tears and pain. Grace. She stands, her mouth becomes a snarl. She is Grace, but she's also not Grace. She's not afraid of me; she doesn't even seem to recognize me. Her eyes are hard. The rain slices the distance between us and, with a shake of her head, the girl they said would never walk turns and runs away.

15th December 2018

David from the Wishmakers sent the charity's minivan to pick us up from the hospital and take us home. I watched the driver while Mum stared out of the window. Mum thinks David blames himself for introducing us to Jon Katrin, that everything that's happened since is his fault. I heard Mum talking to Lola about it on the ward as she gathered up all our Christmas cards from our friends at the hospital.

"David's even looking into allotting some of their fund-raising money to getting us our own car, big enough for the wheelchair."

"So he should. Honestly. None of this would have happened if he hadn't suggested that reporter in the first place."

Mum went quiet then. I don't think she blames David, just Jon. Like she said to Dr. Parker after "the incident," David didn't force Jon to get drunk and smash up our house. That was all Jon's doing.

I knew the minivan was coming for us, but the people standing in our sitting room raising steaming plastic cups of mulled wine was a surprise. Everyone we knew from the street and some we didn't were there. Susie, Zara, Martin, and Sylvia. Someone had hung up a WELCOME HOME MEG AND GRACE *banner in the place where our front window used to be, like a pretty eye patch over the hole the journalist made with his golf club. A Christmas tree vibrated with bright fairy lights in the corner by the kitchen, hurting my eyes, and "Rockin' Around the Christmas Tree" was playing too loud. I knew from the way Mum was looking at me that she knew about the party. I felt sick. I wanted to go to bed. But Mum held my hand, squeezed twice: "Don't worry, I'm here," her hand told mine.*

Everyone cheered when I wheeled myself into the sitting room. Then no one really seemed to know what to do. I hadn't actually done anything they could congratulate me on, apart from staying alive again and it's hard to say "Well done you for not dying again" without sounding mental.

Susie came up to me first, looking like a doll in her Santa hat, and replaced my beanie with a scratchy elf hat before kissing my cheek.

"Welcome home, babe."

I love Susie, but it was Cara I wanted to see most. I asked if she was coming later.

"Ah love, she's at college, English mock A-level today," Susie said, holding up crossed, manicured fingers.

Standing behind a plate of mince pies, Dr. Parker waggled his gray eyebrows at me and Mum squeezed my hand. I smiled. And then everyone else pressed their lips against me, like I was some lucky symbol they all wanted to touch. But it was all right because Mum kept holding my hand, so I knew I was doing OK.

David called Martin a hero because Martin had been watching from his and Sylvia's house when the reporter went crazy. Martin saw him stagger out of his car, heard him shout Mum's name, and then Martin called the police. Martin seemed to be enjoying the party, liked being congratulated. Whenever anyone asked him what happened, the words bubbled out of him like a shaken-up can of Coke. He put his hand on the back of my neck while a photographer—not Ben—took our photo, with Mum holding my hand on my other side. The Cornish Chronicle is running an apology for printing the article. Susie said the editor should've been fired but Mum is glad he's getting a second chance—he has a young family, apparently. Everyone apart from me ate cake and drank fizzy drinks, and everyone talked about what a bastard that journalist was. Mum kept squeezing my hand and looked pretty and happy.

Sylvia, Zara, and Susie cleaned up after the party while

Mum, at last, helped me to my room. Cookie was asleep on my bed, like she'd been waiting all along for me to come home. While Mum unpacked my things and got my syringe of food and medicine ready I looked at the Christmas and Get Well Soon cards people sent while we were in the hospital. A lot of them were from people we've never met. They were all open so I knew Mum had already read them. She'll have put any money sent safely in our red box at the back of her wardrobe, like always. Banks scammed Granddad out of loads of money, so we don't trust them anymore. The cards said the usual stuff, how brave we are, that they're sorry our lives are so hard. Some say their dad or husband used to be violent. They tell us stories about how they used to be hit with frying pans; they're trying to tell us they know what it's like, that we're the same. But none of them say their dad killed their brother. So none of them know what our lives are like. They really don't.

Once I was ready for bed, as a treat, Mum asked me to log into our Meg and Grace Facebook page, to post a thank-you for all the nice things people have said online. Over three thousand people have subscribed to our page and Mum says they've been really supportive. It's how she does a lot of our fundraising.

Home at last! Thank all you lovely people for your help. It means the world to us both during this really tough time. Biggest thank-you of all to my mum, who is always by my side. Merry Christmas, everyone!

I added I love you, Mum *at the end without her even asking. I knew she'd like that.*

The phone started ringing then. Neither of us said anything. It's better to pretend it's not happening. But he wouldn't stop ringing and ringing, and Mum shouted at the phone to leave us alone and I hated him even more for making her upset when she had been so happy.

"I think I'll sleep in your room tonight, Gracie."

I heard her checking the locks before she dragged the roll-up mattress into my room. We both know who keeps calling. But neither of us dares say his name. That's the biggest secret of them all.

Lots of love, Grace xxx

12

Jon

The last time I was in Ashford police station was after I was arrested on Meg's lawn. The police had to yank the golf club from my hand. The station smells familiar, institutional, like a hospital or a school, of bleach and sand on vomit. I think only fleetingly about telling Upton about Grace's real name and birthdate, about *GoodSam*, but I'm too wired to think through what the implications could be for withholding information—besides, they might know already, and I don't want to give Ruth any more ammo, any reason to keep me away from Jakey. So I won't risk it, not now.

Upton leads me into a gray, windowless interview room. The metal table is pushed up tight against a wall; it's bolted, as are the four chairs, to the floor. There are microphones in every corner of the room and the beady eye of a camera at each end. There's another door in the far corner. Upton sits down on one of the chairs and points to the chair opposite. "Please."

I sit, dutifully. I'd anticipated a briefing, but from the way Upton is leaning forward across the table, the way she glances at her hands clasped in front of her, I have the feeling she's about to tell me something big. She takes a deep breath before she starts to talk.

"My colleagues are preparing to speak to the press right now, but I wanted you to hear from me. The body of a young woman was recovered this morning, at the Point."

I feel myself wince but she keeps her gaze steady and professional.

"You didn't know?"

I shake my head. I'd only heard about the dress, not a body. I remember all those missed calls from Cara.

"I've been busy with another . . . commitment. Is it . . . ?" I can't say her name, as though saying it will make the possibility of her death, her drowning, more real.

"We knew there were members of the public who saw the body. We've had to move quickly, before there's too much speculation on social media. We were able to push through the tests, and forensics just confirmed the blood types don't match. It's not Grace. We're about to release a statement in the next few minutes, but I wanted to let you know."

It's as though an invisible rope relaxes around my throat. There's still a chance she's alive.

Upton looks at me; spidery red veins lattice the whites of her eyes. I realize she probably feels the same as me, exhausted but wired.

"We are still searching the area." Her eyes dart to her watch. "Look, Simon's going to be brought in here any moment. I want to be gone when he arrives to talk with you." She rests her elbows on the table. "I'm sure you're aware how unorthodox this is, allowing a suspect to speak with someone outside the force, but Simon's given us reason to believe Grace might still be alive, so that's why we're going to these unusual lengths."

I think of Adam Rufton again, the claims of police negligence and rigidity in dealing with his case. Upton, it seems, is trying to learn from her colleague's mistakes.

"I know you've met Simon before, you know how his illness makes him paranoid, distracted. He says he'll only talk to you. We have no idea what he wants to tell you—if anything—but just try to keep him on the point and don't put too much pressure on him. We'll be recording everything."

I nod and Upton keeps talking.

"There have been some concerns from my superiors about having a journalist meet with our prime suspect—"

"I'm not going to write about it, at least not until Grace is found, if that's what you mean."

Upton's shoulders visibly drop an inch and immediately rise again as a heavy-sounding fist bangs against the door we entered through. She stands and says quietly, "Good luck, Jon," before leaving through the second door.

I don't have a chance to tell her to wait, that I'm not ready.

But the fist bangs again. I don't know what to say so I call out, "Come in!"

As the door opens, my leg starts to shake, and I imagine the people watching the CCTV of me in the adjacent room, the comments about me being nervous, and I force my leg to still. I feel overwhelmed suddenly. I'm not a formal interviewer and what interview technique I do have is rusty. Upton didn't even suggest any questions. I thought she'd prepare me more, but clearly there's no time. I close my eyes briefly and picture Grace. I remind myself this is a chance to help her, that she needs me to get this right.

The door opens with a heavy metallic clang and Simon shuffles in, handcuffed to a short but thickset detention officer. Simon keeps his head down, pliant as a whipped puppy. He's wearing grubby jeans that bag around his legs and a navy sweater. The DO steers him into the chair opposite me. To stop myself from staring, I pour water for us both into plastic cups. It's only when he hears the door shut behind the DO that Simon looks up at me. It's as though all his sorrows have been carved into his face. The lines around his mouth and eyes are so deep he looks like he needs to be sewn back together. His hair is matted and his stubble patchy and rough. His face is strangely lacking expression, like he's someone who has lost all faith in the goodness of the world. I have the impression that if I punched him he wouldn't even flinch.

I can't remember how I was going to open the interview because now he's in front of me I realize I was wrong. I'm not here as the interviewer. It was Simon who wanted to see me. I don't know why, but maybe it's because he knows I'm a father, because he knows about Jakey's illness, about all the crap online and about my arrest. He knows that, for a while at least, I was close to sitting where he is now.

"Hello, Jon." His voice is a rasp but he smiles briefly, as though we're back in the café in Plymouth, not in a police station. "How's your boy? What's his name again?"

Acid rises to my throat, I force myself to swallow. I glance at the camera; I don't want to say his name out loud in this room where the air seems to hum with other people's sadness and regret. I clear my throat. "Jake . . ." I cough; my mouth tastes sharp. "Jacob."

Simon keeps his empty eyes on me; a corner of his mouth twitches, like he's trying to stop himself from smiling again.

"That's it. Jacob. Is he better?"

I nod, feel heat rise to my cheeks.

"You look embarrassed, Jon." As he says the words I catch his eyes flickering, fast as a snake's tongue, back and forth in his sockets.

"I'm not, I'm just—"

"You're not used to the questions being about you, is that it?"

There. Again. His eyes flare. Something's wrong. His mouth twitches and I realize he's not trying to suppress a smile, he's trying to stop from mumbling to himself. Something's seriously wrong with him.

I realize I'm staring, so I look down at the table, pick up my water. Simon sees my hand shaking. I hope the people behind the camera don't. Simon waits for me to answer.

"I didn't think the questions would be about me, no."

Simon shrugs. "That's fair enough. Everyone wants to ask the questions, no one wants to be the person who has to answer them—ever noticed that?"

He raises his plastic cup to his mouth with both hands. He drinks and licks some water across his lips. The corner of his mouth twitches again, and I catch the beat of two syllables but I can't make out the words. He closes his eyes quickly to compose himself before he asks, "You know the date today?"

Out of habit I glance at my watch, but I know without having to look.

"Sixth of June," I say slowly. "The anniversary of Danny's death."

Simon widens his eyes at me. "Twenty-one years." He glances down at his hands, his fingers splayed in front of him, as though he needs them to calculate the number of years gone by. "Twenty-one years of reliving that day, a lifetime of wishing I was dead instead of my son."

His voice doesn't crack, but for just a moment his mouth becomes a thin, hard line. Grief has grown around Simon like ivy, twisting and squeezing until at last it swallowed him whole. I glance at the camera. Upton said I only had ten minutes; this might be my only chance to find out the truth.

"Simon, we need to talk about Grace." I keep my head turned away from the camera and my voice low as I add, "Or Zoe."

His eyes widen when I say her real name, flash with recognition before his forehead creases. "Grace?" he whispers. He won't call her by her real name, not here. His gaze searches the boxy room around us, as though he expects to find his daughter hiding in a corner.

Without warning he stops searching, stares back at me. The left side of his mouth curls upwards again as he says, "She was always such a little thing, so small I could pick her up with one hand." He raises his right hand to demonstrate. I fear for the imagined baby in his hand. "But I wasn't allowed to see her. Not since everything. She said I was too dangerous to be near her."

"Who said that? Meg?"

His eyes trace around the room again, as though his whole dead family are in here with us. At last, his eyes come back to me.

"She said after Danny that I shouldn't be near children, that I was dangerous, that I'd hurt them even without trying. She said I pushed her down the stairs."

"Did you, Simon? Did you push Meg?"

The corner of his mouth twitches again, as though he's struggling with the words inside him. He can't contain them, but he can't release them either. Again two syllables escape, but I still can't make out the meaning.

He starts shaking his head. "No, no," he says, and at first I think he's crying, but then I realize he's shaking with laughter.

"I don't know, I can't remember." He raises his hands to his head and he starts pulling his hair so hard it looks as though he could rip his scalp clean off his head.

"But you'd been calling the house, trying to speak to Grace recently, hadn't you?"

"Grace wanted me to call so I did. I kept trying, again and again."

"How did you know Grace wanted you to call?"

"I don't know, I don't know."

He cries out in a damp sob, it sounds like laughter has become tears. But his eyes are dry. Suddenly he stills, becomes calm again. It's like talking to many different people at once. He clears his throat as though he's been sitting here, perfectly composed, all along, but I see his eyes skip, his teeth chatter again around the words he can't say but when he does talk it's with almost alarming clarity.

"Look, I was a mess after Danny's death. Meg kept saying it was my fault, and it was easy to believe her. I couldn't live with the guilt. Then Grace was born too early. She said it was my fault again, the stress from Danny's death. Grace's illnesses were my fault. I believed her. I thought it was better for Grace if I stayed away."

His eyes sweep the room. I worry I'm going to lose him again.

"Tell me what happened next, Simon."

His eyes widen when they land on me.

"One night I got a phone call from the hospital. They couldn't get hold of Meg, but my number was still linked to her record. They told me Grace was sick, meningitis they said. I drove straight to the hospital, but Meg had already taken Grace home. I still had a back-door key so I let myself in. I just wanted to see her, that was all."

"But you took Grace away."

"I just, I just wanted to talk to her, make sure she was OK . . ." Simon shakes his head emphatically.

"But you couldn't leave them alone, could you? You kept calling them, over and over, but they ignored you until you took Grace away again, didn't you, Simon, after you murdered Meg?"

He becomes very still, his pupils black and bottomless, and he stares over my shoulder and says as calmly as if this were just a chat about the weather, "I wouldn't hurt Meg."

"That's not the same as saying you didn't," I say as Simon starts moving his head frantically, as though there's something stinging him inside. I think about saying her real name again or telling him I know Grace's real date of birth, but I don't want to send him over the edge. Suddenly he stops, blinks, and relaxes again.

"You have to find her. You have to find Grace, Jon."

"I need your help. I need you to tell me where she is."

"Why would I ask you here if I knew where she was?"

I don't have an answer, so instead I ask, "Why me?"

"Because you know what it's like to have a sick kid; you know what it's like when the whole world hates you. We share all that, you and I."

I reach for the elastic band, but there's nothing there so I press my thumbnail into the soft part of my palm to stop myself from shouting that I'm nothing like him. He lifts his hands and points a finger at me.

"But there's one big difference between us. You have the power to tell the world the truth."

"Simon, what is the truth?"

But he squeezes his eyes shut and starts shaking his head again, back and forth, back and forth, chattering nonsense, and then he starts ripping at his hair with angry fists. He stands up quickly and leans across the table, so close I can almost see the anger, the pain, boiling inside him.

"The truth is . . . the truth is that I don't remember what the truth is . . . that's all . . . I don't remember," he shouts, then starts to shake with sobs. I hear the key turn in the lock. Simon raises his hands to his face and, turning away from the cameras, wipes his face in the heel of his hands, but as he does so, he lifts his hand a little and I see his mouth is fixed in a hard line. He mumbles those two syllables again, but this time just clear and loud enough for me to hear.

"The twins."

"You could have warned me he's fucking lost it." I'm pacing, almost shaking with adrenaline, when Upton walks into the interview room. I sound angrier than I feel, taut as a wire. *The twins.* What did he mean?

Upton holds her hands up. "I know. You're right."

"So why the hell didn't you tell me?"

"We had a choice: risk you being pissed off or risk you behaving differently around him. Look, two doctors have confirmed he's coming out of a psychotic breakdown and paranoid. He self-harms if anyone says he's unwell; it's like torture to him. We wanted you to treat him as normally as possible. That's what he craves and that's why we think he asked for you. You treated him normally when you met before and you did again. We are trying to learn from the Adam Rufton case, we don't want to make the same mistakes again."

"Adam Rufton was murdered because you lot didn't listen."

"And I'm working as hard as I can to try to make sure that never happens again. I want to listen. I want to know how you knew Simon had been calling Megan."

I can't let Upton know I've read Grace's diary, so I try to sound casual. "If my wife kept me away from our son I'd be calling every minute of the day to try to see him." My shoulders ache as I shrug. "It was an educated guess."

Upton keeps her eyes on me, nods slowly—she looks like she's working hard, trying to figure out why I'm lying.

"He's clearly unwell. What's going to happen to him now?"

"He's going to be transferred to a secure psychiatric hospital immediately. I'm going to keep questioning him there as much as I can. I need to make sure he doesn't get so stressed that he suppresses what happened to Grace."

"What if he can't help?"

Upton looks away. She can't answer me so instead she says, "Thanks for coming in at such short notice, Jon."

We shake hands and I'm relieved. I want to get out of here, need to get out of here, now. The bleach feels like it's coating the back of my throat, makes me want to gag. I need to breathe, to think.

It's pouring with rain as I drive away from the station. I haven't slept in thirty-six hours but I don't want to go back to the flat, I need some space. The closest beach to the police station is about five miles away. Ruth once told me the locals call it Goat Beach. Granted, it's no beauty spot—it's overlooked by an industrial center and the pebbles are always covered in drink cans and used condoms—but at least it won't be busy. The rain has darkened the day, the lights are already on outside the boxy buildings, lighting up the back of the beach. I trip over the pebbles and slide over a couple of tendrils of seaweed that lie slick like long, wet hair. I've never seen another person down here so, for me, it's perfect. My phone vibrates in my pocket but I ignore it. I need to shake off the connection with Simon, make sure his madness hasn't rubbed off on me. I open my body to the wind, like Ruth does, and let it creep under my T-shirt and down my back, let the air freshen and cool. I let myself shout out to the sea, before I feel self-conscious and lie back on the pebbles to look up at the sky. My phone vibrates again. I toy with not answering it, but then I think it could be Jakey so I look at the screen.

It's Cara. I want to be alone but I also feel an urge to answer. I want to tell her about my conversation with Simon.

"Cara."

"Where the fuck have you been?" She's out of breath, she sounds like she's been running.

"Long story. I only just heard the police found a body, but—"

"I know, it's not Grace." She cuts me off. I thought she'd sound relieved, but she only sounds tense.

"What's wrong, Cara?"

"I can't tell you over the phone. Where are you?"

"You know Goat Beach?"

"That shitty little spot near the industrial estate?"

"Yeah."

"I'll be there in ten minutes."

I wait for Cara at the top of the beach, next to an abandoned pram. She's wearing a red raincoat, her arms wrapped around her chest like a straitjacket. As she gets closer I see she's shaking and there's mud between her toes, but her eyes are wired, full of stars, and for a moment I think she's taken something. But as soon as she starts talking I know she's sober.

"I saw her."

"Cara, you're shaking. Here, take this."

She watches as I take off my sweater and hand it to her, pauses before taking it.

"Look, let's go and sit in my car, it's warm, we can talk there." But she shakes her head. No. She hugs my sweater to her.

"I *saw* her, Jon."

I feel myself frown.

"I saw Grace. Or Zoe, or whoever the hell she is."

Of all the crazy things I've seen and heard today, this is the craziest.

"It was Grace, but it was like she'd become someone else. She was, well . . . I saw her run. I saw her *run*, Jon."

I let Cara tell me everything, in one great flow, about Danny's grave, how she went to the graveyard and how Grace ran into the trees, how she thinks Grace followed a path, but that she was too quick for Cara.

"Grace must have known where she was going; she just disappeared. But it was *her*, Jon, I know it." She pauses, finally taking a breath. "You don't have to tell me I sound mental, I know I do. Please tell me you believe me. I know no one else will."

I look at her. Even in the gloom her eyes are bright. Everything today, especially the body being found, all of it is too much for Cara. I should never have got her involved in the first place.

"Cara, please, let's just get in the warmth and talk this through."

She starts shaking again, this time not only with cold but also with gulping sobs that ripple in waves through her body. "Just say you believe me about Grace." Her words are broken through her chattering teeth.

I pause for too long. She knows I don't, knows I can't.

She turns before I can think what to say, walks quickly back towards her car.

"Cara, wait, I didn't say I don't believe you, I just want us both to calm down. When was the last time you ate something, had a proper sleep?"

She stops abruptly and looks me directly in the eye, her gaze like a challenge. She doesn't blink.

"Grace isn't dead, Jon, and she isn't locked up somewhere."

"But Cara, Grace hasn't walked for years and she hasn't had any medication for four days now. It's medically impossible she'd be on her feet, let alone running."

"Fine. Don't believe me. But I'm taking the diary back," Cara says, her eyes filling.

I glance towards my car, where the diary is stashed in the footwell. Cara follows my gaze and immediately starts walking, shielding her tears from me. I call after her but she doesn't pause or turn back. I watch as she peers through the window of my car, then curse myself for not locking up as she opens the passenger door and grabs the brown envelope with the copy of Grace's diary inside. I decide to let her go. She needs to calm down, to rest, and I need some time to think and figure out where we go from here.

It's 5 a.m. and I'm slumped on my sofa, where I woke an hour ago after a few hours of fitful sleep. I'm still numb with exhaustion but too full of adrenaline to sleep anymore. The window is wide open to the dawn but all I can hear is the morning chorus, no one is out calling for Grace anymore. I close my eyes and rub my hands over my face. Flicking the telly on, I look for something banal enough to send me to sleep again. I can't find anything so I flick across to YouTube. There's a scroll bar with "recommended for you" videos to watch on the side. The first is one I've watched before, it's a short video the Wishmakers made when they completed the renovations on Meg and Grace's bungalow. I let the video play and my eyes blur as Grace's high-pitched voice chatters away, the camera following her as she wheels herself down the hall.

"And this is our amazing, amazing new bathroom. Look, the bath has these jets, which are great for my muscles, because they get really tight from always sitting down . . ."

I sit up on the sofa. Right, it's time for bed. This is ridiculous.

"And this is our specially built medicine cabinet." Grace taps in a code and the doors for the largest medicine cabinet I've ever seen open with a small click. I pick up the remote, hit the red button to turn it off, but it doesn't respond; the batteries are running out.

"The cabinet was Mum's idea, she's much better than me at keeping track of all my meds . . ."

I stand closer to the television, aim, and press the red button again and again. Fucking thing.

"It's a relief one of us is organized. I'm such a dreamer that I . . ." The camera zooms in on the cabinet and the rows of carefully organized pill boxes. I'm inches from the screen. The boxes have their labels turned out, facing the camera. They're all for Grace, but something to the side and just behind them catches my eye. It's a piece of light green paper, a slip for a repeat prescription for Meg, not Grace, folded in half and tucked into the side of the cabinet. My eyes pounce, immediately recognizing another familiar name, one I've heard and spoken myself many times recently.

"Now I want to show you my special bed, which is really cool." The camera moves on, following Grace's chair as she maneuvers out of the bathroom and starts to glide down the hall. I stand still as my mind races. I know what I saw, I recognized the name of the doctor on the paper: Dr. Nina Rossi. She told us she wasn't ever their doctor, so why was she prescribing Meg drugs? I turn the television off, pulling the plug from the socket, load the video on my laptop, and freeze the frame. The prescription slip is small on the screen, but now I can see two names clearly. Dr. Rossi was prescribing Meg OxyContin, a powerful opioid. Maybe it was for her back pain, but in that case why didn't she get it from her own GP? I glance at my watch. I had thought about springing a visit on Dr. Rossi this morning to find out if she knew about Grace's real name and age, but now questioning her is urgent, imperative. If I leave in two hours I'll miss the traffic. I could wait for Dr. Rossi at work. It's a bit of a mad plan, but I'm beyond caring now. I feel alive with energy again, and I need to know why Dr. Rossi lied.

13

Cara

By the time I get home, Mum's on her own, bleary-eyed and disheveled, her FIND GRACE T-shirt thrown over a chair. She's sitting on the sofa in her bathrobe, holding a large glass of red wine, the bottle empty on the coffee table in front of her. She turns slowly towards me, chin raised, defiant in her drunkenness. Her hair is flat at the back where she's been resting her head. None of this feels real. I feel like we're bad actors in one of those melodramatic soap operas Mum loves.

"I was wondering whether you'd bother coming home," she says. The wine has made her teeth look rotten.

"Do you want a cup of tea, Mum?" I ask, wishing I could tell her Grace is alive; better than that, she's alive and *well*. I won't, though. I know she won't believe me, and I can't take any more humiliation. Besides, it'd only make her worry about me more and she doesn't need that, not now. She looks almost swollen with grief and I can see that she can't fight it anymore. I try to think of what she wants to hear, something comforting, but nothing comes.

"What the hell have you been doing, Cara?" she asks, clumsily pulling herself to sit upright on the sofa. I'd forgotten my feet are caked with mud, and the skin on my arms is red and lumpy with goose pimples.

"I went for a walk. I just needed to clear my head."

Mum narrows her bloodshot eyes. "You went back to the Point?"

"Yes," I lie.

Mum likes to be right, especially when she's drunk. She nibbles her bottom lip. "You're braver than me. I don't want to go anywhere near that place." She looks distant as she talks, and her voice shakes. "That poor, poor girl. You know they're saying it was a suicide?"

I nod. She's talking about the dead girl—the girl whose name we don't even know, whose navy dress was ripped from her body by the rocks and the waves. The dress didn't have stars on it. Maybe tomorrow, once the shock has settled, Mum will feel some relief that it wasn't Grace's body they found, but a young woman is still dead. None of us can be pleased.

She blinks and, taking a gulp of wine, comes to a clumsy stand, holding on to the back of the sofa for balance. She's drunker than I thought. Mum gets combative when she's been drinking. Trying to reason with her when she's like this is like wrestling with smoke.

"I'm sorry about earlier, Mum. I shouldn't have said anything with all those people—" but she cuts me off.

"You want to know something awful I realized after you left

the salon?" I know she's going to tell me, even if I don't want to hear. Her breath is sour as she speaks.

"I was jealous of Meg. Can you believe it? Even with all the shit she went through, losing Danny, Simon being an evil bastard, and Grace's illnesses, I was jealous. You know why? You know why I was jealous?"

I shake my head, frightened of what she's going to say.

"I was jealous of how close she was to Grace. I was jealous of how she knew everything about her girl, jealous of how Grace worshipped her mum. I was jealous of how they never left each other's side, their in-jokes, how they always said they were each other's best friend." As she talks, Mum starts crying, her tears falling where so many have gone before. She pulls out a ragged tissue from her sleeve, wipes her eyes, and takes another gulp of wine.

"I know how bloody awful it sounds, Car; you don't have to look at me like that. I know how lucky I am to have you, a healthy daughter. But there have been times, Car, times I wished you weren't quite so independent, times I wished you needed me."

My throat constricts with guilt and regret. It spreads through me like soup, hot and thick, and I don't know how to turn it into words.

"I do need you, Mum." I sound meek as I reach for her hand. She squeezes it once, but then quickly lets me go.

"No you don't, Car, not really, not the way I need you. You're like your dad that way, he was always off doing his own thing, he never needed me either."

Her voice hardens whenever she mentions Dad, especially when she's drunk. I don't want to argue about him, not now, not after today.

"Maybe you should go to bed, Mum, you must be exhausted."

She shrugs in a resigned kind of way that shows I've just

proved her point, that I'm casting her aside again, just like always. She moves unsteadily back to the sofa.

"You go on then, Car." Her voice slurs. "I'm going to stay here and finish my wine and think about how I've screwed my life up."

I know she wants me to rush to her, throw my arms around her, and tell her she's wrong, that she's the best mum in the world. That's what Grace would do. The old Grace. But I feel empty. I don't have anything good to give her and besides, I know she won't remember any of this in the morning, so I turn away.

"Good night then, Mum." As I say it, I hear her gently start to sob again.

I sit on my bed and stare at the Wishmakers forum on my phone. In the sitting room Mum turns on the telly to a noisy chat show, waves of laughter filling the silence. It still stings that Jon doesn't believe I saw Grace, but that doesn't mean it didn't happen. I'm on my own now and there's only one thing I can do that makes sense to me. I open up a new message on the forum and in the "to" field type in *GoodSam*. I spent the drive home composing this message in my head so I know exactly what I want to type. But now that I'm here, I pause. What if *GoodSam* doesn't know anything about Grace after all and he shows my message to the police? They'd either bring me in for questioning or lock me in a mental hospital. Either way, it wouldn't be good. But what if he does know something, anything, that could help? Him exposing me is a risk I have to take. I start to type.

> Hi. I messaged you because I know you knew Grace Nichols, the missing girl? This is going to sound crazy but I think I saw her today. No one else will listen to me but . . .

I stop. What was I going to say next? I remember Grace's face that day, when she told me about *GoodSam*, how her skin flushed, how a light seemed to glow behind her eyes. It was the first and last time I ever saw her like that. Maybe it was just a short-lived crush, but maybe not. I keep typing.

I think you were special to Grace, and I hope she was special to you too. If you know anything, please, please get in touch. I promise I won't say anything to anyone. I just want to find Grace.
C.

I press Send before I can change my mind and, holding my phone to my chest, lie back on my bed, on top of the duvet. I think about how pissed off Jon would be if he knew I'd messaged *Good-Sam* without telling him, but I try not to care. After all, he's in the wrong. I'm the one who should be annoyed. But there's still a part of me that wishes I could ask his opinion, talk all this through. I stamp it out, remind myself that he let me down. Mum's always saying I'm like Dad, that I don't need others the way other people do. What if I am? It might not be such a bad thing after all. It means I can do this, I can help Grace alone. Mum's slurred words come back to me, how she was jealous of Meg, how she wishes I were more like Grace. I harden my heart. I need to focus on Grace now, not Jon or Mum.

I refresh the forum and stare at the screen. Twenty minutes tick by. I picture the new Grace—Zoe—the person I saw today, the too-big coat, the snarl on her lips where there was once always a smile. She stared at me with cold eyes, a stranger, as though I was the one doing something wrong, before she started to run. I couldn't move, I couldn't even say her name. My legs seemed to sink into the soggy ground, my body cut off from the rest of me. She knew those woods, she knew where she was running. What would have happened if I'd been braver and kicked off my flip-flops and chased her across the sodden grass and into the trees? The scene plays out in my mind, me running after her, calling her name. Perhaps she would have stopped then, perhaps she would have told me who she really is. Perhaps she would have told me what happened that night, who killed Meg. I take out the photocopy of Grace's diary and skip through to the last entry, the one marked 19 December. The abrupt ending doesn't feel like Grace, not the Grace I thought I knew. Perhaps she stopped because she wanted to write about *GoodSam* but felt she couldn't for some reason, not here anyway. My thoughts run messy, crashing into each other, when suddenly my phone buzzes on my chest.

Hi Cara. Meet me 5:30 am tomorrow at the place where you and Grace used to fly kites.

My heart is hammering as I read *GoodSam*'s reply, then re-read it to make sure I'm not imagining things. I know the place he means, it's a grassy patch overlooking Angel's Bay. The last time Grace and I went was a couple of years ago, Grace driving her chair so close to the edge it scared me shitless. "Have you ever thought what it'd be like to drown?" she had asked, uncharacteristically dark, staring at the waves below.

"I thought you were afraid of the sea."

"I'm not frightened of the sea, I'm frightened of drowning," she said, glancing at the gray foam below one more time before turning her chair around.

I told Mum about it that evening while we ate fish and chips on the sofa. Mum must have told Meg because suddenly Meg didn't want me taking Grace to Angel's Bay anymore.

If *GoodSam* knows that place, that we used to fly kites there, then he must know Grace well. Maybe he's even with her right now. The thought both warms and chills me. I want nothing more than for Grace to be alive, but I feel thrust into a world I don't know, a world where everything I thought was real is fake, a world where miracles happen, the disabled walk, and the dead come back to life. But I don't trust it; I can't until I know the rules. I watch but don't feel my thumbs as I type my reply:

I'll be there.

19th December 2018

The glass in the sitting-room window has been replaced. It looks exactly the same as it did before he smashed it in, but since those temporary plyboards cut out all natural light it feels like a new beginning, like the house has had an operation and can see again. I sat in the window this morning while Mum got herself dressed. It was a blustery day, I watched an empty beer can clatter under Martin and Sylvia's hedge opposite. I saw a few of our neighbors, on their way to their lives. Sylvia was first, in a beige wool coat and scarf, holding a plastic bag full of books going to the library. She gave a double thumbs-up when she saw the new window and I did one back. Susie was next, holding a hand to her hair and putting her head down against the wind as she trawled for her car keys in her red leather bag, tucking her phone under her chin to make a call as she reversed out of the drive. Then came Dennis, an umbrella tucked sensibly under one arm, like he was off to work in a bank, not to stand behind a display of dead animals all day. He told Mum at our welcome-home party that he walks to his butcher's shop every morning. He absentmindedly patted his stomach as he said it. It had started to rain by the time Cara slammed the front door behind her. It was the first time I'd seen her in a couple of weeks. My breath became ragged and my PEG tube bit into my stomach as I leaned forward in my chair to knock on the cold window. I wanted to shout her name, but I knew that'd worry Mum, make her come running.

Cara was in a hurry. She didn't hear me so I sat back in my chair and just watched her. She was wearing denim jeans, a black knitted scarf, a sloppy old army jacket, and the Dr. Martens she wears every day now she's a student and not a receptionist anymore. Her hair was scrunched up in a loose bun on top of her head. It wobbled from side to side as she started running down the pavement to catch the 09:16 bus to Plymouth. Her backpack strained and as she ran I watched the zipper slide lower and lower, until the weight tipped, making the zipper slide all the way down and books fly out onto the pavement. Heat bloomed around my palms where I pressed them against the cold glass as I watched Cara shout swear words into the sky with white, icy breath. She kicked one of the books, which made me giggle, before she bent down to pick them up. She was muttering to herself and I wanted to wheel out there and help her. Maybe she could pull a sickie and we could go to the beach again, like we used to.

But then Mum called my name, told me to hurry up, said we didn't have long and she had to get me ready for physical therapy. For the rest of the day I made up stories in my head about what could have happened if I had gone out to Cara. In the best one Cara and I were like sisters again, Dad was out of our lives, and Mum was always happy because I wasn't sick anymore.

Every week after physical therapy, no matter what the weather, Mum drives us to Danny's grave. The sky was gray today, but at least it wasn't raining. Mum tucked blankets around my legs and I wheeled myself down the path while she talked to Danny. She says there are some things that are just between a mother and her son. She says I'll understand one day, perhaps, if I can have children. She seems to talk to him so easily. I've tried, but nothing comes out. Today while she was talking to Danny I wheeled down the wobbly paths to read the graves I already know well.

Old favorites are "BELOVED BY ALL" PENELOPE GRAY, OCTOBER 2ND 1882—DECEMBER 28TH 1899. She was only seventeen when she died. I imagine her ghost as grumpy, pissed off she went just before the turn of the century. Then there's WILLIAM KETTERIDGE, "LOVING FATHER, HUSBAND, AND SON," 10TH MAY 1921—22ND NOVEMBER 1963. I always stop to stroke the etching of his cold name. I picture a good man, a man who thought that being a loving dad was the most important role in life, and to prove it he wanted "FATHER" before anything else on his headstone.

Today I played a game where I tried to find dead people who died when they were my age. When I couldn't find any, I turned back to see if Mum had finished. She wasn't talking *to Danny anymore. Instead she was kneeling, holding on to his headstone as though she'd fall forward onto his grave without it keeping her steady. She reached for my hand as we left the cemetery and I noticed fresh soil under her light pink fingernails, from where she'd been pulling weeds from Danny's grave.*

I can't tell Mum this but I hate it when she cries over Danny. I hate it because it reminds me there's a part of her that will always belong to him, a part I can never know and will never heal. Another secret.

Lots of love, Grace xxx

14

Jon

My eyes burn as I close them and lean back on the sofa. My head is a nest of speculation, it won't let me rest. I've been reading up on OxyContin. Nicknamed hillbilly heroin, it's one of the strongest pain medications a GP can prescribe. I couldn't see from the prescription slip how much OxyContin Dr. Rossi prescribed Meg, or for how long, but the withdrawal sounds horrendous. I leave the flat just after 6:30 a.m. The morning is a watery light blue, a whole orchestra of birds still celebrating its arrival. Aware I haven't slept enough, I drive slowly on the empty morning roads. I turn the radio on and then off again—there's enough chatter in my head about Meg, Dr. Rossi, and these pills without adding anything more to it. It's only half past seven by the time I arrive. The office doesn't open for another hour, so I push the driver's seat back as far as it will go. My eyelids grate like sandpaper against my eyes as I let them close.

I wake with a start forty-five minutes later. There's a gray-haired woman tapping on the window of my car, her face pinched and cross like a rag doll with the thread pulled too tight. I smile at her as I point towards the office so she knows I'm waiting for it to open. Her eyes move left and right, left and right before she finally looks up towards the sky and walks towards the entrance, unlocking the door with a shaky hand. I walk across the road, buy a takeaway coffee, and wait—with forced patience—in the parking lot for Dr. Rossi.

She arrives twenty minutes later, driving an old red Saab, and heads straight for a parking space in the far left corner, clearly her spot. She's in another orderly two-piece suit, black shoes with rubber soles. She almost walks straight past me—she looks pre-occupied, like she's running through to-do lists in her head. She stops with a jolt as I step into her path.

"Hello, Dr. Rossi," I say, my voice light.

She blinks at me a few times before recognition sinks in. She says my name like it's the answer to a question she's been puzzling over.

"Jon!" Her eyes are drawn over my shoulder. "What are you doing here?" She tries to match my light tone but it's obvious from the way her lips thin and her eyes narrow that she's far from pleased to see me.

I take a step towards her and she flicks her head. Her short gray hair fans out around her.

"We need to have a talk."

She frowns. "I don't have to talk to you about anything."

"I know you were writing prescriptions for Megan when she wasn't your patient. I know that at one time Megan was taking OxyContin, thanks to you."

Dr. Rossi's face flares red from her neck, her eyes pinballing from me to the office and back.

"I have no idea what you're talking about."

"I have proof. Proof that would be easy to share with the police, and that is exactly what I'll do if you don't follow my instructions. OK?"

She blinks hard, as though trying to wake herself up. I open my palms towards her.

"It's up to you—either me, or the police."

"Yes, yes, I understand."

"Good. I'll give you a few minutes to tell reception they need to cancel your first appointment this morning. I'll be waiting in that car"—I point and she glances towards it—"in the road just to the left of the café. If you're not there in five minutes I'll be calling the police and giving them the evidence that links you to Megan. You got that?"

She fixes her jaw, and nods. "I'll be there in five minutes."

Then she turns sharply away from me and walks towards the office entrance, as though I was just a smear on the asphalt she had to step over.

Four minutes and forty seconds later the passenger door opens. Dr. Rossi winces as she nudges away the rubbish in the footwell to make room for her feet. I wait until she's shut the door and put her seat belt on, and then we drive silently away. I stop a few minutes later, on a tree-lined residential street. She looks surprised.

"Here? You want to talk here?"

I shrug. "As good as anywhere, unless you want to be somewhere more public?"

She shakes her head. In her lap she makes her hands into fists, but otherwise she seems calm.

"OK. Are you ready to tell me why you gave Megan those pills?"

She sighs, looks up to the sky through the windshield for a moment, before turning towards me. Her face is impassive as she talks.

"It all happened so long ago it feels like another lifetime. Grace and her mum were registered with my colleague, Dr. Marsh, but because Grace's health was so complex everyone who worked at the office knew them. We all knew, of course, about the son's death, and they were always so sweet, so smiley. They'd bring muffins in for the staff, that sort of thing. So, as you can imagine, there was a lot of goodwill towards them. Megan became close to our then administrator, who put her forward for the two-day-a-week admin role. Everyone who worked at the office thought it was a good idea, a good way to support them both." She glances out of the window, sighs, before she continues. "One night, Dr. Marsh was on leave and I was working late with Dr. Brannagh— Jeremy. We thought we were alone, but we weren't. Grace had the last appointment with Jeremy. We thought they'd long gone, but Megan forgot something and came back to Jeremy's room. We hadn't shut the door properly." In her lap, Dr. Rossi's knuckles are white. "She saw, well, she saw us. Together."

The thought of Dr. Rossi having an affair was so far from my mind, so far from my comprehension, I have to stop myself from crying out in surprise. She keeps her gaze fixed forward, determined not to look at me. "I was married, of course; it was a reckless, stupid thing that shouldn't have happened. We were both senior practitioners at the clinc. Megan was smart enough to know the repercussions would be serious, both personally and professionally."

Dr. Rossi comes to an abrupt stop.

"So she blackmailed you into giving her drugs?"

Dr. Rossi rolls her lips together.

"You have to understand—she could have destroyed everything: my marriage, my relationship with my children, my career, my reputation. My whole life ruined by this one mistake, this one moment of insanity."

I understand now why she seems so robotic, why she holds herself clenched like a fist; it's to avoid ever giving in to impulse again.

"She blackmailed me. Made me prescribe the OxyContin."

"Did she say what she wanted it for?"

Dr. Rossi shakes her head. "She always claimed she had chronic back pain from when she fell down the stairs. It must have got worse over the years, lifting Grace in and out of her chair. I think she developed a dependence."

"She was an addict?"

Dr. Rossi nods. "She was on it for years. When you called after she was murdered, I was sure Cara somehow knew about it. Megan told me she'd kept the prescription slip as proof of my involvement, to maintain her hold over me. That's why I agreed to meet you and Cara. I thought somehow you knew."

We both stare out of the windshield. The silence seems to swell with questions.

"You said Meg was doing an admin role at the practice, so presumably she would have had access to patients' records?"

Dr. Rossi keeps her face turned away as she replies, "She would have been trained in how to use and update records, yes."

"So she could have edited a patient's record?"

"Of course—why do you ask? Do you think she was—" but I cut her off with a shake of my head. She clearly didn't know about Grace's real name and age, and there's no point in telling her now. So Meg would have changed Grace's details herself. Even though Meg and Grace were well known, the office must hold thousands of patient records, and in the unlikely event someone queried Grace's it would have been easy for Meg—this wonderful mother—to convince them they were getting confused. I need to keep pressing Dr. Rossi while I still can.

"You said Meg fell down the stairs, but she always claimed Simon pushed her."

Dr. Rossi turns to me. "I didn't believe a single thing that came out of that woman's mouth."

I don't want the tension to slacken, for her to find an excuse to stop talking, so I keep asking questions.

"Did Simon know Meg was blackmailing you?"

Dr. Rossi shrugs. "I have no idea. After they left Plymouth he registered under a false name at the office. He made an appointment with me. He wanted to see Grace's medical records."

"Why?"

Dr. Rossi shakes her head again. "Frankly, I think they were both mad, him and Megan. And no, before you ask, of course I didn't let him see the records."

"Did he say anything else?"

"He didn't have time to say anything else, to be honest. As soon as I figured out who he was, I told him to leave but he wouldn't, he kept asking to see Grace's medical records. He became quite aggressive, kept on saying again and again that he had to tell me something, something important about Grace. He grabbed hold of my wrist, which is when I called for help."

"Did he mention anything else? Maybe something about Grace's age, her birth certificate?"

Dr. Rossi shakes her head. "No, he just kept rambling on about her medical records even as my colleague called the police to have him removed. I really don't see why any of this is important—"

"Do you think Simon killed her?"

Dr. Rossi's eyes dart away from my face.

"Who knows? It's the most likely conclusion. Megan was an addict, she probably abused him for years, drove him mad until he snapped. Or perhaps they were both taking the drugs. I wouldn't put it past them."

"What about Grace? How was she with Grace?"

Dr. Rossi shakes her head emphatically. "That's the only thing I couldn't fault her on. Even though she was screwed up, taking God knows what, she always seemed to be an impeccable mother. She'd research Grace's illnesses, find out about new treatments, that sort of thing. She'd never miss an appointment. Dr. Marsh said Megan was always alert and completely present in their appointments. She'd even take notes sometimes. He said he felt she'd lay down her life for that little girl. I thought the drugs were probably her way of coping."

"So what happened? Why did she leave when she had two senior doctors on the hook?"

Dr. Rossi stretches out her fingers and then makes fists again.

"A few of the nurses reported some of their meds and supplies were going missing. We had a meeting about it. Jeremy and I knew it was Megan, of course, pocketing what she could find when rooms were left empty; thought she was selling it on. Then things escalated when the daughter of an elderly patient with dementia claimed her mother's watch had gone missing during an examination with Dr. Marsh. I'd seen Megan talking to this patient, so I immediately had my suspicions. There was no way we could prove anything, of course. The daughter couldn't even prove her mother had lost the watch at the office and not somewhere else so it never came to anything. Still, with the meds disappearing and the accusation from the patient, Jeremy and I thought we'd found a way to get rid of her, but then she just disappeared without a word, without warning. Dr. Marsh was worried—he felt it was out of character—but Jeremy and I convinced him not to pursue it. We were just so relieved to have our lives back."

"Where's Jeremy now?"

Dr. Rossi swallows. "Heart attack, three years ago."

I nod, feel Dr. Rossi twitch beside me.

"And now Megan's dead you never thought about going to the police with any of this?" I don't bother keeping the anger out of my voice.

"I thought about it, of course I did, but we kept our secret for so long. We both had so much to protect, and now that Jeremy's dead I couldn't do it to his widow, his kids. I can't destroy their memories of him."

"I don't think you're trying to protect anyone other than yourself." I sound bitter, angry. She turns to me then; her face is flushed but her eyes are hard.

"Oh come on, Jon, you of all people know the extremes we're capable of when people we love are threatened." She must have read up on me, knows about the photo of Jakey, the whisky and the golf club. She knows I have no right, taking the moral high ground.

"Look, what are you going to do now, with all of this—with everything I've told you?" she asks.

"I don't know. Not yet. I've done a fair bit of asking around, but no one's ever mentioned Megan's toxicology being anything other than normal."

Dr. Rossi raises her eyebrows.

"You're surprised," I say, as a fact.

She nods. "I never thought she'd get off the drugs, not the amount she'd taken over the years."

We fall into a heavy silence.

I turn to Dr. Rossi. "What are the main side effects of Oxy-Contin?"

"Well, short term, besides numbing pain it can cause vomiting, stomach pain, headaches, that kind of thing."

"And what if someone takes an overdose?"

"Then things get more serious: respiratory problems, swelling of the face, throat, tongue, cardiac arrhythmia, seizures . . . all sorts of nasty stuff."

Something starts buzzing in my chest. I don't recognize it at first, it's been so long since I felt it, but eventually I know. It's the feeling of making a discovery, of flipping a slanted world and finding it makes more sense upside down than what you thought was the right way up. I can't move, can barely breathe, I'm just staring straight ahead.

"Jon? Jon, what is it?"

I turn the key in the ignition.

"I need to go, I have to go. Right now."

I leave her outside the office and drive away before she has the chance to question me again.

A few moments later, I pull into a quiet road, let my head drop to my hands. I need peace to order my thoughts, to try to make some sense out of them. Simon would have known Grace's real name, her real birthdate—why wouldn't he tell someone? Was Meg blackmailing him too? Or did he have another reason not to tell the world the truth? There were no drugs found in Meg's system and no one has ever mentioned her being unwell with any withdrawal-like symptoms. Meg certainly didn't seem like someone addicted to drugs when I met her and, besides, when would she have found the time to get off them while caring for Grace around the clock? Dr. Rossi mentioned that Simon could have been taking OxyContin too, but when I picture someone suffering from addiction I don't see Meg and I don't see Simon. I see someone else completely.

I'm propelled back to a small, clammy hospital room. It's nighttime and Ruth's asleep in the chair by Jakey's bed. He's so small under the blankets that I get up to check he's still there. I stand by his bedside and am surprised to find he's awake. He's too weak to cry or say anything; he just looks at me with complete resignation, like he's already agreed to die, and I know he wants it to be over. It was like he was begging me to make the pain stop and in that moment I would have done anything to help him, to end his suffering. Thank God Ruth stirred. She watched as I stroked Jakey's cheek with one finger until his huge, empty eyes finally closed, like he couldn't bear the sight of the world anymore. I blink the memory away, then I see Meg by Grace's bedside, Grace looking at her mum with the same imploring eyes, her tiny body pumped full of chemicals, begging her mum to help her, to make it stop, and as her thin body rattles with pain I see Meg reach for a bottle of pills.

15

Cara

With just a few hours before I meet *GoodSam* I know I won't sleep so I don't even bother trying. I open my laptop and google "Missing Grace" to check for updates and click on a new video link. Suddenly, Cookie, with a mewl, leaps onto my bed and curls herself into a shell shape in the space between my crossed legs. I remember how she used to curl up and sleep on Grace's legs. I scratch her ear, lean in close to hear her purr, and whisper, "You probably know more than anyone, don't you, Cookie?"

The video is a series of short interviews with people from Summervale. It opens with Sylvia and Zara side by side outside the salon. Zara, in huge gold hoop earrings and gold eye shadow, talks, and Sylvia casts shy glances at Zara, nods along at everything she says.

"Grace was, well, Grace was an absolute ray of sunshine, she was the smiliest little girl I ever knew. Even when she must have been in huge pain she'd smile through it all. She used to come into the salon and she'd always have us all laughing, cheer us all up."

But, if Jon is right, Grace wasn't a little girl, she was a young woman. Neither of them knew Grace, not really. They only saw her how they wanted to see her, as bright and false as a Disney character. It was just so much *nicer* for everyone if the disabled girl was happy. I see Grace, staring at me through the rain by her brother's grave, how she walked with such ease, as though she'd never even sat in a wheelchair. Zara and Sylvia have no idea, but the sweet Grace they talk about in the video doesn't exist. But Zoe does, and she's the riddle I have to solve.

Next up on the video is Dennis outside his butcher's shop, hands on hips in his white apron.

"When they first moved here Grace was in one of those manual wheelchairs, but you could see she was nowhere near strong enough to shift the thing: her arms were like twigs, you know. Anyway, everyone in the community collected money and held fundraisers, ran marathons and what-have-you, and we raised over two thousand quid to get her the powered wheelchair so she could operate it herself with the joystick and not have to be pushed when she came to a hill or whatever."

The interviewer says something I don't hear. Dennis smiles in response and his cheeks grow into round red apples of pride.

"Yes, we're a very close-knit community, that's what we're like down here on the estate: we all look after each other, doing shopping for the elderly, visiting the sick. We like to help each other out, do what we can for our neighbors, you know."

Dennis trots out his neat little lies. I don't remember anyone coming to visit Granddad when he was bedbound after his stroke, and there were reports last year of a retiree dying in their bungalow from the cold and no one noticing until spring. Most of what

Dennis is saying is bollocks. Before Meg and Grace moved here the neighbors wouldn't say hello in the street. Even Dennis was just "the butcher" until Meg told us his name. But Meg and Grace changed us: everyone would stop to say hello, to ask after Grace as the brave mum wheeled her broken daughter down the road, as though ignoring them would be like turning away from a lost, frightened toddler crying for help. Meg would welcome the sighs, smiles, and arm squeezes like a prima donna accepting flowers at the end of a performance. It was as though they flirted with us until we fell in love with them, as if they knew that one day plastic-faced news reporters would be asking questions and they'd have us to tell the world how wonderful they were.

The camera cuts to the outside of the salon. I stare at the photo of Grace and Meg in the window, the one where Grace is holding on to her IV and Meg is holding on to Grace. It makes me think of the photo I showed Charlie, and as I stare I hear the phlegmy rattle in his voice again. I remember how his finger shook over the photo before he started shouting.

"She's sick, don't you people understand? She should never have been born! She's sick."

But I've seen Grace standing, watched her run. I know she's not sick, not anymore. Is it possible the doctors misdiagnosed her? I remember Dr. Rossi, how suspicious she seemed: *What do you know?*

Was she worried we'd uncovered malpractice? That she could somehow be held responsible? But if Grace had been misdiagnosed, if she wasn't as sick as she thought, why didn't she tell the world? Why aren't we celebrating instead of mourning?

My alarm wakes me at 4:45 a.m. Cookie has disappeared and my laptop has slipped down the bed. My heart leaps so hard in my chest it makes my ribs ache. It's time.

I dress quickly, jeans and an old cardigan, my Dr. Martens. Just before I leave, I shuffle through a drawer and find the rape alarm Mum was given at a self-defense class Meg organized in the community center a couple of years ago. I shove the alarm into my pocket with my phone.

The TV is still on in the sitting room, Mum collapsed in front of it. Her wine glass has fallen, empty, on its side on the floor. She's snoring softly, the air thick and sour around her. I think about putting a blanket over her, but I worry she'd stir, ask where the hell I'm going at five in the morning, so I settle for picking up her glass. At least when she sees I've gone she'll know I had one small thought of her. I'm about to leave when I turn back and whisper "I love you" into her sleeping ear.

The morning is chilly, but noisy with birdsong. Angel's Bay is just over ten minutes' walk away. At the end of our road I go through a passage that takes me onto a public footpath, which eventually leads either down onto the beach or up into an open field overlooking the sea. Before she got her powered chair I used to push Grace all the way. She'd pretend to help but usually she'd be too excited, her attempts halfhearted. I didn't mind; those were the days she'd still let me help her. I remember how her upper body would shift and jive around in her chair, but I never saw her legs move. It was like they weren't part of her at all. Did they work all along?

I'm pleased I've arrived at the clearing before *GoodSam*. A thin barrier of barbed wire separates the end of the grass from the cliff and the drop below. I'm too far from the edge to see, but the waves sound restless, agitated, and here the gulls drown out the songbirds. There's no one around. I stamp my feet to extinguish a small puff of fear that's risen inside me. I'll make sure we stand way back from the edge. I remind myself I know this place well, know the few hiding places. I try to ignore the voice inside that whispers, "But so could he."

He arrives soon after. I know it's him, not just because he's the only person I've seen this morning but because there's something about the purposeful way he walks. He doesn't seem to notice or care about the scenery. Instead, he walks with both hands in his pockets, his eyes fixed on his black shoes. He's wearing a black hat and his black bomber jacket is zipped high up his throat. He doesn't lift his head until he's in front of me. He's tall and whippet thin, with an angular head so sharp it looks like it must hurt to rest it anywhere. He has a small gold hoop in one ear and on his neck, above the collar of his jacket, there are two black flicks of tattoo ink, like the fork in a snake's tongue. His mouth is sloppy, turned down, like the taste of his own mouth disgusts him. He's nothing like the smiley cartoon face online, nothing at all like the sweet, bashful kind of boy I imagine Grace would pine after. I feel small in Mum's red raincoat. His cold eyes settle on me. One side of his mouth lifts as though he finds me funny. I think about the Grace I saw in the graveyard. She had the same hardness in her eyes. I force myself to talk first.

"I saw Grace yesterday."

His smirk becomes a full smile. "You thought you saw Grace yesterday." His voice is a guttural rumble, his vowels round and soft, Cornish.

"You wouldn't be here if it wasn't her. How did you know about this place?"

I hear the same plumpness in my own accent. He shrugs his thin shoulders.

"You've been pretty upset recently, haven't you, Cara? You might not tell people what you're feeling but I know you're upset.

Who's to say you didn't just see someone who looked a bit like Grace and got overexcited?"

His eyes are slits, as though even the bleached colors of early morning are too bright for him. I shake my head.

"So why drag me all the way out here then? Why not just ignore me? I know you know something. And I know what I saw. I saw Grace."

"Yeah, but you know how it sounds, don't you? A local disabled girl is missing and you see her able-bodied and well, running around in a graveyard?" His voice is only just about a whisper. "You think anyone's going to believe that? C'mon, Cara, where's your evidence?"

He looks as though he's trying not to laugh. How does he know so much? Grace must have told him everything—my name, the day she saw me . . . but did she tell him willingly or did he force it out of her?

"I have evidence."

I want the lie to be small but powerful, but he doesn't even flinch.

"Don't bullshit me. We both know you don't."

"How do you know? The only way you could know is if you've got Grace. She's telling you everything."

Without taking his hands out of his pockets he steps towards me. I feel suffocated by his height. I take two steps back.

"You need to stop, Cara. Grace wouldn't want you to be in any danger, would she?"

He's so close I can see his Adam's apple moving below the zipper of his jacket. I take two more steps back, the barbed-wire fence getting closer. He presses on again, close to me, trying to trap me.

I take another step back and the barbed wire presses against my back through my thin coat. I hear the sea, boiling and messy below. *GoodSam* looks at it over my shoulder.

"You know, I remember there were a bunch of teenage kids who used to dick around up here, cliff-jumping. Then one day one of them landed on a rock, smashed both his legs and his spine into little pieces."

He moves towards me again, so close I can see myself reflected in miniature in his eyes. I strain back, I can't bear to touch him, I cry out, but he ignores me as the barbed wire bites into the skin on my back.

"The lesson being that you need to be careful of what you can't see, because what's just below the surface can be worse, far worse, than you ever imagined."

"I'll go to the police," I say. He hears the tremble in my voice. It makes him smile again.

"No you won't. What would you say? You saw a disabled girl running away from you? They'd laugh at you—think the trauma had got to you. If she wanted to be rescued, why would she run? Come on, Cara, think! We know everything about you. We know where you live, where you work. I went past your mum's just now. She's on her own, isn't she? You've seen what happens when we get angry. Don't do it to your mum, you're all she's got now." The hairs all over my body rise as his words flow like a flood of freezing water through me.

"I keep thinking, about a barrel of petrol and a match," he says in his quiet voice. "What a show that would be."

I see Mum asleep on the sofa, then her eyes flip open and her skin starts to bubble and melt. I press my hands down onto the barbed wire behind me, feel it slide out of me, the shock of it makes me panic. I try to move away from the edge, but he won't let me go, he forces me back again. I cry out as the barbed wire presses like a dagger but he just keeps talking, his soft words like drugs straight into my blood. I try to twist my face away from him, but he's everywhere.

"I know all about you and you don't even know my name." He's smiling again. I turn away, cover my face with my hands as he whispers right in my ear.

"That's it, Cara, good girl, keep your eyes and your mouth shut and you'll be safe, but open them and I swear to God you'll wish you listened to me."

I feel him pull away, but I don't move my hands, don't open my eyes. Fear has welded them shut. I fall to my knees, low, like I'm about to be executed. My breath is hard and jagged, my lungs feel full, sharp, small sacks of broken glass. I feel a line of blood ripple down my back. I smell the earth, ageless and wet with dew. I see Grace snarl and run away through the graves. I see Meg's forehead smashed, blood dark and sticky, then I see Mum's eyes flash open and I curl myself up tighter and I pray for it all to stop, to end now, and I keep low, curled on the ground, and hope the early morning sun will bleach it all away.

4th June 2019

If someone's reading this it means I've either been arrested or I'm dead. Either way, at least one person—you—will know what really happened to me, Zoe Grace Megan Nichols. Everything people think they know about me is a lie. The truth is this: I was never the sick one. She was.

Those are the only words I want to write. I could write them again and again and never grow tired. But this isn't a diary for me. I'm writing this for you, whoever you are. An explanation of sorts, so you know who she really was, how she made me sick, kept me small and stunted, her eternal little girl. I need you to know that when she squeezed my hand she was controlling, not comforting, me. When she read medical journals she was looking for ways to make me sick, not heal me. She kept me in a wheelchair until my muscles became so weak they forgot how to work and all the while she called it love. I need you to know all of this.

Before I got meningitis I don't think I'd ever seen her smile or heard her laugh. We lived each day in numb silence, as if Danny had only drowned the day before. She said it was Dad's fault, all this sadness. She threw herself down the stairs in front of him, though she told people later he had pushed her. He called her a crazy bitch before the front door banged shut after him for the last time. Mum would only take me out of the flat to visit Danny's grave after that. I ate sugar sandwiches I made myself. I didn't grow. I drew faces onto my fingers and called them my friends. Then, one morning, my skin seemed to be full of red-hot ants and there was a rash, like scales creeping up my arm. I couldn't move my neck. Everything went black and when I woke Mum was running with me boiling in her arms, screaming through the hospital, and, just like that, my life changed. Suddenly she noticed me. She stroked my hair, told me I was a good girl when I swallowed the pills she gave me. She kissed me and lied to the doctors about my symptoms, she wouldn't let me leave my bed for weeks. I remember the nurses telling Mum how small I was for my age and praising her for her courage. I've often wondered if it was then that she started to lie and pretend I was three years younger. It wasn't hard. No one would question such a devoted, loving mum. I was almost nine the first time she told me she loved me and I knew I'd do anything—even lie to the world about who I really was—to hear her say it again.

We got older, but I still didn't grow. I knew if I tried, if I really tried, I could move my legs more than any of the doctors thought, but it'd make Mum angry so I imagined they were made of stone and stopped moving them completely. My body ended at my waist. Mum said it wasn't my fault, but my muscles didn't work properly. Mum was my world. I believed her and so did the specialists. They did physical exams and more tests and said I had high levels of creatine kinase in my blood, which can be a sign of muscle disease—but can also be a sign of being forced to swallow statins. But the doctors didn't think of that. Why would they? Mum was perfect. No one questions the mother of a sick child. So instead they shook their heads, looked at the fake test results Mum got off the internet, prodded my wasted body a bit more before they said, "The most accurate diagnosis we can make is that Grace has muscular dystrophy. It's exceptionally rare in females, but it can happen. I'm so sorry." That night Mum made us chocolate mousse and we watched Disney films. It felt like my birthday.

I thought I was happy when we moved to Ashford. Mum told everyone I was seven. I knew it was a lie, that I was older, but I was always in my wheelchair then, shaved head, skinny, and thin as the drug addict I'd become. She called me Grace, she said it suited me better than Zoe. So Grace I became. Again, no one questioned Mum. She said being younger meant I could be her little girl for a few more years, and that changing my name helped keep Dad away, helped her keep me safe.

Years passed. I spent whole seasons in bed. She started giving me a new pill, bright pink. It made my mouth so slippery I couldn't swallow food anymore. Dr. Parker said I had dysphagia and Mum pretended to cry when another doctor decided it would be best for a PEG tube to be fitted in my stomach. I threw one of those pink pills across the room so Mum locked me in my bedroom without anything to eat or drink. She shouted that she'd never love me as much as she loved him. After two days I took the pill and a few months later I had the operation.

It was after the PEG tube was fitted that everything started to change again. People kept telling me I was going to be an adult soon, able to make my own decisions. I tried to stop them because it made Mum clench her jaw, grind up more pills. That's when I knew that somehow I had to escape. I was slowly starting to understand: Mum was addicted to attention, and who would get more attention than the mother of two dead children? Then, at last, we wanted the same thing, Mum and me. We both wanted Grace Nichols dead.

16

Jon

It takes me a while to compose myself enough to start the drive back to Ashford. The methodical nature of driving helps calm me, softens the horrifying images I have of Meg giving Grace drugs she didn't need. As I pull on to the highway my phone starts ringing. I shuffle it out of my pocket expecting to see Cara's name, but it's not Cara calling. It's Jakey. I click the speaker button and answer.

"Hi, mate."

"Hi, Dad."

"Shouldn't you be at school, Jakey?"

"Yeah, but I've got the dentist's this morning, so Mum's dropping me at school later." His voice is monotone, the vocal equivalent of heel-dragging.

"Everything OK? You sound a bit low."

"Auntie Emma came over last night." Ah. Ruth's twice-married and newly single best friend from her schooldays, who is in a determined man-hating phase. A hundred quid says I am the current target.

"Mum thought I was in bed. They'd been drinking wine and I heard them talking about you. They were saying some really shitty stuff, Dad."

"Jakey, don't swear."

"You do, so does Mum and Auntie Emma, all the time." There's a small squeak to his voice, a reminder that adolescence is right around the corner.

"Yeah, well, if you want, when you're in your forties, you can swear. Look, mate, I really want to talk to you face-to-face about what's going on, so how about I come over later, after school, and we can go and get burgers at that new American diner place Mum hates."

"Are you getting divorced?"

"No, mate!" I say it like it's the most ludicrous thing I've ever heard. "We're just going through a rough patch. Remember when you and Fred fell out for a bit? Well, it's just like that."

"I'm not friends with Fred anymore."

"OK, well, it's not just like that. Look, let me speak to your mum and I'll pick you up around six and we can have a proper chat—sound good?"

"Yeah, sounds good, Dad."

I know there's more he needs to say.

"Dad . . . are you getting close to finding that girl, Grace?"

"I think so, Jakey. I hope so."

There's the slightest tremor in his voice as he asks, "But you will find her, won't you?"

"Eventually, yes, we'll find her."

"Promise?"

"Promise." I regret it as soon as I've said it.

Jakey breathes out, relieved.

"Good."

"I'll see you later then, mate. Love you."

"Love you too, Dad," he says and my heart aches with each word.

I've just got back to the flat when Cara calls. I haven't heard from her since she ran away from me on Goat Beach, so it's a surprise.

"I need to speak to you," she says, her voice taut as a wire. "I'm coming over."

Something's happened. She doesn't sound angry with me anymore. She sounds terrified. It's still probably not a good idea for her to come here, in case anyone sees, but I can tell she's not in a mood to be told anything and, besides, I still feel jumpy from my meeting with Dr. Rossi. I need to offload, to ask Cara if she saw anything to confirm my suspicion that Meg was giving Grace extra drugs, drugs she didn't need.

Five minutes later the buzzer echoes through the flat. It's been so long since anyone came over it takes me a moment to find the receiver behind the old coats hanging in the hall. She walks into the flat like she's been here a hundred times. She barely looks around. I start talking as soon as she's through the door, eager to tell her everything I've learned from Dr. Rossi.

"Cara, I'm glad you called: you won't believe what I've found out. I was right about Grace's name and age. I was watching that video—you know the one, where Grace shows the camera the drugs cabinet—when I saw a name on one of the prescriptions . . . Jesus, Cara, what's wrong?"

She's standing in the middle of the tiny hall, her whole body

219

rattling. Only now I notice that her raincoat and the knees of her jeans are covered in mud. There's a smear across her face as well. Her skin is a strange color, almost blue, like the veins beneath have frozen. She looks even worse than she did at the beach. My first thought is that she's rowed with her mum, and Cara, being Cara, slept outside to prove a point. I usher her into the sitting room and clear piles of old newspapers from the brown cord sofa that came with the flat. I make her sit while I put the kettle on. I don't have any blankets or shawls—soft things were Ruth's department—and it feels weird bringing her my unchanged duvet, so instead I dig out my sleeping bag and wrap it around her on the sofa. I hand her a mug of sweet tea and am pleased to see as she sips that the rattling has become more of a shiver.

I grab a chair from the kitchen and sit opposite her. She closes her eyes and lets the tea warm her hands and face. I give her as long as I can bear before asking, "Cara, can you tell me what happened?"

"We need to stop, Jon." Her dry lips quiver around her words. "We have to stop all of it, it's too dangerous, we don't know what we're getting into. We just need to stop." She keeps her eyes fixed on her tea. "I met *GoodSam*," she says quietly, addressing the mug in her hands.

"You did what?" I wasn't expecting this.

"I saw Grace, Jon, I *saw Grace* and I couldn't just do nothing, pretend I hadn't seen her. I had to do something."

How fucking stupid of me. I should have guessed she would do something like this. If I'm honest, I'd probably have done the same if it had occurred to me to contact *GoodSam*, but I'm still livid with her for putting herself at risk.

"So you met up with a possible lead, someone we know nothing about, on your own and without even telling me? He could be a fucking kidnapper for all we know, Cara!" Simon has been transferred to a secure psychiatric unit, and Upton and others are trying to press him for information as much as they can. I still think Simon knows more than he's admitting but, having met him, my instinct is he's telling the truth—he doesn't know where Grace is, and I remember how clear his voice was: "I could never hurt Meg." That means the killer is still out there, it means *Good-Sam* could know where Grace is, he could be dangerous, and I'm livid with Cara for being so stupid.

"That's just it. I don't think he kidnapped her. I don't think anyone did."

I stare at Cara. Her face is pinched. She looks like I feel. Is she, like me, starting to question the authenticity of Grace's illnesses? If I'm right and Grace wasn't as sick as we thought, then it is possible Grace could walk, or even run. It is possible that Cara saw her in the graveyard.

At last Cara pulls her eyes away from mine. She lowers her head and starts sobbing into her chest.

"Oh shit, Cara," I say clumsily. I sit down on the sofa next to her. "God, I'm sorry, I'm sorry I didn't believe you."

Cara starts shaking her head to show that's not why she's crying. "We have to stop now. This, this person I met, he said stuff about my mum, about what he would do if we didn't stop . . ." Her voice trails away. She looks up at me and I see the fear, bright and alive behind her eyes. "And he said if we went to the police he'd hurt Mum. So we just . . . we just have to stop everything, OK?"

Her eyes seek reassurance. I look away, because I know I'm going to have to lie.

"OK, if that's what you want, OK."

"I mean it, Jon."

"I know you do," I say but I sound angry, frustrated, so I repeat, softer this time, "I know."

I pat her shoulder and she takes a sip of tea.

"Are you sure the person you met was *GoodSam*?"

"I don't know, but whoever he was, he knows Grace."

"Can you tell me a bit about him, what he was like?"

Cara rubs the heel of her hand over her eyes, like she's trying to wipe the shock of the last few hours away. She keeps her eyes closed as she says, "He was probably about thirty, white, tall, and really skinny."

"That's good, Cara. You remember what he was wearing?"

"Black, all black. He had a tattoo on his neck but I couldn't see what it was because he had his coat zipped up high like he was trying to hide it, but it was long and black, right here." She shows me on her thin neck.

"On the left?"

She thinks for a moment. "Yeah, on the left."

She opens her eyes, turns to look at me as she says, "Whoever he is, he's dangerous, violent. We have to stay away from him, Jon."

"Cara, if we don't do anything an innocent man might go to prison, and if we can't go to the police then, what choice do we have?"

"That's what I'm saying: we don't have a choice. We just have to stop everything. You promised." Her voice rises, her anxiety quickly escalating; she's terrified.

"OK, OK." I make myself sound calm, not wanting to upset her again. I want to point out I haven't promised anything, but I'd sound like a pedant and she's too exhausted, too traumatized to hear any more now.

"Do you want anything to eat? I could make you some toast,"

I say, forgetting I don't have any bread, or any food for that matter, but she shakes her head.

"No thanks. Would it be OK if I stay here for a few hours, just lie here and try to sleep for a bit? I can't face going home right now."

It's not ideal. I want to call Dave straight away, offer him money I don't have, and see what he can tell me about this bloke with the neck tattoo, but Cara's already snuggling down into the sleeping bag, yawning.

"I may have to go out for a bit," I say and the sleeping bag shrugs and mumbles, "I can let myself out," before it seems to sigh and then still.

I close the sitting-room door gently behind me and text Dave in the kitchen.

I need to talk to you. It's urgent.

Dave, most likely excited by the thought of another all-expenses-paid trip to the pub so soon after the last one, calls me back after just a few minutes. His voice is echoey; he sounds like he's in the toilet or a changing room, like he's gone somewhere private to speak with me.

"Dave, thanks for calling, mate."

"Yeah, you said it was urgent so I'm guessing you want to meet for a pint later?" He lets out a laddish snort of laughter. I feel unspeakably sad suddenly. I've duped this lonely man into confusing work with friendship.

"No, well, yeah, maybe. Look, I need some help. I'll pay—a hundred quid?" I stop myself from calling him mate.

"I'm listening."

"I need you to ID someone for me. Someone local, white male, anywhere up to midthirties I'd say, tall, slender build, with a tattoo on the left side of his neck. Someone who's been in trouble before."

The pause stretches, awkward, even across the phone line.

"I don't know, Jon, that's not really—"

"Just run a few searches, ask around a bit. He's local and most likely well known to you lot."

Dave pauses again. It makes me uneasy so I say, "OK, two hundred. I'll give you two hundred quid just to ask a couple of questions."

"Two hundred and a few pints when I finish at five?"

"OK. Done. I'll meet you at half past."

I spend most of the afternoon at the kitchen table, rereading old articles I find online about Danny's death and scouring a few photos Ben sent through from the *Chronicle*'s archive. The articles are old, sparse on detail. They mention the family from Plymouth staying for the weekend in Port Raynor Caravan Park, but mostly they're interested in what the council is going to do to stop any more accidents in the future. The photos are more helpful. There are a few of a much younger, healthier-looking Simon, his arm protectively around Meg's shoulders. It must have been a hot day. Meg's wearing a flowing caftan; her body is well hidden in most of the photos, but in one her right arm is curled around the dome of her lower belly, as though she's giving herself a hug. Grace was born that September so she would have been around six months pregnant when the photo was taken. I try to remember how big Ruth was at six months, but I can't, not really. I stare at her belly until my eyes start to blur, and at some point I must drop my head onto the table because I wake two hours later with a crick in my neck and my glasses squashed across my face. I stand and move slowly into the sitting room but Cara's already left, the sleeping bag carefully rolled up at the end of the sofa. I understand why she's terrified, but if I'm right and Meg was giving Grace drugs, then that changes everything. If she wasn't kidnapped but ran away from Meg herself, she doesn't need to be rescued, she needs to be found for questioning, to find out what happened that night. Her own father's future is on the line—and so is mine. There's no way I can stop now.

The Red Dragon is quiet at half past five; the few lone drinkers stare dull-eyed into their fast-emptying pints like fortune-tellers searching for answers in tea leaves. The bank only let me take out a hundred quid. I'll just have to convince Dave I'm good for the rest. He's already sitting at a round table, his legs curled under the small stool like a fat jockey. I wish I could ask him straightaway about the envelope sitting on the table in front of him, but Dave needs a chat first and I need to keep him on my side.

"All right, Dave. Pint?"

I get the drinks and let Dave talk about football while the envelope burns between us. He catches me looking.

"OK, mate, I can take a hint," he says, "but first . . ." He rubs his fingers and thumb together a few times and I hand him the hundred quid.

"I'll get the rest to you tomorrow."

Dave looks at the notes in his hand, raises an eyebrow. "And there's me thinking all you city lot were loaded."

"I'll get the rest to you, Dave, I promise."

"To be honest, mate, I feel like I'm robbing you for the hundred, never mind two. Let's call it quits."

I nod dumbly. Acts of kindness always take me by surprise.

Ruth would call me a cynic, say it's the Londoner in me, but I prefer to be surprised by kindness rather than anticipate it.

"So, anyone in the records match the description I gave you?"

Dave's stool wails beneath him as he leans across the table towards me and says, "Not exactly."

"What do you mean, 'not exactly'?"

"OK, so no one matches the description. No young man with a tattoo on his neck."

My heart sinks. I realize how much I was hoping he'd find him. But Dave raises a finger.

"However," he says, "one of my colleagues reminded me of the Craigs."

Dave takes a pull on his pint, savoring the moment.

"The Craigs?"

Dave wipes a bit of foam from his top lip with the back of his meaty hand. "The Craig family have been known to Ashford police since well before my time. They've been petty criminals— shoplifting, that sort of thing—probably since shoplifting was invented. They travel around a bit, always keeping in the South West, mostly Cornwall but sometimes as far north as Taunton. It can be hard keeping tabs on where they're living. They've given us the runaround a few times."

"OK, so the guy with the tattoo is known to you, then? He's one of these Craigs?"

"Not exactly, Jon. Stop rushing me."

I feel my phone buzz in my pocket but it's easy to ignore. The only important thing is happening right here, right now. Dave takes another lazy pull on his pint and slowly slides a thick finger under the flap on the envelope, pulls out a mugshot, and hands it to me. The photo is of a young man, wide-eyed but vacant-looking. He looks like he's in his late twenties but could be older, his neck skinny and long as a cormorant's, with a pronounced Adam's apple and sharp cheekbones. His eyes are wide but full of regret, like a schoolboy after a telling-off.

"So he got the tattoo after this arrest?" I ask, bored by Dave moving so slowly, but he smiles at me and shakes his head.

"This is Anthony Craig, who's been arrested by us twelve times since he was sixteen—drink, drugs, fighting. Arrested him myself once, found him a bit of a softie actually. That last time was for grievous bodily harm—beat some poor bloke to a pulp outside a pub. He pleaded guilty and got six months but was out in four." Dave scrunches up his face before he glances over his shoulder, as though he thinks one of the old drunks propped up on the bar might be listening in, and says, "I don't have a photo of Robert, or Robbie, Craig"—he pushes a finger into the bony chest of the kid in the photo—"Anthony Craig's identical twin brother."

That one little word is like a triple espresso straight into my veins.

The twins.

I thought Simon's ramblings were just a part of his psychosis. I never thought he could be trying to give me a clue.

Dave keeps talking. "Robbie Craig used to work at that tattoo place in town and, according to a couple of the boys at work, Robbie's the type who thinks getting tattoos is some kind of hobby." Dave stabs the photo of Robbie with his forefinger again. "I've never met him, but apparently he's the one we need to keep our eye on. A couple of them even reckon it was Robbie, not Tony, who beat up that bloke, but, for whatever reason, it was Tony who took the flak."

It must be them. I take a gulp of my pint to try to hide my excitement.

"So they're from Ashford, are they?"

Dave shakes his head. "Couple of hours north, near Rainstead. Their folks used to work in tourism, a hostel or something, before their mum died of cancer when the boys were still nippers. The dad couldn't cope, ran the business into the ground, got into debt, and moved to Spain when the boys weren't even ten years old. They were in and out of the care system after that, which is when they started getting into trouble."

Was Simon in touch with these Craig twins all along? Maybe it was through them that Grace communicated with her dad—asked him to try to call her. I take another gulp of beer to try to hide the smile I feel creeping across my face. But it's too late. Dave's eyes narrow at me and he looks guilty, like he's just told someone else's secret.

"What's this about, then, Jon? Nothing we should be involved in, I hope?"

I shake my head like Dave's being crazy. In my pocket my phone starts vibrating again. Again I ignore it.

"Just about old Mr. Leeson up at Franton Farm. He reckons he saw a skinny bloke with tattoos out with a couple of big dogs in one of his fields. He thinks they could be the ones killing his sheep."

Dave chuckles, amused I'm wasting my time on Mr. Leeson. He shakes his head at me and says through his laughter, "Rather you than me, mate. Rather you than me."

"So is this Robbie still working at the tattoo place?"

Dave wipes an invisible tear of laughter from his eye and shakes his head. "Apparently not. One of the boys reckons Robbie's been trying his luck with long-distance truck driving, says he got his license sometime last year. I had a quick look and it turns out he's registered with some place out near Rainstead, up on the north coast. JPH Haulage, or something like that. Why all this trouble for old Leeson anyway, Jon?"

I shrug, trying to make myself seem casual as my mind cartwheels with the new information. "Someone had to start taking him seriously."

My phone rings a third time. I'm sure Dave's told me all he knows and I'm ready to go now. The phone call is perfectly timed. My heart freezes as I see the number for New Barn Cottage.

"Where the fuck are you?" Ruth sounds dangerous. She's not shouting, but her voice is thick with rage. I imagine the muscle in her neck twitching. I search around my head for somewhere other than here that I should be. I thought our meetings with Dr. Bunce were over. I look at Dave, point at my phone as I move away towards the toilets. Ruth starts laughing, joylessly, down the line.

"You forgot, didn't you? Our son has been waiting for you for the last forty-five minutes, Jon. You were taking him out for 'boys' burgers' after school, he said."

"Oh fuck." I see Jakey waiting outside the house, checking the time on his phone, staring down the road for my car, checking the time again, and my heart withers to ash.

"Can you put him on?"

Ruth pauses. She knows how important it is for Jakey and I to have a good relationship, for us both.

"Wait a minute," she says and I hear her feet running up the stairs. I picture her hand pushing Jakey's bedroom door open, picture him facedown and burning with rage on his bed. Ruth's muffled voice comes through the receiver, she sounds conciliatory, pleading, but Jakey's reply is short and angry and I know he won't talk to me.

"He doesn't want to talk to you at the moment," Ruth says, playing the peacemaker. Brownie points for Ruth.

"OK, OK, that's fair enough. Can you just tell him one thing for me?"

Ruth makes a gravelly sound in her throat, like she's about to lose it with me

"Please, Ruth, just one thing. Tell him I'm sorry, and tell him I'm going to find Grace. I'm going to find Grace for him."

Ruth snorts down the phone. I hear her trudge back downstairs as she says, "Jon, are you losing your fucking mind? Is that what's going on here? You can't even keep a burger date with our son and you're trying to play the hero?"

She waits for me to lash back at her, but I bite my tongue.

"You're delusional, Jon," she says and hangs up.

Ten minutes later I've left Dave in the pub with his hundred quid and am on my way home. I'm furious with myself for forgetting my promise to Jakey, but my anger is weighted by the realization that I might just be able to keep my bigger, far more important promise. I might be able to find Grace, or at least find out what happened to her. I heave my guilt onto a distant shelf in my mind, somewhere I rarely bother to reach. I need to think now. On the drive an endless loop of questions is running through my head, about the twins and why and how Grace got mixed up with them. Grace led a sheltered life, she'd be the last person to come across career criminals like the Craigs. Why would one of the twins be interested in a disabled kid unless there was something connecting them, something I can't see? Could it be the pills Dr. Rossi prescribed? Simon knew about the twins, so it can't be a coincidence. Could he have known they were involved with Grace's disappearance? The way he said it—*the twins*—it sounded as though

I should already know them. But then again, he wasn't making much sense at the time; I have no real idea if he can be trusted.

The twins. I think about the first time we met in that busy café, wonder whether Simon mentioned anything then. Maybe I didn't pick up on it before, too focused on the article. It's worth a shot.

As soon as the front door shuts behind me I clatter through the flat searching for my Dictaphone. Simon's interview tape is still in the machine. I find it at last, under some unopened mail on the kitchen table. Simon's voice is a squiggle as I rewind the tape back to the moment when he talked about the day Danny died. Then his voice crackles, alive in my kitchen.

"Then I saw those boys. They were only about eight, identical. I thought it was a bit odd they were on their own, running like hares down the path to the cove."

I rewind, press PLAY again. "They were only about eight, identical." Rewind, play: "identical." I listen to Simon say the word "identical" again and again until the word itself seems to break down and starts to sound like another language entirely, and suddenly everything around me feels sharper because it's starting to make sense. Somehow Grace got involved with these twins, these brothers, the same eight-year-old boys who were there all those years ago, on 6 June 1998. The boys who watched Danny drown.

17

Cara

After I leave Jon's flat I get the bus home. I don't like being out-side, it makes me feel exposed. I see his thin face in every stranger. For the first time since all this happened, I just want to be home.

Mum seems surprised but pleased when I collapse into her arms. I breathe in her particular mix of hairspray and the pear-drop smell of nail polish. She strokes my hair and I feel a little safer. She doesn't ask where I've been and neither of us mentions the row. I don't even care anymore if she knew Grace and Meg were lying about Grace's age, if she knew Grace's real name. She would have been trying to protect Meg, trying to be a good friend and keep her secrets. There's no harm in that. Besides, those things are nothing compared to the revelation that Grace can walk, even run. The only thing that matters to me now is that Mum and I are together, safe. It's a sunny day so Mum draws the curtains in the sitting room and brings me hot drinks while I lie on the sofa. I keep my eyes open. Whenever I close them I sense him, as though he's waiting for me in the thin space between my eyelid and eyeball. He's always smiling at me. I'm grateful Mum doesn't ask any questions. She just seems relieved to have me home. I listen to her whisper to Zara on the phone in the kitchen.

"You were right, Zar, she needed time, just like you said. Repressed trauma."

I imagine Zara smiling, congratulating herself on being right.

"I'll keep a close eye on her: she needs to be reassured that Simon can't get to us. Poor love has had a worse time than any of us, after all. I'm going to take a few days off, stay here with her, if that's OK with you?"

I'll let her think it's Simon I'm frightened of, not *GoodSam*, with his sharp teeth and cruel, laughing eyes. My back itches where the barbed wire broke through my skin. I curl up, tighter. I want to stay here forever, tiny and hidden from the world. I try not to think too much, but it's the fear I can't control. It comes for me like a frost, sudden and silent, leaving me petrified. I see Grace's spilt chair again, the sticky dent where Meg's forehead once was. I feel the force of the blow from the lamp again and again, like a fist to my stomach. I hear the sound horribly dulled as he crushed the precious alleys and paths full of Meg's life, her memories, her joy. I wonder what part of her he killed last.

At some point during the afternoon the doorbell rings and I hear Martin and Sylvia asking questions about me. I wonder how long it'll be until the whole estate knows that I've finally crashed, as I'm sure they all said I would. Mum runs me a bath and afterwards, when my skin is pink and steaming, she makes me get into bed and without me asking brings beans on toast for dinner. She sits on the end of my bed, propped up on her elbow, watching me, smiling with every mouthful.

"This reminds me of when you were little, Car, remember?"

I don't remember a specific time, but Mum does.

"It was just after your dad buggered off. You cried so hard you made yourself sick."

She says it with a small smile, like it's a happy memory, not one full of misery. She pats my leg through the duvet. I feel like her pet but I don't care.

"I think we should both take a few days off work. I want you to recover properly from everything. You rushed too much last time, that's why we've ended up back here. But this time I just want you to take it really easy for a good few days, OK?" She takes a bottle of unmarked pills out of her cardigan pocket. "Meg gave me these a few months ago when I was going through that patch of insomnia—do you remember?"

I don't, but I nod.

"They're just pills to help with sleep, they sort of melt everything negative away so your mind doesn't churn right before bed. Once you've finished eating I want to see you take a couple and then you'll have a good night's rest and we can see where we are in the morning . . ."

Mum's other cardigan pocket starts to glow and vibrate with a phone call. She looks at the screen and says, "It's only Zara, I'll call her back later." She drops the phone back in her pocket; it stills for a moment. She frowns at my half-finished food, before taking out the phone, which has started ringing again.

"You should answer it, Mum," I say, flicking a few crumbs off the duvet. "It might be something important."

She gives me an "Are you sure?" look before sitting up and pressing the answer button.

"Zar, I'm just busy now with Cara, she's—" but Mum doesn't

finish what she's about to say. I hear Zara's voice, small but urgent on the end of the line.

"Oh God, really?" Mum says. My bed rises as she stands. I feel all my back muscles tense.

"You're sure?" Mum sounds almost excited.

Zara babbles some more on the other end of the phone. I tell myself it doesn't necessarily mean something bad. Knowing Zara, it could be anything from Grace being found to an unexpected sale in Topshop.

"God," Mum says, phone clamped to her ear as she walks across the hall and stares at the pictures on the hall wall. "I can't figure out whether this is good news or not. So it's a secure unit, is it?"

I'm out of bed now. I don't want to miss anything.

"What is it?" I mouth at Mum but she just shakes her head. She needs to concentrate.

My insides twist and I think of Jon. Has he gone and done something stupid? Got himself arrested again?

Mum's nodding along with whatever Zara's saying, before at last she rounds off the call.

"OK, Zar, well, thanks for letting me know. Pop over for tea tomorrow if you want. Cara and I will be here." She turns to me, smiling at the thought that we'll be here tomorrow, together. She hangs up, drops the phone back into her pocket with a long exhale.

"What is it, Mum?"

She takes my hand and, turning towards me, says, "I don't want to upset you, Car, but you should know. It's not . . . it's not nice but it may help you feel a bit safer." She's trying hard to smooth away the smile that keeps creeping onto her lips. "Simon Davis tried to kill himself this morning."

I feel my body twitch involuntarily. Mum doesn't notice, and keeps talking.

"You know Zara's cousin Remi is dating a police officer? Well, he told Remi and of course Remi told Zara." Mum lowers her voice to a whisper. It sounds mean, too gleeful for the words. "He was in a secure psychiatric hospital but he got a razor from somewhere. He must have made such a mess." I see the dark red rust color of Meg's broken head.

"Oh, Car, you look terrified. Sorry, love, I didn't mean to upset you." She pulls me into a hug, rocks me back and forth. I smell all the chemicals on her. I can't breathe.

"Shhhh, shhhh," Mum sighs into my ear even though I'm not making any noise. At last she lets me go, still holding my hand, and smiles at me sadly.

"Come on, get back under the covers." I let her lead me and she sits back on the end of my bed. It makes me think of all those times I saw Meg sitting on the end of Grace's bed.

"I can't decide whether I'm glad they caught him in time so we can fight for justice, or if I wish he'd managed it, saved us all the pain of the trial," Mum says.

I swallow and try to look like I don't care either way.

"Mum, I'm feeling really knackered again, I think maybe I'll try to go back to sleep if that's OK." I wriggle down under the duvet. Mum smiles and strokes my hair.

"You want me to stay with you, Car? I don't mind." Under her palm, I shake my head.

"I'll be all right, Mum, I promise, I just want to sleep." I hear her pick up the bottle of pills she left next to me.

"I'm leaving two here for you, by your water glass. I think you should take them."

"Maybe later. Thanks, Mum."

Outside, the sky is the inside of a shell, all pink and peach. Mum draws the curtains against it, as though the beauty of it will make me feel worse.

"Good night, darling." She leans over and kisses me. "Love you."

"You too, Mum."

I don't realize I've been holding my breath until at last Mum closes the door behind her and I feel my lungs relax. There's a buzzing sound in my head, like my thoughts are all out of tune with each other. Simon tried to kill himself. I can't imagine his desperation, the loneliness of knowing the truth but feeling the world turn its back. Simon didn't kill Meg and he didn't try to hurt Grace. I bet Danny's death wasn't his fault either. I think all this, but I can't prove any of it, and I'm presented with a choice: either I join everyone I love and ignore my instincts about Simon or I fight for him because I know he's innocent and he can't fight for himself. As soon as the question takes shape in my head, I've answered it.

I pick up my phone from my bedside table and scroll through my contacts. The sound of meticulously planned laughter echoes out of the sitting room; Mum's watching one of her talk shows. Jon picks up after just one ring.

"Cara, how are you feeling? Any better?" His voice is softer than usual.

"Yeah. Look, Jon, Mum just told me something."

Jon swears softly when I tell him about Simon. I don't mention the razor; I don't want to picture any more blood.

Through the phone I hear the sound of a car door slamming shut.

"Where are you going?" I ask in a loud whisper.

"It doesn't matter, Cara, you need to stay at home, be with your mum for a while."

As he says it I know he's wrong, I don't need to be here. I need to know who Grace really is—whether she's being held against her will or not. I need to know whether *GoodSam* or someone else was waiting for her in the shadows at the graveyard, whether they're controlling her. But then I remember the way she looked at me, the sneer on her lips, the fact she was lying to us all about being able to walk, about her age. She didn't look like a victim. This isn't over. Not yet.

I pull off the duvet. My legs feel heavy from lack of use after only a few hours and I shake them back into life. Mum folded my jeans neatly on the chair in my room. I grab them and start to pull them on as I keep the phone fixed to my ear.

"You spoke to the bloke you know in the police, didn't you?" I say, knowing I'm right—it's what I'd have done if I were him. He knows something.

Jon doesn't say anything for a while, weighing whether to tell me or not. I cup my hand round my mouth, force myself to talk quietly.

"Look, I'm the only one who's seen *GoodSam* or whatever his name is. I'm the only one who's seen Grace since she was taken, I know what she looks like now. You think even if you do find her that she's going to talk to you? A reporter who's screwed her and her dead mum over once before? Of course she won't. She'll never talk to you, Jon, but she knows me. Remember how she talked about me in the diary? She always looked up to me. She'll listen to me."

Jon's quiet on the other end of the line, thinking. I know he wants to keep me safe, but he also knows I can help. At last he says, "Look, if I agree to this it's on the understanding that you'll do as I say."

"Of course."

"No bloody running off and meeting up with psychopaths on your own. Understand?"

"Yes, yes, I promise."

"If I tell you to stay or if I tell you to go somewhere, you do it without messing around, without even questioning me."

"Agreed."

"And, Cara, do your mum a favor: don't just disappear, talk to her, let her know you're OK, that you'll be safe, and that you'll be back tomorrow. If you do all that then we have a deal."

"Thanks, Jon."

I have no idea what I'm going to tell Mum. I grab a T-shirt out of my drawers. "I'll meet you at Goat Beach, same spot as before?"

"I'll be there in ten minutes," he says.

Underneath the concern, there's a hint of excitement in his voice and I think he's secretly pleased I'm coming along. I want to ask him what he knows, where we're going, but I know it's best for us to talk in person.

"See you soon, then," I say, before I hang up. I finish getting dressed and grab my backpack, shove in some overnight stuff before picking up a notepad and chewed pen. *Mum—I'm sorry. I can't tell you where I've gone but I promise I'm safe and will be home tomorrow. Please try not to worry too much.*

I pause before I write, *I love you. Cara x.*

I open my bedroom window and, dropping my bag outside to the ground first, I crawl through the open window and jump down into the golden late afternoon light, the smell of cut grass and warm asphalt immediately filling me with hope. I start walking quickly towards the park and remember the only piece of advice my dad ever gave me, when I was small and terrified of the dark. He told me that monsters are always scarier when you stay and wait for them, that if you call them out and look them straight in the face they're usually not as bad as they seemed. Now, as I walk towards *GoodSam*, I find myself hoping that, for once, Dad was right.

Raynor Beach
5th June 2019

I didn't think I'd ever get away from her. I tried to tell a nurse once—"Mum gives me pills I don't need"—but the nurse looked at me as though I'd slapped her clean across the face. I was going to tell Cara but Mum got there first. She saw us becoming close and stopped us from being alone. Then Cara stopped visiting altogether and I felt a new space open up inside me, a hollow where hope used to be.

A part of me gave up. I thought I'd be lying next to Danny soon, my grave freshly earthed. I saw us—Danny and me—as ghosts in the cemetery, together at last. It didn't sound so bad. I took all the drugs she gave me and I fell deeper into the lie my life had become. No one knew who I really was. I didn't know who I was, not anymore. I was lost even to myself.

It was winter, soon after the operation to fit my PEG tube, when everything changed. Mum had given me so many different drugs I'd been out of it for days. I was on the sofa, wrapped in blankets and, as a reward for being so sick, Mum let me look at our Facebook page. I only had a few minutes, but it was enough. A message flashed up from a boy: Tony Craig. He was so thin in his picture I thought at first that he was sick too and just wanted someone to talk to, but when I opened his message I saw I was wrong.

Hello Grace,

You won't remember me but my name is Tony and I was there when your brother died. I knew he was in trouble in the water, so did my brother. I wanted to help but I couldn't. I've felt guilty ever since. I want you to know that I still think about him and I'm sorry. I met your dad a few months ago, he told me you were sick and that I should help you. He wasn't in a good way, I'm sorry about that too. I don't know what I can do really but I want to make things right so here I am. I can't make up for my past, for letting your brother down, but maybe I can do something for you. Anything you need, just let me know. I'd like to help if I can.

Cheers,
Tony

His message was brief but powerful. It changed me. I admit I was angry at first. If this Tony and his brother had helped Danny, then he might have been saved and all our lives could have been so different. But what's the point in being angry? It won't change anything. Instead I focused on the fact that Tony had spoken to my dad, that he wanted to help me. I felt a sort of blooming inside. Before I deleted his message I replied, asking him to set up a profile on the Wishmakers forum. I told him to use the name GoodSam because he was my Good Samaritan. I told him to find ForeverGrace.

GoodSam and ForeverGrace started messaging each other every day. I just wanted a friend, a normal friend. He told me about music he liked, gigs he was going to, he even said he'd take me to one. He didn't understand when I said I couldn't, that Mum would never let me. I didn't mean to tell him what she was doing. The words just fell out of me and then I couldn't get them back. After that we didn't talk about music anymore. He said I was brave, thanked me for being honest with him, said that he wanted to be honest with me. He told me he'd had a bad life. That his mum died just a few months before Danny drowned, that a couple of years later his dad left him and his brother to fend for themselves. He said he only realized recently that the guilt of not helping Danny all those years ago still consumed him, made him angry, prone to violence. The twins were put into separate foster homes when they were teenagers and Tony fell in with a bad crowd. He told me he'd just left prison but said he was different now. He'd taken a course while he was in prison that made him realize how he could change his life. He wanted to be a better person, to make up for mistakes he'd made in the past. He was in Plymouth when he saw my dad, walking along a road. Tony tried to talk to him but Dad got upset, angry. But a few days later Dad contacted him and said the only way Tony could make up for not helping Danny was to help me. Tony said we weren't so different, me and him, we'd both been trapped in lives we didn't choose. He said he was my friend, that he was going to help. At first he said we should call the police, tell them what Mum was doing to me, but I said no. Even after everything I didn't want to punish Mum. So Tony started making up plans for how I could get away. I thought we were playing, messing around, like I know friends do. But I know nothing about friendship and didn't know anything about Tony, not really. He wasn't joking. I said I wanted her to wake up one morning, come into my room, and find me gone. I told him I just wanted a chance *at a new life. He said he understood. But it's only now I know he didn't, he didn't understand at all.*

At first, I just watched her. Counted how many pills she took from each bottle, how she ground them all up together in the pestle and mortar, how she mixed them with my food before sucking it all up into the plastic syringe and fixing it to the hole in my stomach. She let me count out my pills. Then, after a while, she let me grind. She was watching me grind my pills one evening when the doorbell rang. While Mum talked to Susie about what color she should dye her hair I hid three of the pills in my underwear and ground up some extra acetaminophen so Mum didn't notice the difference when I showed her the powder. She kissed me, called me a good girl, before I leant back on the bed and lifted up my top.

It took months, but I hid more and more pills. I started going through withdrawal, my body shook, but I was hardened to the pain. Mum said she loved me even more. I stayed in bed, slept all day. But as the drugs left my system and I started to feel stronger, at night when I heard Mum snoring across the hall I'd practice my walking. It was painful at first, my bones felt dried out and brittle, my muscles weak and floppy like wet spaghetti. But slowly my bones and muscles hardened and as I got physically stronger it felt more and more possible. I started to believe I could get away. That I could live.

We decided we'd do it in the summer, June 3rd. We deleted our messages to each other. No one was ever supposed to get hurt, but it still felt safer that way. The plan went like this: I'd pump Mum full of the pills I'd been hiding and while she was sleeping we'd take the red box of donations. It was my money, after all. There must have been a few thousand pounds in the box—Tony said I had to give it to him for getting me away. He would take me some-where safe to change my clothes, my appearance. Then, at first light, Tony would take me to a place called Rainstead where his twin brother, Robbie, would smuggle me to Holland in his truck. Tony said everyone wanted to get into the country, no one was interested in people trying to leave. He made it sound easy. After all, everyone was looking for a disabled teenager, not an able-bodied young woman. But I didn't understand then what I see so clearly now. The golden rule—either I'd die or Mum would have to die. We couldn't both survive the truth.

18

Jon

Cara still looks unwell, the skin under her eyes sags with purplish half-moons and she seems smaller somehow. She's fully alert, though, sitting forward in the passenger seat next to me, and she's not shaking anymore, which is definitely a good sign.

As we drive, I tell her everything. I tell her about how mad Simon seemed in our meeting, how he whispered in my ear. I tell her about meeting Dave, what he told me about the twins, and I tell her about Dr. Rossi, how Meg blackmailed her for years and how Meg was able to change Grace's name and birthdate on her medical records. I explain we're driving to a haulage company just outside Rainstead, which Robbie Craig registered as his place of work. She takes it all in, her eyes wide. I thought she'd be swearing, livid that I kept on digging when she asked me not to, but she seems beyond recriminations now. She just wants to find out the truth. I wait until I find a quiet lane to pull into before I stop the car to tell her what Meg was doing to Grace. I turn to Cara. She's confused, but knows me well enough now to know I have something important to say.

"Have you ever heard of Munchausen by proxy?"

Cara shakes her head.

"I'd only heard of it at work a couple of times, but I did some reading last night. It's a mental-health problem where a caregiver fabricates and induces illness. I don't think Grace was ill, Cara. I think Meg was."

As my words land, Cara's face twists with confusion. She starts shaking her head. "I don't . . . I don't understand."

"Meg stole, bought, or got drugs through blackmailing people. She forced the drugs on Grace, to give her the symptoms for epilepsy, muscular dystrophy, heart problems—all of it. Her illnesses were fabricated by Meg. That's why Grace could run away in the graveyard. Her legs always worked, they were just forced not to."

"Why, why would she do that?" Cara's voice is a whisper. Her eyes flit about my face, desperate for an answer, an answer that will make everything I just said less horrifying. But I can't give her one.

"Cara, maybe we should talk about—"

"Just tell me! Why did she do it?" Cara's almost shouting. She won't be fobbed off, she needs answers.

"Partly money maybe—think about all the fundraisers and support they received—but I think the real reason was deeper. Like everyone, I think Meg just wanted to be loved. She wanted people's attention, their admiration, their respect. Maybe she thought she deserved it after Danny died. Maybe she was so delusional, her illness so entrenched, that she even believed Grace really was sick. I don't know yet."

I've said enough. I don't mention how this revelation totally reframes Meg's murder because, next to me, Cara has gone very still. She's staring at something only she can see, her face full of a private horror and deep sadness, a place only for her and Grace. She opens the car door.

"Cara, please don't—"

"I just need a minute on my own."

I nod. I understand some things shouldn't be shared. She disappears behind the car and in the rearview mirror I watch as she walks into a field and, hidden behind a hedgerow, drops to her knees on the sun-hardened earth. She covers her head with her hands and she starts to shake with sorrow and rage before I look away.

She comes back to the car a few minutes later, her face puffed and her eyes red and raw, but her expression is hard, set. I ask if she's all right and she just nods and says, "I'm fine." We drive the rest of the way in silence, the unsettled kind of silence that seems to hum with thoughts. Neither of us knows how this is going to play out, neither of us even wants to guess.

As we near Rainstead, Cara starts to move around in her seat.

"You all right?" I ask again, turning my head to look at her. She nods, looks at me for a moment, and I know that, for now at least, the shock has passed and she's as determined as me to find out how this will end.

The headquarters for JPH Haulage and Sons is down a track that opens onto a muddy space about the size of a football pitch. There are a few truck cabs parked at the far end. The office is a green modular building on stilts, it's warm looking against a large wall built out of cinder blocks. I notice there's razor wire strung across the top. Cara reaches to open her door.

"No, Cara, you're staying in the car."

"Don't be like that," she says but then I take her wrist, probably firmer than I need to.

"We had an agreement that you'd do as I say. Don't make me regret bringing you with me." I'm using the same warning tone I use for Jakey when I need him to really listen to me. She looks at me. I know I sound patronizing, but at least she recognizes I'm serious. She nods, I let go of her wrist, and she shuts the door.

"Keep the doors locked and the engine running, OK?" She doesn't argue. I feel her watching as I walk towards the office. I find myself worrying, of all things, that all this trauma will make Cara lose her spark, her courage. I push the thoughts from my mind and make myself focus on the sign that hangs inside the door in front of me: OUT OF HOURS PLEASE RING THE BELL FOR ASSISTANCE.

The bell feels sticky under my finger. There's black paper stuck up in the glass panels of the door so whoever is outside can't see what's going on inside. I try the bell again and a sharp female voice calls from inside.

"Larry, that you?"

I take a deep breath, try to keep London out of my voice.

"No, I'm not Larry, I'm just here to ask after some work."

The modular building quivers as heavy footsteps approach the door.

"Oh. Not from the council, are you?" She sounds Cornish born and bred.

"Not from the council, no." I soften my vowels in a way I hope sounds authentic. A key rattles in the lock before the thin plastic door opens, followed by a puff of stale cigarette smoke. Her large body fills the doorway. She has thin, wispy hair and small eyes like raisins stuck in the thick dough of her face. She doesn't try to hide what she's doing as she looks me up and down. I suddenly feel lost, totally out of my depth. I struggle to remember why I'm here.

"What's yer name?"

"Jon, my name's Jon."

"You wanting work, are you? Cos we're not taking anyone new on, not now, so if yer here for work yer may as well leave right now."

She bends her head and hacks a cough that sounds well rooted into the crook of her arm. There'll be no charming her, I know. My only chance is to be upfront.

"I'm looking for someone, one of your drivers."

"Oh yeah?" Her dark eyes move across my face.

"Robert Craig—he's one of yours, isn't he?"

"Might be," she says. "What's it to you?"

"He's an old mate of mine. I used to know him and his brother when they lived in Taunton."

"Oh. Well, see, that sounds like bollocks to me, Mr. Jon." She laughs. It becomes more of a splutter before breaking into a thick, phlegmy cough when she sees my face. "I know that's bollocks cos no one who actually knew Robbie would ever call 'im Robert." She rolls the Rs in "Robert," taking the piss.

I stand my ground even though I feel my face burn.

"Look, I'm just an old mate like I said. I used to know the two of them, Robbie and Tony, when they were small. I'm in town for a night and wanted to see if Robbie's around for a pint, is all."

The woman starts fishing around in one of the large pockets of her stretched hoodie. She finds what she's looking for and pulls out a pouch of green tobacco. She starts rolling a cigarette with one hand, as though her fingers were designed for the work. It's rolled, licked, and lit in a matter of seconds. One beady eye winces as it fills with smoke. Her lips move around the cigarette as she talks.

"As it happens, yer in luck. Robbie pissed me right off, canceling his trip to Holland at the eleventh hour last week. Said it was family bother, but we all know what that means. Only family he's got left is that bloody brother of his. Look, I don't give two shits whether yer a mate like you say or not, just make sure the little prick turns up tomorrow morning for his trip. Tell him from Mandy that if he don't, then we don't want ter see him here again. Hear?"

I nod.

She scowls, waits for a second before growling, "I said, hear?"

"Yes, yes I got it. So, do you have his address?"

She snorts at me, like having an address is the poshest thing she's heard of in her life.

"I might be pissed off with 'im but I'm not that pissed off. I'm not going to give yer his fucking address or his number so don't even bother asking."

The paper from her cigarette sticks to her lips as she pulls it free. A curl of tobacco is left on her bottom lip.

"What I will tell yer is that it's a tradition for blokes before a trip, especially a long haul, to go to the Bull in Rainstead the night before. They think it's good luck to drink themselves even more stupid before they go."

Rainstead is just a few miles down the road. I smile my thanks at her. She looks flatly back at me and says, "If yer here for trouble, mind, don't you let onto him or anyone I sent yer or y'll have a whole fleet of hard bastards on yer back. Hear?"

I nod and slowly start to back away. As I do, she looks over towards my car, sees Cara in the front seat, looks at me again with her suspicious eyes, and without warning slams the door, the whole modular building shaking as she stamps heavily back to wherever she came from.

If Cornwall were a family, then Rainstead would be the distant cousin no one ever likes to mention. It wasn't always this way. I remember Ruth telling me that when she was a girl her mum would drive all the way to Rainstead to buy fish. It was a small fishing port back then, quaint and unchanged for generations before quotas took effect, suffocating business for independent fishing companies. The coastline had become a graveyard of small boats. Sometime in the late eighties, the council built a one-way system that coiled around the town, literally in the shape of a noose. It didn't take long for the high street to go the same way as the fishing boats. Now, faded signs are the only clue that there used to be shops behind the boarded-up windows and doors. The only surviving places are a bookie's, a pound shop, a Tesco's, and two pubs. Cara shrinks in her seat as we pass the Bull, where Robbie and his mates will be drinking tonight. The second pub, the Lamb, is up on a hill on the road out of town, as though the building itself is desperately trying to find a way to leave Rainstead. I pull into the parking lot to turn around, go back the way we came in the hope we'll find a B&B, when Cara nudges me and points to an old wooden frame that says ROOMS AVAILABLE hanging by the front door. I don't see any TripAdvisor stickers or hygiene scores stuck to the door.

"We'll find somewhere else," I say, pointing the car out of the parking lot, when Cara says, "Don't be a stuck-up Londoner. Come on, it's only for one night, it'll be fine. You park, I'll see if they have rooms free."

I'm about to tell her it's a Friday night in bloody Rainstead, of course they'll have rooms free, but I bite my tongue. I should be glad Cara seems to be perking up a bit. I park and she comes back after a couple of minutes.

"Thirty quid each, shared bathroom, sound OK?"

I panic, try to think which of my credit cards has any money left on it.

"God, Jon, you look like you're about to puke. I'm going to pay for my own room if that's what's freaking you out." As she hauls her backpack out of the passenger footwell she says, "Oh yeah, and I told them you're my uncle," before she slams the door.

My room is small with thick, dusty carpets and a wobbly-looking single bed. The rooms are joined by a tiny bathroom. I have to turn sideways to walk through it into Cara's room. She's sitting on her bed, frowning at her phone. She drops it quickly into her bag when I knock on the half-open door. She sees my eyes follow the phone into her bag.

"Before you ask, no, I'm not messaging *GoodSam*. I just got a few messages from my mum, that's all."

"Everything OK?" I ask and Cara gives the sort of exaggerated nod I recognize from Jakey. It means Susan is probably not OK, far from it, but I remind myself Cara is an adult. I don't have the time or energy to lecture her now. It's coming up to 8:30 p.m. and I want to get to the Bull—I can't risk missing Robbie.

"If it's all right with you, I think I'm going to stay here," Cara says.

"That's no problem," I say, nodding.

In fact I'm relieved she's not going to put up a fight. There's no way I was going to let her come with me. Perhaps her encounter with Tony has made her more risk averse, more rational, which is no bad thing.

"Just stay in here with the door locked, try to relax."

252

"Yeah, I will. Just make sure you get a photo of him, OK? Pretend you're on a video call or something, take a photo, send it to me, and then I can make sure it's the same bloke."

I wave my phone at her and nod to show that I know what I'm doing.

"Call me if you need me, all right? I'll just be down the road, and don't forget to lock this door," I say as I open the door to the hall.

She salutes me.

"Good luck, Uncle Jon."

I shut the door and wait for a moment, until I hear the lock slide closed. Good. It makes me feel braver, knowing she's safe. I walk quickly away from the pub in the warm evening as though trying to outpace any doubts. I pause by a walker's signpost just after the pub parking lot. The arrow pointing to the left catches my eye. I hadn't mentioned anything to Cara; I knew we were close, but not this close. The sign says PORT RAYNOR BEACH; the place where Danny died is just a mile away. Port Raynor lighthouse, one of the few still operational in Cornwall, two miles. I'm relieved Cara didn't see the sign. I know she'd want to go to the beach if she had. Aware Cara could be watching from the window, confused as to why I've paused here, I start walking again. But with each step I feel my courage wane and I have the vertiginous feeling that I'm walking away from life as I know it, that everything is about to change.

19

Cara

It's only when I feel the lock slide in the door and I am alone that I feel my whole body release a breath I didn't know I was holding. I sit on the edge of the bed and try to shuffle my thoughts into some kind of order. Everything Jon said in the car about Meg, about what she was doing to Grace, was mad, completely insane, but I know now that doesn't necessarily mean it's not true. Intellectually, I think he's right, but I won't believe it, can't believe it in my heart, until I hear it from Grace herself. I remember Charlie, how his leathery face twisted in anger—"She's sick!" Was his shaky finger pointing at his daughter, Meg, not Grace like I'd assumed? I remember how Grace used to slump lower in her wheelchair when Meg was close, how she seemed to become sicker, more fragile. A pain flames in the middle of my forehead. Every thought, every memory feels like a tiny sharp hammer inside my head and the sharpest hammer of all, the one I know I won't be able to answer or understand for a long time to come, is why didn't Grace tell me what was happening to her?

I stand to look out of the window. The high street below is empty apart from an empty crisp packet that floats along, caught by a breeze in the gutter. The early evening summer moon hangs low in the sky as though it's keeping an extra-close eye on Rainstead tonight. In the distance a lighthouse winks out its warning. I watch as Jon walks down the hill towards the Bull. With his flimsy raincoat, Converse, and black-rimmed glasses he sticks out like a sore thumb. I should have got him to change into a tracksuit or something. He stops to look at a sign, like a foreigner just off the boat from a distant, more tasteful, and prosperous country, then carries on walking. I press my hand to the grubby window and without even knowing I'm going to say anything, I whisper, "Come back safe, won't you?"

Then I feel stupid and drop my arm to my side.

I pull the curtains closed and sit back on the bed. There's no TV and I don't want to look at my phone, it'll only make me feel guilty. Mum's tried to call twice and sent a few crazy-sounding text messages. I texted her back before Jon left: I'm sorry, Mum. I'm really fine. I'll be home tomorrow xxx.

I lie back on the unfamiliar, overly springy bed and feel the beat in my temple thud against my hands. I regret sleeping the day away—there's no way I'm going to sleep until Jon's back. I decide to go downstairs, ask if they have any acetaminophen for my head.

The pub has low ceilings and the same thick, heavily patterned carpet as upstairs. There's a well-trodden path, the color of Marmite, running through the center of the carpet, leading to the bar. Although it's not busy, I glance around the few drinkers, checking faces, make sure he's not here.

The barmaid is chatting to a woman of a similar age. As I get closer I hear their local accents. They could have grown up with each other, neighbors, the other's history as familiar to them as their own. Just like me and Grace, or what Grace and I could have been like. The barmaid is the same woman who checked us into our rooms. She's maybe somewhere in her fifties, bottle blond, a little plump, kindly looking, but her smile is hesitant, as though she's learned not to trust people she doesn't know.

She reluctantly moves away from her friend and bends across the bar towards me.

"What can I get you?"

Suddenly it feels rude to ask for headache pills without at least paying for a drink, so I say, "Pint of Coke and a bag of salt and vinegar crisps, thanks." I emphasize my Cornish vowels. I want her to know I understand, that I'm the same as her. She hears, smiles, warmer this time, and nods before half filling a pint glass with ice and pouring my drink.

"So I'm guessing you're not here for a holiday," she says. "You and your uncle must be—"

"Visiting family?" I say, more of a question than a statement. It sounds like total bollocks, but she just nods again. She knows it's none of her business. She puts my bag of crisps on the bar and I hand her coins from my pocket before she turns back to her friend. I pick up a sticky menu and pretend to study it for something to do. My head throbs, but being here, distracted from my thoughts of Grace, seems to be easing it slightly. It hits me that the barmaid and her friend probably know the Craig twins—one of them could have sat on the stool I'm on right now. I hate thinking about Robbie, the man with the tattoo. The thought that he has a brother, a twin, sends a trickle of fear down my spine.

I finish my drink quickly and am about to ask for the painkillers before heading back upstairs when the barmaid's friend runs her fingers through her short brown hair and says, "Course, I tried to tell those lads we've had two deaths because of the rip currents in that one cove, but did they listen? Did they heck. Just shrugged like I don't know what I'm talking about, like I haven't lived here my whole life, and then ran off towards Raynor with their surfboards."

My stool creaks as I strain to hear them. The noise makes both women look up at me, surprised, as though they'd forgotten I was there. I know it would be easier, safer probably, to ignore the sudden lick of curiosity in my stomach, to quietly go back up to my room and stare at my phone until either Jon sends me a photo or I fall asleep. But I know I won't, and besides, the friend raises her eyebrows at me like I've just elbowed my way into their private chat.

"Sorry, sorry, I couldn't help but hear," I say, "but I'm from Summervale, near Ashford. You probably heard about Grace Nichols, the disabled girl who was kidnapped? Meg, her mum, was murdered?"

Drip, drip.

Both women listen, their eyes round, expectant as I keep talking.

"Well, I knew them a bit and I'm just curious. Is Raynor Beach near here? That's where Grace's brother, Danny, died, like twenty years ago, wasn't it?"

I watch the two women thaw with every word. Now a connection has been made, their smiles open up like arms flung wide. The barmaid's friend shuffles her stool towards me. She has a short list of names tattooed in scrolling text on her upper arm.

"Oh God, you knew her, did you? That Grace Nichols? Honestly, when I heard what happened to her, I thought I was going to be sick, and to think it was her own dad too. Thank God he's locked up, that's all I can say. I just wish they could throw away the key. Bloody nutter. I bet everyone in Summervale's spitting with anger. Imagine if anything like that happened round here, Gillian, to one of ours, we'd all be spitting, wouldn't we?"

The woman doesn't stop to see the barmaid shake her head and doesn't seem to hear her as she says, "Can't even imagine, Luce, can't imagine."

"God and the poor mum, what was her name again? Meg. Megan. That's it. The poor woman. I heard she was nothing short of a saint to that girl, literally laid down her life for her daughter." Gillian nods along as keeps talking and I try not to wince as they praise Meg. I don't want to piss Luce off, so I just sit and make all the right noises as she babbles on.

"And to think she'd already lost her boy. Remember, Gill, Christie was working at the chip shop round the corner when it happened." She turns back to me and says, "Christie's my ex—mother-in-law. Anyway, Christie said she heard the ambulance from way off, couldn't believe it when it stopped just outside the chippie and the paramedics went running down the path, towards Raynor. Christie said for weeks after that she couldn't get the poor woman's screams out of her head. She said she knew, as only a mum can, what those screams meant. Poor soul."

At last, Luce stops talking, drains the last of her white wine.

Gillian shakes her head at the memory, but then a gruff male voice from across the bar barks, "Gill!" and with a roll of her eyes she walks away to serve the man.

Luce takes a big breath, as though she's about to start talking again. I leap in, my headache forgotten, before she does.

"So he died here, did he? Danny?"

She looks at me, slightly despairingly, like I haven't been listening, like I'm being dim. She nods a couple of times, slowly, emphatically.

"Yes, just a mile down the coastal path at Raynor Beach."

She nods in the direction of the lighthouse before her eyes glaze over and she's shaking her head again and saying, "That poor, poor woman. And she was pregnant too. I remember one of the ambulance boys told Christie later that she was pregnant. At the time I was surprised her pregnancy was never mentioned in the news reports, but then I thought she must have lost it and didn't want the bloody world to know."

She's wrong, of course, the baby did survive, but only just. I wonder whether Grace in utero felt her mother's screams, whether those screams echoed around her brand-new heart. There's a brief silence before Luce continues.

"I was just saying to Gillian: Raynor looks like the most peaceful spot in Cornwall, but those rip currents are bloody lethal. Some of the old boys even reckon it's cursed." She wrinkles her nose. "But it's just them currents, they'll whip you off your feet, even in shallow water, and hold you under like a bloody crocodile until you stop kicking. The council do bugger all, of course. If it was popular with tourists round here they'd be signs and lifeguards and all sorts. Can't have one of those nice rich people from London drown, can we?" As Gillian walks back to us she lifts her glass and waves it at her friend. By the time Gillian has filled Luce's glass I've made my excuses and got down from my stool. I let the pub door bang behind me as I walk into the warm night.

I don't make a conscious decision to go. It's almost like I've been here before. My feet seem to know the way. They know they have to take me to the place where a whole family was destroyed so many years ago. I have to go to the place where Danny died.

5th June, 2019, later

Raynor Beach

He arrived at 1 a.m. I was standing in the kitchen, lit by the streetlight pouring through the window, waiting to let him in through the back door. He kicked off his shoes outside and put plastic covers over his feet. He said it would be better for me, for both of us, if he didn't leave any trace that he'd been in the house. The reality of him being there was overwhelming, his online avatar become flesh. He was like a miracle. I raised my finger to my lips, "Shhh."

I showed him the three syringes I'd made up—stuffed full of the drugs she used on me. Ketamine, OxyContin, and sleeping pills, all crushed and mixed with water. I could draw a syringe with my eyes closed. I'd fixed the needles and pushed the air out of each one, the liquid inside rising like nectar at the end of the needle. In return, he showed me the ties for her arms, the gag. He smiled, and as they caught the light I saw how his teeth looked like they'd been filed to sharp points. Mum's snores grew louder and he followed me down the hall.

We paused outside her door to check we were ready. His jaw was flexed, his eyes wide, already focused on what was behind the door. He licked his teeth as he pulled the hood of his coat over his head, carefully zipped it all the way, gloves already on. For the first time I realized this man who knew the secret of my life wasn't the kindhearted person he made me believe he was. He had lied to me. He wasn't here to atone for past crimes, he wasn't interested in rehabilitation. I could feel the anger in him, the violence.

"Well, are we going to do this or not?" he whispered. His voice was light, a reminder that this wasn't a big deal for him, like he wanted me to know he'd done much worse.

"We tie her up, we inject her, we take the money, we leave." My voice was only just audible as I said the words I'd written to him again and again.

She didn't stir until Tony was standing directly over her. He leaned down, grinning, inches from her face. She opened her mouth to scream but Tony was too quick. No sound came. He punched the gag into her mouth so deep she wouldn't be able to cough it out. Her eyes bulged in panic, her limbs started to lash about. But Tony had already pulled her right arm hard above her head and using one of mum's scarves tied it to the bed frame. I wanted to tell him to be gentler, but there was no time.

"Get her other fucking arm," he shouted at me. I tried, but she lashed it away like a whip before making the hand I used to hold into a fist and punching the opening in my stomach. All the air left my body as I felt the tube travel through me. The pain pushed me back against the wall and the syringes fell from my pocket, my secrets exposed as I dropped to my knees. I held my stomach, pressed the dressing around the tube hard to keep any blood from spilling. Mum was thrashing, still on the bed. She'd pulled the gag from her mouth and screamed just once before Tony, straddling her now, pushed a pillow hard into her face. She bucked and twisted beneath him, trying to unseat him with the strength that I know only comes when there's nothing left to lose.

Tony swore as his feet and knees slipped against the sheets, he couldn't keep her back and hold the pillow *against her face. He leaned his weight forward, his palm flat, pushing all his weight down against the pillow. He looked wildly around the room for help. That's when he saw it. Next to him on the bedside table was the iron lamp that used to be Granddad's, stout and heavy. Bracing himself against the pillow he pulled it from its socket in one quick flick. He released his hand and Mum threw the pillow off her face, gasping like she'd just been dragged out from underwater. He turned the lamp upside down and raised it, high above his head. He paused, as though giving Mum time to recognize this moment so she knew this was how it ended. I heard a sound. It started as a murmur and turned into a shout. I realized it was coming from me. "No, no, no, no!" Mum turned towards me, no longer than a second, but I knew we both saw something in the other that was entirely new. For the first time in my life it felt like we truly knew each other. She made the shape of my name with her mouth, my real name, but no sound came before the lamp flew down fast. I screamed as one of its curled feet struck her forehead. Her limbs tensed and she made a sucking sound as he pulled the lamp away and brought it down, harder, again, again, harder. Until her face couldn't be called a face anymore and there was no life left in her body. It just lay there, completely emptied. Tony was left panting above her, the lamp shaking in his gloved hand. He blinked at it, as though surprised to find it attached to his arm, before he dropped it to the floor. He slowly stood up and stared down at Mum bleeding quietly beneath him. Then, his head cocked to one side, like he was admiring his work, he turned to me. There was blood splattered across his face. His eyes were fired, crazed with life, as though he'd sucked all Mum's strength out of her and it now flowed directly through him. He looked at me and, smiling, raised one finger to his lips.*

"Shhh."

20

Jon

The Bull smells like the bottom of a laundry basket, of old sweat and stale beer. I notice the group of blokes as soon as I walk into the pub. I glance at them. They've taken over an area in the pub to the right of the bar with a dartboard and pool table. I don't want them to see me so I keep my head down as I walk straight to the bar. I order a pint, not because I want one, but because I think it'll make me stand out even more if I have an orange juice. I feel raw, exposed, out of place. I shouldn't have worn this stupid raincoat, the fashionable glasses. I take the coat off, but the glasses have to stay. I find a small table close enough but—with the door between us—not too close to the men. I sit and only then look at them.

There are six of them, two sitting at a table and the others crowded round the dartboard. They all look like a variation of the British bulldog: short or shaved hair, white skin made red and an-gry by the sun or black and wrinkled by the tattooist's needle. A couple of them are younger than me but the rest look like they're in their fifties or older. Most of them have huge bellies, taut as drums, full of beer. They have wide, easy smiles. They throw noises back and forth to one another—roars and slurs—but they all seem to understand each other perfectly. They wear gray polo shirts and slack-looking jeans. Their part of the pub is already littered with empty pint glasses, they've clearly been here for a while already. The biggest one fires three darts at the board, one after the other, like missiles, and the others bang the table with their palms and shout. I don't know if they're congratulating him or laughing at him. The two at the table have their backs to me and are much quieter, only moving to take the odd sip of their pints. They seem separate from the group, watching from the sidelines, not even talking to each other. The one on the left looks older, his back is curled, and he's wearing a flat cap, but the bloke on the right, closest to me, is younger. His hair is short, light blond, and from here his neck looks too long and thin to hold the weight of his head. One of the older blokes comes over to him, slaps a red-raw arm over his shoulders.

"Your round, lil' Rob," he says, slurring slightly.

The seated man turns and I see a black streak like a lightning bolt on the side of his neck. It's him, exactly as Cara described. Robbie Craig. He heads towards the bar with slow, viscous movements, like he's melting, but there's also a careful grace to him, as if he has every movement planned out well in advance. While the barman—without having to be told—pulls six amber pints, Robbie glances up at the clock hanging behind the bar, his jaw tensing, relaxing, then tensing again. His fingers drum the bar, he's forcing himself not to hurry. He doesn't look like a man having drinks with mates—I recognize due diligence when I see it. There's somewhere else he wants to be, somewhere else he *should* be.

I look at his eyes, his mouth, his hands; have they seen, spoken to, and touched Grace? My chest tightens and I have to take a big gulp of beer and look away, to get my shit together. I take my phone out of my pocket, flick the camera on, and fix Robbie in the viewfinder. I try to look like I'm searching for a signal, and just as my thumb lands on the red button one of the fat-bellied older men at the bar slaps Robbie on the back, blocking him entirely. Shit. The fat bloke has a drinker's nose, bulbous and red like a cartoon. He takes a pint off Robbie and, after swallowing a few deep gulps, makes a sound like air being released from a tire. Relief.

"So, Robbo, word is you've got the southern route—all the way down to Sorrento, isn't it?"

Robbie says something I don't catch, he tries to steer past the man, but he's awkward, trying to hold five pints.

"Bloody typical. Favoritism, that's what it is. Mandy sends you off to look at all those Italian girlies in their bikinis—even after you were a no-show for the Holland job—and I'm off to the fucking sour-faced north again."

Robbie shrugs, tries to move away, but the bloke suddenly looks like he's having a lightbulb moment. His eyes widen, his brow lifts, beer spills over Robbie's hand as the bloke grabs his arms and says, "Wait a minute, Robbie, you little swine, you're not shagging fat old Mandy for the best trips, are you?"

The others turn towards him, sensing sport more interesting than darts. But Robbie just shakes his head, his tattoo flashing.

"Nah, mate. I'm too knackered from shagging your missus," I hear him say.

There's a beery, excited rumble from the others and for a moment the smile below the red nose drops, his hands ball, and I think he's about to punch Robbie, before he suddenly smiles again, broader this time, and slaps Robbie on the back, spilling more beer as he does so.

"Cheeky bastard, that's exactly the kind of thing your dad would've said, isn't that right, lads?"

There's another low rumble of agreement before Robbie slowly makes his way back to the table, greeted with nods of thanks as he hands out the glasses. I turn away quickly as the red-nosed bloke looks over at me, his eyes narrow, before taking another long pull on his pint. Coldness runs through me. Does he recognize me? But then he moves over to a bald guy who's quietly watching the others play darts. Red nose says something, starts laughing in the bald guy's face, but the bald guy flicks him away like a mosquito. Robbie says something to the guy in the flat cap, careful not to involve the others, who are all gripped by the dartboard again. The older bloke nods slowly. It looks as though Robbie's asking for advice. The man talks for longer than Robbie, but he doesn't look at him. He hardly moves his head, but makes small gestures with his hands, as though explaining something. Robbie stares at him intently, taking it all in. Then he seems to repeat something the older man has just said, who nods as Robbie talks. After just a couple of minutes, the flat-cap man shrugs his heavy shoulders as though casting off a heavy weight and the conversation is over, but not before, under the table, in a practiced sweeping motion, Robbie passes him a small roll of notes, which he takes and puts into his breast pocket without even glancing at it, like he knows Robbie wouldn't dare be so stupid as to shortchange him. There's a shout and some swearing from the darts players but the two seated men stay perfectly still while a couple of the others give each other high fives. Red nose shouts, "Fucking bull's-eye, mate!"

Even though he's still got half a pint left in front of him, Robbie stands. He nods once respectfully to the man next to him, who nods back.

"Oi, oi, I'm done," he shouts to the others. They swear at him, call him a pussy. Robbie's jaw tenses again but he chooses to ignore them. They turn back to their game. None of them seem too disappointed to see him go. Robbie shakes a few hands, slaps a couple of backs. I catch him looking at the clock again before he makes his slow, sloping way to the door. Before he leaves he stares at me for just a moment, and as our eyes meet in that brief second I see the thin face from Dave's photo. They're almost identical: the sallow cheeks, the sharp cheekbones, the prominent Adam's apple. But where Tony's eyes in the photo were dulled, as though ashamed, Robbie's eyes are bright, alert, and emotionless. In that moment I have the feeling that Robbie's dark eyes have seen things I can't even imagine. I make myself count to twenty before I get up and, without looking at the other men, follow him out of the pub and into the warm night.

He's in a hurry, walking fast. I have to jog a couple of paces so I don't lose him completely. The lighthouse flashes like a searchlight in the sky, urgent, as if we're all convicts and Rainstead one huge prison. Robbie walks quickly up the steep high street, away from the sea, and for a mad moment I think he's heading to the Lamb, that somehow he knows Cara is there. I start running towards the hotel and look up to see, with relief, that the curtains in Cara's window are drawn. I have to get to him, stop him before he can get anywhere near her, but then he makes a sharp left at the sign for Raynor Beach. Thank God. I stop, try to get my breath and my hammering heart to calm. But as I start to follow this man who threatened Cara, who probably murdered Meg, I think about

Jakey, and regret washes over me like nausea. He still hasn't called me back or answered my texts. And as I move deeper into the night I wish I could hear his voice, just for a moment, because his faith in me makes me brave and now, like never before, I need to be brave.

21

Cara

The moon casts a silvery path, as if showing me the way towards the beach, while the lighthouse keeps its beady eye open, searching for danger. I feel like they're on my side, my team, here to keep me safe. I try not to let myself think too much. I know if I do I'll let fear take over, run back to the pub. I don't know what I'm doing exactly, but I feel like I need to see the place Danny died, where it all began. It's like an invisible string is connecting me to Grace, leading me there. I feel like I'm sleepwalking, but I don't want to wake up. I stop at the sign where Jon paused just half an hour earlier, then take the path signposted Raynor Beach, opposite the empty fish and chip shop that Luce's ex-mother-in-law works in.

I start to follow the path, which bends down towards the sea. The salt in the air seems to fill my lungs, the sea glugging to my left, calling me on, a warm breeze gently pushing behind me. At times the path gets rocky and I have to crouch to clamber down short but steep drops, lift myself over stone stiles. Nettles and overgrown gorse bushes sting and grab my skin with tiny sharp mouths, but I ignore them. I'm getting closer, I must be. To my left the sea no longer gulps and sloshes but has become a low, steady roar. Suddenly the path opens onto a small grassy patch; the lighthouse sweeps its beam over a cove below. I've been told enough times never to go near the edge at places like this, the ground might look secure but it could be false, a weak grassy overhang, the stone and rock underneath eroded, licked back into the sea. It's not clear how to get down into the cove and, for the first time, I hesitate. My eyes start to adjust to the gloom. I tell myself I'll just go down and see it, just for a moment—I've come all this way, after all. The path is steep and narrow. I bend low and use my hands to help me along. I slip a couple of times but stop myself from crying out.

With the moon bouncing off the water and the sea-slick rocks, the cove is lighter than it looked from above, the night more navy than black. Stars like benevolent spirits seem to smile down at me. The cove is almost a perfect horseshoe shape. The sea strokes the sand where the two meet so gently. I can see why Simon thought this was a good place for his family, a safe place. I decide to sit for a moment, then I'll make my way back. It seems impossible that this flat, soothing sea stole a small boy and planted the seed for so many years of sadness and pain. I close my eyes but the noise of falling rocks makes them fly open again. It's the noise I made as I came down the path. There are no voices and whoever or whatever it is doesn't make any other sound. I listen hard. Above the sound of the sea I hear the steady crunch of small rocks being disturbed, rubbing against each other. Footsteps. I shrink back. Who the hell would be coming down here now, in the dark? Could Jon have seen me go, followed me? But why wouldn't he have shouted after me?

I see Robbie's dark eyes, his thin arm pulling back before sending the heavy lamp crashing against Meg's skull. *Drip, drip.* Please, *please*, I beg the sky, don't let it be him. They're getting closer, footsteps steady, they're coming down to the beach. If I don't do something he'll see me. I have to move, I have to move now. I slowly come to a crouching stand and then run behind a large boulder. I push myself close, its cold bulk reassuring against my cheek. The footsteps stop as the person steps down onto the sand. It's worse not being able to hear them. He could well have seen me from above. Perhaps he's already holding a rock in his hand, testing its sharpness against his thumb, nice and heavy. *Drip, drip.*

I don't know where he is. I'm too frightened to turn around in case I see him behind me so instead I hold my breath, gather my courage, and force myself to look up, over the edge of the boulder. My veins jolt as soon as I see him. He's looking out at the sea, his back towards me, wearing an oversized coat, the hood over his head. He starts to walk across the sand, towards the darker side of the beach, towards me. He walks carefully, with a slight limp. He looks smaller, much smaller than I remember. The wind picks up from the sea and a gust almost pulls his hood back. I see a flash of short, spiky light hair, before a hand rises to put the hood back in place. But it's too late, I know what I've seen. The lighthouse searches the cove, flashes over us both. I move out onto the sand, my cold limbs oiled with adrenaline. I keep my eyes fixed on her, terrified that if I blink or turn away she'll vanish again. Like me, she's keeping to the shadows like she shouldn't be here. I call her name loud and clear in the night:

"Grace!"

6th June 2019

Raynor Beach

The night it happened, Tony carried me into an old car-avan, Mum's blood still on his face. It left a stain on one of the stars on my dress. He didn't say a word, just left me in the filthy, empty bathroom, the tiny bathroom suite the color of well-stewed tea. He came back with a sleeping bag. The next few days were a blur. I was in shock from that night and still in withdrawal from the drugs. When I opened my eyes, everything around me vibrated, but it was worse when they were closed—that's when Mum would come for me, her face crumpled and bloodied. But in my dreams she'd give me the drugs I now craved. Sometimes I heard low voices, hands changed me out of my clothes, cleaned the wound in my stomach. The caravan shook with weather and footsteps. I don't know how long it took, but at last the fog started to lift from my mind and when I woke the bathroom door was open.

They'd changed me into leggings and a blue hoodie that smelled like deodorant. I wondered who had worn it before me. There was a bandage on my stomach. I tried to walk, my legs like chewing gum, but slowly I made my way out of my bathroom cell. They were both there, Tony and his brother Robbie, the one with the tattoo. Tony had told me about him. Mum's red box was open and empty in front of them on the plastic table. I couldn't look at Tony without seeing Mum and he didn't look at me. I stood in the middle of the room and Robbie pointed at the empty box and said, "It's not enough."

I knew where to take them. She'd been stealing for as long as I could remember. She told me she stole to pay for the drugs I needed but now I think it gave her a thrill. And she was good at it. She stole from friends' houses, from old people in nursing homes, and hospitals. Apart from that GP office in Plymouth where Mum worked for a little while, no one ever suspected her. Even if they did, no one would ever dare accuse her. The whole of Summervale would turn against anyone who uttered a single word against Cornwall's most adored mum. Just ask that reporter, Jon Katrin.

When we got to the cemetery I played up my confusion, said I couldn't remember where Danny was buried. I knew three of us searching for one small grave would draw attention—they had no choice but to leave me alone. I didn't know how many days I'd been in the caravan exactly. It was only when I stood in front of his grave that I counted the number of times I'd watched the sun rise and fall out of the grimy window and worked out the date: June 6th. The day Danny died, Mum's birthday. I knew the twins were watching, so I mouthed a silent "happy birthday" to her in the pouring rain as I dug up the wet earth at the foot of Danny's grave. I lifted out the blue box I knew I'd find there. I only had to peek inside to know it was enough. It had to be enough. Even in the dull light the brightness of the diamond rings, the gold watch, and necklaces stung my eyes, so I shut it again and put the box in the pocket of Robbie's coat, just like he told me to. I wanted them to see me do exactly as they said. I know what they're capable of now. I've survived so much for so long. I have to survive them.

22

Jon

Robbie uses the flashlight on his phone to light the path in front of him, which is good—it means I can keep a good few paces behind and not risk losing him. The light glimmers through even the thickest gorse bush. I walk as carefully as I can, mindful of loose rocks and lifted roots. In the distance, the huge yellow eye of the lighthouse winks. My heart beats hard in my chest, like a third set of footsteps. I think only about the next step and the one after that. I don't let myself think what he'd do if he found me following. After half a mile or so the path opens out into a small grass clearing, the sea growling like a guard dog on my left. Robbie shines the flashlight ahead of him, between two dense bushes. It doesn't look like a path, but he wraps his coat around him to protect against the sharp thorns before he dives between the bushes. There was a path here once. Again I force myself to wait, count to twenty before I follow. The thorns tear at my rain-coat like long nails, trying to pull me back. I freeze, but ahead I see Robbie's light flickering, moving forward and up; he didn't hear. Temporarily reassured, I push forward. The overgrown path opens a little, like it's been used a few times recently; some of the brambles look freshly broken. Without warning, the path gets steeper, and at times I have to use my hands and claw the ground for balance. The sea, behind me now, sighs and moans and the lighthouse keeps up its rhythmic beat; like a strobe light it catches time in pulses. From afar there was comfort in it but now it makes everything too strange. Up ahead I see there's a shadow, darker than the others, and as I battle my way towards it I think it's a huge rock, but when I get closer I realize it's too uniform, too big, to be a rock. It's a rectangle, a small caravan, dark and almost choked by brambles. It's clear no one's had a holiday here in years.

Ahead, the phone light dances on and I follow, past more aban-doned caravans. Suddenly, the light from the flashlight disappears and darkness falls like a blanket. I duck down; I feel more ex-posed without the light. I don't know where he is, where he's gone. I count to twenty again. I want to turn around, bolt back to the warm glow of the pub. I'd order a whisky to settle myself and then I'd call Upton, tell her everything I know. But what if it's too late by then? If I go back now we may never know the truth about Meg, about Grace. I owe it to Simon, to Cara, to myself. I think of the promise I made to Jakey, see him waiting for me, glancing at his watch. I've broken too many promises already.

Bending low to the ground, I make myself move forward. Without Robbie's flashlight it's hard to see which way to go, but then my eye catches a flicker. To my right there's a small light, no bigger than the light from a match. But it's there and it's all I have so I decide to go towards it. I keep my eyes on the light and my shin smacks against something hard and flat. I yelp in pain, fall to the ground biting my tongue to stop from calling out. My mouth fills with the coppery taste of blood. I clutch my leg and wait for the pain to subside. My hands are damp as I lift them off my leg. I'm bleeding, but there's no serious damage done. I stand slowly and, pulling my coat over my hand, move the nettles to the side to see what I crashed into. It's a sign on top of another sign. The top one says PRIVATE and the one below says PORT RAYNOR CARAVAN PARK. I remember Simon in the café, telling me he booked a caravan for Meg's birthday, the weekend Danny died. I remember Dave telling me the twins' dad used to work in tourism—thought he ran a hostel, but wasn't sure—could it have been a caravan park? The nettles nip at my ankles, and as I walk on the light grows, the glow welcome in the darkening night. The light is coming from another, larger caravan. The overgrown yard is dotted with the forgotten skeletons of family life, an abandoned child's bike, a rusty small trampoline, all being slowly digested by brambles and ivy. There's an old Volvo parked carelessly at an angle, its nose almost touching the front of the caravan. I stay crouching behind a tiny, moldy pile of logs. The curtains in the caravan are drawn, but they're flimsy, easy to see through, though from here I can't make anything out, just the occasional shadow, nothing more. The caravan rattles and groans as someone walks about inside. Words are spoken but they're too muffled, I can't make any sense of them. More words come soon after. They are shorter, angrier, like punches thrown in a fight. One of the voices starts shouting and, as the door flies open, I shrink back, careful to keep myself hidden.

"Well, where the fuck did she go?" Robbie pushes himself in duplicate out of the caravan before the thin door bangs shut behind him. It takes Tony a moment to regain his footing.

"I told you, Rob, I don't know." Tony's voice rises higher than his brother's. "Don't look at me like it's my fault. I told you that valuation bloke was too far away, that I'd be late. I got back ten minutes ago and she was gone. And all the while you were in the pub."

"I was only in the fucking pub, Tone, to pay for the border tip-off. And I'll look at you how I like. This is your mess, remember? *Your* mess. You think I'd be here if you weren't my brother?" Robbie pushes Tony in the chest a couple of times. Tony's hand forms a fist at his side, but even in the darkness I can tell he's holding it loosely, halfhearted, intended to boost his own courage rather than to be used against his brother.

"And how about when I stood up to get you out of a worse mess, Rob? Huh? Four months of my life in a shithole just to save you from having to go through it. You owe me."

Robbie's head drops. He sighs like he's tired of being reminded of the debt he owes his twin. He pauses for a moment.

"The money?" he asks.

Tony hunches slightly. It's all he has to do to let his brother know the money is gone.

"Fuck!" Robbie shouts at the sky, before he turns back to Tony, his eyes bright and wild even in the darkness. "I told you, Tone, how many times did I tell you this was rotten from the start, but you couldn't let it go, your fucking conscience, all because of that kid all those years ago."

Tony keeps his head low, like he's heard this many times already.

"I just want to make right some of the stuff I've done wrong, the stuff I'm not proud of. Prison changed me, it changed me here." He presses his fingers to his forehead. "It made me realize something. That moment when we didn't help that kid, even though we knew he was in trouble, that split-second decision is what made everything after go to shit."

"I've heard enough of your reformed-character bullshit, Tone. You wanted to say sorry because when you were a little kid you didn't save a toddler from drowning? Send flowers, write a fucking card, that's what most people do. But not my sensitive brother, no, what do you do, Tone? You get involved. A woman is fucking dead and the whole of the South West is searching for her psycho daughter who could put you in prison for the rest of your life because you wanted to *say sorry*?"

Robbie's face is red from shouting but Tony doesn't glance up once. He can't look his brother in the eye.

"I told you what her mum was doing to her, Rob, she needed my help, I had no idea what she was really like." At last he looks up at his brother. "She'll be heading into town, won't she, Rob? What if she goes to the police? What if she tells them all those lies she made up, about what happened to her mum?"

There's a whimper in Tony's voice and I realize he's not only afraid of his brother, he's also afraid of Grace. She has power over him. He knows something about her, about what happened, and it terrifies him. Robbie hears the fear in his brother and, moving forward, he puts his hand on the back of Tony's neck. Tony rests his forehead on his brother's shoulder. It looks like a position they know well, one they both seem to find soothing.

Robbie's voice is calmer as he says, "We just need to find her. Let's start by looking in town. She won't talk to anyone and she won't go to the police, she wants to disappear as much as we want her to disappear. That's why the plan is going to work. When she's back we'll not take our eyes off her for the next few hours. We'll get her on that truck first thing tomorrow morning and once she's away, lost somewhere in Europe, we'll never hear from her again. It'll be over."

Tony lifts his head, blinks at his brother like these are the words he wants to believe.

Robbie looks out towards the sea as he says, "She can't have got far. Let's go and get the silly bitch." He turns and is about to start walking when Tony grabs his arm.

"There's no need to hurt her though, is there, Rob? Please, you don't have to hurt her."

But Robbie shrugs his brother's arm away and, without saying a word, he starts to walk down towards the sea, Tony just behind him. I cower back behind the pile of logs, terrified they're going to come directly past me. I step back; a branch snaps under my foot. To me it sounds as loud as a gunshot. Robbie stops, but Tony only turns his head slightly. Robbie's jaw tenses before he says, "Badger," and they both keep moving.

Robbie leads. He takes a different track from the one we came up just a few minutes earlier. He walks straight ahead from the caravan, crushing the stinging nettles under his boots while Tony trips along behind him, an identical shadow.

I wait until they're almost out of sight before I start following. This time there is no path. The brothers move quickly, almost running down the steep hill that leads to the sea, trampling the nettles and brambles as though they are soft as lamb's grass. I remember Simon called them hares. They grew up here, they know this place, and these hills, these secret tracks, as well as they know each other. They are directly on course to hit the light from the lighthouse on its never-ending sweep when suddenly they vanish. Their timing is perfect: the light doesn't catch them, and I don't know where they've gone. It is absolutely silent, I can't even hear the sea. Wherever they are, they aren't moving, or making a sound. Either they've gone so far ahead I can't hear them anymore or they've stopped. I feel out of my natural habitat, like a swimmer in unknown waters, soft belly exposed to the sharks circling below. The light from the lighthouse seems to be searching just for me. I shouldn't be here. With each flash of light I think I see eyes in the bushes, shiny and black as they watch every move I make. My skin prickles and a small voice I didn't know was part of me, never needed before, whispers in my ear that the game has changed. I'm not the hunter anymore. I've become the hunted. I start to run.

23

Cara

She puts a hand against a large rock next to her for support. She doesn't turn towards me but I see her whole body tense, suddenly alert when she hears her name. She freezes, like she's trying to decide what to do. Run or stay. Finally she speaks.

"I'm not Grace."

I move quickly away from the sea, towards Grace, towards the dark caves. The wet sand sucks around my feet. I don't want to spook her but I need to get to her quickly. All my senses feel sharpened, the wind whips my skin, the waves roar, I smell the salt from the sea but I keep my eyes full only of her, fixed on her back. I won't let her get away again. She still hasn't moved. Run or stay. She looks like she's waiting for me. Stay.

She's just a few paces away and I force myself to slow. I'm whispering her name, again and again, like the more I say it the more real this will become. She lifts her hand from the boulder and I watch as she pulls her hood down, exposing the back of her head. Her hair is spidery and fair, like a newborn. I'm only a couple of paces away from her now. She keeps perfectly still as the light whips around the cove, as if searching for secrets, for us. My breath catches, my skin pricks with the realization that this is what I wanted: to find Grace, to be with her alone. Silence stretches out between us, the last before we both say and hear things we can never change. A silent goodbye to the Grace Nichols I thought I knew.

At last she drops her hand from her head and slowly, with a limp to her right, turns around to face me. Her eyes meet mine, and as we stare at each other I realize that I never really looked at Grace before. Just like everyone else, I assumed I knew what she looked like, who she was. But I only saw what I was told to see. I only saw her limitations, her illnesses, an impenetrable wall between us.

But tonight I see a whole world within her.

My lips make the shape of her name again, but it sounds wrong. She isn't Grace anymore. Grace will always be the little shell in a wheelchair, hiding beneath her hat and behind her glasses. This woman who stands before me, smiling now, with a gaze that feels more like a challenge than a welcome, is someone else entirely. This is Zoe.

"Cara," she says. Her voice sounds calmer than the air feels. She smiles again, briefly showing the small teeth that used to cause her so much pain. She takes a slow, hesitant step towards me. She speaks like she moves, slowly, like she's still learning to trust herself.

"You know, I used to have all these fantasies about how I'd escape. In one of them, you'd come and I'd tell you everything. I'd show you my legs, how I could make them move more than I ever dared let on, and then you'd take me away." All that time she was desperate for me to see her, as I see her now. All that time she needed my help and I couldn't see beyond my own fear of her frailty. She shakes her head gently.

"But you're too late, Cara. I'm already away from her, I'm already free." The light flashes across her face. She's no longer a seventeen-year-old girl, she's not even twenty to me now. She seems older than anyone I've ever known, worn down by years of abuse and pain.

"You're not sick." The words sound too short, too simple. I know the answer, but I need to hear her say it. The person who used to be Grace shakes her head.

"Not since I was a little girl," she says. She keeps her eyes on me, holds her hands palm upwards to the sky, as though to prove her health.

I keep moving slowly towards her. We're so close now that when the light comes round again I see the gray shadows below her eyes and I see her fear as she glances up, towards the cliff behind me. She's on guard, watching for someone. There's fear in her eyes as she scans the cliff top—the twins aren't her protectors, they're her captors. We might not be safe here. But before I can think about what we should do I need to hear about Meg from Grace. I need to know why, in case it's the last chance I get.

"Why did she, why did Meg . . ." My voice is barely audible. I find I can't finish, but Grace's ears are sharp.

"Why did she do it?" Grace sighs, tips her head back, as though the answer is somewhere out there, in the night sky, too big for this small beach. I see her life beating in her neck. Apart from occasionally looking towards the path that leads down from the cliff, Grace is composed, and her quiet control helps me stay calm. She lifts her head, meets my eyes again before she says, "Do you remember visiting me in the hospital a few years back? It was Christmas Day. Susie made you come in with her."

Mum had to drag me to the hospital. I moaned all the way. I wanted to be with my friends, flirting and laughing in the pub, not trapped in a stale hospital.

"Remember when our mums went to talk to the nurses?"

I don't. I only remember Grace so thin it was painful to look at her, but I nod.

"You told me a story about a time when Chris tried to kiss you, but you moved and he ended up slipping over in the mud?" I'd forgotten the story I exaggerated to entertain her, but now I remember Grace in her hospital bed, her bone-sharp shoulders shaking so hard with laughter I was worried she'd dislodge the needle in her hand.

I nod again.

"What happened when Mum came back in and she saw me laughing with you?"

I panic. I can't see what she wants me to see. In my memory, Grace just keeps laughing and laughing.

"Think about it, Cara, think hard. What happened when Mum came in?" I focus on the fringe of the memory. I remember thinking Mum and Meg would be pleased that I'd made Grace laugh after so long. Grace kept laughing when they appeared in the doorway. Mum looked uneasy; she kept casting quick, nervous glances at Meg because her face was frozen, a fixed mask of rage. She stared at Grace as though her laughter appalled her. Finally, Grace sensed her mum's stare and stopped laughing immediately. She looked winded, as though she'd just been punched in the stomach. Laughter extinguished, as easy as snuffing out a flame. When she saw the way Meg was looking at her Grace let out a small whine and then her eyes came back to meet mine. Her mouth opened and started to move. She was trying to say something to me before she started to gag and her tiny body started flipping in her bed. Suddenly she was heaving. I touched her arm, it was wet with sweat but I was too clumsy, too slow, and Meg had to push me out of the way to bring a cardboard tub under Grace's mouth as she quietly vomited. I edged away from her bed, towards the safety of my own mum, and I buried what I thought I heard Grace say into the deepest, most hidden coils of my brain: "Help me."

"You remember, don't you?" the new Grace says now. I taste salt on my lip, touch my face; it's soaking. I didn't even notice I was crying. She hasn't answered my question but she's shown me how far I was from seeing what was in front of me. How far I still am from understanding the depths of Meg's abuse.

"I have so many memories like that. Times someone almost found out what she was doing to me. But it was like none of you wanted to see the truth so you became blind to it, to me. So I studied you and others instead. I watched you. I was good at watching people. I had to be, it was the only way I'd learn anything about the world. Through watching you I learned what I could about relationships, about being a young woman. I listened to Susie moan to my mum about you, about your arguments, problems you were having, her fears for you. You taught me so much without even knowing it. Like it or not, you are part of my awakening."

I feel my mouth move to say the only thing I can think of.

"I'm sorry. I'm sorry, Grace . . . Zoe." It's the first time I've said the name, her real name, but she doesn't acknowledge it—apologies are no good to her.

She doesn't speak for a moment, just stares out to sea as though expecting something or someone to wash up on the moonlit waves before she says, "You know, I've never been here before, to the place Danny died. I thought about it a lot over the years, how it would be to come here. I thought it'd be different somehow, that maybe being here would help me make some sense of everything that's happened."

"Does it?" I ask.

"No. It doesn't. It's just a place, isn't it? It's just a beach." She looks at me with a mixture of confusion and something like pity, and I know now is not the time for me to question her. She needs to feel safe, to trust me again, and I have to let her take the lead. After so many years of abuse she needs to feel in charge now.

"Why are you here, Cara?"

I'm surprised. I thought it'd be obvious.

"I've been trying to find you."

"No, I mean, are you here to help me?" My heart aches with the memory of all those times I could have helped her, when she begged me to take her somewhere, just the two of us. But for the last few years, Meg had such tight control over her that she kept her inside, in her chair, away from the world. I wanted to relieve her pain somehow but I felt blocked by my own awkwardness, my own fear of doing something wrong, making things worse, not better. Grace is still waiting for my answer.

"I'm here to find out the truth."

"Now?" She almost laughs. "After so many years, now you want the truth? OK. OK. Fine. Here's the truth."

She burrows into the pocket of her coat and pulls out a small notebook, folded in half. It's dog-eared and almost falling apart, not at all the sort of thing Grace, the old Grace, would have. I don't take it immediately, as though taking something physical from her will make all this real.

"Cara, take it, please," she says, shaking the notebook between us. "I've written everything down. What really happened."

"That other diary?"

"Most of it was bullshit. I knew she'd be reading every word. I want you to read this. Share it if you want. I want you to know what my life has been like and what really happened that night." She waves it at me again. I reach out and take it. It feels like I'm holding evidence from another world. Old or new, I can't tell. The light comes round again and I see her hand is still shaking, even without the notebook. She's not as calm as she wants me to believe.

"I wanted to tell the truth about everything, about the night he murdered Mum." She swallows, closes her eyes briefly as if trying to smother the memory. *Drip, drip.* I wish I could tell her that since finding Meg I think I understand, in a small way, how hard it is to escape, to forget the past. But I haven't suffered a lifetime of abuse and pain. I don't know what it is to believe cruelty is love. Grace's eyes follow the notebook as I slide it into my own coat pocket before she glances back up again towards the cliff. I don't let myself imagine the twins up there, in the darkness, watching us.

"There's one thing I need you to know."

I don't trust myself to speak, so I just nod at her to keep talking. It's like she knew I was thinking about the twins.

"I want you to know I would never have told Tony anything about my life, about Mum, would never have replied to his first message if I'd known who he really was. I know you met Robbie, that he frightened you, but Tony's worse. If I'd known what he would do to her, what he was capable of . . ." Her voice trails off, as though lost for a moment in how things should have been. "When you read the diary, you'll know. She was only supposed to go to sleep, and when she woke up I'd be gone. He promised me he wouldn't hurt her. Even after everything she did to me, all the agony, I still didn't want to hurt her."

Her eyes are swollen with tears when she looks at me.

"I need you to believe me, Cara. Please, tell me you believe me." And suddenly she's Grace again, the little bird in her wheelchair asking whether an armful of balloons will carry her far, far away, begging me to help. She's the Grace who is goodness without end, the Grace who is incapable of lying, the Grace I miss. Looking at her, listening to how she wanted to protect Meg even after everything, I think that maybe Grace hasn't gone completely.

"I believe you."

She smiles a brief flash of relief and gratitude before she asks again, "So, will you help me?"

"How?"

"It's simple, Cara. The twins will be coming back to the caravan soon. They wouldn't risk leaving me alone for too long. If I don't get away they'll kill me. I'm dangerous to them now because I know what Tony did to her and they won't trust me now I've tried to get away. You can help me by letting me go. Right now. Let me have a chance at a normal life."

"Gr—Zoe, please don't ask me that. Let me call the police. They'll protect you, I promise. You haven't done anything wrong, they'll see that. You can't get away from the twins on your own. Everyone will know what she did to you, what Tony did to her. No one will blame you, everyone will want to help you."

As soon as the words leave my mouth, Grace shakes her head.

"I've spent my whole life being pitied and feeling different. I don't want that again. I just want a normal life, Cara. If I stay here I'll always be the girl this happened to. I'll never escape my past, I'll never escape her."

Suddenly I realize how little she knows of the world. She thinks she can just escape, after everything that's happened, leave everything behind and start a new life.

"I just want a chance to live my life the way I choose. That's all. That's all I want." She makes it sound so simple, so reasonable.

She moves towards me, takes my hand in her own. Her skin is cold and the realness of her flesh almost makes me shout out. My instinct is to pull my hand away from this stranger but I don't, because I need this connection to her, need to feel the softness of her, the pulse of her life in my hands. She squeezes my hand. My skin warms where we touch.

"Please, Cara, let me know what it's like to be free."

As the light comes back around again, I see tears have been rolling down her face and I see the sweet girl she once was, but I see so much more in her as well. She's books and books of unwritten diaries, she's undiscovered even to herself.

Suddenly, I hear raised voices. They sound like they're coming from up on the cliff. Grace has heard them too; she's turned towards the cliff, her eyes hard as she focuses on the sounds. She drops my hand like our touch is burning her. I can't make out the words, but the voices are just loud enough for me to recognize him. Jon. His is the loudest voice; he sounds panicked. I don't recognize the others but I'm sure it's the twins. I reach out for Grace but she's moved away from me.

"Just let me go, Cara, please," she says, moving deeper into the shadows as though she too wants to be taken by the place that took her brother. I realize she's giving me one more chance, one more chance to do what I never could—to help her, to really help her. And then I hear the unmistakable sound of rocks falling.

24

Jon

There's laughter as I start to run. Robbie wants me to know we've switched positions, that he's just behind me now, on higher ground. The light from the lighthouse passes over me again and again and again. It seems to know exactly where I'm going, following me. I don't care about making noise or drawing attention anymore. Now the darkness is safer than the light. I start to run down the hill. Robbie's laughter turns into a whoop, he's just steps behind me. Tony is close by too, although I don't know where exactly. The light swings round, I feel like an animal perfectly positioned in a rifle's sights. I don't have a plan, all I can do is run towards the sea. The brambles lash against my legs as though trying to claw me to the ground. The whooping gets louder as I run faster, faster downhill. There's a rush as one of them comes close behind me, so close I hear his legs pumping through the undergrowth, his breath rhythmic, so much calmer than my own.

It's Robbie, and he makes a high-pitched chattering sound. He's laughing at me, teasing me like an animal trapped and running desperate circles in a cage. My heart is a drum in my chest but my legs are elastic, they stretch onwards towards the sea. My right foot catches on a snare of bramble, twisting my ankle. I shout out as it sends me forward, but manage to catch myself in midair. I don't fall, but it sets off a fresh round of laughter from Robbie. I keep running. In every wave of light from the lighthouse I see the edge of the cliff getting closer. Tony runs alongside his brother now. I wish he'd do something to stop Robbie, but his loyalty is with him, not with me. I have the feeling they aren't even trying, they don't need to, they know there's nowhere I can go. I limp on, like a mouse half mauled to death by a cat. I know it's pointless, but the instinct to keep moving is too strong. One on the left, one on the right, I can only keep going forward, flying down the hill until suddenly my feet feel lighter because, without warning, the brambles have disappeared, there's nothing biting at my ankles with tiny razor teeth. I'm on the grass. The light glides round. I'm standing on the grassy clearing I passed just a few minutes earlier. I'm closer to the edge than I thought. My adrenaline and fear want me to keep running but I know if I do I'll run off the edge. There will be rocks below, hard and cold, waiting for every soft part of my body. Those rocks will kill me for sure. I force my legs to stop. I'm so close to the edge the beach is directly below. In the next lick of light I see the twins come towards me. They're panting, Robbie enjoying the end of his game, Tony a few paces behind. Black again. They disappear.

"Who the fuck are you?" Robbie, left or right, I don't know.

"I, I, I . . ." I stammer, making him laugh again. The light moves round. They're getting closer, creeping slowly like predators, keeping to the longer grass. They're still a few feet away, eyes fixed on me.

"Perhaps now is the time you tell me why you've been following me, *Mr.* Jon?" He knows my name. I remember Mandy from the haulage company called me Mr. Jon just a few hours ago. She must have told him I was looking for him, that she sent me to the pub, and roused his suspicion. He saw me just before he left the pub, knew I'd been watching him.

The black, when it comes again, feels darker because of the brief light.

"I thought I'd lost you on the path on the way up. But you were hiding, waiting for us, weren't you?"

"Rob, you don't have to—"

"Shut up, Tone."

I have to try to reason with them. They need to believe I can help them. I feel every cell of my body, light with fear. I see Jakey waiting for me outside New Barn Cottage. I could lie, pretend I didn't hear them talking outside the caravan, pretend I don't know that Grace has something over Tony, that he's scared of her, that I don't think Tony's capable of murder. But it would serve no purpose. I have to let them know I heard everything, I have to take the risk. My breath is still ragged from the running, forcing me to talk in rapid, short bursts.

"I heard you talking. Tony, I heard what you said: the lies Grace would tell the police, that if she did, you'd go back to prison. I know she's involved with her mum's murder. If you tell me the truth, maybe I can help."

I hear one of them shuffle and Tony asks, "How can you help?"

I swallow. At last my breath is becoming more regular.

"I can act as a witness. I can tell the police everything I heard, tell them Grace was blackmailing you. I'm a journalist, I'll help you prove your story. But you have to tell me the truth about what happened to Meg and Grace. That's the only way."

"You must think we're fucking idiots." Robbie's voice is a growl out of the darkness before the light flashes round again. Tony has moved closer to his brother, he looks like he's ready to hold him back if he needs to. Robbie's eyes are fixed on me; his cheeks are red and his lips wet. I'm surprised he hasn't moved forward, closer to me.

"You think we're going to believe a fucking journalist? You've been buzzing around like a fly on shit. You're not here to help Grace, you're not here to help my brother—"

"He might be serious, Rob," but Tony's drowned out by the sound of rubble falling, hitting the rocks below, a cruel, strangely hollow sound.

That's when I realize why they won't come any closer. They don't need to. The ground starts to crumble beneath my feet; my stomach rises to my throat. I think I hear Robbie laugh as I look at Tony, his face frozen in horror. More rocks fall, in a trickle this time. I close my eyes, hear Tony call out something that isn't even a word, but it's too late, there's nothing he can do, nothing anyone can do. I'm glad my eyes are closed, it makes it easier to see Jakey clearly; smiling, healthy, and happy as the earth falls away beneath me.

25

Cara

Grace starts moving away from me. I try to go after her.

"Grace, no, please don't—" but I stop talking because from across the beach I hear another steady trickle of stones falling before they smash hard against the sharp rocks below. It's the sound I was always taught to fear as a child. A scream—Jon—comes just seconds later, followed by more falling stones. I cry out. Time slows down, seems to move in frames as I run a few paces towards where I think he fell before my head catches up and I realize I'm leaving Grace, letting her get away. I stop. Everything is quiet, except for the sound of the sea sighing with its endless work, moving tiny stones back and forth, and the blood pounding in my ears. I can't hear either Jon or Grace anymore. Jon might be dead. If he is, I should stay with Grace and call Upton. That's the best way I can help her. She might not think she needs us, but she does. But what if Jon's not dead, just badly injured, dying?

I can't help them both. I'm stuck, the scales perfectly balanced, and with every ragged breath I take I know Grace is getting away and Jon's life could be fading. I look towards where Jon fell and then I look back to where I was talking to Grace. The scales tip and I start to run up the beach, towards the path and the foot of the cliff. Even though there's a risk of landslide and falling rocks hitting me it feels safer here, my body pressed against the side of the cliff where they won't be able to see me. I hear the twins, still up on the cliff above as the wind catches their voices. I'm too far away to make out the words but I'm close enough to hear that one of them is upset. The other is trying to calm his brother, keep him from getting too close to the edge, to the place where Jon fell. I hear the word "accident." I force myself to wait. There's no sound or movement from the rocks where he fell, no sign whether Jon survived the fall. The voices above have died but I force myself to stay, my cheek pressed up against the chalky cold foot of the cliff. I wait for my breath to slow enough for me to breathe in time with the waves. Even though I can't hear them, the twins could still be up there and I know they'd kill me if they found me. Suddenly a tiny light—a flashlight—on the headland catches my eye. It's moving, like someone is running. My breath catches with relief as I realize they're not coming down the path, they're heading back towards town. They must think that's where Grace will be heading. It makes sense. It's where most people would go. But Grace isn't most people.

My voice is small as I call quietly into the darkness.

"Jon?"

The silence is so loud the emptiness is almost like a reply.

"Jon?"

The beam from the lighthouse is approaching. I'm terrified of what it might reveal, terrified of it showing me Jon bloodied and unmoving, his eyes open, forever gripped by the shock of his death. The light tracks across sharp black rocks, their surfaces pockmarked with barnacles and drenched in seaweed. I see the sand around him first, splattered red with blood from where he fell. The human bulk of him in this hard place makes me cry out, a sound I haven't heard before, and I run towards him. I kneel in the wet sand but I can't touch him. Not yet. He's as still as the hard rocks underneath him. One of his legs is bent at the knee, kicking up towards his hip at the front, the wrong way. His arms look like they've been stretched away from his body and then flung back; they sag around him, making his clothes look empty. I can't see where the blood is coming from. His eyes are closed, thank God, but his face is strangely empty, as though he's already left his body. My hand shakes as I stroke it against the cold skin on the back of his hand.

"Jon," I whisper again and again, as though trying to call him back from wherever he's gone. My tears fall and wet his face. Without warning his cheek twitches as one of my tears splashes just below his eye. But it's dark so I can't be sure. Another falls and again he seems to wince, as though my tear is adding to his pain. He makes a low gargling sound, like the breath itself is trying to decide whether it should stay with him or move on. Blood trickles from the side of his mouth as the gargle becomes a word.

"Grace," he says. His eyelids ripple, he tries to cough against the blood in his mouth. "It was Grace."

I wipe my own tears from his face, say his name again, but Jon doesn't respond.

26

Jon

Six months later

The trees tracing the edge of the football pitch glow orange in the winter sun and the ref's whistle blows as Ruth helps me out of the car.

"It's started!" I say, wanting her to hurry, but she's fussing with my laces. I wish she wouldn't. It's not like I notice whether they're done up or not. Ruth senses my impatience.

"Don't rush me!" she says. Without looking up she taps my knee and I smile down at her blond head. It's good, this gentle teasing, it feels like a milestone. Ruth was the first person I saw when I came out of my coma; she barely left my side for two weeks. Whenever I tried to talk about us, apologize for being a twat, she'd kiss my forehead and tell me to shush.

It's been raining a lot recently. The parking lot and sports field are slick with mud. I feel Ruth's arms strain behind my chair. I try to help by pushing my wheels forward but it's not very effective. Mud sprays behind us, Ruth sounds out of breath, and we've barely moved. I picture Jakey pausing in his game to scan the people watching on the sidelines, trying to find our faces, masking his disappointment so his teammates don't tease him later.

Ruth groans, but my chair doesn't move an inch. This is pointless.

"Shit. Look, you go on, Ruth, we're already late, shout extra loud for me. I can get myself back to the car," I say, leaning down hard on my right wheel to turn around.

"No, no, come on, I can get you there, I just need to . . ." She pushes the sleeves of her jacket up, tries to get purchase on the slippery ground. I move about an inch. "Ruth, please, just stop. Look, what matters is that one of us is there, OK? You can come and find me at halftime. I'll listen to the radio, have a snooze, I'll be fine."

She comes round in front of my chair. She's frowning, her lips twisting around the words she's stopping herself from saying. We've talked a few times about accepting things are going to be different, limited. I got Alex, my physical therapist, to have a quiet word with her, explain that sometimes it feels better to accept my limitations rather than constantly battle them. He told me later what her response was: "Are you sure you've met Jon?"

But this Saturday afternoon she listens to me. She nods, kisses my chilly cheek with her warm lips. Gives me the car keys and heads towards the shouts and calls from Jakey's game.

I start to haul myself back to the car. Alex reckons in a couple of months I'll be walking with a cane, but Alex is paid to be optimistic. The docs said I was lucky to keep my leg. As well as the leg, I broke three ribs, my pelvis, both arms, my cheekbone, and my collarbone. And that's just what was broken, not counting the bits that were punctured and perforated. Perhaps it sounds trite, but almost dying saved me. I know what matters now. Listening matters, family meals matter, being there for my son matters.

"Jon, mate?"

A tall man strides in front of me. He's wearing a blue hat with a yellow pom-pom, and inside his navy puffer I catch a glimpse of a wool sweater with a reindeer stitched on the front, even though it's only December 2. He's in his midforties, grinning like he's got the funniest joke in the world on a loop in his head. He bends towards me, resting his hands on his thighs like he's greeting a small dog. I can't remember his name but I think I met him at the last match.

"Hi," I say, nodding at him. He points at his chest.

"Tim," he says. More grinning. "You heading to the game, mate?"

"Actually, I'm just going back to the car."

"Uh-oh, St. Bethell's losing again, are they?"

I wonder if he gets cold teeth from all that smiling.

"No, it's just, it's a bit muddy, with the chair, getting over there was a bit much, so I'm going to just wait in the car," I say clumsily.

Tim looks down at me and towards the pitch and then back again to me. His smile falls for just a moment before he says, "The hell you are, mate. I'll get you over there."

"No, no, really, I don't think . . ." but Tim has already disappeared behind me, grabbed the handles. He slips a bit at first, but I can feel his strength through my chair.

"We'll be there in no time," he says. Even though I can't see him, I'm sure he's grinning again. He doesn't say anything for a moment, perhaps building up courage before he says what I knew was coming.

"I hope you don't mind my asking, mate, but I'm curious. You were involved in the Nichols mess over the summer, weren't you? That Grace girl, or whoever she was?" He was more eager than I thought. The wheelchair jerks through the mud, my head bouncing, jolting me in my seat. I could tell him he's got the wrong bloke, but he knows my name, knows Jakey, he'll know I'm lying. So I decide to say nothing. He doesn't seem to notice or mind that I'm not keen to talk.

"What's your theory, then, on what happened to her after she got away?"

I clench my jaw but remind myself what Alex says about being mindful about where I hold tension. With effort, I relax it. Tim leans over the back of the wheelchair so he can catch my answers.

"There is no theory, there's only what happened. She'd been studying people driving for years. She took the Craig twins' car, managed to drive herself to the haulage depot, and hid in the empty cab of one of the trucks, the first batch that left at midnight that night. No one knows where she ended up because those trucks went from Oslo to Sorrento. The twins were picked up the morning after, trying to board a boat from Plymouth. Traces of Megan's blood were found on Tony's coat and her DNA was in the caravan. They're in prison now. That's all there is to know."

Tim has been leaning forward too much. He's got my wheels stuck in a particularly sticky patch of mud. He pulls me back a few paces for a run-up.

"And what about the girl, the neighbor who let her get away?"

My jaw clenches again and this time I know, no matter how hard I try, I won't be able to release it. Ruth told me Cara came to the hospital twice while I was unconscious. She left flowers. She kept calling until Ruth persuaded me to let her visit at the end of September. Both my arms were in plaster and my leg was still a

301

formless red sausage with pins sticking out like someone had been practicing voodoo. Cara stood awkwardly by my bed in the spare room at New Barn Cottage, her eyes skittish, unable to find where to rest. She looked younger than ever, just a kid. What had I been thinking, getting her caught up in the whole business?

"Well, at least you look a bit better than last time I saw you," she said.

I laughed; it turned into a cough that hurt my chest. Cara's eyes widened in alarm. She glanced towards the door, looking for help. I shook my head, telling her not to bother, I was fine.

We talked clumsily about other things—Cara's place at Bristol Uni, Jakey's summer football camp—until Cara bit her lip and blurted, "I'm sorry you think I did the wrong thing, letting Grace leave that night."

The weight of her words landed heavy in my bones. I felt exhausted just hearing her name.

"I don't think you did the wrong thing. I just wish we'd got more answers."

"But you read the real diary, what Meg was doing to her, it was . . . it was torture. If she'd stayed she'd have been charged with accessory to murder, she'd have escaped one prison and gone straight into another." Cara's voice was strained, her words too practiced. I don't say that if I'd had my way Grace would've been charged with something more serious. I took a deep breath that made my ribs scream.

"Look, I don't want to argue about this. There's no doubt, no doubt that Meg was sicker than any of us imagined. But does that justify her murder? There were so many other ways Grace could have got away. There were people she could have told about what Meg was doing to her."

"She tried, Jon! You've read her diary, the real one. She tried telling me, telling that nurse. Meg had total control, not only over Grace but over all of us. Even if one of us had listened to Grace, heard the truth, I doubt we'd have believed it."

"That doesn't justify murder."

"But she didn't murder anyone."

"Tony has withstood every questioning, every test. Both of them confessed to their role in my fall but have resolutely denied Tony's involvement in the murder." I was getting angry now.

"So?"

"So if we'd been able to question Grace, maybe we'd have more answers."

"Yeah, but don't forget, Jon: if we'd had more time with Grace, you wouldn't be lying here now."

Cara blinked, glanced down at her feet. I saw a tear drop to the floor.

"Look, Cara—"

But she didn't want to hear. She just turned on her heel and ran out of the door.

That night in June comes back to me in sharp fragments of memory. Like stepping on a piece of broken glass when I thought all the shards had long been swept away, it cuts just as deep each time. Of course I'm grateful to Cara, bloody grateful to her for saving my life. I don't blame her for anything. I blame myself. I was the one who fell, who forced her into making a decision between saving me or freeing Grace. What I can't do is pretend that a dangerous person on the run God knows where is a good outcome. Other lives could be at risk because of me. It's that thought, not the painful knitting back together of my bones and muscles, that keeps me awake at night.

Cara's right, we all should have listened more carefully to

Grace—or Zoe, as she is now. She planted the diary at the murder scene, I'm sure of it. She knew Meg was reading it so she only had good things to say about her, only bad things to say about her dad. Meg would have approved of the way Grace portrayed him, pleased to know the tales she'd carefully woven about him were taking effect. As for Grace, she must have known Simon would be the main suspect. Whether he was calling or not, I don't know, but I don't think for a minute that Grace didn't know what she was doing, that her diary wouldn't add fuel to the fire, giving the police and the community someone to focus on. She was treading a fine line and she did it beautifully.

Her second account, written after the murder, still wasn't the whole truth. She'd spent her life studying the best, after all. She knew just how many secrets to give away and how to bury the truth even deeper. I knew when I heard them talking outside the caravan that Tony and Robbie weren't manipulating her; she was manipulating them. She knew she could frame Tony for Meg's murder, that everyone would believe her over a man who'd been in trouble with the police since he was a teenager. She was the victim of years of abuse, but she was also her mother's daughter through and through. After all this I'm in the same position I was a year ago, after I wrote the article for the *Chronicle*. What I believe to be the truth is totally at odds with what everyone else wants to believe is true.

Shouting from the game brings me back to the football pitch.

"Sounds like someone's scored," I say to Tim, but he doesn't hear, he doesn't care about the football, not now, not when he's getting the details of a great anecdote he can dine out on for months.

"I heard that you don't think it was the twins who did it."

"Did what?" It's facile to play stupid but I'm tired of these questions. The part I'm trying so hard to forget is the only bit everyone wants to talk about.

"Killed the mum, of course. I read somewhere you thought that Tony Craig didn't do it." He's slowing his pace, trying to eke out the time he has to question me. My leg throbs and my head feels heavy, stuffed with all these questions I'm always asked but have promised Ruth I'll never answer, not honestly, anyway. She wants to forget almost as much as I do.

"Mate, trust me, I've said all kinds of crazy shit since the accident: just ask Ruth—it's the morphine. Whatever you read, or thought you heard, forget it. Honestly, I don't remember any of it."

I have the lie down pretty perfectly, but every time I say it a little bell chimes in my head.

You win, Grace. You win again.

"So you think he did do it then?"

"All I know is that those twins put me in this effing thing." I hit the side of the chair.

"Yeah, right. The bastards."

But Tim's not interested in what happened to me. My story is clear, you just have to look at me to believe it. He wants the other story, but he can't have it.

"What about the dad?" Tim isn't going to let his chance with me escape so easily. "You saw the interview with him on *The Morning Show*?"

I tried to watch it but I didn't get far. The presenters, sitting next to Simon, looked a bit uneasy perched on the edge of their orange sofa, but Simon seemed better than ever before. His dark eyes still crawled like shiny beetles around the studio, but he seemed to fill his own skin at last.

"So, Simon, tell us, did you ever suspect Megan was abusing your daughter?" The presenter did quite a good job of masking her discomfort. Simon cleared his throat carefully before he started speaking his rehearsed words.

"Well, Katie, Megan was a master manipulator. She'd blackmail me to keep my suspicions to myself. She'd threaten to accuse me of rape or being violent and she'd remind me that everyone would believe her over me." Although he'd probably been told not to, Simon stared right into the black eye of the camera. I felt as though he was talking directly to me.

"I wasn't in a good place at the time. I was unwell myself after Meg blamed me for our son's death and wouldn't let me see Grace. I lost sight of what was real and what wasn't. I knew Meg was lying about Grace's name and age, of course. I suspected she was up to something else but I didn't know what. I came close to telling a doctor the truth once, but I'm ashamed to say I lost my nerve. Meg could have ruined me, got me locked up. You see now what she was capable of."

I didn't know if it was sweat or tears, but Ruth saw the droplets running down my face.

"Maybe we'll watch this another time," she said, flicking the television off and wiping my cheek with a tissue. I'm relieved that, so far, there hasn't been another time. The truth is I think Simon knew Grace was involved in Meg's murder, he knew she'd do anything to get away from her. He didn't come forward when the police were looking for him because he wanted to give her the time to get away, to escape. That's why he didn't tell the police about her real name and age. He let the world think it was him and that she was someone else to protect her, to give her a chance. He was, in his way, trying at last to be a father to her.

"Mate?" Tim asks, pulling instead of pushing my chair as though he's trying to jerk an answer out of me.

"No, I never saw it." I sound the full stop at the end of the sentence. People like Tim don't want to know what I know, not really. He thinks he does, but he doesn't, because if he did he wouldn't be able to smile so much. Instead, he'd lie awake night after night and he'd see a hundred different Graces, one a waifish shop assistant in Paris, another a beggar in Munich, another a waitress in Rome, all of them walking with the same barely perceptible limp.

We're almost at the pitch now. Ruth is standing just outside a small group of mums and dads. She's bundled up in a scarf and hat but she's still moving from one foot to the other to keep warm. She's shouting, "Good pass, Leo! Come on, Bethell's!"

My heart constricts with love as soon as I see her and I start impatiently pushing myself along. Now the ground is firmer, I don't need Tim anymore, Tim and his questions about something that can never be made right. I need Ruth and I need our future.

"Thanks for your help, Tim, I can take it from here," but Tim keeps pushing me along.

"Thanks, mate, I can take it from here," I say, louder. Tim stops pushing and moves round to the front of my chair. He looks like he's thinking about shaking my hand, so I keep pushing myself on, towards Ruth, and say with a nod, "Appreciate your help."

There's a small note of failure in his voice as he calls after me, "Any time, mate, any time."

Ruth claps her hands together when she sees me, kisses my cheek, and I bite my tongue when she says Tim is a good bloke. I wave at Jakey. He skip-runs a couple of joyful paces when he sees me and waves back. Ruth holds my hand until Jakey has the ball and he's running fast up the wing. We let go of each other to clap but then the ref blows his whistle, someone's offside, and through the gaggle of parents groaning at the ref, laughing with each other and calling encouragement to the muddy players, I see a young woman in a blue coat. She's standing at the opposite edge of the football pitch. She has blond hair that looks too perfect to be real and she's staring straight at me. When she knows I've seen her she smiles and raises her finger to her little rosebud lips.

Shhh.

Then the ref blows his whistle and I blink and realize it wasn't Grace but another woman in a blue coat and a familiar wave of relief and fear washes through me as I remind myself that even though we don't know where she is, Grace is not here. Grace is gone.

27

Cara

"Welcome to your first tutorial. It's wonderful to see you all here."

Dr. Mackenzie makes a point of trying to look each of the twelve of us in the eye as he scans the table, like he's making a toast. Some look away, embarrassed, giggling quietly, but I look straight back. I want to show him I'm ready, that I'm where I should be, here in his large office at Bristol University that smells like leather, the air humid with concentration.

"As most of you know already, I'm Dr. Mackenzie and this place where you find yourselves now is where we shall, all of us, be meeting every Tuesday and Thursday, two to five p.m. for the next year. Perhaps some of you will come to love this place, while for others, I'm afraid, it may feel like your own personal penitentiary." There are shy titters from around the group. "But I hope, at the very least, it will be a sort of mind gym for you all. A place to sweat out ideas, take a few punches and give a few—considered and well placed—in return. Here, together, we will try to understand some of the most ethically challenging acts committed by humans and, in turn, try to formulate a framework for how we believe society should respond to those acts. It will be hard work for us all, and for some it may feel distasteful at times, perhaps even morally and spiritually confrontational, but it is my belief that in order to understand people and therefore the world in which we live, we have to understand all different types of people and expressions of humanity, even if to us they may seem inhumane. So, there we are. Now, before I go on, and I will go on and on and on"—more polite laughter—"I want to meet all of you and for you to meet each other. So, let's go round the table and if you could introduce yourself please, and explain a bit about why you're here, champing at the bit to study criminology." Dr. Mackenzie opens a large white palm towards the guy sitting to my left. Next to him there's a girl who's scribbling notes already and then, I realize, my stomach plunging, it'll be my turn.

The first guy stands, color flushes to his cheeks. He looks like he was knitted specially to go to university. He's wearing a plaid shirt under a wool V-neck sweater, and brown cords. He takes his glasses off before he smiles confidently at us all.

"Hello, I'm Jamie. I did my A-levels at Harrow before working abroad . . ."

I suddenly feel like laughing. I wish I could take a photo to send to Mum. She'd hoot if she saw this place, these people, me in the middle of them. She cried when the acceptance letter came in the mail and was still crying when she pulled me into her arms.

"I couldn't be more proud of you, Car," she said, a little too loudly, into my ear. Although she'd never say so, I know she'd be even happier if I was studying history of art, or anything other than criminology.

While Jon was in the hospital I told Upton everything Jon had told me about Meg, what she was doing to Grace. Upton interviewed Dr. Rossi and slowly others came forward, and then there was a flood of stories. Nurses remembered seeing Meg fiddling with Grace's IV, doctors admitted feeling uncomfortable with Grace's test results but bowed to pressure from Meg, friends realized it must have been Meg who stole their earrings. Meg forced such a cocktail of drugs into Grace that even she started to believe Grace was unwell. Her conditions and symptoms baffled most doctors and if there was ever a hint that anyone was becoming suspicious she'd move Grace to a new doctor. They didn't move to Ashford for a better life, they moved because Meg thought—correctly—that the aging Dr. Parker could be more easily manipulated for referrals and prescriptions. She didn't make those trips to London to get the best care for Grace, she made them to pick up illegal drugs and fake genetic test results that led to Grace's muscular dystrophy diagnosis. She carefully researched which drugs to give Grace to weaken her heart, which drugs would cause her to have seizures, and which drugs would stop her being able to swallow. Meg was smarter than any of us knew, her deceit well researched and her tracks carefully covered.

Mum moved a few months after Grace left. Our bungalow sold for far less than it should, but too many people had seen it on the news. People move to Cornwall to live close to the sea, not the scene of a brutal murder, but Mum didn't care. It gave her enough to buy a tiny two-bed flat in the center of Ashford. She's decided, on the advice of her therapist, to get to know her new neighbors slowly. Mum had a breakdown, or in Zara's words "needed a bit of a rest," when the truth about Meg came out. Zara and Mum closed the salon for a month. She told me Meg had taken the photo of Jakey in hospital and persuaded Mum to post it online.

She said she was sorry before she started crying again. I told her—honestly—that I don't blame her. We were all under Meg's spell.

I helped Mum take down all the photos of Meg and Grace late one night because she didn't want anyone seeing us. I caught Mum staring at a photo of the two of them, both leaning forward to grin into the camera, Meg holding Grace's hand between both her own. Mum's eyes glazed in concentration as she said, "I used to think it was the cutest thing, you know, the way they always held hands."

I looked closer: in the photo, Grace's fingers were swollen red, flushed with blood. Meg was always touching Grace, on her hand, her shoulder, her leg. But like Grace said, it was never to hold her daughter, or to reassure, like when Mum holds mine. It was a way for Meg to remind Grace that she was in charge. Her touch was a warning.

Mum and Zara are back running the salon again now and Zara dyed Mum's hair blond on the first day they reopened, which I take as a sign they're both looking forward.

Dennis is just "the butcher" again and Sylvia does her nails at home now; she says it's to save money. David Raffin hasn't been seen in Summervale since June. Martin has been heard saying he always had his suspicions about Meg but no one believed him. Meg and Grace pulled us all together but, when the truth came out, they pulled us all apart again.

"So I'm really delighted to be here and look forward to getting to know you all." The room breaks around me into gentle, supportive applause as Jamie, now the color of a poinsettia, sits down. Dr. Mackenzie turns with a smile to the note-taking, black-haired girl next to me. She's less red, but far shyer than Jamie.

"Hello everyone, my name's Rose-Marie and I moved to the UK from Hong Kong . . ."

Jon didn't want me to visit when he was recovering at home. I felt it as soon as I walked into his room. The atmosphere around his bed was unfriendly, like a hand gently pushing me away. I tried not to let my disappointment show. I'd wanted to tell him about my plans to become a journalist. How I was going to study criminology and then do a postgrad in journalism. I thought he'd want to hear, but he didn't ask and I lost my nerve to tell him. He'd written me a card thanking me for helping him, for calling the ambulance. He didn't even mention Grace.

Turns out Jon's instinct was right from the beginning, from the first time he met Meg and Grace. He knew it was wrong that Simon was being kept from his daughter. He wrote the article and withstood the attack as well as he could. It makes me less angry with him now—I know he blames me for letting Grace go—which is definitely a good thing. It means I'm more likely to leave him alone.

"Thank you," Rose-Marie says in a tiny voice before crumpling back into her chair.

I feel all the eyes in the room turn to me and my heart seems to have risen up from my chest because it's now beating in my ears. I'm not sure I can remember anything, not even my own name, let alone the reason why I'm here. My hands are clammy against the table as I stand. I force myself to look at the curious faces, wonder whether any of them will become my friends. At the end of the table, there's a tiny girl sitting next to Dr. Mackenzie; I hadn't noticed her before. Her nose just about reaches over the tabletop, she's wearing a baggy gray beanie, and behind her huge glasses her little eyes are fixed on me, like an X-ray. I look away from her, make myself smile, dig my thumbnail into the side of my finger, swallow, and speak.

"Hi, I'm Cara. I'm here because over the summer I learned

for myself how even the worst crimes and the people who commit them often don't fit neatly into the categories of guilty or innocent. I want to understand the space between guilt and innocence, I want to explore how the penal system could change to better help and rehabilitate someone who is both victim and perpetrator." A couple of people nod in agreement and others tap their pens against empty writing pads. "I'm really happy to be here," I add, and as I sit gratefully back down I glance across the table. Grace is still there, smiling her wonky smile at me. I know she's not real. I glance down at my hands, make myself blink, and when I look up again Grace is gone.

Epilogue

He arrived at 1 a.m. I was standing in the dark kitchen, waiting to let him in through the back door. I'd already cleared the house of any evidence of what she's been doing to me—leftover vials and bottles of drugs—put all our dark secrets in a black bag for the garbage men to take away. I didn't want the police finding them, confusing the investigation into my disappearance. After so long I couldn't risk anyone guessing the truth, not now when I need time to escape. He kicked off his shoes outside, just like we agreed. Down the hall, Mum snored. The reality of him being there was overwhelming, an online cartoon become flesh. He was like a miracle. I raised my finger to my lips.

"Shhh."

He followed me down the hall. We paused outside her door, to check the other was ready.

"We tie her up, we inject her, we take the money, and we leave," he whispered.

Her door opened easily. She was snoring, greedy and undisturbed by the yellow streetlight that seeped from the window like an infection. The air around her smelled off, like sour milk. She was turned towards us, her mouth slack, her cheek squashed against her pillow, her thin curls stuck to her forehead. I felt all my hatred and all my love as I stared down at her. She started to stir. I smiled. Her puffed eyelids parted, lazy at first and then, when she saw me standing smiling above her, they opened wide.

"Grace, what are you . . ." She tried to sit up, but Tony was quick, he pushed her down, half lifting himself onto her bed, pinning her arms above her. She screamed my name and I punched the gag into her mouth. Tony shouted, "Now!" and I watched her face crease with horror when she saw the syringe. I felt warm, knowing she knew what was about to happen. I had become her and she was me. She knew the pleasure in my power and I knew her fear. All this passed between us without words. I wanted the moment to stretch out, to solidify so it would last forever, but Tony shouted again, "Now!"

She started bucking beneath him. I aimed the needle for her arm, started to push, but she thrashed and the syringe leapt out of my hand, falling to the floor behind me.

Tony swore. She looked like she was going to erupt beneath him. All my senses surged. I knew the lamp was there. I yanked it out of the socket and my arm dropped under its weight. Tony watched. It took him a moment to understand as she squirmed, grotesque between his knees. He loosened his grip and she rose up beneath him like a cresting wave, making him fall back. But I already had the lamp above my head. I paused. I wanted her to see me, above her like this. She looked at me in a way I've never seen before, like I was a stranger to her, a person in my own right. Her eyes were wide with surprise, and then I catapulted my arms forward. The curled, iron foot of the lamp landed between her eyes. Behind the gag, she made a dull, sucking sound. Her clawing arms dropped as her strength started to fall away, like a battery finally dying. She fell back onto her pillow, her eyes so wide I could see their roundness as they spun in their sockets. Blood started to roll down her forehead from a wound I couldn't see.

Behind me Tony started mewling like a kitten.

"Christ. What have you done? We have to go. We have to go right now," he said as more blood seeped, warm and rich, from her head. I felt a flash of anger. He was weak, this man who had let my brother drown. I didn't want him there for that moment, that pure, perfect moment that was just between Mum and me.

He started edging towards the door. He was shaking, desperate to leave.

"Wait for me in the car." I was in charge now. I gazed back at her, wanted to wipe her blood all over her face, but I knew I had to think about evidence, about the future. My future.

Tony's shadow loomed across the walls as he left the room. I was glad. I lifted the lamp above my head again, the weight made it drop harder. The curled foot struck her forehead again and again. When my arms were tired and my gloved hands couldn't lift the lamp anymore she made a wet, grunting sound, and as her eyes filled with blood she kept them fixed on me. I watched as the darkness came for her. And as I watched her life slip away, I felt my own glow and I became alive, reborn. Grace was gone, and Zoe stood in her place.

Author's Note

A friend and I once had a discussion about how all stories are based on real life to varying degrees. I've thought about that a lot recently and am inclined to agree. *Grace Is Gone* is no exception, as the novel was inspired by the story in Missouri of mother and daughter Dee Dee and Gypsy Rose Blanchard.

Dee Dee was diagnosed posthumously as having Munchausen by proxy or fabricated illness, which is described by the NHS as "a rare form of child abuse. It occurs when a parent or carer, usually the child's biological mother, exaggerates or deliberately causes symptoms of illness in the child." Dee Dee inflicted years of unfathomable suffering on her daughter—forcing her to have unnecessary surgeries, making her live in a wheelchair, fabricated endless medical emergencies for her, and even told the world she had the cognitive capacities of a seven-year-old when she was, all along, a healthy young woman. Together with her then boyfriend, Gypsy Rose plotted and carried out her mum's murder to escape the horrifying abuse. *Grace Is Gone* is inspired by these real-life events but it is a work of fiction and all the characters and events are products of my imagination.

I found Gypsy Rose's story absolutely devastating, but the more I thought about it, the more her story raised broader questions in my mind—questions which in time became the bedrock of Meg and Grace's story. It is a story about what happens when maternal love—possibly the fiercest type of love—mutates and goes wrong. Meg and Grace's story is also, to my mind, about justice and redemption: like Cara at the end of the novel, I found myself wondering whether murder in extreme circumstances can ever be justified? What if I'd experienced such horrifying and debilitating abuse as Meg inflicted on Grace, who would I be? What if I tried to tell the world, but no one believed me? Would I be driven to commit the ultimate crime to escape?

Would you?

Acknowledgments

I'd like to start by reassuring you that none of the characters in this book are inspired by anyone in my family. James, Otis, Edward, Sandy, Tim, Catherine, Eloise, Joshua, Rose, Alex, Laura, Leo, Barnaby, and Chloe: you can all breathe easy! Thank you for being terrible material for a psychological suspense novel.

I'm absolutely indebted to my incredible agent Nelle Andrew whose dedication and passion is second to none and whose gentle parental advice has helped see me through some of the tougher moments of being an author and a new mum.

Huge thanks to my two editors at Little, Brown, Lucy Malagoni and Lucy Dauman ("The Lucys"), for guiding me through with such skill, grace and calm, good humor.

I'd also like to thank Kate Hibbert, Andy Hine, Helena Doree and Sarah Birdsey, the fantastic foreign rights team at Little, Brown.

My thanks also to desk editor Thalia Proctor, copy editors

Zoe Gullen and Mari Roberts, and to proofreader Jon Appleton. Thank you for rescuing my appalling grammar.

My thanks also to Steve Panton for the fantastic cover design that made me feel so excited I almost went into early labor.

Deep gratitude to Dr. Tim Hall and Dr. Deepa Shah for their professional wisdom and for taking the time and care to respond so thoroughly to my very dull questions. Thank you.

Personal thanks for the love and support to "The Berlin Five"— Marlies Lenstra, Rebekka Benzie, Charity Garnett, and Becky Murrell. I love you all.

I am indebted to my friend Tor Garnett for her wisdom: "Manage your energy and not your time." Thanks also to my friend and fellow author Lulah Ellender for the sage advice and professional first read.

My gratitude to the Ladykillers for sharing all the highs and lows. It is excellent to be part of the coven.

To my darling godkids—Maalu, Dash, Sephy and India—I love you all but please put this down, I'm sure you're not old enough to read it yet!

Thank you to my son, Otis, for being with me—literally while I wrote this book and for arriving when it was mostly finished. You have changed the world for the better just by being you. I love you.

Thank you to my husband, James, for always saying "I love you" even when I've done nothing but snarl and talk about how tired I am. I love the life we've made together. Finally, to the readers of this and all books—thank you!

This book is dedicated to my wonderful parents, Edward and Sandy Elgar. Thank you feels so inadequate for all the love you share, but it's all I have—so thank you.

About the Author

Originally from the Cotswolds, Emily Elgar studied at Edinburgh University and went on to complete the novel writing course at the Faber Academy in 2014. Her debut *If You Knew Her* was an international bestseller and received rave reviews. *Grace Is Gone* is her second novel.

Emily lives in East Sussex with her family.

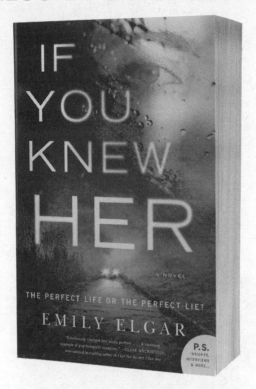